THUNDERCRACK

The big gun came whipping around, angled down, and fired. Six hundred yards away, the suit talent at the other end of the projectile's trajectory offered no resistance, none at all. One minute there was a man in a suit; the next minute there was a man in a suit with a burning hole a foot wide through his chest. The man fell in a fog of blood, and the suit, already fractured by the impact of the projectile, simply shattered like glass on the stones.

I'm in a war, Joss thought in increasing horror. *A real war . . .*

Other Exciting Adventures in the
SPACE COPS *Series*
by Diane Duane and Peter Morwood
from Avon Books

KILL STATION
MINDBLAST

SPACE COPS
HIGH MOON

DIANE DUANE & PETER MORWOOD

AVON BOOKS • NEW YORK

SPACE COPS: HIGH MOON is an original publication of Avon Books. This work has never before appeared in book form. This work is a novel. Any similarity to actual persons or events is purely coincidental.

AVON BOOKS
A division of
The Hearst Corporation
1350 Avenue of the Americas
New York, New York 10019

First AvoNova Printing: May 1992

AVONOVA TRADEMARK REG. U.S. PAT. OFF. AND IN OTHER COUNTRIES, MARCA REGISTRADA, HECHO EN U.S.A.

Printed in the U.S.A.

RA   10   9   8   7   6   5   4   3   2   1

ONE

JOSS O'BANNION WAS SINGING. THIS IN ITSELF wasn't so unusual, but Evan had some slight trouble with the way Joss did it. Joss inevitably sang in a key that would probably be called M, if any other human being ever tumbled across it; and he sang loudly, so that the confines of their little ship rang with the sound. Evan thought to himself that the computers would shudder at it, if they could hear. He hoped they couldn't. He wished *he* couldn't.

In addition, the songs he sang were not exactly the sort that Evan had been used to when being trained in song as a child.

"They crash him, and his body may burn!
They smash him, but they know he'll return,
To live again! Captain—."

"Stop a moment," Evan said finally, unable to bear it anymore. "Just you stop. *Joss!!*"

Joss put his head out of his cabin and looked down toward the front of the ship, where Evan was sitting in *Nosey*'s command chair. "Need something?"

"Quiet would be nice," Evan said. "What *was* that caterwauling?"

"*Captain Scarlet* theme. Don't tell me you never heard of *Captain Scarlet?* It was a—"

1

"Possibly there are things it would be better not to know about," Evan said. "It sounded like you were strangling a chicken. A good job we didn't have an open comms channel; Mars control might have thought a murder was taking place."

Joss snickered and held up a cube. "I've got that one, too."

"What?"

"In space, no one can hear you scream," he said, yet another of his obscure quotes, and vanished back into his cabin again.

"I wish no one could hear you *sing*," Evan muttered. He was answered with fiendish laughter and what sounded like another chorus of *Captain Whoever-he-was*.

Evan sighed and sat back in the control chair. *They've partnered you with a nutcase, Glyndower,* he thought, and made a wry face at himself. Surely Joss had been no more crazed about this three-weeks' holiday, and his attendance at the Triplanetary Video, Solid and Holo Collectors' Convention, than Evan had been about the prospect of seeing his old buddies at FAF Sydenham Upper. It was going to be nice to see Huntley and Laker and so many of the rest of the lads with whom he had done suit training, all of— what was it now? Five years ago? There would be a lot of drink taken, a lot of singing, probably no better than Joss's, to tell the truth—and a lot of suit talk. That was what Evan looked forward to the most; probably as much as Joss looked forward to trading and buying his weird entertainment vids with other weirdos similarly inclined. And Joss probably considered Evan's madness to see the newest suits to be just that. No accounting for tastes . . .

The proximity alarm went off. Evan tapped the console to shut it up, hit the comms circuit and said, "Mars approach Phobos, Solar Patrol vessel CDZ 8064 *Nosey* for preinsertion."

"SP CDZ 8064, reconfirm filing and execute."

Evan hit the control that would pass their flight and landing plans to the approach computers for reconfirmation. A second later the automated OK came through, a stream of characters on one of the console screens, and

Phobos approach said, *"On automatic. Override alert in six minutes."*

"Noted, Phobos. We'll check in then." Evan tapped the comms off again, swivelled around in the command chair, and called, "You've got six minutes to finish your packing before they want you up here."

The singing broke off. "I'll be done long before then," Joss said cheerfully. "I'm only bringing the cream of the collection."

Evan rolled his eyes. What the "cream" might be of a collection of ancient vids that included things like rubber singing mice, and spacecraft like malfunctioning electric irons, spitting smoke and sparks out their rear ends, Evan hardly dared to speculate. The things that people used to consider entertainment often horrified him, but they enchanted Joss, who had been collecting them for longer than the two of them had known each other.

Joss tossed the first of his bags out into the commonway that led to the front cabin. "I'm going to make a pretty penny," he said, all glee.

"Selling some of your treasures, are you?"

Joss held up one cube as if it were platinum. "Auction for this one," he said. "The *complete* 'Mr. Ed.' "

"Oh dear," Evan said, and concealed his vast relief that Joss was finally selling *that* one.

Joss smiled a little and ducked back into his cabin. "What about your buddies?" he said. "Have you got your schedules worked out yet? Going to spend the whole three weeks taking suits apart and drooling over the newest negative-feedback systems?"

"Not the *whole* three weeks," Evan said, as mildly as he could. Joss snorted, over the sound of cases being snapped shut, and came out into the front cabin.

He sat down in the right-hand seat and gazed out. Mars was already quite large in the cockpit window; ruddy and gibbous, the surface beginning to be streaked more emphatically than usual with canals, the north polar cap hazy around its edges, beginning to contract as the CO_2 of its dry-ice component started to sublimate away.

"Springtime on Mars," Joss said, leaning back in his seat. "Romantic, isn't it?"

"I prefer Paris," Evan said. "Warmer."

"Only about fifty degrees."

"Centrigrade," Evan said. "Also, you don't have to wear breather apparatus on the Boulevard Saint-Germain."

"Picky, picky," Joss said.

"And since when are *you* in search of romance?" Evan said. "Mister cool-and-collected."

Joss looked at him sidelong. "Even a cop has his moments. I seem to remember that *you*—"

"I seem to remember how *you* bugged my bedroom, you voyeuristic little paddy chink!"

"It was a security matter," Joss said, blushing hard. Evan smiled. Anytime he wanted to get Joss, these days, he mentioned that. It had become almost too easy.

The insertion alarm went off, and Joss jumped up with the air of someone about to do something immensely important. "Get out of my chair, you grudge-nursing petty-minded Taff," he said. Evan got up, still smiling; they changed seats.

"Put your belts on," Joss said, fastening his.

"Why? You planning to crash us again, like at Willans that time?" But Evan belted up.

"Here go the retros," Joss said. A moment later Evan felt the kick as the iondrivers cut out temporarily and the chemical rockets cut in. "Retrofire," Joss was saying to approach control. "Proceeding as filed."

"Welles pad two three," said approach control, some bored young woman from the sound of it. *"ETA from over-ride alert, twelve minutes."*

"Gotcha, Phobos, good day," Joss said.

They watched the planet grow and grow till it filled the front window. "Some sandstorms down there," Joss said, looking with interest at one that had to be covering some tens of thousands of square miles along the equatorial line.

"It's the time of year for them, isn't it?"

"Won't bother us," Joss said. "I'm not leaving the Hilton for the next week."

Evan doubted this. For one thing, he doubted that the Hilton had enough restaurants to keep Joss interested. It would only be a matter of hours before he had gone forth, no matter how bad the sandstorm, in search of Mars's best gazpacho, or something else equally obscure. So he merely said, "Mmf," and watched Welles start to become something you could see.

It was the biggest city on Mars, the oldest, and the oddest-looking, since it had been built in about six different waves of construction. The styles of architecture included everything from domes to internally insulated and sealed concrete blockhouses to glasteel skyscrapers to carefully concealed underground construction, to the "neo-exhibitory" style that said it was all right to build above ground again, in the loudest colors and strangest shapes you could find. Welles looked like the egg-laying site of some strange alien creature, littered with a farrago of the odd things that had hatched from the eggs, all sprawled about together in a great flat plain that had once been the floodplain of a river in the days when Mars had enough water to have rivers, or for that matter, floods.

"There's the flatport," Joss said, with some satisfaction, pointing off to one side of the growing city. "We're right on."

"You mean you're *not* going to crash us for a change."

Joss looked at Evan with narrowed eyes. "It wasn't my fault the last time," he said. "But I warn you, keep up the way you're going, and it may be my fault shortly."

Evan tried not to laugh out loud.

They descended in a silence that grew to a thin scream that was the best the atmosphere could do, even after some fifty years of first-stage terraforming. Lichen grew here, happily, and some simple mosses and club mosses, several of them genetically tailored for the maximum production of oxygen from minimal CO_2 and imported to Mars from Earth, at ridiculous expense. Horsetail mosses were struggling in the equatorial areas, grown under plastic in huge plantations and coddled like tender tropicals; they grew only in the summer, released a great deal of oxygen during their growing season, and were harvested as vegetable matter for processing at the end of it. It would be a long, long time before Mars would be a place where you could walk outside without needing a breather; and it would be even longer before it was as warm as, say, Wales.

Nosey banked rightward under computer control, righted herself. Joss watched the controls, but touched none of them. The landing at Willans, which Evan had been teasing him about, had been at an independently owned station, with little money and a lot of maintenance problems. But they were landing at the capital city of one of the Federated Planets, and ATC here could be safely assumed to know what they were on about. Evan hoped.

"Coming in," Joss said, "Look, there's the Hilton."

"You mean the one that looks like the two balls and the—"

"Your mind is in the gutter, you know that," Joss said affectionately. "Yes, that one."

"I'll make a note in case I need to find you."

"Heaven forfend," Joss said. "Contact in about thirty."

"Ready," Evan said. The ship corrected attitude, settling on her underjets; slowly the Wellesian cityscape began to rear up off on one side of them as they settled. The screen to one side of Joss showed a schematic in vertical axis of their landing, the circle-and-square of the landing pad matching perfectly with *Nosey*'s orientation grid. *Nosey* flared; pink dust kicked up around them on all sides; and they were down, sitting on her skids under the violet, star-pointed sky of day, while the dust settled around them at .31 gee.

"Welcome to Mars," Evan said softly.

"Party!" Joss said, leaping out of his seat as fast as his unbuckling of straps would let him, and headed back into the companionway for his cases.

Evan smiled, got up, and went to get into his suit.

THEY SAW *NOSEY* SAFELY BESTOWED IN ONE OF the underground "parking garages" accessible from the main field by ramps and elevators, left her on voice seal, checked her in with the hangar attendant, declined on-site customs handling, and made their way through what seemed like half a mile of underground corridors to the Welles immigration facility.

Immigration was rarely more than a formality for people carrying Solar Police badges, and they passed through quickly, attracting only the usual stares from the tourists queueing at the three desks in the worn-looking little pre-fab dome. Only Evan was in uniform, meaning his suit. He didn't have to be at this point, but it was simpler to carry his luggage this way; and he would be wanting the suit when he went visiting Sydenham High. *Poor stripped-down thing that it is,* he thought. He tapped his badge as they paused at the desk, and Joss showed the bored-looking Immigration man his own. *I just hope they have the grace not to laugh at it too hard.* The tourists, for their part, were all staring at him as if he were from another planet. The stories about powered suits, and the men who wore them, had become pretty fantastic over the years, and doubtless most of these people thought that Evan's suit came equipped with nuclear weapons on the outside and a psychotic on the inside. *Well,* Evan thought, *one out of two* . . . And the stories were occasionally of use . . . espe-cially if they kept someone from shooting at him.

Customs was slightly more interesting than Immigra-tion. Evan had to declare his suit, not being on Mars in the line of duty, but he had all his paperwork ready, and handed the Customs man the datasolid while watching Joss and his own Customs officer with interest. Joss had his solid-satchel open, and the Customs lady, a short, swart creature with close-cropped hair, was sorting through it with an expression of slightly revolted interest, like a gar-dener looking for slugs. "Any obscene material?" she said.

Joss looked at her wide-eyed. "Madam! That would be in contravention of sixteen different statutes of four plan-ets and nine administrative areas, which I won't bother quoting to you since you know them as well as I do. I can offer you 'Scooby-Doo,' the original 'Lone Ranger,' and eighteen successive years of the Eurovision Song Contest, but obscene material—!" He paused, looking thoughtful. "Then again, I suppose you could make a case that the Eurovision Song Contest—"

"Go away," said the Customs lady, and pushed Joss's bag back at him. He shut it and headed after Evan.

Evan was laughing softly as Joss caught up. "Thought you were going to have a kitten there," he said.

Joss looked at Evan sidelong. "Yes, well," he said, "I didn't bring the *manga,* so you can just stop looking at me that way."

Evan put his eyebrows up. "Too valuable to sell here, eh?"

"Evan," Joss said severely, "the Customs regulations—"

Evan snorted at Joss. "Come on," he said, "let's get to the hotel before you strain my credibility any worse."

The Hilton was the senior hotel in Welles, and looked it. About half of it, the oldest half, was underground; the rest had been built as a skyscraper, one of the van der Rohe revival type, and looked like nothing so much as the box that some smaller skyscraper had come in—all flat glass, reflecting the scatter of buildings all around. They took a little smart-rail cart to it—a small open "bus" that followed a guide-strip buried in the floor of yet another underground corridor.

"This place is a regular warren," Joss said, glancing around at the accesses to various other levels of corridor and tunnel.

Evan nodded. "They've had more time to dig here than elsewhere," he said, "and the ground under Welles is more stable than other places—less worry about marsquakes. They've gone twenty or thirty stories down, now, but no one seems to want to go much further when the costs of building aboveground have finally come down. Even here, people would rather see the sky, I guess. Here we are—"

They were in front of what would have been the entrance to a grand hotel, if people habitually buried such underground. The Hilton's outer shell might look ascetic, but whoever designed the entrance had been working in the Late Decadent school; broad steps carpeted in red, with brass stair-rods, came curving down to the little circle where their smartcart had left them. All around were white ersatz-Corinthian columns, and much more polished brass, and in front of the diamond-paned glass doors stood a doorman with more braids and medals than some generals Evan had seen.

Joss looked at it all and held his peace as they made

their way in. There was one good thing about the suit, Evan reflected: when you were carrying your own luggage, no one tried to take it away from you—they tended to be afraid they might accidentally set something off, and not survive the encounter.

Reception was more of the same: white marble floors, antiques on pedestals, carved teak and etched glass. They checked in and were given keycards, and went off to find the lift, a glass and brass confection that looked like something that Tiffany dreamed on a bad night.

"Are you sure we shouldn't have gone to the Marriott?" Evan said as the lift door closed on them.

"We get the convention rate here," Joss said.

Evan sighed. They were well paid, but not enough so that there was exactly money to burn on this holiday. "It must have cost them a pretty penny to import all this bumf. Let's see . . . at about a thousand credits a pound—"

Joss laughed. "When they first built this place, they thought it was about to become the cultural and industrial center of Mars, because of all the archaeological work, and the mining. Then that didn't pan out."

"Ouch."

Joss grinned. Puns were something that Evan had long despaired of breaking him of. "Listen, the place is worth seeing for the sake of the craftsmanship alone. You don't see work like this anymore. Do you know how long it took them just to do the wood carving in the bar?"

The lift stopped; they stepped out into a corridor tastefully done in ivory and gold, with a carpet so blatantly crimson that it vibrated even in the subdued lighting. Evan was tempted to flip down the protective shields in his helm. "What room are we?"

"It's a suite. Seven twenty-three."

They found the room and keyed it open. Evan stepped in, put his case down, and then said, "Oh, no."

"Oh, come on, Evan!"

The sitting room was out of old Hollywood, by someone's bordello. Emerald-green brocade swag curtains were everywhere; the pile of the cream-colored rug was an inch deep; the furniture was all trying hard to be Louis Quinze, and failing. Evan sighed and looked around. "Are *all* the rooms like this?"

"I think some of them may be worse."

Evan wasn't sure he could imagine anything worse, or that he wanted to try. "All right," he said, and looked into one of the bedrooms, and winced. "I have never slept in a four-poster bed before," he said, "and I'm not sure I care to start now."

Joss looked into the other room. "I don't think you get a choice."

"Oh well." He took off his helm and began to look around. Really, the place wasn't badly equipped; wet bar, all the comms equipment you could want, a snack blaster. This wouldn't be a bad base for a couple of weeks, but he was damned if he was going to bring any of the lads from Sydenham up here. There would be talk.

"There are two bathtubs in here," Joss's voice said, slightly surprised, from his bedroom's bath.

Evan went for a look at his own, and was surprised. "Here, too. What's the other one for? Laundry?"

He was far enough away that he couldn't hear Joss's reply, except for the tone of voice that it came in, which suggested he would rather not hear the words anyway. Coming out, Evan looked with mild approval at the bed, which was big enough to need its own postcode. It was nice that they were finally building beds that 'someone over six feet tall could sleep in without hanging over the edges. There was more comms equipment in here, and another bar.

"Nice big closets," Joss said from the sitting room. "Want something to drink?"

"Mmm, in a while," Evan said, starting the series of coded flexes that undid the internal catches on his armor. It *was* a relief about the closets. There was nothing so annoying as a hotel room where you had to leave the suit lying on a chair or something all day, because there was no room for it elsewhere. And the closets had a voice seal on them as well. Very, very nice. "All right," he said, "Make that a Scotch and water."

"What kind of Scotch? What kind of water?"

Evan laughed and came out to have another look at the

wet bar. After a few minutes he was continuing his revision of his first impression of this place. The bar was, to put it mildly, well equipped; this was somewhere he could bring his buddies to drink without too much embarrassment, even if the place did look like a bordello otherwise.

"Come on," Joss said, "dump your armor and let's go have a look downstairs."

"You just want to get into the restaurants," Evan said, sitting down and taking off his greaves. "Glutton. Wait till I can make a call or two. And aren't you supposed to call HQ and let them know we're on-site?"

Joss grumbled, but got out his comms pad and keyed in the combination for Solar Police HQ. "They don't care, anyway," he said. "They've kissed us good-bye for a couple of weeks."

And we're envying you every minute, said a voice in his head after a moment, through the implant he wore just below his ear and about an inch in.

"Tee," Evan said, "we'll send you postcards."

You said that when you went to Willans. You didn't send us anything. *Fibber.* There was about a three-second pause between speak and hear, this far out from Earth orbit; but it wasn't enough to really be a problem. Telya was liaison with their commanders back at HQ, as well as research assistant, comms expert, and gofer. Her title was "expediter," but it might as well have been "know-it-all." She was invaluable, almost the third part of their team. Evan had often wondered to how many other sop teams Telya was almost-third; but that she was not permitted to tell— and (Evan suspected) wouldn't tell anyway, just for badness's sake.

"All right. What should we send you? Postcards from the archaeological diggings? Pictures of man-faced rocks?" Evan looked around him and added, "Examples of the weird life-styles of the natives?"

There was a pause. *I can see it through Joss's pad. Bozhe moy. Joss, you said you were getting a discount— now I see why! They give you sunglasses when you check into this place?* And there came a great peal of laughter from somewhere on the Moon.

Joss, sitting on one of the Louis-something settees in the

sitting room, looked vaguely discomfited. Evan burst out laughing. "Give him a break, Tee," he said. "Do you know how long it took them to do the woodwork in the bar?"

"All right, all right," Joss said, "so the place is tacky. But it's *colossally* tacky. No half measures."

No argument there, bwana. You're going to need a taste transplant when you get back.

"Well, we'll worry about it then," Joss said. "Any messages?"

Yes. Lucretia says, you two be perfect little gentlemen as always, and have a good time.

"As always!"

There was no response from the implant.

"There's wishful thinking, if you like," Joss said, shutting his pad down. "Well, they know we're here. Let's go get something to eat."

Evan raised his eyebrows. "Do you ever think about *anything* but food?"

"Yes," Joss said, "but you're tired of hearing about the vids, you keep saying. There's a terrific Chinese place downstairs—"

"You just wait a few moments," Evan said. "I want to make a call myself." He finished shedding his armor, opened his case, unfolded the portable rack, and set about hanging everything up neatly.

"Your mother must have been tough on you when you were little," Joss commented from the next room.

"Yes," Evan said, "she always made me put away all my weapons systems before I could have any dinner." He picked up the helm last of all, did a quick battery check on it, and placed it on the top of the rack; then sat down on the bed, pulled his bag over, extracted his own pad from it, and told it a commcode.

Its screen lit up a moment later with the image of a handsome young woman in uniform. "Commander Huntley's office."

"Evan Glyndower calling," said Evan. "Is Chris there?"

"One moment, sir." The screen blanked, then lit again.

"Evan! You're early." The face that looked back at him was grinning from ear to ear, and smudged on one high cheekbone with joint lubricant. Chris Huntley pushed her dark hair out of her face and laughed at him. "You caught me in the shop."

"Nothing serious, I hope."

"Routine maintenance," she said. "Takes longer than usual, with this new suit they've issued us."

Evan smiled too. "I want to see this baby."

Chris waggled her eyebrows at him. "Just wait till you do. I want to see your face when you get your hands on the new augmented-plasma cannon—"

Evan sighed. "Pity I can't take one home. What's the schedule?"

"Most of us are on ops tonight. Tomorrow would be better."

"Tomorrow it is then. Lunch?"

"Lunch and after. Then dinner out with the crowd."

"You're on. See you tomorrow."

"Out," Chris said, and the pad's screen went blank.

"There," Evan said, getting up. "Five minutes to change, and *then* we can go see about your dinner."

"You said you were going to see 'the lads,' " Joss said in an accusing tone of voice. "Some lad!"

"Did you tap my channel again, you nosey little—"

"Not me, son. *You* left the linkage open. Think you wanted to brag. If I'd known the FAF weapons officers looked like that, I might have reconsidered my choice of careers."

Evan snickered as he went off to change, greatly cheered all over again by the prospect of visiting the "lads," the suit troops, and by the prospect of the good talk about old times, and how the military suits were so much better than the downgraded, disarmed civilian monkey models issued to poor unsuspecting EssPat officers. "You mean you can even think about such things when you're here in a hotel full of other vid freaks? You astonish me."

"Shut up and get on the stick. I'm hungry."

DINNER DIDN'T COME ANYWHERE NEAR SO quickly, of course, for first Joss wanted to go downstairs and register his presence with the convention message service. There was a lot of private horsetrading that went on before and after the open auctions; all kinds of wheeling and dealing and some price-fixing went on among the more aggressive traders, and Joss wanted to make sure that several of them knew he was there. And after he had registered, nothing would do but that he drag Evan into one of the program rooms in the subground part of the hotel, and stand there in the back of a smoky little room, laughing and clapping at one obscure entertainment after another. Evan put up with it as a sort of history lesson; yet another example of the weird things that people considered entertaining in older and more benighted times.

Eventually they got free, mostly by Evan threatening to go off to some other restaurant—a prospect which Joss couldn't handle. They made their way out of the hotel and down one of the long causeway tunnels leading away from the hotel entrance; then to an escalator up into a park-dome, and up out of the dome by several lifts.

"Good-o," said Evan as they stepped out of the last one. "It's still here." He headed across the atrium to the entrance of the restaurant. As such things went, it was understated: shaped like a peak-roofed Chinese arch, painted dark green and a somber crimson picked out with gold. There was no calligraphy, just the single word, *Sichuan,* above it in red neon, and even the neon, in small, neat letters, managed somehow to be tasteful. The whole thing looked no different from other Chinese restaurants that they had seen in the past, even the one on Willans Station—though there the pillarwork had been of stressed steel and an integral part of the station's structure.

Joss glanced at Evan, a slightly cockeyed look. "Wait a minute. *Still here?* You mean you know this place?" He looked like he was about to say a bad word or two. "I thought *I* was going to introduce *you* to it!"

"A man has to eat somewhere," Evan said, grinning. "And when he's just spent his duty hours sneaking round the archaelogical digs with which this planet is all too well provided, he likes good food to take the taste of Martian dust out of his mouth."

"You were in a suit," Joss pointed out. "The dust wasn't anywhere near your mouth."

"*Diw!* After those vids you made me watch, you're a fine one to let reality get in the way of a good line!"

The door opened and two couples came into the atrium. They were chatting together, laughing and looking generally well fed and content, which made Evan feel still more satisfied. Indeed, his satisfaction was shading perilously close to smugness as they got close enough to the door to breathe a bit of the air the couples had brought out into the open area with them. *Sichuan*, like everywhere else in an enclosed environment like this, would have very efficient atmosphere scrubbers, but the faint, tantalizing aroma that mingled garlic and ginger, sesame oil and hot-bean paste, had managed to escape regardless.

Evan looked with vast amusement at Joss's grin. "Any second thoughts?" said Evan. "Italian, perhaps? Or Yaroslav Vsevolod's Russian place upstairs?"

"Bugger the Russian place! Until later in the week, anyway."

Evan chuckled. "Should be just a bit better than your ruddy puppet-shows. 'Anything can happen in the next half-hour,' indeed! You have no idea, Joss-*bach*. This place has the best Chinese meals I've ever been privileged to fork over my fillings—and yes, I use chopsticks, and I don't have fillings, but don't let facts interfere with the alliteration."

"I take it they have *sake*?"

"They have, boyo. And *shaoxing*. Oh yes, and *mou-tai* and *kaoliang* for those foolish enough to want them."

"Such as certain sops I can think of. Come on, man, are you going to stand out here gabbing while my stomach sings me to sleep?"

THE INTERIOR WAS DIMLY LIT BY THE INDIRECT lighting built into the walls, and by the illuminated fountain set squarely in the middle of the floor. There were fish in it, carp and thumping great black-patterned goldfish, and they came up to watch Evan and Joss go by in a way that suggested they, too, had become addicted to the food in this establishment. When neither EssPat officer offered anything to eat, the fish submerged again, one of them blowing an expressive bubble of disapproval that people could be so stingy.

In the usual way of restaurants, none of the clients seemed to see them come in, and at first they also went unnoticed by the scurrying waiters. That wasn't a problem for either man: both, and Evan particularly, were far too used to heads turning and an awkward silence settling over anywhere that warranted a visit from uniformed sops. Anonymity was a pleasant change—until the lean Chinese in the short-sleeved shirt glanced up from his datapad behind the cash desk, did a classic take, and stared. It was a stare of such intensity that for the briefest instant, Joss felt the beginning of a twitch in his gun-hand. Evan had been on Mars before, on Patrol business, and it was likely enough he had left some enemies behind him once that case was closed.

"Cooking the books, David?" said Evan. "Then I'll have mine hot and sour."

The Chinese smiled, in a way that gave immediate lie to any inscrutability he might have claimed. "Evan! Evan Glyndower!" he said, pronouncing it properly. "Welcome back to the Big Red One!"

There was grinning and handshaking, laughing and introductions. Joss looked at Evan in a way that indicated he was making mental notes about David Liu. Probably one of them was that even in the midst of his surprise, the Chinese had taken care not to refer to "Officer" Glyndower—though there had been just the tiniest hesitation in David's speech as he took in the civilian clothing and edited the rank from his greeting. For his own part, Evan watched David favor Joss with a quick, cool look of assessment, and apparently label him "safe." David shot him a look that seemed to say, "No uniform on him, either?" but said nothing.

Joss was looking a bit thoughtful after shaking hands with David. Probably, Evan thought, he had noticed the calluses on the edge of that small, delicate-looking hand.

"Kung-fu, aikido and a little jeet-kun-do," said David,

answering at least one of the questions that were ticking through Joss's mind. He smiled, a quick twitch of the mouth that seemed a much more appropriate expression than his earlier wide grin. "It keeps me fit."

It also makes you quite heavily armed, thought Evan as David found them menus. One of the waiters came over to say that their table was ready. David looked towards it, and shook his head. "I think a larger table," he said, then glanced quickly at Evan. "That is, if you still generate as many plates as I remember?"

"Probably more," said Evan. "Joss likes Chinese food, and Lon never did." Out of the corner of his eye, Evan saw the look of surprise start to cross Joss's face, and then stop when he saw the policeman watching. He was a bit surprised himself, really. It was unusual, even now, for him to bring up his late partner's name in conversation. Lon Salonikis had been killed at the beginning of an ugly drug-bust on the L-5 station, Freedom II, and for an uncomfortably long time, Evan had both blamed himself for not being there, and regarded Joss as something close to second best. When that went away, so did mention of Lon's name; until now, and for the simplest of reasons. David had known the dead man when he had been Evan's partner that last time on Mars, and his reticence over asking questions was nothing more suspicious than plain, old-fashioned good manners.

They ended up at a considerably larger table, seating for at least four and maybe six, and when David left them to stalk around the restaurant and make sure that everything was in order, Joss gestured at the expanse of white linen and cleared his throat expressively. "I remember a man who told me he couldn't even *look* at a chocolate cake without putting the fit of his suit at risk," he said. "So what's with all this? Low-cal potstickers? Fat-free duck?"

"Vacation." Evan's grin was wicked. "Three weeks of it. And not even Aunty Gwyneth's cooking could put on so much fat in a fortnight that I couldn't work it off in the week that's left. Sichuan food—*this* Sichuan food—is no problem at all. And anyway, though the appetizers all come on their own plates, each portion's quite small. Just about right, really."

"It's your waistline, Officer Glyndower. And your suit that might need elastic gussets let into the seams before it lets you into it again."

"Your concern is duly noted, Officer O'Bannion. Now have some of these pickled veggies before I scoff them all."

The food began to arrive shortly afterwards, and the usefulness of the larger table immediately began to be obvious. What with small plates, little bowls, and tiny dishes of sauces that ran through the whole spectrum from mild to murderous, Evan did indeed generate a surprising amount of crockery. And those were just the appetizers. There were soups as well, and the addictively crunchy hot-pickled vegetables that had begun the meal and kept appearing in bite-sized quantities throughout it, with the spicing stepped up just a little more at every appearance.

"Sops found fed to death on Mars, film at eleven," said Joss after the first delivery of plates had been cleared to make way for the next.

"*What* at eleven? Never mind, you're just being obscure again." Evan lifted his sake cup in a toast. "Here's to obscurity of all kinds, including sitting here and minding nobody's business but our own."

"I'll second that," said Joss, reaching to where the bottle—no nonsense with little flasks here—sat in the silver bucket of boiling water whose billowing clouds of steam had turned as many heads as a powered-suit might have done, when it was first brought out of the kitchen and set at the end of their table. He refilled Evan's cup and then, regardless of proper etiquette, topped up his own. "Here's to all the perpetrators who don't know where we are—"

The silver bucket made a noise like *ptank,* and there was a splash as hydrostatic pressure tried to compress its noncompressible contents; then it began to piddle two long streams of scalding water from the matching holes that had been punched through its sides.

Smallbore ultra-high-velocity projectile weapon, said a helpful little voice inside Evan's head as everything began to run slow. *Single-shot setting. So far . . .* That much was obvious. If any of the half-dozen UHV sluggers on the market had sprayed them at full auto, not even David's head chef could have worked out which had been *ma-po dofu* and which had been the customers eating it.

Customers who, because they were on vacation, were not just out of uniform, but unarmed.

There was one recurring problem about floors, even in a quality restaurant like *Sichuan*. They were bloody hard. When Evan slammed down in a shoulder-roll to take him out of the line of fire—whichever direction *that* might be—the impact knocked most of the useable air out of his lungs. The transmitted shock of another slug chewing through the oak planking far too close to his gut knocked out the rest as effectively as a kick to the solar plexus, leaving him rolling for the shelter of something hard and solid, but concentrating even harder on trying to start breathing again.

There were screams from the other patrons as they huddled in booths, or ducked behind tables that were as much use as the proverbial wet paper bag. As yet they were safe enough, because the gunman was still trying for aimed shots; Evan heard two more directed at Joss as he huddled, wheezing, behind the carved stone fountain. The spaced, muffled whack of sound-suppressed single shots. But if patience or whatever time had been allowed for the hit ran out, then the guy would most likely flip over to automatic and just shred everyone in the place.

"It's the only way to be sure," said an unwanted quote. Then he heard the thud.

It wasn't the gun. This was a meatier noise, and anyway, he heard the gun an instant later when it hit the fountain's parapet and fell into the water, to the outrage of the fish. Groping for the weapon in more than two feet of water and nearly two dozen startled fish, Evan peered over the fountain to see what Joss had done.

He had done nothing, though from the look on his face as he surfaced from under a chewed-up table and a thoroughly ruined dinner, he looked entirely capable of doing something right now. Something very nasty, involving chopsticks and sensitive orifices.

The gunman was still there, near the doorway, except that now he didn't really qualify for the title since David

Liu had kicked the weapon out of his hand and by the looks of things, fractured the gun-hand's wrist in the process. It didn't stop the man from doing something very stupid. Rather than running while he had the chance, he dropped into a horse stance and poised the hooked fingers of his useable hand.

David also had just one useable hand. In the other, braced, balanced and still unspilled, was a bowl of *dandan mian*, prepared especially for Evan and Joss. Turning away to set the bowl down was too dangerous, and using it as a weapon was unthinkable—for one thing, there were few schools of martial arts that gave training in the offensive use of noodles.

Evan Glyndower nodded thanks, then glared at the would-be assassin. "You're under arrest," he said.

The man made a little forward jerk with his left arm, and suddenly his hand sprouted the blade of a knife. It poised for an instant between his fingers as he took aim, and in that instant David Liu spun on the toes of his left foot and kicked with the edge of the right. The heel of his solid, sensible, restaurant-manager's shoe came up and out like a hammer and took the man with the knife between upper lip and nose, at a rising angle that lifted him clear of the floor.

The autopsy would later reveal that he was dead before he hit it again, but the man who had killed him had no need of a coroner to know it.

Sichuan's manager stared at nothing for a few seconds, while he regained his composure and the restaurant regained something that was a little less than panic. That did not prevent it from emptying almost between one breath and the next. Only when all the other customers were gone did David straighten up and square his shoulders. Then he turned to Evan and shook his head. "I am gravely out of practice," he said apologetically. "That was too hard, and too high."

"But it wasn't too slow," said Joss. "That was what mattered. Thank you."

Evan nodded. "Twice."

David shrugged. His face was impassive again, hiding whatever expression might be behind it. "He tried to hurt my friends," he said, "and look what he did to my restaurant. I just wish I could find out why."

"The old gang," said Evan, "from the archaeology scam. We were never quite sure that we'd rounded them all up. It seems not."

"I see." If there was any condemnation, any anger, any opinion at all in the way that David spoke those two words, neither of the sops were able to hear it. "These noodles have gone cold," he said, changing the subject for the sake of changing it, "and the rest of your meal is . . . upset." Which was a polite way of observing that the food and the furniture and the tableware had all become inextricably mixed with each other, and were good for nothing except entry in an exhibition of Futurist art. "Let me close the doors until the police arrive, and after that we can start again. For the meanwhile, Evan, I think that I would like a drink. *Mou-tai*. And I will not tease your fondness for it, just this once . . ."

THEY DIDN'T HURRY DINNER, BUT NEITHER DID they prolong it. The local police arrived, and looked the scene over, and took initial statements from Joss and Evan; they would be wanting to see them tomorrow, they said, though the expressions on their faces said they would really rather not have any closer contact than necessary with the men who provoked attacks like this. Evan kept his thoughts to himself for the time being. He was composing the beginning of his own report in his head, and damning his bright idea that they should come to Mars for a nice rest. *Joss was right,* he thought; *we should have gone to the dark side of the Moon and just vegetated.* Then he threw the annoying thought out. *Never mind. This doesn't have to spoil the rest of the holiday, unless we let it.*

David sent them home with an extra carton of dan-dan mian and a resigned look. "No such thing as peace and quiet around you," he said. "There never was. How long are you going to be on Mars?"

Evan shook his head mildly. "If this kind of thing keeps up," he said, "that's a good question."

"Two weeks," Joss said. "You cheer up, dammit."

"Come back again," said David, "after we clean the place up. I never did get that *really* hot dish made up that I promised you."

"Oh, well then," Evan said, mock-heartily. Half his mucous membranes, he thought, had already vanished under the onslaught of the chillies before the firefight had begun. He might as well lose the rest of them. "You're on."

They said their good nights and headed back for the hotel.

"You never told me that people were trying to kill you when you were here last," Joss said.

Evan shrugged. "Things got a bit rough sometimes."

Joss snorted. "Maybe you should stay in your iron underwear the rest of the trip."

"I am going out by FAF Sydenham," Evan said, "where everybody else has the same underwear, and anyone who tries to shoot you in it gets a rude surprise. Everything will be fine. I'm just worried about *you* now. Sitting there in that hotel, out of uniform, not armed—and you've been seen with me."

"No one is going to crash a convention full of vid freaks to try to get at me!"

"Oh? And think of the innocent bystanders."

"Damn," Joss said. "You and your bright ideas about coming to Mars for a nice rest!"

"Joss," said Evan gently, "shut your face."

They got back to the room, and Evan went for his pad to begin drafting a message about this madness to Lucretia. From across the room, Joss said, "Oh, God."

"What?"

"Look at your pad."

Evan fetched it out of the drawer where he had left it. It was flashing and beeping and doing everything but jumping up and down. The screen was flashing NOTIFICATION/URGENT. He sighed and hit the buffer dump.

The screen began to scroll with a message routing, the usual weird codes, and then the message. ACTIVATION, it said, among a lot of other things, and then the code address for Sop HQ on the Moon, and then the body of the message:

SP VESSEL CDZ 9093 MISSING FROM MARS ORBIT / FLIGHT PLAN FILED DESTINATION OLYMPUS MONS SP BASE / NO RESPONSE FROM TRANSPONDER / INVESTIGATE LOCAL DAWN / REPORT SOONEST / ABSTRACT FOLLOWS / LUCRETIA.

Evan breathed out unhappily, and in some puzzlement. "Now what the devil," he said, shaking his head. "Since when do we do planetary traffic searches?"

"Since the piece of traffic in question is carrying an all-spectrum Solar Patrol coder/decoder prototype," Joss said from the sitting room.

Evan blanched, and swore, and lost his appetite for the rest of the dan-dan mian.

TWO

THE ABSTRACT WAS ALREADY IN THEIR PADS, AS
it turned out. And if they couldn't find the missing ship, it
was going to be a matter of some considerable concern.

Communications was the one thing that held the Solar
Patrol together. Without fast, accurate, secure communications, no police force could function—especially no force
spread among four planets and nine administrative areas.
The Patrol spent more each year on comms hardware and
software than on any other aspect of their organization, including salaries and spacecraft.

The past year had seen the Patrol suffer some setbacks in
this area. After all, what science could devise, science could
analyze—especially when the criminals doing the analysis
had such interest in breaking the codes and locked channels
that the Patrol used to pass information about them. The
coded satchel-packet system that HQ had been using for the
past eight years or so had been broken, this past year. This
by itself wasn't a major problem; the people in Patrol cryp-
tography had been expecting a crack, and had long been
working on the next, less defeatable system that would replace satchel-packet technology when it was broken.

The new system was ready now. Joss looked at the long
string of letters after its name, in the abstract, and sighed.
In some ways, the tech people were as crazed for exciting-
looking acronyms as Evan's friends in the suit business.
PENMBSBF: Polled-Export Node-Matrix Barricaded

Sidebound Bundle Filing, the new system was called, which did nothing whatsoever for Joss as far as understanding was concerned. But the abstract made it obvious that this new system was the absolute state of the art in secure communications over long distances, and pretty near unbreakable . . . until the next time. Attached to the abstract, in Joss's pad, was another article, a more detailed one about the system. For curiosity's sake alone he opened a window on the padscreen to look at it . . . only to find it full of words and phrases like "nontossed bundles," "nutshell routing," "premessage scan control," "unschedules," "Z-particle behavior masks," and some even odder technical terms, like "wazoo."

Joss put the second article away and went back, rather gratefully, to the abstract. A prototype hardware/software package incorporating the new system in a small satellite had gone out from the Moon in the missing ship for trials on and around Mars. Everything had been uneventful . . . except that the ship missed its landing ETA. It had not informed Mars Control, or anyone else, of anything going wrong. It was simply gone.

Evan came out of the next room and looked over his shoulder. ''It might be nothing," he said. "A systems failure or some such."

Joss looked up at him with a crooked smile. "Bets?"

"Not me," said Evan. "Not the way our luck runs. You think someone snatched it."

Joss sighed. "If the SP's communications haven't been completely secure for a while," he said, "nothing seems more likely than someone getting wind of this prototype being shipped out, and deciding to catch one and take it home. I would, if I were a crook. At the very least, I'd look for someone to sell it to. At best, I'd find someone who could figure it out on the quiet, then use the knowledge to break into the system later. They won't trash all this research just because one prototype goes missing."

"Which makes it all the more important to find where the thing has gone," Evan said. "Have we got a flight plan on the missing ship?"

"Right here." Joss touched the pad; it brought up a sectional map of Mars. "Here's the Mars Control en route supplement," he said. "The ship would have done normal orbit injection here"—he pointed—"and then it was scheduled to use this flightway, Rexam, over to Niton Slot, near Olympus Mons. The log says they called the Rexam ATRCU center on time, just a position check. But nothing was heard from them after that."

"So they would have been running along this line . . ." Evan traced a line from the end of the Rexam flightway to Olympus Mons.

"Somewhere there, yes. Nothing much but archaeological and mining camps out that way. And this place."

Evan looked at the sectional map, and stared. " 'Tombstone'? Is someone famous buried there?"

Joss shook his head. "Your classical education really *was* pitiful," he said sadly. "Never mind. That's its name, and the name of their nav beacon, too."

Evan sighed and headed back to his side of the suite. "It's just as well I didn't unpack," he said. "It's not that long till local dawn. If I were you, boyo, I'd have a quick kip."

Joss looked after Evan, squinting in confusion. "Will you please speak English?"

"Only if forced," Evan said from the next room, amid the soft electronic squeaks and pips of armor being status-checked. "I said, better get some sleep."

Joss thought sadly of how much sleep he had been planning to get. There was going to be breakfast in bed after it, and then a slow leisurely stroll through the exhibition space downstairs, and the delight of starting to sell off his collection to an appreciative audience. *Dreams, idle dreams,* he thought, and turned down the bed. Then he said, "Want to see a vid before you turn in?"

The growl with which he was answered was definitely not in English. Electronics continued to cheep and blip in the next room.

Joss grinned a little, rummaged through his bag, came up with a solid, and slotted it into the room's viewer, turning the volume down very low.

"They crash him, and his body may burn!
They smash him, but they know he'll return—"

In the next room, someone began saying something soft and heartfelt in Welsh.

"I'LL FLY HER IN," SAID JOSS, AND FOR ONCE EVAN didn't even bother to object. *Nosey*'s course from Welles Spaceport to the Niton Slot area was a simple ballistic arc, scarcely even leaving atmosphere before starting descent and finals.

"There's your town," Joss said at one point, nodding at the window. Evan, in *Nosey*'s other front seat, craned his neck.

"That's a town?" he said softly. "That's ten sheds and a landing pad."

Joss chuckled. "You've lived in smaller places, to hear you tell it."

"With one pub and one fueling station, yes . . . but we didn't call them towns! Hamlets, possibly."

Joss shrugged. "We'll worry about it later. This is the line the ship would have been on. Peel those eyes."

Evan flipped his helm's visor down and went to augmented vision. Joss made himself briefly busy at the instrument console, instructing the ship's sensors to look for the usual SP distress frequency squawk, and adjusting the sensitivity as high as it would go; if the vessel had crashed, the squawk might be operating at very low power, or only sporadically. "I'm going to do a standard quartering pattern between here and Olympus Mons," Joss said, bringing up the autopilot screen and laying down a basketweave grid on it. "It's about the best we can do until some more help arrives."

"Right you are," Evan said.

And he said little more for the next two hours, as *Nosey* took them back and forth across the rosy Martian landscape, under the violet-black sky. It was fair weather for searching, at least; the day wasn't far enough along for the wind to have risen much, and the dust was fairly quiet. But as time went on, and the landscape warmed, it would get worse.

Joss spent the time alternating between looking out the

windows and trying to coax more sensitivity out of his instruments. Both were fruitless. Evan was much better suited to see anything on the surface than Joss was; and as for the instruments, Joss was beginning to suspect that there was simply nothing out there for them to detect. His mood blackened. It took a great deal to destroy an SP vessel's ID transponder—the things were admirably shielded from any merely mechanical trauma, and had no moving parts larger than submolecular size. You practically had to nuke them to get them to shut up. *And we would have noticed a nuke ... I think.* Otherwise, the only way to stop one sending was to take it apart with the correct tools, and shut it down on purpose.

Joss frowned. He had seen such things done with civilian transponders. He didn't think it could be done with SP ones, though—at least, not by civilians. They didn't have the right tools, for one thing. *At least, they don't as far as you know ...*

Joss sighed and went back to watching the autopilot bring the ship around for one more long banking turn. Evan was still staring out the window.

"How long now?" Evan asked.

"Two hours, ten minutes."

Evan shook his head. "There's nothing out there but red rocks and more red rocks," he said. "And dust and gravel. Dammit, Joss, how can we even be sure we're in the right place? We've nothing to go on but probabilities. And no transponder trace still, I take it—" He looked hopefully over at the console for a moment.

"No such luck. I think we need more help."

Evan sighed and flipped up his visor. "But this area is still our best bet. We just need more detail. And some local knowledge."

Joss nodded glumly. He hated it when his machinery proved unequal to a task. "Back to that town, then?"

Evan snorted. " 'Town.' Yes. Let's see if we can get some help from the people there."

"They probably won't have much in the way of equipment. Sand skimmers and such."

"True. But they've seen this landscape a lot more often than we ever have and they'll be able to notice small things gone wrong with it in a hurry. A pile of rocks and sand that means nothing to us will be obvious to them as something that wasn't there last week. And even in a place like this, with miles and miles of nothing but miles and miles, the local people notice everything. Let's go."

Joss took the controls himself to bring them in, having his own opinions about what Tombstone's ILS system might be like. He didn't want another repeat of the near-crash back at Willans. For one thing, Evan had enough ammunition already, without gathering more—and for another, in any argument between Mars and something hitting its surface, the planet invariably won. Joss had no desire to lose one of those arguments.

When they were in sight of the "ten sheds," Joss opened a comms channel. "Tombstone approach control, this is CDZ 8064 requesting landing clearance, over."

His only reply was the faint sizzle of static, and Evan raised his eyebrows. "They might well be out looking for the downed ship," he said.

Joss blinked at the prospect. "All of them? Leaving the place deserted? Not even a duty controller?"

"Oh aye, they'll do that all right. Happened a lot when I was stationed here before." He grinned suddenly. "Not a single accident, either—but a lot of cardiac arrest."

"Wonderful. Just wonder—"

"Incoming vessel, this is a recorded message. ILS indicates there is presently no other traffic in the area. Please therefore commence a manual approach to the pad and make surface transit to Parkbay Three when done. Thank you. Tombstone Control out."

"A recorded message?" echoed Joss, in tones of near-theatrical disbelief. "The control tower is an answering machine?!"

"There's an improvement," said Evan with some satisfaction. "Some places, when I was here last, didn't even bother."

"I'm liking this place less and less," said Joss, "and I haven't even *seen* it yet."

"Now don't judge a book by its cover, boyo." Evan was grinning again, even wider than before, and finally Joss gave up and laughed.

"This is a book in a plain brown wrapper," he said. "And the original cover's been ripped off and sent back to make somebody a quick buck."

"You're speaking in tongues again."

"Just goes to show how much you missed in school by not reading comic books with the rest of us." He turned his attention to *Nosey*'s proximity sensors. According to their readouts, Tombstone's crappy traffic control had been telling the truth, but Joss remained wary, trusting the screens and his own eyes more than any recorded or computer-generated voice. It was bloody irregular; he didn't like it; and fortunately, he didn't have to.

Nosey swept low over the single mangy-looking landing pad, support jets swirling up the usual cloud of Martian dust as Joss deployed her crawlers instead of the more usual strut-and-skid landing gear. It was rare nowadays that a ship had to taxi anywhere: few were capable of detuning their multiple kilotons of thrust low enough to simply trundle the vessel forward, rather than taking off again and in the process flattening whatever happened to be behind the thrusters' efflux nozzles. If movement was required after landing, it usually involved either EM-repellor sleds and a tractor tug, or slideways built into the floors of the pads themselves. Expecting that out here would be like ... Joss's mind hunted for an appropriate simile, and failed miserably. Like expecting an unexpected thing.

Accidents weren't unexpected, though. He noticed that the landing pad and the half-dozen parkbays that ringed it were all equipped with reinforced blast berms to channel any explosions upwards. Considered kindly, it would avoid some cack-handed pilot scouring off the pad's meager facilities with over-enthusiastic use of taxiing thrust.

And considered with the bleak eye of cynicism, it would contain the aftermath of a fumbled approach by someone not used to Traffic Control By Answering Machine. The only thing missing had been the beep, after which Joss might have left a message the Chief Controller—assuming there *was* such a thing in Tombstone—wouldn't have forgotten in a hurry.

The clunk as *Nosey*'s crawlers made contact with the

Martian surface was encouragingly solid, and since Joss had identified Parkbay Three on finals, there was still enough forward momentum remaining for the ship to simply roll from pad to parkbay with just the smallest goose from her rearmost attitude thrusters. Of course, since they were now facing the wrong way, getting out again would almost certainly prove more eventful.

"Tsk!" said Evan. "They don't even offer valet parking."

"I wouldn't take it even if they did. This has got to be one of the scruffiest, sleaziest, down-at-heel—"

"What about refreshingly unchanged, full of character, rich in period charm . . . ?"

"I've scraped period charm off my boots before, Evan. It's called leaving the horseshit in the street."

"No horses on Mars, last time I looked."

"You know very well what I mean! C'mon. Let's see if we can find this bloody decoder, and then get back on vacation."

After fifty years of terraforming, there was no longer any need for cumbersome space suits, and the astronauts who had first walked on the Martian surface like foil-wrapped Michelin Men would have envied Joss and Evan the lightness of their Semi-Hostile Environment Life-support equipment. The heaviest parts of the SHEL gear were its powerpack and breather system; the rest looked like a late twentieth century fighter pilot's pressure suit, a sealed, lightly helmeted coverall whose surface was decorated with pockets, pipes, and wires. Sop SHELs had a few extras that went beyond the shields on each shoulder: enhanced comms equipment, light body armor built into the structure of the SHEL so that its presence wasn't obvious, and provision for all the targeting sensors that might accompany whatever sidearm the officer chose to carry. Even then, both the civilian and the sop SHELs were for daytime wear only. It would need many more years, and a deal more terraforming, before the Martian night became hospitable enough for more than lichens to take liberties with it—and despite what perps might think, a sop was higher up the evolutionary scale than that.

Tombstone looked no more appealing from the surface

than it had from the air, and to Joss's jaundiced eye, more
than the settlement's name was reminiscent of what he had
seen of Earth's Old West period. Granted, all of that had
been on entertainment vids, but—except for the color of
the dust and the shape of the buildings—the atmosphere
was right. Horseshit in the streets would have been entirely in keeping.

And men with guns.

That thought was what prompted Joss to engage a little
more than the usual voice-locks when he closed *Nosey*'s
ramp. Ignoring Evan's eyebrows, which lifted considerably, he patched a low-intensity Watchdog program to the
ship's defensive systems and dared Evan to object. There
was no objection, at least nothing audible. The low-
intensity setting was safe enough; at least it wouldn't try
to blast the maintenance staff, assuming Tombstone had
any—unless they were the sort of ill-intentioned people
who confused maintenance with sabotage. That had been
tried already, before Watchdog, and it had only been by
great good luck that Joss, and Evan, and *Nosey,* hadn't all
gone up in the same big bang.

"We've already been shot at," said Joss, not caring that
he sounded the teeniest bit defensive. "I'd rather not take
any chances."

"No objections here, boyo," said Evan. "So why don't
you let me put on the suit?"

"Because I don't think we'll need that level of firepower to help us find the decoder."

"Yet we've already been shot at, as you so properly
point out. And you think we need the Watchdog." Evan
tilted his head to one side, waiting to see how Joss would
wriggle out of this one, and Joss grinned despite himself.

"We might also need the good citizens of Tombstone,
who know this part of Mars better than the pair of us. I
think they'd be more willing to help if one of us didn't arrive in town wearing an ambulatory tank."

"Ah, hearts and minds. Just like they taught us in the
Service. Why didn't you say so before . . ."

★

THEY WALKED THE SHORT DISTANCE FROM THE pad to the town center. Even if the distance had been much longer they would still have walked, since Tombstone boasted neither a slideway nor a cab service. Joss looked up and down the dusty main street with the weird feeling that he had indeed fallen into one of his own vids. There should have been tethered horses in a street like this, and high-fronted clapboard buildings instead of the low geodesic domes. He was half-expecting the first person they might see to be wearing a Stetson—which, balanced on top of a SHEL helmet, would have been *really* weird.

"This place is well named," said Evan behind him. "It's a ruddy ghost town." Joss half-turned, wondering if his partner was picking up on the same Western images and making some sort of closet vid-watcher's joke.

That was when the shot went between them.

No projectile this time; it was a thin needle of violet light laced with sparks where its energy ionized stray particles of dust, and it came so close that Joss could hear it sizzle. He and Evan were already diving in different directions, clawing out their own guns in midplunge to fire back. Except that there was nothing to shoot at. The slaved HUD eyepiece of Joss's helmet had gone active directly after his Remington left its holster, but the thing's motion and thermal sensors saw not a single target. Three hundred yards away, there was the fast-decaying heat signature of a beamer's discharge flare, and that was all.

Joss picked himself up off the ground, breathing hard and wanting to hurt something. "I," he said slowly, "am getting tired of being shot at. Bullets, and now beams. Sooner or later one of them is going to *hit* me."

"Maybe," said Evan. "But that at least was only a warning shot." He stood up and dusted himself down, then returned his own gun to its holster and so disengaged the targeting eyepiece. "Whoever loosed it off was easily close enough to hit either or both of us, if hitting was what they wanted."

Joss nodded agreement. With any sort of particle beamer, three hundred yards was point-blank range. "Warning of what?" he wondered. "That they know we're here? Hardly a surprise, if Welles Control advised them two hours ago. Warning to get out of town? Same thing: they'll already know this is a straightforward search-and-locate mission. We'll not be staying to enjoy the scenery."

"You love your mind games, you know that?" Evan smiled, and if it was a sour sort of expression, that was only to be expected in the circumstances. "I'd say it was just a greeting to the cops, and a little reminder that the inhabitants of *this* Tombstone are carrying more than Colt Peacemaker .45s. We've been warned, all right, and with a beamer so we'd get the message loud and clear."

"Okay, so you've been paying more attention to the vids than I thought. Question is, who did the shooting?"

"We may never know, Joss-*bach*. This is the Mars I remember from the last time. Those archaeological sites weren't in the basement of the Hilton, mind. This is the outback, where you can tell a man by the length of his, ah, barrel."

"Gun machismo. Bloody marvelous! I *knew* I didn't like this place."

"Not even its bar?"

That was something Joss hadn't expected. Granted, the past few minutes hadn't given him much opportunity for sightseeing, and granted, the domes had as much individuality as a tray of eggs, but the second dome up on the left did say BAR AND SALOON in letters big enough that he shouldn't have missed it. The calligraphy left a bit to be desired, but its meaning was plain enough. This was their first stop. Joss groaned under his breath. There always seemed to be a brawl of some sort at the beginning of their investigations; the sop uniforms, and Evan's size, seemed to attract the sort of barfly who needed to prove something. The brawl this time looked more inevitable than most, since there had already been enough proof that the natives were restless. At least whichever one of them had been carrying the beamer. But in any case, in a place like this, the bar was likely to be the best place to get information, and find out who to talk to.

"I'll make an exception for the bar," he said, "but only if it turns out to be useful. Otherwise, I hold by everything I've said."

"Your objections are duly noted, Officer O'Bannion."

Evan dusted at himself again, and straightened the equipment webs that had been knocked slightly askew when he threw himself out of the line of fire. "Now; let's go see who's at home."

They paused between the outer and inner locks of the bar-dome to take off their breather gear as manners dictated. Even out here, keeping them on would be considered impolite, a veiled insult cast on the premises' own facilities. Then they stopped. Joss could tell from the look on Evan's face that they had both been struck by the same thought at once. It would be very easy to get rid of unwanted visitors by means of an airlock accident, and despite the way that Evan had dismissed the warning shot—Joss never, *never* dismissed being shot at—that shot had made it obvious enough that visitors in sop uniform were very unwanted indeed. *Manners be damned,* thought Joss, and thumped the cycle button with the heel of his hand. They kept their breathers on until the inner lock had closed behind them.

Whether it was the insult suggested by their breathers, or the presence of two strangers in a town that didn't attract such casual visitors, or the sop uniforms they wore, all heads turned and all conversation stopped. All that was missing was for a honky-tonk piano to tinkle on for a few notes before going silent in its turn. Joss wasn't surprised; this was what was *supposed* to happen in bars like this when the strangers in town stepped through the door. He would have been more concerned if nobody had paid them any attention, because then he'd have started to wonder what was hiding behind the pretense of normality. This stillness and hostility, veiled or open, was the true normality of such a situation.

And Evan's looming presence behind him might have had just a bit to do with it as well.

He unsealed the breather system and clipped it in place on the shoulder of his SHEL. Pointedly, though, he did not take off his helmet. For a couple of centuries now, any cop who came into a drinking emporium with his hat or cap or helmet on was there about official business; equally, taking the headgear off meant that its ex-wearer was off-duty, and looking for nothing more than a drink. There had been many occasions down the years when a rookie's forgetfulness had caused panic and spilled pints. Joss had seen it happen more than once in his own career—and on the very first occasion, had been the cause.

There was no wild scramble for the door, which relieved Joss slightly. Together they stalked up to the bar. Joss felt a number of eyes looking with interest at his holster, and noticing that it was still secured. This of course meant nothing in particular, since its positive fastener had long since been replaced with something that didn't obstruct a fast draw; but Joss wasn't about to point that out to anyone. For the moment he contented himself with running a speculative gaze along the rows of bottles. Their labels were familiar, and sometimes even their shapes, but their contents were another matter entirely. Pink gin was usually mixed to order, with Angostura bitters. It didn't normally come that color in the bottle, and especially not the harsh cotton-candy shade that was presently hiding behind a Tanqueray label.

" 'Dewars never varies,' " said Evan, coming up behind him. "So why is it blue?"

"No idea," said Joss. "I'm a stranger here myself."

The barman had been doing traditional barman things since they came in, like polishing glasses and running a cloth over the countertop. In fact he was doing them with such energy that it was obvious he didn't have time to serve any more customers. It was equally obvious that if he polished that single glass or scrubbed at the farthest section of countertop too much more, he was going to eventually wear them both away. He was watching Joss and Evan with an expression that both sops knew all too well. It fell short of actual hostility, but it had the blunt, closed look of a man who thinks that if he's unhelpful for long enough, the people he doesn't want to see will go away. It might have worked with the locals, but officers of the Solar Patrol had been made to feel unwelcome by professionals, the sort of people who used heavy weaponry to make their point. A rude barman didn't count for much.

Finally Evan rapped his knuckles on the counter. It wasn't an especially loud noise, nor even particularly impatient, but in the quietness of the bar, where conversation had just about risen back to a murmur, the three sharp taps sounded as if they had been delivered with a gun-butt. The barman jumped to be of assistance, and Joss sighed inwardly. It looked like Tombstone was another of the all too many places he had been, where the only thing that gained respect was violence or the threat of it. Just once in a while, it would be nice to have a duty assignment where the worst a sop could threaten would be the withholding of a tip.

"Good morning," Evan said, in a tone of voice which suggested the morning's goodness was going to have something to do with the bartender's cooperativeness. "Solar Police. Glyndower." He nodded at Joss. "O'Bannion."

"Morning," said the bartender, and said it as a curse.

"An SP ship went missing somewhere in this area last night," Evan said. "We need to talk to the local PPD officer and start up a search. Can you tell us where his office is?"

"Fifth dome down on your right as you go out," said the bartender.

"Thanks," Evan said. He looked at Joss with an expression that said, *Which of us goes?*

"You go ahead," Joss said. "Sun's over the yardarm somewhere. I might have a quick one." And he took his helmet off.

"Right."

Evan headed back for the airlock, and Joss went back to contemplating the drink bottles behind the bar. He wasn't quite sure what he wanted yet; the peculiar colors of things that evidently weren't what their labels claimed had taken the edge off his thirst, and the atmosphere in the bar wasn't helping.

He sighed. "All right," he said, "what's the local poison, my good man?" It was a setup remark and he knew it, and intended it as such; if he was going to chat with these people, they might as well make the usual jokes at his expense.

"Well," said the bartender, "the cops usually have cyanide."

"Straight up, or on the rocks?" Joss said amiably.

The bartender laughed. At least, he stretched his mouth

and forced three syllables that sounded like "ha-ha-ha" past his teeth. "That's a good one, Officer! I'll remember that! Ha-ha-ha . . ." It sounded no better and no more sincere the second time around.

"Anyway," said Joss, "I'm flying today, so better give me something soft. Ginger ale, whatever. But my partner will want something with a little more oomph to it when he comes in. Whiskey and water. Very weak."

"Scotch, Irish or bourbon?"

"Irish. That green one on the end shelf."

The barman picked up the indicated bottle, looked at the label, shook his head and put it back. "Sorry, sir," he said, "that's vodka. Our Irish whiskey is here."

"The *orange* one?"

"Yes, sir. Bushmills. From the North of Ireland."

Joss eyed the liquid dubiously; it wasn't even the color of oranges, but an eye-searing Air Rescue fluorescent. The strangest part of all was to discover that it actually smelt like whiskey. "Comes from the North of Ireland, eh?" he said. "Its ancestors might have done, but this one missed the boat a long time back. It looks like Bush travels no better than Guinness." He shook his head and shrugged. "Oh, all right. Just don't forget the water. Lots of it."

Directly after he had served the drinks, the barman found something else to do back down at the far end of the counter. Joss watched him go, picked up Evan's glass, and sniffed warily at it. *No duty was ever paid on this,* he thought. *And for such a small settlement, there's much too much hard liquor on the shelves. The colors have to be somebody's idea of a joke; without barrel aging, everything from whiskey to brandy to Campari is going to come out looking like plain white spirit.*

He drank his ginger ale thoughtfully. *That's probably what got us shot at this morning. Just someone nervous about their still.* Possibly once people got the idea that he and Evan weren't particularly interested in the stills, they might loosen up a little. He hoped so. There was a ship missing out there that needed to be found.

The barman started wiping the counter again. Joss began discussing the weather with him in a good-natured way that suggested he didn't care whether he got an answer or not, and was quite willing to keep talking until the bartender said something. Nor was it as inconsequential to talk about the weather here as one might think. If a dust storm blew up unexpectedly, it could make a surface search that was already no picnic into a real bitch of an assignment. There was a chain of geosynch weathersats keeping a close electronic eye on variations in the Martian climate, but they could only monitor and report, not control, and the sort of dusters that most concerned Joss could blow up and then blow out in a matter of a couple of hours. In those few hours, they could cover tracks, crashsites, even change the base topography of a given area, so that only longterm residents could find their way about.

"You have any people here who work as guides?" Joss said, after a little. "We may be needing one or two."

"Some," said the bartender. "They're mostly out at the mining sites; they come in every now and then. Or if someone messages them from Scott's place."

Joss filed this information away and turned a bit to look at the rest of the bar. The patrons were divided about fifty-fifty between staring at him and staring at their drinks. Joss caught the eye of the nearest, a dour-looking creature with a bald head and a black mustache that was climbing around to his ears, and lifted his glass at him in salute. The man favored him with an expression that wasn't quite a death wish, and at the same time looked at the glass with interest.

"Same again for him, please," Joss said, and waited for the bartender to serve it up. It was something blue, with ice. Joss raised his eyebrows, picked the glass up and brought it over to the man's table, sitting down across from him.

"Nice weather we've been having," Joss said, and smiled.

"What you mean 'we,' kemo sabe?" the man said.

Joss's grin spread dangerously. "Seen that vid, have you?"

A little of the death wish fell off the man's annoyed expression. "You know that's a vid?" he said, sounding surprised.

"I have a full collection of the originals," Joss said

softly, *"and* all six of the parodies. O'Bannion," he said, holding out his hand to the man.

"Fiesler," the man said, "Laurenz Fiesler." He took Joss's hand and shook it, bemused.

"And what do you do, Mr. Fiesler, besides watch entertainment that most people of our time consider too odd to bother with?"

Fiesler smiled a bit. "Mostly I mine lichen."

"Is that anything like 'mining moisture'?" Joss said.

Fiesler laughed out loud that time. "I've seen that one too. My mother used to show it to me when I was little." He took a long swig of his drink. "Nope. You've never been to Mars before, have you, O'Bannion."

"First time for everything."

"Well, this isn't like growing club moss. The lichen here is the same kind that lives on Earth, but a little hardier. Likes the rock, lives right flat to it. The only way you get it off is to scoop up the rock and pulverize it."

"Sounds hard to do without hurting the lichen."

"It is," Fiesler said. "Three different processes. Ultrasound, mechanical compression, agitation. A lot of equipment that used to be used on the dig sites goes for that now. Then wetting, compacting, compression again, baling—and the lichen goes out in big bricks, like shoe boxes, to the club moss farmers mostly."

Joss blinked. "What do they want with it?"

"They use it for fertilizer." When Joss blinked again, Fiesler laughed at him a little. "Mister, you know how much it costs to haul fertilizer up here from Earth? It's not economically viable. Except for human waste and the meat and vegetable matter left over from food processing, this is the only usable organic matter on the planet. There's lots of it, it's got pretty good nitrite content, it's a renewable resource—we spore over the areas we've mined—and it's all over the place."

"Makes sense," Joss said. "But what do you do with all the rock you have left over?"

"The chaff? We sell it to the plascrete companies over by Welles. Saves them the processing costs of going out and pulverizing it themselves."

"Nice racket," Joss said.

Fiesler looked at Joss from under his eyebrows, which were almost as thick as his mustache. "Not as nice as some," he said, *sotto voce*.

Joss tried not to look too interested. "Oh?"

Fiesler drank his drink, swallowed reflectively, looked off toward the door, and said, "Some people around town aren't going to be real glad to see you here. And some people *are.*"

Joss admired the slightly zenlike quality of this statement and sat quiet for a moment, waiting to see what else might be forthcoming. But Fiesler didn't say anything, and Joss noticed that there were looks being directed toward them from various nearby tables.

He took a drink of his ginger ale and said, "Much more of the digging going on around here?"

Fiesler shook his head. "Not as much as there was a few years back. That first metal find, it got everybody overexcited. Me, I'm not sure it was ever anything but a hoax. I'm not sure the scientist people know what they're talking about, either."

Joss nodded, unwilling to start arguing the point. It had been about eight years ago, now, that someone digging for subsurface ice had found a layer of iron oxides. Nothing special about that, at first; except that on analysis, the oxides were shown to be not of naturally-occurring iron. The carbon traces in them indicated that they had been produced by the rusting down of a half-inch-thick layer of solid steel.

At that point, man had only been on Mars for about sixty years, and the discovery was made far from any of the originally established settlements. Many people insisted that this was some kind of elaborate hoax. Others pointed out that it seemed farfetched that anyone would have buried a steel plate half an inch thick, half a kilometer wide and *eighty* klicks long under the Martian surface, just as a joke. Besides, carbon dating indicated that The Strip had been rusting there for some thousands of years. Indeed, the Martian climate being as dry as it was, it would have taken at least that long.

The discovery had set off the predictable rush of digging, "finds," publicity, accusations, counteraccusations, more digging, and around and around. Joss had been slightly amused by it at the time. There was something about Mars that had always made Earth people a little crazy, causing them to give undue credence to tales of canals, alien princesses, dry sea bottoms, stones shaped like human faces, and endless other tosh. This, he had thought at the time, was just one more manifestation of the desire to find that someone else had, once upon a time, lived in our solar system with us. Joss had thought that now that people were living on Mars, it would correct the situation. Instead, it seemed to have made it worse. There were still archaeological digs going on all over the planet, for the question of how The Strip *had* gotten there had never been resolved to anyone's satisfaction. And, as happened wherever people were digging for unique archaeological materials, there were also threats, thefts, protection racketeering, blackmail and occasionally murders. It was those crimes which had first brought a certain Welsh EssPat suit specialist and his then partner to Mars, where they had handled the case with such efficiency that there had been few perps left to stand trial.

Joss put this business to one side of his mind for the moment. "Do you tend to work close to this area, Mr. Fiesler?" he said.

Fiesler shook his head. "Not me. I come here to shop—stocking up today. I keep my rig south and west of here, as a rule. The stone all around here, clear to the Mountain almost, has been mined out and respored. It'll be a few years before it's ready to mine again."

Joss nodded. If this were true, Fiesler wouldn't be likely to have seen anything. "Did you work this area before, though?"

"A couple years back."

"Would you recognize any changes in it, you think?"

"Probably. The worst you get around here is dust; it drifts up against things, but it can't do much more than change the terrain, at least not in the short term. We get the occasional marsquake, but since things are pretty flat around here to start with, it's hard for anything to fall down. Cracks, you get. Big ones. Not much else."

Joss nodded toward the wall, in the direction of Olym-

pus Mons, cocking his eye at the door: the airlock was cycling. "Don't know how you can call terrain that contains
that 'mostly flat.' "

Fiesler smiled at him just a bit more widely. "You get
used to it after a while."

Joss shook his head. "Used to a mountain twelve klicks
high?"

The inner door opened up, and Evan was standing there.
He flipped up his visor. Joss looked at the expression on
his face; it was not one he had often seen before, and as
surreptitiously as possible he loosened his weapon in its
holster.

Evan looked around the room and said, "Someone get
on the horn to Welles PPD, right now."

Everybody in the bar stared at him.

"Sorry," said Evan, "but someone's shot your sheriff
and left him in the street."

THE GRAY-PAINTED DOME AT THE FAR END OF
Tomestone's single street carried neither the crest of the
Solar Patrol nor that of Mars PPD. Instead, right above the
outer lock, someone had painted a silver star with the
word SHERIFF printed across it.

And someone else had all but obliterated both the star
and the word it carried with a burst from an ultra-high-
velocity heavy-caliber slugthrower.

Joss's first urge on seeing the place was to turn to Evan
and say, "This has to be a joke, right?" But what lay in the
rutted dust of the road, in front of the dome, removed any
humor that might have been latent in the situation.

The whole top of the man's body was gone. Or not precisely gone; bits of it were lying here and there, gray or
pallid white, or white but oozing red from within—
shattered bone, shreds of lung and brain. The dome was
spattered, though all the spattering was freeze-dried now,
in this thin air, and frost was forming over what larger
pieces hadn't already sublimated all their water away. An
old-fashioned chainsaw might have done the same job, but
not as neatly—if that was the word wanted here. The rest

of the man lay in the street—not really twisted, for it's
hard for just half a body to twist. The combination of frost
and drying out made it look like half an unfinished shop
mannequin, with untidy flaps of red-and-black leather
sticking out where the rest would eventually be fastened
on.

"They waited till he came through the office door, shot
him and went away," said Evan. "There's no sign of any
attempt to force the outer doors, as far as I can tell."

"So he saw them, and knew them, and was coming out
willingly," Joss said.

"Sounds like it. Let's make sure no one touches the
caller panel . . . though the odds of it carrying any useful
prints are minimal. No one goes barehanded in this cold,
not if they want to keep their skin on. Then they did the
sign." Evan cocked an eye up at it in chill annoyance. "A
calling card of sorts, I suppose."

"Whose calling card? Why did they do this? And who
the hell *are* they?"

"Now that, Joss-*bach,* is the number one question. And
this whole vicious little business puts rather a different
complexion on what brought us to this pesthole. Officers
on the spot and all that."

"Not in this case. We may have found it, but we don't
get to wrap it up. Tombstone may have—" Joss paused as
one of the crowd who had followed them from the bar
handed him a dingy blanket given him by someone behind
him. He took the blanket and settled it over the sheriff's
remains. "They may have *had* an elected sheriff as its local law-enforcement officer, but it comes under the jurisdiction of Mars PPD in Welles. What we do—no matter
what we want to do, and as to that, I'm not sure yet—is
wait till Welles gets a murder squad out here . . . and then
go about our business. Of which we have plenty."

For just a few seconds, Evan Glyndower looked very
angry indeed at the thought of doing nothing. Then he
shrugged as training regained precedence over emotion.
"You're right, of course. We've already left too many
traces over the evidence as it is. And what we have to handle, PPD aren't equipped for."

He said it calmly enough, but he looked like he hated

every word. Joss knew exactly how Evan was feeling. Beneath his own veneer of calm, the same slow fire of rage was burning like a sourness in his gut. And yet orders were orders, and police procedure was there to be followed, not flouted—especially not by the blue-eyed boys of the Solar Patrol. Had the breather mask not been in the way, he would have spat some of the sourness out onto the ground. As it was, he had to be content with no more than a long, deep breath that only served to fan the fire.

"Come on, Evan. Let's get back to *Nosey* and report this."

"And then let's do some aerial recon." Evan stared at the blanket-covered half-corpse, and his big hands closed into fists like hammers. "Because if I don't get away from the way this town smells for a few hours, I'm afraid that I might really hurt somebody . . ."

THEY WAITED UNTIL THE PEOPLE FROM PPD ARrived: a group of three grim-looking cops in dusky red SHELs, who moved into the sheriff's old dome and started to dust and spray the place for prints. Evan and Joss went off to do their recon, and when they came back three hours later, the Welles cops were still there. Nothing had changed, except that the corpse was gone from the street; someone had brought in a flitter, and the half-body lay there in the back of it, swathed in a black pressure bag.

Joss was in a fouler mood than he had been before they left. The search they were presently conducting was hopeless. There was simply too much terrain around here to be covered without some help; and there was no sign of the team that was supposed to be sent from Welles to help them search. Nor, as it turned out, would there be any sign of them very soon, Tee had told them. There were only three SP ships based on Mars with enough range capability to undertake a search. Two of them were still out on searches for private craft, and the third was down for servicing and might be functional later this week.

"Damned budget cuts," Evan was muttering. "How the

bloody hell are we supposed to get anything done around here?"

"It's all your fault," Joss said. "You're the one who keeps pulling off the impossible. You get a reputation for being a miracle worker, and next thing you know, you're saving the galaxy."

"Not me, Joss my lad. You with your great bulging brain, it's *your* doing that gets us into these things."

Joss rolled his eyes a bit and headed over to the most senior of the cops, a little man with a lined dark face and a rather frustrated look. "Officer Latham," he said, "have you found anything out?"

Latham looked at Joss with weary humor. "Officer O'Bannion," he said, "these people have no interest in telling us anything. The Welles County courts could subpoena them, but I don't see that it would do any good, since it would take months, maybe a year, to get the paperwork through the system here; and they wouldn't tell us any more then than they're telling us now." He leaned against the flitter. "All we can do is take this poor devil to the morgue and tell the Probate people to process his will, if he had one."

Evan came over and looked at the flitter, then at Latham. "Certainly there has to be something more that could be—"

Latham looked up at Evan with a total lack of the nervousness with which most people regarded "suit talent." "It would be nice if there were, Officer Glyndower. Look, this place isn't even officially a *settlement*. There are no local authorities, no town council, no local statutes, nothing like that. There's nothing but the people who live here. The only writ that runs here is general planetary law, and we have the devil's own time enforcing it. People who come out to places like this to live don't do it for the sake of finding structure in their lives! They come out here to the middle of nowhere to get *away* from law, and rules, and supervision. That they should have a sheriff—" He laughed softly, just a breath of sound with no humor to it. "They were just worried about being shot at and not having a witness that they had an excuse to shoot back. Poor old Joe—" He looked at the flitter, looked away again.

"He deserved better," Latham said. "I never did understand why he stayed in this job, but—" He shrugged.

Joss nodded. "Well, then," he said, "we'd best let you get on with your work. We have troubles of our own. If we can help you in any way—"

"We'll give a shout," Latham said.

The two of them started to make their way back to *Nosey.* The swift Martian night was starting to fall; the sky was all black now except for a thick line of violet right around the horizon, and a blur of dust kicked up by the rising wind veiled the sun as it started to dip below the barren horizon.

"We should stay the night here, I suppose," Joss said, thinking a little sadly of the Hilton. "If our help should arrive suddenly—"

"Yes," Evan said. "And then tomorrow morning—if there's no help, we're going to have to find some other way to do our job."

Joss rolled his eyes. "Ah, eternal duty," he said. "The improbable we do immediately . . . the impossible takes a little longer . . ."

"And less time, the sooner you start," Evan said, and strode ahead.

Joss smiled a bit and followed him off into the dark.

THREE

EVAN WOKE UP ANNOYED—MORE SO THAN HE
had been for a long, long time.

He was used to hostility from small towns, and used to
it on Mars; but this time it seemed to him as if more effort
was being spent on being nasty than was strictly necessary.
There was something going on.

Of course there's something going on, he thought unhappily. *When is there not, when the SP sends you somewhere?* But still, it was true. The little scams and rackets
they had been getting whiffs of, didn't merit this level of
anger and fear at all. Nor, he would have thought, did they
merit what had been done to the sheriff, except that small
towns had their own small levels of priority. It was all too
possible that the dead man had been more heavy-handed
than his predecessor, and somebody had objected to it in
the most direct way they knew. After all, using a plasma
beamer on Joss and himself just to say "go away" was
scarcely what one could call subtle.

He sighed and got up to make himself tea. Joss was
probably still asleep. He had been late to bed, filing some
kind of report with HQ; typical of him, to be so conscien-
tious on a day when people had been shooting at him and
other people had been getting blown away right on their
own doorsteps. *Then again,* Evan thought, pulling his uniform singlet on, *that's one of the ways he deals with it, I*

suppose. Structure. We all have our ways of structuring our responses. Me, I make tea.

The little galley was scrupulously clean, which was Joss's fault again. For all his jokes about tidying up hotel rooms and such, Joss was a stinker about keeping the ship neat. *Probably because it's his first one,* Evan thought . . . then laughed at himself; it was his first ship too.

He nuked a pot of water and fished two teabags out of the little plastic bin where Joss kept them, thought again, picked out a third, and dumped them into the water. Then he sat down to think.

They were going to have to try to do a more detailed overflight today. Too much of yesterday had been occupied with the murder of Tombstone's sheriff. Probably that waste of time was one of the things Joss had been putting in his own report. Evan resolved to have a look at Joss's pad a little later.

Meanwhile, while the tea was brewing, there was always his own pad to look over. He fetched it from his stateroom and brought it into the galley, checking the clock on it. Early, early morning on the Moon; not much better here. He keyed his implant on.

"Tee?"

There was the usual three-second pause. *What are you doing up this early?*

"Busy day. Tell me something: What access to surveillance satellites have we got available here these days?"

Another pause, and then a sigh. *Not much more than we used to . . . and there's been a change of ownership. The reconsats all belong to the Space Forces now. Security.*

"Terrific," Evan said. "All right. I want whatever pictures we can get of the Niton flightway corridor. Here—" He pulled the pad over, brought up the maps Joss had given him, told the pad to be touch-sensitive, and stroked a circle around the area he was interested in. "This bit. Can we get pictures of that? The last forty-eight hours, and as high-res as you can."

I'll do what I can. It may take a while. You know how they are.

"I thought we were supposed to be on the same side," Evan said. This was true; but it was equally true that the

Space Forces saw the Solar Patrol as beat cops, not to be trusted with "sensitive" information; and the Patrol, by and large, saw the Space Forces as superannuated "peacekeeping" troops with too many guns for their own good, and an inflated notion of their own importance in the great scheme of things. "Anyway, tell them that lives are at risk and so on. See if you can't light a little fire under them. If you don't have any luck with that, sic Lucretia on them. *She'll* have fun with them."

Will she ever, Telya said, with only thinly disguised glee. Lucretia loathed the Space Forces more than most. *Anything else I should pass on?*

Evan considered mentioning Tombstone's murdered law officer, then dismissed it. Knowing Joss, it was already in last night's report; a brief reference and nothing more, since local trouble, however brutal, had no relevance to their present mission. "This place is a dump, everybody hates us because they don't know us, and no one wants to tell us anything."

Sounds like the usual.

"Tell me about it. Why can't we ever be sent somewhere classy?"

I don't know . . . I thought you had been. The Hilton—

"Your low blood sugar is showing. Go get me those satellite shots."

Will do.

The tea had become properly black. Evan poured out a cup and didn't bother with the sugar or the milk as he scrolled through the files presently resident in the pad. Here was a new one: this would be Joss's report of last night, a copy left for Evan with Joss's usual thoughtfulness. He read through it, finding a nasty and accurate precis of the previous day's happenings.

Evan lingered for a moment over the description of the conversations in the bar, and Joss's evaluation of them.

Much local "private enterprise" in evidence, most of it illegal or marginally so (distilling, etc). However, there are hints of some more powerful influence (or influences) operating in the area as well, either controlling or trying to control various aspects of the

town's economy. Difficult to tell whether any of this
is germane to our reason for being here.

General affect of the people we've met so far has
been inappropriately nervous, but this possibly has
something to do with the local law officer having apparently been murdered.

Evan snorted a little at the phrasing. What they'd seen
had hardly been a suicide ... But that was just Joss being
his usual correct self, refusing to definitely posit murder
until a court had agreed with him.

The initial response to this being the arrival of Solar Patrol officers rather than those of the Planetary
Police Department, may have served to aggravate
rather than alleviate an unpleasant situation.

Evan drank his tea and thought about that. Normally,
people who had just lost their only policeman would welcome the appearance of another, *any* other, especially
when the place was as marginal and isolated as Tombstone
was. But the reaction to their appearance, even on other
business, was anything but welcoming.

*Maybe they're afraid that what happened to their last
cop will happen to us* ... That at least would be under-
standable. The last thing the people living in this quiet
place would want would be more shooting and more killing, which would only draw more sops, more attention,
more trouble. Or maybe, as the report suggested, they
were afraid that the attention and the trouble had arrived
already.

Well, I don't think I'll be shot, Evan thought, finishing
his tea. *At least, not this morning. It's time to put the
SHEL aside, and let whoever needs to know just how much
potential trouble* has *arrived.* He rinsed and dried his cup,
put it away, and went off to get cleaned up.

About half an hour later he was in his armor and tapping out a note on Joss's pad: *Going out for the morning
paper. Back shortly.* He took his own pad, headed out of
Nosey, sealed her up, and strolled into town.

There were very few people abroad, and those whom

Evan passed looked at him with extreme suspicion, and sometimes crossed the street to avoid him. In his present mood, he didn't mind. On Mars he was in no position to walk around with his visor up, and with it down, he was quite aware that he presented a more than usually threatening image—that featureless, steel-silver surface, showing any onlooker nothing but a distorted reflection of his own unnerved face. At the moment, that was fine with Evan. Let them think about his presence a little—that he was likely to be a bit more difficult to shoot than their last cop had been—and it might make his job and Joss's a little easier.

Meanwhile, though, he had other business on his mind than threats. He made his way toward the shop-dome they had passed yesterday. Evan was thinking of his mother, who had said to him a long time ago, "If you want to find out what's happening somewhere, *cariad,* go down to the corner shop and get a pint of milk and a loaf, and don't hurry. You'll find out soon enough."

He walked up to the dome, slapped the control for its outer lock. There was a grumbling of machinery, but no action—the thing was stuck. Evan sighed, put his pad down for a moment, placed his gauntlets flat against the sliding door of the outer lock, and pushed. Complaining, the door slid back. Evan stepped in, pushed it shut again, made sure it was sealed, and waited for the airlock to pressurize. Nothing happened.

He sighed again, and did what he had done so many times on Mars before: turned around and kicked the outer lock door, hard.

Air began to wheeze into the lock. Evan shook his head. There was something dodgy about these old Goodyear seals—always had been. *Well,* he thought, *actually, the problem isn't the seals. The problem is that the sealing* mechanisms *are all fifty years old, and no one has money or the time to replace them.*

The lock finished pressurizing, and as the inner door opened, it sounded the sort of electronic chime that usually announced a customer's entrance into a shop. Evan smiled faintly at the familiarity of it, then stepped in and looked around.

The shop was less dingy than he had expected, and more crowded. Most of the floor space of the dome was taken up with shelves stacked up fifteen feet high, or seven feet high around the edges; on the shelves were every kind of thing that a mining community could be imagined to need, with hardware getting the best look-in. Drills, both pneumatic and laser, new and used, and parts for them; a lot of parts for skimmers and sandsleds, almost all used; SHELs and stillsuits and regular clothing, folded up on the shelves; toolkits and small appliances (all used again); and off to one side, the food shelves, with big bulk bags of flour and sugar and other such staples, and smaller luxury items in slightly beat-up wrappings, and in every language imaginable, looking as if they had come a long way. Evan smiled and put his visor up. It was the kind of place where you might find anything, if you had all year to look, and didn't mind that it had had five previous owners.

"Can I help you find something?"

The voice was not the snarl he had half been expecting; and to Evan's astonishment, it was a British accent, from somewhere in the Midlands, if he was any judge. He turned and found himself looking at a big round dark man in atmosphere-tight coveralls, with his breather gear hanging off over one shoulder like a casually thrown-back necktie. The man was looking at him with curiosity, but no hostility, which made a pleasant change.

"Yes, you can, actually," Evan said. "I was wondering if there's anywhere in town that I might be able to send a dox."

"You can do that from here," the shopkeeper said and sounded slightly pleased. "Over this way. Might I ask how you come by that accent?"

"Honestly, I hope," Evan said, and followed the man off to one side of the dome. Here, on the side opposite the door, there was a lock leading into another dome, and more shelves were stacked up against the dome wall proper, all filled with paperwork, more foodstuffs, a cash register, a credit terminal, an adding machine dating back to the early 1900s at least, and much other bumf. "I'm from Wales, at any rate. Evan Glyndower, Solar Patrol."

The shopkeeper laughed. "Pleased to meet you, Officer Glyndower. Scott Virendra, from Birmingham, England. Some time ago." He put out a hand, and Evan shook it carefully—one had to be careful not to squeeze, when wearing the suit. "What did you want to dox?"

"Uh, I've got it here." Evan held up the pad. "If you have a standard LP-12 interface—"

"Yes indeed, right here." The man bent down and came up with a grimy plastic bag full of cables, and began rummaging through it. "Someplace here—ah." He found one, untangled three other cables from it, and plugged one end into his dox machine, an ancient model that was doubling as a bookshelf for about half a dozen paperback manuals on skimmer repair. "Straight text, or graphics?"

"Both."

"And how were you going to pay for that?"

"Cash."

Virendra looked at Evan with just a touch of skepticism, but it was good-humored. "You have pockets in that thing?"

Evan laughed and undid one of the forearm hatches, coming out with a small wad of paper scrip. "Not in the usual places."

"Here we go then," said the shopkeeper, and plugged the cable into Evan's pad. "You want to dump your material to the machine, we'll see if we can get her to work."

Evan nodded, tapping at his pad. He had come up with a much-edited version of Joss's report, which he was doxing to HQ; Lucretia would probably be astonished by its arrival, at least until she received the more private message, via the implant and Telya, explaining what was going on. There was nothing sensitive in the document he was sending now, but Evan had added a couple of shocking lies about the ship they were hunting, and he was curious to see if they might surface later, and where.

While the transfer was running, Evan looked around him and said, "Does the town have a newspaper? I was hoping to pick one up."

"We have a broadsheet," Virendra said. "Not much news here. We have a clipping service with the IP wire, it sends us headlines and things. Mostly our paper has ads in it."

"Local papers don't change much," Evan said with a smile. "Sounds like our old one in Llangollen."

"I was in Llangollen once," said Virendra, and that was all it took: he was off in gossip mode, at full gallop. Evan reckoned that it would take about fifteen minutes before the gossip topics got off Earth and made it to Mars.

It was actually about twenty-five, but Evan didn't mind. Virendra wasn't just a gossip, he was an *entertaining* gossip, and that made all the difference. He was also—from the police point of view—a mine of information, since though without doubt his stories had been embroidered over many tellings, there was a core of meticulous observation in them all.

That, Evan realized in retrospect, was why he hadn't minded the lengthy preamble. His ear had long since grown bored with fiction, since as a sop the fictions he most frequently encountered were straightforward lies. Virendra's anecdotes weren't lies, although they were a lot of other things, and their exaggerations were obvious to someone who knew a little of the truth behind them. In his verbal wanderings around Wales and the English Midlands, he had mentioned places and events that Evan knew—and had done so with enough accuracy that once his embellishments had been stripped away, the statements could stand up to cross-examination in a court of law. Evan made a mental note of the fact. People like Scott Virendra were occasionally a bloody nuisance, especially if they collared you in the bar, but just as often they were a gift to the police. The only drawback in a little community like Tombstone might be in convincing him that talking to Evan—or Joss, assuming Officer O'Bannion ever arose from his downy couch—wouldn't somehow incriminate his friends. If he needed convincing. Evan smiled a bit at the thought, for at the speed that Virendra was talking, he had said the wrong thing half a dozen times already. To the right, or more properly wrong, police officer, there was probably more than enough evidence to bring him down to the nearest precinct house for a little more "assistance with enquiries."

"Who's out there, Dad?" The voice came from beyond another doorway, one Evan had noticed and then dismissed as yet more storage space. Apparently it also doubled as living accommodation, for the person who came out through it was the first besides Joss and himself that Evan had seen in Tombstone without a SHEL or skinsuit. "Dad, I said . . . *Oh!*"

That, or variants on the theme, was what most people said when they saw the suit, and Evan was wearily familiar with almost every nuance of pronunciation. This, however, was somewhat different. Not only was it said by a rather pretty young woman, but its tone conveyed more pleasant surprise than he was used to hearing. She was as tall and dark as her father, but very much slimmer, and she was wearing her hair in a single heavy black braid that was very traditionally Hindu, and to Evan's mind must have been the very devil to deal with when wearing a skinsuit's helmet.

"Ah, Kathy. This, Officer Glyndower, is my bookkeeper, purchasing manager and daughter, Katherine."

"Sounds like your priorities are in the right order as always, Daddy dear," said Kathy, but she was smiling as she said it. "Good morning, Officer. I'm glad you're here."

Again Evan offered the immobile armored fingers that represented a handshake in the suit, but Kathy Virendra pumped his whole forearm up and down in vigorous greeting. Now that she was over her surprise, she seemed enthusiastically pleased to see him, graflar armor and all. Neither the reaction nor the sentiment were much in accord with what Evan had encountered yesterday in the bar, but he wasn't going to object on that score.

"I take it," she said, sizing up both him and the suit with a long, thoughtful stare, "that you're here in this walking tank to nail the bastards who shot Josef?"

"Kathy!" Virendra sounded scandalized, even though to Evan's ear it was the mechanical outrage of someone going through the motions. He had a feeling that Katherine had a rough tongue when she let it go, and her father had long since tired of trying to keep a curb on it. Or on her, probably. Children grew up quickly in places like Tombstone, and among the first thing they learned was a wider

and more colorful vocabulary than those living a more settled existence had need for—though if "bastard" was the
worst she could think of in an attempt to shock the new
boy on the block, he had gotten off lightly. Evan almost
smiled, but concealed it in time, thinking that even ordinary school playgrounds were often the location for rawer
language than most army boot-camps. Not that Kathy was
a schoolgirl; far from it. He put her age at the late middle
twenties, young enough to be passionate about things, but
old enough that those passions weren't just teenage flight-
iness.

"Not this time. My partner and I were sent here on other
business. We were probably still in the air when your sheriff was murdered. But we advised the PPD in Welles, and
their Homicide squad came out yesterday afternoon."

"The PPD." Kathy Virendra made the acronym sound as
if it applied to a disease rather than an organization. "Yes,
I saw that bunch of useless farts. And as usual they
couldn't find their own arses if someone tied their hands
together."

"Katherine!" said her father again, and this time Scott's
anger was more apparent. "Moderate your language,
young lady—"

"What is this 'lady' crap? Daddy, you know as well as
I do what's been going on around here, so why pretend it
never happened? I saw what was left of Joe, and nobody—
not even dear Mamma—could pretend hard enough to
make something like *that* go away."

"You saw?" Evan was somewhat surprised, though not
as much as he might have been in other circumstances.
Life in the Martian outback taught children more than how
to swear like troopers; the uglier forms of death were more
common out here, and thus the need to come to terms with
it. "That wasn't something for a young woman to look at."

Kathy gave him another of those up-and-down looks,
and set her fists on her hips. "Officer Glyndower," she
said, "nobody's spoken to me like that for a long time, and
I'll take the compliment as intended rather than the insult
it could be. This isn't the lobby of the Hilton, and even the
accidents around here tend to be messier than in town. I
didn't just see what was left lying in the street, I was one

of the people who made sure he wasn't left there. You wouldn't have noticed me—people in SHELs all look alike anyway—but Josef Chernavin was my friend. *Our* friend."

Evan lowered his head in silent apology, feeling just a little ashamed of himself. He didn't normally say something that was so out of place, and knew he should have realized the implications of his words before they left his mouth. "Sorry about that," he said at last, and then smiled a small, wry smile. "Looks like I've been spending one leave too many with my old Mum in Merioneth, see? Very old-fashioned lady, she is. Wouldn't like Mars at all, no." Kathy and her father were watching him, and he nodded slowly as if confronting a great truth. "Too much dust— and her with such a thing for tidying, too."

Virendra chuckled, the sound of a man who knew exactly what Evan meant, but Kathy just rolled her eyes. In amongst all the earlier gossip, Evan had picked up enough references to Scott's wife for him to form some small opinion of why there was no Mrs. Virendra on Mars. Their divorce, he guessed, had been amicable but inevitable, and looking now at the offspring of that marriage, it was small wonder that Kathy hadn't stayed with her mother. The surprise was that she had stayed with her father for so long, because she was definitely one of those children his mother called "a hawk hatched by chickens." Willful was another and less kindly way to say it.

"Well, Mister Sop Glyndower, I don't think you're here to do the tidying, so what brings you out here if not to hunt murderers? The scenery? The weather? Or is it all a big sop secret?" Kathy was sitting on the edge of the counter now, swinging one leg and daring him to take exception to her impudent tone.

Evan contented himself with a glance at her father, a glance heavy with implications of what he, Evan Glyndower, would do with this cheeky little minx if she was his own child. Quite apart from anything else, even if he'd overestimated her age by ten or so years, she was still too old to be playing the brat—or at least, to be playing it without reprisals. "Hardly a secret, if anybody bothered to check the answering machine that pretends to be your traffic control system," he said. "Welles Central logged a flight plan, advised ETA—*and* purpose of mission, in case we needed help on the ground."

"About the crashed ship? Then it's for real?"

"Of course it's real! For pity's sake, why would we . . ." Evan's voice trailed off as realization dawned, and if, as in Joss's weirder vids, that realization had taken the form of a light going on over his head, Evan felt sure that his light would have been no brighter than a glowworm's armpit. "You thought that we'd put out a wide-band crash alert as a *cover?*" The girl stared back at him, looking satisfyingly embarrassed, and Evan felt for the first time in this conversation that he had actually managed to score a point. "Mister Virendra," he said, ignoring her, "however long you and your daughter have been out here, it's too long for her."

Virendra raised his shoulders in an elaborate shrug, managing to imply without a word that he'd been saying the same thing for so long that he'd gotten bored repeating himself. "It is nonetheless unfortunate that we must rely on the officers of the PPD. Though I would prefer that she moderated her language somewhat, I—and others in this town—share Kathy's low opinion of the force. Far from capturing whoever committed this horrible crime, they are more likely to stir up a hornet's nest with their investigations, and be well out of harm's way when the stinging starts."

Evan relaxed a bit inside the suit. It was starting: Virendra had begun to say the sort of thing that careful prompting—but never anything so unsubtle as interrogation—could lead in all sorts of interesting directions. Except that on this occasion, Virendra took the step himself, with a candor that almost caught Evan Glyndower off his guard.

"You and your companion were in the bar yesterday," he said. Evan nodded; it would have become common knowledge in Tombstone before they had ordered their first drink. "And you were doubtless impressed by the variety of alcoholic beverages which so small an establishment can offer its patrons." Again a nod, but this time Evan was paying a great deal more attention than his casual glance might have suggested. "I must confess to you, Officer Glyndower, that not all those drinks have reached Tombstone by legally acceptable routes."

Hearing it said aloud by one of the locals was a surprise; hearing it phrased with such oblique delicacy was hilarious. Evan started to guffaw, but caught it halfway and turned it into a cough. "I do beg your pardon," he said, and coughed again, several times. "Oh, excuse me ... when a tickle catches me like that, I just have to let it take its course. It's the dust here. Once you crack this thing's faceplate, there's no defense."

"In that case, Officer," said Kathy Virendra, who had seen through Evan's performance and was now very cool and missish at her father's confession being greeted with concealed laughter, "I hope for your sake that nothing else cracks it." She grinned, very slightly.

"I'll drink to that," said Evan, wondering a bit at the phrasing, but letting it go. "Mister Virendra," he said carefully, "I'm presuming that you've weighted up all the implications of what you've just told me, so I won't issue cautions, and so far as you're concerned, this conversation will never have taken place." Evan knew that he was stretching his authority by such a statement, but at the same time, the Solar Patrol charter did permit its officers to exercise a certain degree of flexibility in their interpretation of the law. It was one of the first documents to have written in black and white what every sensible policeman knew: catching a misdemeanor was all very well, but not if it let a grand felony go undetected. Evan knew there was something bigger here than smuggling or bootlegging. He could feel it, almost *taste* it.

He gazed at Virendra for a few seconds. "We'd guessed about the drinks already," Evan said. *Well, it wouldn't do to let them think they'd pulled the wool over our eyes altogether, now would it?* "The speculation was in terms of percentage proportions—how much smuggled, how much locally produced, that sort of thing. Cop stuff. But there's not the market for a lot of smuggled alcohol in one small town, so let me suggest this to you: that the only booze not distilled locally was the stuff that originally filled those bottles in the bar, and that probably comes in quite respectably, one bottle at a time? Am I right so far?

Virendra had gone as pale as a man with his ancestry could manage, but he nodded agreement and even managed to give Evan a slight smile. "It would have to be one bottle at a time, or illegally," he said. "My family has run shops since the middle of the twentieth century, and the farther goods have to travel before the point of sale, the higher the price they command when they reach it. The hardware you saw out in the warehouse-dome is all essential equipment, vital for work—or for life, Officer Glyndower, just simple survival! Most of it has already been owned two or three times, reconditioned, serviced, fitted with spares, stripped down, rebuilt—"

"I get the picture."

"If such necessities must be reused to destruction because they cost so much to ship here, then can you begin to imagine what prices luxury goods command? You can buy Glenwhatsis in the big hotels in Welles, but have you ever considered what's involved in first getting it over the sea to Skye, and then to Mars? When all those overheads are added to the price of a drink, then only the wealthiest can afford to drink it—and they do so, Officer Glyndower, not because it's good, but because it's expensive, foreign, and not for the likes of people like us! Well, I tell you with pride that the whiskey and the gin and the brandy we make here tastes just as good as theirs, and the miners can afford to drink it. They drink it proudly, because it's their own; they made it themselves, or their friends did; and most of all, it owes nothing to anyone else, because it's Martian!"

"Quite so," said Evan softly. "Knocked the dust out of the cushions, that did."

"What?" Virendra looked blank, as if he had taken a wrong turning somewhere.

"What the preachers used to say in Wales, when they were bargaining for their speaking fee. 'For one sovereign I will preach you a fine and learned sermon, and for two I will preach so that there are tears in the eyes of the women, but for three sovereigns, look you, I will preach to knock dust from the cushions!' " He grinned a bit. "Will you have your three sovs now or later?"

"You're making fun of my father," said Kathy Virendra. Her voice was tight and angry, an unpleasant edge to it that Evan fancied had been honed in too many situations just like this. There was nothing wrong with being defensive of yourself or your family—he had been that way himself—but Kathy had brought it to a level of pugnacity that went beyond the defensive and into the offensive. And she was that, all right. For all her good looks, she was one of the most offensive people he had met in a long while, and for less reason than most.

"I was not making fun of anybody," he said, and if he sounded tired, it was because he was growing tired of her. "I was just impressed by his vehemence. There's nothing wrong with being proud of achievement and eager to do better—otherwise not one of us would be sitting on this planet and drawing wrong conclusions from what each other says. So, and I know it's hard for you, just be *quiet.*"

Kathy stared at him with her mouth open and drew breath to say something; then wisely thought better of it and subsided into a chair behind her father's desk, looking fairly chastened.

He turned his attention back to her father. Scott Virendra was watching him with a furtive wariness that Evan recognized from other investigations. It was the look of a man who's just thought back over what he's been saying, and realized that he's said far too much. That was true enough, and it was far too late to change. Evan studied him in silence for several seconds and then said, very gently, "Now then; *what* hornet's nest?"

"You've started, Dad," said Kathy. "So you might as well finish. I think Officer Glyndower's going to be a more sympathetic audience than the PPD. At least," and she gave Evan a smoldering look from eyes the color of coffee, "I hope so."

"Normally that would be a matter for the courts to decide," said Evan, making the pronouncement sound as formal as he could. He had been smoldered at before, and it was always best to nip that sort of thing in the bud before people started jumping to the wrong conclusion over an officer's relationship with his witnesses. "But I *did* say that this conversation would go no further. So let's hear all about it. Start with the sheriff. He was a local man, local enough to have many friends in Tombstone. What was his connection with the bootlegging? Graft? A percentage cut?"

"Nothing."

"Now that I don't belive. There had to be something in it for him."

"All right then, how about a drink that he could afford to buy whenever he felt like it, rather than something he had to save for?"

Evan's mouth quirked. "Try a better one, Mr. Virendra. Booze isn't *that* expensive."

"Maybe not in Welles City, Officer. Or anywhere else with an off-planet landing facility. But out here, it's another story. All we have is an atmosphere pad. Everything we own comes in through Welles or Herschel, and though they can't put too many surcharges on the essentials like the stuff I carry in this store, when it comes to luxury goods everyone's a middleman, right down the line. We can't play one against the other the way the big hotels can do; we have to pay what's asked, or do without."

"Or make your own."

"You see?"

"I think I do, after all. But didn't your sheriff tell you that one of the Excise and Duty regulations says it's perfectly legal to make beer and wine at home, so long as it's for domestic use?" Evan didn't quote the regulation; for one thing, he didn't know it off the cuff, and for another, it would have made him look a real bureaucratic prat.

"That's all very well, Officer Glyndower, but it doesn't cover distilling. I know, because Sheriff Chernavin checked through all the regulations for us."

"But Joe turned a blind eye to it," Kathy chipped in, "so long as the stuff was local produce for local consumption. He saw everything, of course, but he said nothing. He didn't need to: nobody was getting hurt, except maybe the big city distributors, and he figured that they were doing all right as it was.

"He figured nobody was getting hurt, eh? Until he got

himself blown away in front of his own office. I've seen some examples of cutthroat business practice in the past, Mr. Virendra, but isn't that taking matters to extremes?"

Scott Virendra's eyes widened slightly as he realized what Evan was implying. "It wasn't the distributors, Officer Glyndower!" he said hurriedly, waving both hands in the air. "I wasn't suggesting that, indeed no!"

"Then who?" snapped Evan. "If you're so certain who it wasn't, then you must have a fair notion of who it *was*. Well?"

"It was . . ." The merchant faltered, looking sidelong at his daughter. She ignored the glance completely, staring instead at Evan as though trying to read him in the same way that he had read her father. There was no moral support for Scott Virendra from that quarter, and after clearing his throat as though what he was about to say had stuck in it, he faced Evan again and said, "It was Harry Smyth's crowd."

"Harry Smyth's crowd." Evan said it as though he was tasting the words and finding them lacking in flavor. Certainly they were lacking in conviction. In a place called Tombstone, he found talk of "so-and-so's crowd" or "the such-and-such gang" of convenient villains in black hats, less than impressive and too fanciful by half. They'd be complaining about rustlers next. Rather than treating Virendra's statement as evidence, any cop worth his badge would regard it as just one more of the man's exaggerations and dismiss the whole thing—that was if he didn't charge the merchant with deliberately wasting police time and a whole flurry of other petty offenses. And yet . . .

Evan remembered another time, not long past, when the crime that he and Joss thought they were investigating was claim-jumping. No potential gold mines, certainly, just asteroids viable for exploitation. It had all led to the same thing, old crime or new: somebody who had done all the work of exploration and testing had seen that work go for nothing when the men with the guns muscled in. Some of them had backed down; others had objected, and had gotten shot. Just like Sheriff Josef Chernavin. *What was* he *objecting to?* thought Evan. That was why he didn't laugh, didn't throw out all the other information he had gleaned, and why his voice was much more gentle than it might have been when he said, "All right, so we've got this gang. Why did they murder your town sheriff?"

Virendra shook his head. "I don't know them. Not well. They aren't seen around town much. As for Joe, all I can think is . . ." He sighed, shook his head ruefully. "I think maybe the local stuff got too popular. You must have seen it, in Welles—the bright colors are hard to miss. There are people in town who think it's fashionable to drink the local rotgut . . . more fashionable than the imported stuff, even."

Evan knew exactly what Virendra was talking about. He had seen moonshine sold the same way in fake mason jars in North America, and *point!* in stoneware jugs in Ireland, and brown death in white glass flasks in Iceland, and *raza* in clay bottles in Turkey. *Drink the exciting, deadly, delightfully crude booze of the natives!* was the sales pitch. *Get a* real *hangover!*

"So then," Evan said, "your Harry Smyth saw a way to turn a quick profit from something the local law permitted. How long ago?"

"Ten months, maybe a year. It didn't count for much at first. There wasn't enough money involved to make it more than a sideline—"

"A sideline from what? What was his main business?" Evan came in hard and sharp again, jumping on the questionable word before Virendra could retract it. Standard low-level interrogation practice; maybe "sideline" was just a turn of phrase the merchant used, and maybe it indicated that he knew more than he had intended to say.

"Mining, probably." Evan quirked an eyebrow, but said nothing. "He has to be a local man, Officer, or he wouldn't know where to put the pressure on. That means he has to be a miner. There's nobody else out here, except me."

"Is that so? Then where do I find this Harry Smyth?"

"I don't know."

"Mr. Virendra, a less tolerant officer than myself could easily lose patience with the number of things that you don't know. Explain that."

"Some of the . . . the bootleggers said that they heard

the men who came to threaten them use just that one name. Harry Smyth. Except that there's no record of anybody with that name in Tombstone Mining County."

"About twelve thousand square kilometers, Officer Glyndower," said Kathy Virendra helpfully. "That's a long beat, even for a cop whose suit does the walking for him."

Evan didn't even glance at her. "Wonderful," he said. "And let me guess: with their breathers sealed, they all looked alike anyway. The face masks are polarized, of course."

"I'm afraid so."

"Oh God. All right, where were we; small scale local industry subverted by anonymous villain and friends for fun and profit. So then what?"

"Designer Drinks," said Virendra simply. "When the hooch went from fashionable to acceptable to popular, demand for it went through the roof, prices went up, profits went up, and suddenly it wasn't a sideline anymore."

"It's not Harry Smyth," said Evan, frowning, "it's Al bleeding Capone." Even though he still needed the details from Virendra, he knew most of the rest already. His knowledge had nothing to do with Joss and his entertainment vids; Prohibition, that particularly stupid and short-sighted law, had been a part of training. So far as the Solar Patrol was concerned, there were no really new and original crimes left under the Sun; only modernized adaptations of past offenses. That was why so much emphasis was placed on historical lawbreaking, to teach the present generation by the past generations' successes. And failures. It had been the passing of the Prohibition regulations that had given truly organized crime its toehold in the old United States, and it had taken well over a century to be rid of it. This was ceasing to be one of Joss's Wild West shows and turning into something very much nastier. Evan found himself thinking about the weapon that had been used on Sheriff Joe: a rapid-fire slugthrower. Call it a—his mind hunted for the reference—a tommy gun. Primitive technology or modern, the effect was much the same, and greed and violence didn't change much down the centuries.

"It took your sheriff almost a year to realize that there

was a protection and extortion racket running on his patch?"

"They kept it a close secret for as long as they could," said Virendra. "The people who mine the lichen around Tombstone are tough—they have to be, to make a living from this desolation. But that toughness is no defense against men with guns. Being tough, standing up to them, was more dangerous than doing what they told you to. A couple of people argued. Told Smyth's mob where to stick their production requirements. And that was when the 'accidents' happened. Do you know what sort of accidents can happen to a lichen miner, Officer Glyndower? Real, ordinary, run-of-the-mill, all-in-a-day's-work accidents?"

Evan thought about the ultrasound pulverizers that were used to separate the lichen from the rocks on which they grew, and about the fragility of SHELs and the delicate organism of living tissue that the suits were supposed to protect, and nodded, just once. "I've been to Mars before," he said. "I know."

"Then you'll know why most people kept their mouths shut, before someone shut them permanently. Until Joe found out."

"Found out about a couple of murders, and didn't report them to higher authority? Why the hell not?"

"Two reasons, Mister Sop Officer," said Kathy Virendra. "First, from what I heard, there was no mention of murder. Those were accidents, remember? Circumstantial evidence, I think you call it. And second, Joe was probably thinking of what any investigation might turn up about *him,* after nearly a year of not seeing anything."

"I think he was probably offered a sweetener to stay as blind as he had been," Scott Virendra said. "Cash, a cut, whatever. That's the way the Smyth gang would have worked. Anything to keep business running smoothly. Anything for a quiet life."

"And he refused," said Evan. That was the generous thing to say. *Either he refused, or he took their money and that put him off his guard. Until they came back with the "tommy guns" and made sure he wouldn't see anything. Bastards.*

"I don't know," said Virendra. "But he could have accepted all the profits from this year and from next, for all the good it—"

A chime drifted in from the outer dome as its lock cycled open, and Scott Virendra bit his words off short. The man looked scared. For just an instant Evan wondered why, and then remembered what Virendra had said about the way Harry Smyth's boys kept their faces hidden. If all that could be seen of them was the blank darkness of a polarized mask, above the insectoid array of a breather's cycling system, then they could be anybody—anybody at all. Even the customer who'd just come into the shop.

Evan could hear the sounds of movement beyond the office doorway, as the newcomer wandered up and down the labyrinthine aisles of the main shop-dome. There was nothing furtive about those sounds, which was just as well. After what he had heard—and more importantly, after what he had seen behind the words, in the expression on Virendra's face—Evan Glyndower's trigger fingers had developed a slight but definite itch.

"Well," he said quietly, "aren't you going out to see what you can sell?"

The merchant didn't move for a few seconds; then pushed himself heavily and, Evan thought, reluctantly, out of his chair and walked towards the door. Then he stopped, and even through the skinsuit he was wearing, Evan could see the changing set of the man's back and shoulders as the tension drained out of him. Virendra stepped back and to one side, out of the doorway, and smiled both in relief and recognition.

The person who came through the door did not seem especially threatening—although as Evan knew from personal experience, that meant nothing where modern high-tech weapons were concerned. But he relaxed nonetheless, set at ease more by Virendra's attitude than by the new arrival's apparent harmlessness. She was no more than five feet two inches tall, red-haired, pale-faced and freckled, and given that coloration, Evan wasn't surprised to hear her introduced as Helen Mary Cameron. Any further doubts as to her ancestry were laid to rest directly as she began to speak, because her voice was heavy with the burr of Scotland.

"I wasna expecting to find you keeping such company, Mr. Virendra," she said, a bit taken aback by the hulking presence of Evan and the suit. "And you, sir—I wasna expecting to see you in here, not with so much needing done around this town."

"Criticism on first introduction is a sign of something or other," said Evan, "but whether it's a good thing or not depends on the reasoning behind it. What's yours?"

"With the sheriff shot dead in the street and those PPD people pulling his office apart, I wouldna have thought you required such a question, Officer Glyndower."

"The PPD have their job to do, Miz Cameron. I have mine. And they aren't the same."

"Be careful, Helen Mary," said Kathy Virendra. She had started to work her way through several elderly ledgers on her father's desk, but the simulation of industry didn't impress Evan in the slightest. "Don't get drawn into conversation with Officer Evan here. Not unless you know exactly where you were at nine o'clock on the evening of the tenth inst."

If it was meant as a joke, it fell flat—and not just with Evan, who had just about had enough of Kathy's remarks. Helen Mary Cameron stared at her past Evan's armored shoulder, and made a noise that the sop would have transcribed as *Huh.* "I was probably up to my elbows in the bloody compression baler, as usual," she said. "Scott, the main hydraulic flutter valve has gone again, and this time I think it's permanent. Have you a BB-220 squirreled away somewhere for a reasonable price?"

"Possibly, possibly. But why doesn't Andrew buy a new baler? He's certainly spent its price in repairs over the past year."

"Because the repairs and the spares cost a little at a time, and new equipment costs a lot all at once. That's why . . ." They wandered off among the racks of hardware, Virendra sounding persuasive and Cameron unimpressed.

Evan listened with mild interest to the discussion. There was nothing for him to learn from it, but the tone and timing of Scott Virendra's speech made an interesting contrast to the way he had spoken only a few minutes before. His nervousness had evaporated completely, despite what he had said about not knowing the Smyth gang because they always wore blacked-out breather masks. It was probably because he and his daughter both knew this red-headed young woman, and had known her for a long time. Probably for as long as Sheriff Chernavin had known the men who came to kill him.

Dismissing that somber line of thought until such time as it would be of some use, Evan wondered what had become of Joss. The question was answered by another chime from the outer lock, and by a voice calling his name. "Over here," he replied, and then, remembering what the outer dome looked like, expanded his directions to, "past the flour and sugar, in the office."

Joss came in after a few seconds; Evan had failed to say where the flour and sugar were, and without the owner as a guide, their seemed to be a lot more of Virendra's store and general warehouse. "Gone for the morning paper, eh? So, what news?"

"Nothing of much use to us," said Evan, aware that Kathy had looked up from her stack of ledgers as if to remind him he had said the conversation with her father would go no further. "Most of it's likely to be the PPD's pigeon anyway, and you know what planetary police departments are like when outsiders start intruding on their patch."

Kathy lowered her head again, and pretended to get on with her work—then sat up very straight with a horrified expression on her face as Helen Mary Cameron came back into the office and said, "How much did they tell you about the Smyth gang?"

Smyth gang? Joss mouthed silently at Evan. Evan waved him to silence.

"No more than what the whole town probably knows already," said Evan. "Bootlegging, extortion and murder. A pretty picture—but none of our business."

"What? But you're police, aren't you? Why else are you here?"

"Search-and-rescue mission. EssPat has a ship down in this area. They sent us in to find it, and bring back the crew. And as for us being police, Miz Cameron, yes, we are—but the criminal offenses which have been taking place around Tombstone are not within our jurisdiction. Unfortunately, since Mars has a PPD, they—"

"—do what they always do! Nothing!" To the sops' surprise and discomfort, she looked to be on the edge of tears.

"Did you know the sheriff very well?" Joss asked, trying to be as diplomatic as possible about the potential relationship.

"I dinna care about the sheriff!" Helen Mary burst out, then recovered herself and shook her head. "Oh dammit, yes I do care, I'm sorry he's dead, but I'm more concerned about my father!"

It spilled out in a rush of words: how her father had gone out three days before in their big cargo skimmer and had headed north from Tombstone into what had become known in the past year as the Badlands. It was the territory where Harry Smyth's gang was supposed to have a hideout, when they weren't behaving like ordinary, hardworking citizens. Andrew Cameron hadn't believed it; any sort of gang headquarters would be too obvious in terrain where every feature was known to somebody or other, and it was far more likely that the Smyth mob had just encouraged that rumor for their own ends. True or not, what Andrew had hoped to find were large deposits of lichen that had gone untouched since the gang trouble first started.

"And I havena heard from him in nearly three days!" she finished.

"Transmitter problems? Or a skimmer breakdown?" For Helen Mary's sake, Evan was trying to look on the bright side, although he had reservations about what might really have happened. If the lichen miner *had* run across something he wasn't supposed to see, then from their reputation alone, Harry Smyth and his followers were likely to ensure that it wasn't reported back in the quickest and most permanent way. "After all, from what I've heard you say already, your father's mining equipment needs fairly constant maintenance if it's to keep running at all."

"He wouldna let the comms transceiver break down."

"But if the skimmer had a lift-drive failure, the impact might have jolted something loose, and no fault to your father. So he may well be sitting out there, waiting for you to gather up a search party and go get him."

"As if I could get a single *man* from this town to go into the Badlands, when they're all so scared for their own skins!"

Joss tapped Evan lightly on the back of the head— tapping his armor would have been a waste of time—and said, *"We're* heading for the Badlands. It'll be an aerial search for our own downed ship, and there's no reason why we can't look for your father while we're at it." He paused, almost a little too theatrically for Evan's taste, and then gave the young woman a speculative stare. "We'll need a local guide for both searches, Helen Mary. How well do you know the area?"

"Well enough." She took a deep breath, as if dismissing her own fear of what might be out in the Badlands, and let it out slowly between her teeth. Then she smiled. "You've got your guide."

"Why," said Kathy Virendra, "are EssPat running this search and not the PPD? You keep saying that you can't interfere in what's happening here because they're the local law and this is their, uh, their patch. This missing ship's down on their patch."

"But it's our missing ship, and nothing to do with them," said Joss, much more amiably than Evan since he hadn't had to suffer Kathy's little comments for most of the morning. "Areas of jurisdiction work both ways, and we just happened to be on the spot. The Solar Patrol looks after its own, and when you're on the spot you do what you can for your buddies, cos they'd do it for you."

"Even if you're on vacation," said Evan.

"You brought that suit on *vacation?"*

"Where I go, it goes. Like a Swiss Army knife, but bigger." He swung around with a thin whine of servos and raised one hand in a salute of farewell to Scott Virendra, then closed his visor down. "Come on, Helen Mary, Officer O'Bannion. Let's go see what we can see."

NOT LONG AFTER, THEY WERE IN *NOSEY,* AND heading northwestward at a good clip. Joss had fastened Helen Mary down in Evan's seat, leaving Evan to make himself as comfortable as he could in the passenger seat. It wasn't really made to fit his suit, but he managed to get the straps to go around it well enough to save him from falling over if something sudden happened—which, when Joss was flying, was occasionally the case.

Joss, meanwhile, was chatting to Helen Mary in the inconsequential kind of way he typically used with nervous civs to calm them down. Evan grinned a little to himself, knowing from experience that this mode lasted only so long with female civilians. After that, Joss started relapsing into charm, which was even funnier.

Through the windscreen, ahead of them, Evan could see a small chip of silvery brightness levering itself up into the violet of atmosphere, the bottom of its irregular disk made jagged by the rocky horizon.

"Ah, the hurtling moons of Barsoom," Joss said.

Helen Mary looked at him incredulously. "The *what?*"

Joss got a rueful look. "Doesn't hurtle very well, does it," he said. "Oh well. Life never knows when to imitate art."

Mary Helen looked back at Evan, uncomprehending. "He means," Evan said, " 'Oh look; Phobos is coming up.' "

"Is that which one it is?" Joss said. "Holy Buddha, look at the shape of it! What hit it?"

"Deimos is a lot farther out," Evan said. "It looks more the way Venus does from Earth. Something hit Phobos a right swipe, all right, but no one knows what. Not Deimos; it doesn't show any signs. Might have been something strayed out of the Asteroid Belt, the boffins think."

Now it was Helen Mary's turn to stare at Evan. " 'Boffins'?"

"He means scientists," Joss said. "Evan speaks a strange form of English, but don't let it frighten you; he's a gentleman even if he *does* pronounce 'schedule' without the *c.*" He tapped at the pilot's console for a moment, setting a course in, and then turned away when the autoguide took over. "Panic and Terror," he said, "valets to the War God: that's who they are. Even if they don't hurtle."

Evan looked at Joss in bemusement.

"You think you have a corner on the classical education

market?" Joss said, turning to the computer console next to him and working at it for a moment. "Hah. Helen Mary, I need to know what kind of comms string your father's skimmer would be using. What model transponder was he using?"

"It was a Hayes-GEC," she said. "A 960. The string was LMNR-1807-RKL."

"Thanks." Joss worked for another moment at the touchpads, then said, "What kind of reach did it have? The usual 500-km squirt-variable?"

"That's right."

"Got it." Joss made one last set of adjustments to the console. "That will hunt your dad's frequency at the same time as the one we're after. Now then—"

He cleared the front screen, displayed a plan-view of the terrain they had searched over the day before. "Is there any likelihood that you can think of that your dad might be in this area? We've done it already, and I'd hate to waste time."

Helen Mary leaned in close and examined the screen, tracing parts of it with one finger. "No," she said, "I don't think so. The problem is, you can never tell—"

Joss looked back at Evan. "Your hunches tend to run in harness," he said. "You have any thoughts on this? I'd sooner go on to new ground. But she's right."

Evan held still and refrained from thinking for a moment; thinking about a hunch, doing anything so specific as looking for a feeling about it, was fatal.

"I think maybe we should go over it again," he said. "I know it seems like wasted time. But you asked."

"Right you are," Joss said, and worked over his console again. The familiar cross-hatch lines of the search grid laid themselves over the map of the area west of Olympus Mons: green for ground not yet covered, red for the area taking a second pass. "Helen Mary, it's going to take about six hours to cover all this ground. Can you keep alert and watchful on a visual search for that long? Tell me if you can't. We can take a break in the middle if need be."

She smiled at him. "Officer, do you know how long and hard you have to look while surveying for lichen? A six-hour run is no picnic, but it's hardly unknown, either. If after six hours I can still tell how old a growth of lichen is within a month from three thousand feet, I shouldna have too much trouble seeing my father's skimmer."

Even if it's in little pieces spread over half a hectare? Evan thought, but kept the thought to himself. The thought of equipment failure was with him, having seen those racks and racks of spares in Virendra's warehouse. There came a time when even the most carefully cossetted piece of equipment could not be run anymore. But people would try to keep it running anyway, simply because of the prohibitive cost of buying a new part. There were always people who were sure that they knew everything that needed knowing about maintaining their own machinery. But they rarely had equipment that could test for factors like metal fatigue. A valve goes in a braking-jet system, a combustion chamber develops a hairline crack, and boom, there you are scattered over the countryside, and no one will ever find out what happened.

Joss was busy with his computer again. "Here," he said, "here's a craft recognition list. Pick your dad's skimmer profile out—I have just about all of the major models here. Had he done much modification on it?"

"Not much. Some to the engine pods—he thinks the commercial exhausts are too small."

"It's touch-sensitive . . . draw them in for me. Three sets of views—there's the plan: touch this for front and side. We have smart side-looking radar . . . it'll rotate what you draw and construct a 3-d version, then match against objects on the ground."

Evan looked over at Joss. "When did you buy *that?*"

Joss smiled wickedly. "I made a deal with one of the people in Parts Procurement at Serenitatis," he said. "He wanted—"

"Don't tell me what he wanted, for pity's sake, I don't want to know!" Evan said. Joss had a slight pirate streak, one which Evan wasn't always sure sorted well with his position as a sop. Still, it was fueled by his creativity, and *that* definitely made him a better sop than many Evan knew, so he had for some time resigned himself to taking the more wicked of Joss's habits along with the straighter ones. *Still,* he thought, *I wonder what he did give the fel-*

low in Procurement? If I could get them to give me some of those new upgrades for the suit—

He sighed, then, and moved up a bit closer to the windscreen, dismissing the thought of his aborted trip back to Sydenham to take *real* suits apart with the lads. Leaning against the bulkhead, he made himself as comfortable as he could and began the business of looking out for a sign of metal, or anything manmade, in any shape, just looking . . .

THEY WERE AT IT FOR HOURS BEFORE JOSS called the break. Helen Mary was still fresh, astonishingly so: she had again and again called their attention to some piece of scrap metal lying on the surface that they had both missed. Mars was not exactly the easiest place to do a visual search; there wasn't even the interesting variation of the landscape on the Moon, flat broken by sudden craters and mountains, terrain all very distinct and separate. Here was just a huge rock-tumble that obscured craters and valleys together; the remnant of an ecology where there was just enough erosion to make serious changes in the landscape over a shortish period of time, say several hundred centuries. Some of these valleys had once had flows of water in them, perhaps as recently as a few thousand years back; though that kind of thing had long since ceased. Wind still worked on the stones, and so did the extremes of heat and cold—cracking valley walls apart, fracturing crater rims, leveling everything out. And the dust and sand blew, rubbing the edges off things, removing any feeling of sharpness or specificity that might make the landscape more interesting or arresting to look at. The only exceptions were the occasional long straight scars where rock had been scalped up by lichen-mining rigs, and the wind and dust had already begun their work on those. Everywhere else, the rounded, reddish sameness of things blurred one's vision after a while, made the mind tired. The radar wasn't tired, but neither had it seen anything, anything at all.

They had almost finished the run over the terrain Joss

and Evan had covered the day before. Joss had set *Nosey* down in a rare little bare patch of a huge field of boulders about fifty kilometers west of the shield boundary of Olympus Mons. Evan made tea and broke a few packs of soup open to be heated in the galley, listening to Joss go on about dead sea bottoms and alien princesses in flimsy clothes.

Helen Mary was sitting back in the number-two seat, smiling and shaking her head at Joss as if he were a creature from another world. "And they laid *eggs,*" Joss was saying, "and they rode around on thoats. If you think of something like a sabertoothed tiger with a lot of legs—"

"Eggs?"

"Legs. And they had radium pistols, and—"

Evan brought the tea in. "You're seeing," he said to Helen Mary, "what I have to put up with. Aren't you going to tell her about the alien war machines?"

"Later. I'm just getting warmed up."

Evan rolled his eyes and went back to lean on the bulkhead again, looking out the windscreen at the bleakness outside. "Rocks," he said, "and more rocks. What a place. I begin to understand why the people taking pictures all that while ago kept seeing faces and such. You want to see something out in the middle of all this nothing. Some kind of pattern."

Joss laughed at that. "True. There may have been something to that face business, though."

Evan looked at him questioningly.

"When the first exploratory team to go out that way finally got to the site," Joss said, "they found that someone had removed the rock."

"Removed it?"

"Well, it was gone."

Helen Mary nodded. "I remember reading about that in school. It was just gone. No one was ever sure whether one of the exploratory team might not have gone out and taken the thing in the middle of the night, or what. But no wind was strong enough to have blown it away . . . it was too big."

Evan nodded. "Some jokester . . ."

"Mars seems to bring that out in people," Joss said.

"The old myths seem to die hard. Even scientists who should have known better seemed to *want* to find signs of life here. Herschel got involved with the fabrication of a hoax himself, though one of the London daily newspapers put him up to it, they say."

Evan thought of the London papers that were still coming out with headlines like, WW II BOMBER FOUND ON MOON, and smiled. "That one," he said, looking out the window, "that one looks kind of like a head. See, you can see the nose—"

Joss guffawed. "Do I smell soup? Let's eat it before it gets cold, and then get going. We've got a lot of territory to cover."

They ate their soup and got back in place; Joss lifted *Nosey* up. The ship lurched a little as it boosted. "Night's coming on pretty fast now," Joss said. "Thermocline's settling."

Evan grunted and concentrated on keeping himself in the passenger seat. The straps creaked and complained about the weight of him and the suit together, but held. "How long is this shaking going to last?"

"Not long . . . it's done now." *Nosey*'s pitching and heaving stopped; she boosted more smoothly. Joss tapped at the control board, then sat back. "It's just that the contrast between the warmer and cooler layers of the atmosphere is pretty extreme, and the spot where the density-change happens is much lower, this time of day. Radar's up." He looked out the screen. "Eyes peeled, everybody."

Another hour went by. There was little real diminution of the sun's light, there being atmosphere of such low density to filter it; but the shadows of the boulders grew long, and confused the view with overlapping patches of darkness and light, as good as any camouflage. Evan alternated between using the vision augmentation in his helm, and just plain squinting, or letting his eyes go unfocused; he seemed better at seeing detail that way. Once or twice he saw pieces of metal, either new or rusty (and hence there for a *long* time, and no use to them) that the others had missed. But it was little consolation to him. Two days, now, the SP ship would have been out in this. An environment with little pressure, not anywhere enough oxygen to breathe, and the Martian night coming on again . . . when the temperatures could drop to -50 or -70 degrees centigrade, and often did. What kind of chance would men have in that if their craft had suffered enough damage to kill their transponder—

An alarm shrieked. "Holy cow," Joss said, and began working over his scan console. There was an image flashing there, a wire-animation outline that Evan at first couldn't make out, and then realized was a piece of an engine pod; the pod of a large craft, not of a little thing like a skimmer. Helen Mary looked at the screen with one of the most desolate expressions he had ever seen, and tears began to run from her eyes, though she made no other sound.

"It's not a skimmer," Joss said, sounding both unhappy and very excited. "Verified SP craft. Or part of one."

"Part—"

"Just you keep your tin pants on," Joss said, and turned, having a word with the forward-facing navigation controls. *Nosey* began to bank off to the right. The wire-frame image stuttered, grew a bit, changed shape on the screen. "Fragmented signal," Joss said. "An artifact of us coming in on direct approach." His hands were working as fast as Evan had ever seen them work before. The image stuttered again, changed shape once more. "There. Another few seconds—"

One of the instruments chimed. "Inertial's got it," Joss said, triumphant. "Locked in and mapped. About—" He studied his board. "Fifteen minutes. Let's not rush it. The wind is kicking up out there."

Evan nodded; sunset acceleration, the rapid shift in local weather on Mars around sundown, he knew too well from old experience. You sat tight until the sun was properly down; the winds could be capricious, and deadly. "Is it definitely what we're after?"

Joss nodded and hit another key; the screen blanked, then came up with the image that the radar was comparing against. It was an atmosphere-capable Patrol cruiser a little bigger than *Nosey*, with much more powerful engines. Evan began to twitch a bit. Local weather shouldn't have been able to do anything to a ship with engines like those . . . not even Martian local weather.

"No transponder," Joss said, tight-voiced. "No transmissions whatever. No carrier, no power readings. Nothing."

Helen Mary shook her head, paused a moment to wipe her eyes. "I'm sorry," she said.

"You're sorry!" Joss turned away from his board for a moment, took her hand and just held it. "Thank you."

She gulped and nodded. Joss looked at her a moment more, then turned back to his work. "A little less trouble with the wind than I thought," he said. "About ten minutes now."

They rode it out mostly in silence, the only one to speak being Joss, as he occasionally chided or praised his instruments. Evan had to smile in spite of himself; Joss habitually talked to the ship's machinery, with varying degrees of affection or annoyance. It would have been even funnier if the machinery didn't occasionally behave as if it were listening.

The engine note changed. "All right," Joss said, turning to the nav controls, "easy down. I'm going to make a low-level pass for the cameras first."

Evan realized he really ought to go sit down and strap himself in, but instead he braced himself more thoroughly against the bulkhead and peered out. They were in an area that was marginally more interesting than most of the terrain they had been over; indeed, they were just now into country that they had not covered the day before. The thought that, had he and Joss gone on for just a little longer yesterday, they might have been here *then,* irked Evan a bit. But he put the annoyance aside, looking out the windscreen. For as far as he could see, big boulders littered the ground; but they did it patchily, not in an unbroken field as they did most other places. There were bare patches, strewn with all sizes of red gravel, with wind-blown dust drifted up against the scattered stones here and there. And there, at the far end of that really big patch, was a long scarred groove, with a great lump of something resting at the end of it. Shapes stuck up from it, and resolved themselves. An engine pod; a skid sticking out at an odd angle. And in the middle of the gravel and the dust, tracks—

"Verrrrrry interesting," Joss said, and said nothing else. He turned to tend to his scanning equipment.

"They're a good ways from the ship," Helen Mary said, looking confused. "Nothing the ship had would have done that, surely—?"

"You're right," Evan said, and his face set grim. "Someone's been here before us . . ."

"There's another bare patch not too far from here," Joss said. "I'll sit us down there. Don't want to mess those up with the thrusters. Evan, go sit down. I don't trust this wind."

"Yes, mam," Evan said, and did as he was told. It turned out to be wise; about ten seconds before landing, *Nosey* began to buck and thrash and sideslip like a mad thing. Evan just managed to get himself strapped in before the ship sat down, hard, with a sound of everything not actually bolted to something else rattling in its place.

There was a second or so of stunned silence, and then Helen Mary said, "Do you always fly like that?"

"Sometimes he's worse," Evan said, and got up.

Joss was getting up too, reaching for the clamps that held his SHEL equipment. "You dim Taff," he growled, "I dare you to do any better. It's gusting to a hundred out there, and the rocks—"

"All right!" Evan said. "Helen Mary, you stay here—"

She favored him with a look, as if he had suggested she go out in her underwear. "Officer," she said, "I live here. I can walk in the wind without falling over. Can you?"

Evan said nothing for a moment. When he had first been on Mars, he had spent some weeks learning the trick of handling the wind, and had also picked himself up off the rocks more than once. He smiled at Helen Mary in apology and said, before he put his visor down, "If I can't, you'll pick me up, yes?"

She smiled back and put her SHEL on.

They went out into the Martian sunset.

FOUR

THEY CAME OUT OF *NOSEY* INTO A SCREAMING
gale. It was odd, Joss thought, how thinly it screamed; a
function of the slight density of the atmosphere, which
was after all somewhat less than that on top of Everest.
But it pushed quite well, and he had to lean into the gusting wind with all his force to stay upright.

Then, of course, the only problem was that it changed
direction without warning, gusting as ferociously to one
side or the other of you as it had into your face or your
back a moment before; so that you staggered one way or
another, and then staggered in an entirely different direction, and did a very poor imitation of a drunk among the
unforgiving stones. Joss looked with concern at those
rocks, which somehow seemed a lot sharper and nastier
than they had while he had been cruising safely above
them. He thought about his faceplate, and what one of
those rocks might do it if he fell the wrong way. It was
guaranteed fallproof, he knew that: the faceplate was made
of the strongest, most shatterproof plastic known to man.
The question is, he thought, bracing himself against a cow-
sized boulder and trying to get his breath and his balance,
is it known to the rocks? And should he crack his faceplate, there was no help for him, no sharing of breather
gear as in the old underwater films. SHEL gear was size-
fitted and wearer-specific, and relied on a positive
pressure-seal to work correctly. Neither Evan nor Helen

Mary would be able to do anything for him. His lungs would freeze, he hoped, before he felt his eyeballs doing so.

Joss hung onto the rocks and took care where he put his feet.

Evan was ahead of him, striding into the wind as if it didn't matter; but all the same, Joss could hear the suit's servos straining and arguing with the pressures working on them from this side and that as the wind shifted. Inside Joss's helmet, a voice said: *"I'd forgotten what this was like."*

"I wish I didn't know to begin with," Joss said, and staggered hard against another rock.

"Buck up, man. Not too far to go."

Joss wondered exactly what was involved in bucking up, and thought it better not to ask: Evan was likely to make some horrendous pun at him by way of revenge for the ones Joss liked to hit him with. Joss busied himself with working his way around another boulder, this one nearly the size of a garage, and found himself staring at something that was not a boulder. It was an engine pod from the cruiser, and Evan was standing over it, expression invisible behind his closed faceplate. The pod was smashed half-flat by the force of its fall, like a chocolate Easter egg dropped on a hot plate.

Joss paused and looked down at the pod, ran a hand over the shipward end of it. "Evan," he said, "this didn't fall off. Look at the section."

"Cut," Evan said. *"With something fairly highpowered. Pulse laser—"*

"I don't think so," Joss said, as Helen Mary came up behind him. "Look at the edges. Polished, almost. No, this was a particle-beam slicer of some kind."

"Impossible. They can't cut that fine—"

"I thought you said the ones on your suits could. Your army suits, I mean; not the stripped-down ones."

There was an annoyed-sounding silence. *"So they can. But they don't have the range to bring down a ship on the wing. And how do you know the cut was fine, anyway? You haven't seen what the—"*

Joss was already heading past the pod, struggling to-

ward the crashed ship. It looked surprisingly unhurt, for
something that had had one of its engines chopped off it
like the drumstick off a chicken. And that engine had
fallen quite nearby. *Someone took the engine off the ship
as it was coming down?* Joss thought. *But if it was already
coming down, why shoot at it? Or had it been shot at at
some other way already?*

The wind came howling across the rock-strewn plain
and hit Joss harder than ever, dust and sand rattling and
hissing against the faceplate of his SHEL. He staggered,
and someone caught him from behind and steadied him.
He looked over his shoulder. Helen Mary was there, bracing him until he found his feet again. He got straightened
out, tapped her on the arm by way of thanks. She wouldn't
let go of him, though. Joss sighed, and resigned himself to
being helped, and they made their way toward the ship together.

It was rather like *Nosey,* or had been—a bit older, a bit
bigger; not an enforcement vehicle like theirs, but a research vessel with enough space to carry some cargo. The
ship was a long slender shape rather like the old rocket
ships in the vids—stabilizers on either side, a big wide
windscreen up front, a sleek pointed nose. And there the
resemblance ended . . . for half the ship's side was missing. Metal and plastic and other materials had burst outward from inside when it crashed; pieces of garbage lay
all over the site, or had lain there, for the wind was rapidly
taking them away.

Joss cursed and stumbled over to the ship with Helen
Mary. Behind them, Evan was stalking along with dreadful
sureness, never missing a step now; he had found his feet
again. Joss came to the ship, reached out and touched one
great blackened rag of steel that was hanging away from
the main body of the craft. There had been fire inside, as
well as explosion. He unclipped the torch from his belt
and shone it into the huge irregular rent. Everything was
blackened with soot, melted by fire.

Evan stepped past him into the hulk. Joss let him:
should something heavy fall down from the ceiling of the
vessel, Evan was much better dressed to cope with it than
he was. His partner vanished into the darkness, his own

torch coming on, picking out here a shattered console, there a seat twisted by fire, all its cushioning burnt away, farther in a door warped out of its frame. Then he disappeared altogether, into the body of the ship.

"Anything?" Joss said after a second or so.

He could hear nothing but Evan's breathing down their commlink, but that at least was reassuring. There was a sound of scraping metal, over the increasing hiss of the windblown sand; something being hauled aside, tossed out of the way; a crash. Another crash, more scrap being thrown out of Evan's path. A sound of rummaging.

Then, *"Diw,"* Evan said. And there was a huge crash from inside that shook the whole ship.

"Evan!!" Joss cried.

No answer.

"Evan—" He started to climb through that gap himself, then stopped as the light wavered through the inner doorway, and that huge silver-gray form came at him again. *"It's all right,"* Evan said. But his voice made it plain that nothing was all right, nothing whatsoever.

Joss was shaken. "No bodies," he said. "Explosive decompression?"

Evan came out through the gap, the shining armor all streaked with soot. "Not at all," he said. "You think there would have been this much of the ship left if they'd crashed from any height at all?"

Joss nodded, then looked in again. "There aren't any bodies," he said. "At least none here—"

"None in back either. I checked. And more." He sounded grimmer than ever. "The prototype's not back there, either."

Joss stared at him. Helen Mary gripped his arm, shook it. "Those tracks—?"

"Someone's been here," Evan said, "and done a little salvage."

Joss shook his head, torn between shock and horror and anger. And worse, it was getting hard to hear Evan above the scream of the wind, the incessant rattle and hiss of the sand.

Helen Mary shook his arm again. "Officer," she said,

"we've got to get out of here! There's a dust storm coming up!"

"Oh no," Joss said, and turned away from her hurriedly, lurched away from the ship, toward the tracks left in the gravel and sand nearby. Helen Mary came after him as he unhooked the little 'Shica vidcamera he used for making records of evidence.

It was almost too late already. The wind was gusting to seventy now; gravel was being whipped around as easily as if it were dust itself, raking across the tracks and abrading them away even as he watched. Joss circled around them as best he could, taking shot after shot, but already the definition of the tracks was being eroded. Another five, ten minutes and they would be gone altogether—

Helen Mary was dragging his arm. "Be careful, don't step on them!" Joss shouted at her, taking more shots.

"Officer—"

A hand closed around his biceps and squeezed, just a little. It was like being caught in a vise. "Come on, you idiot," Evan said, "do you want to lose *Nosey* in this? Come on!!"

Joss took two more last desperate shots of the tracks, then followed Evan back toward *Nosey*—not that he had much choice, with that steel gauntlet around his arm. It was getting hard to see. The sun was almost completely down now, and the air was full of dust; the rattle of it against him was less a sound than a sensation now, like being attacked by angry bees that couldn't sting through his protective clothing—yet. And vision was closing down entirely, Joss realized, as a cloud like a solid red wall came at them and surrounded them. He reached out and caught at Helen Mary just before the world turned dark brick-red.

Together they stumbled back toward *Nosey*. At least Joss assumed they were going toward her; Evan could see in this, at least—thank God for the augment equipment built into his helm. *What's he using, though?* Joss thought as Evan led them weaving around boulders, picked their way over stones. IR *trace can't be any good to him in this. The particulate matter alone would mask out the heat trace—and* Nosey *doesn't leak much heat anyway, not enough to show in this cold—*

He barked his shins on rocks, and stepped over them, and wove around them, through the darkening red-black haze. Evan didn't stop, pulling them along unmercifully. Joss looked up, trying to see the sky, even a star or two for reckoning's sake: he could see nothing but that same red-black fog, scattering the dim sunset light into a directionless glow. It was as if they were on the inside of a frosted glass bowl filled with ocher-colored fog. The blown sand and gravel stung now, the imaginary bees beginning to work through the clothing, the faceplate struck and struck again by a hail of sharp reports like slugs from some antique revolver or machine gun. He thought irrationally of the bullets that had wiped out the sign over the sheriff's office in Tombstone, and thought, *Those were nothing compared to this—*

He rammed into something, hard, and had no hands free to shield himself against the impact. It was the ship. Joss slid sideways along it, still holding Helen Mary by the other hand, and found the outer door, which Evan had found first and keyed open. In he stumbled, dragging Helen Mary after him, and the door slipped shut behind them.

His ears rang with the sudden silence, as the inner airlock door opened for them, and also with the sound of gravel and rocks ricocheting off the hull. Joss dragged himself to his feet, pulled his headgear off and staggered into the cabin to collapse into his pilot's seat. Evan was leaning against the bulkhead again, working at his helm; he pulled it off, looking haggard.

Helen Mary came in from the airlock, slowly and with great care, and sat down in the passenger seat, fumbling at her SHEL gear with shaking hands. When she had the headgear off, she looked at them both and said, "That was too close a one."

"I wish I could say I'd seen worse before," Evan said, "but it would be a lie."

Joss shook his head. "Every day," he said, "I come to respect that silly tin suit of yours more. How were you *seeing?*"

Evan looked at him, bemused. "Are you daft? I couldn't see a thing. The IR trace was wiped right out by that dust. It's one of the suit's few weaknesses."

Helen Mary stared. "Then how did you find your way back?"

"I memorized the way we came," Evan said. "It's not hard to do; it gets to be a habit, after a while. They teach you how, in suit school. They have to. After all, what would happen if one day your inertial trackers broke down in the midst of something crucial where your visibility was obscured? A firefight or some such? You'd be dead." He grinned, not entirely a pleasant grin. "They spend too much on our training to let us get dead easily. Wastes the taxpayer's money, don't you know."

"Here's to the taxpayer, then," Joss said, with feeling.

The ship rocked slightly. Evan and Helen Mary looked at one another, then at Joss, with slightly panic-stricken expressions.

Joss shook his head. "Forget flying in this," he said. "We're here for the duration. You don't want to *think* what the air turbulence above a storm of this sort is like."

"But we might flip over!" said Helen Mary.

Joss shrugged at her. "There's always that chance. We're a long way away from any tie-downs. But there's nothing we can do about it." He stood up, finding with slight surprise that he was trembling all over. "For my own part, I'm going to get something to eat, and maybe even something to drink, since I think we're going to be here a little while, and I won't be flying anytime soon. Anybody else?"

He was not quite trampled in the rush to the galley.

TWO HOURS LATER THEY WERE STILL SITTING there, the three of them crammed into the space around the little table that was really meant for two. Evan had shocked Joss by insisting on tidying the supper containers away after they were done with them, but the bottle of wine was still there, about half full. All three of them were gazing at it with expressions varying between interest, weariness and concern.

"I had some real wine once before," Helen Mary said. "About four years ago, at a friend's birthday party."

"What kind?" said Joss.

"Some brand called Cheap Red. No, really," she said as he started to chuckle. "It had a brown paper label and everything, with the name stenciled on it. 'Twas from *Earth*," she said, slightly indignant at his amusement. "We thought it was pretty good." She paused and looked at the bottle in the middle of the table. "It wasna as good as *this*, though. . . ."

Evan said, "No, I guess it wasn't." He peered at the bottle curiously. "What does this noble vintage say? Hmm. Chateau d'If—"

"Never you mind about that," said Joss indignantly. "It was a present."

"From that nice lady on Willans? That's right, she grew her own grapes down in the greenhouse tunnels there, didn't she? The lady with all the grandchildren, that you were dating."

"You were dating someone's *grandchildren?*" Helen Mary said in great shock.

"Do not believe everything this man says to you," Joss said. "He will, as his people quaintly put it, have your knickers in a twist in short order. Anyway, I was *not* dating her grandchildren." He glared at Evan. "The very idea."

Helen Mary mouthed the words "knickers in a twist," shook her head, and reached for the wine bottle.

"Here, let me," Evan said, and filled all their glasses, finishing the bottle off. "Joss. Your attention."

"I hear and obey, O tin-plated one."

"That pod. Cut off the main craft."

"Without a doubt. And then tracks."

"They were fairly deep," Evan said.

"A heavy vehicle," Joss said. "At home, I would suspect something armored. But here—"

They looked at Helen Mary. She nodded. "Anything that's used out here for long periods needs a fairly hard or heavy shell," she said. "Most people opt for just plain

heavy—it's cheaper than hard, even when you take the extra fuel consumption into account. Metal is cheaper, even
here, than sending to Earth for the high-resistance lami-
nates."

"Lichen miners have vehicles like that," Joss said.

She nodded, very matter-of-factly. "They'd better, considering that most of their work involves plowing up the
stones. Every now and then you have to buy new bolt-on
armor for the front of the chomper."

"The only problem," Evan said, "is that those big
chompers move very, very slowly, because of their weight.
They have no need to hurry, after all. If a lichen miner had
been to this site in even the last forty-eight hours, we
would have come across it on our way here."

"Always assuming that it didn't go over Mons way, or
into some other piece of territory that we haven't covered
yet."

"So we'll keep our eyes open for it tomorrow," Evan
said, "when we see if we can't find some hide or hair of
Helen Mary's da. But meantime, I don't think it was a lichen miner that made those tracks. Do you?"

Joss got up, squeezed out of his seat against the wall,
and went out for a moment, coming back with his 'Shica
and its little portable display screen. He hooked the camera up and started scrolling through the shots he had taken,
with Evan and Helen Mary craning to see them.

"Damn that wind," he said. "Damn the timing of it." As
if in annoyance, the ship rocked a little with a particularly
bad gust. "But look at that," Joss said, pointing at the fifth
picture he had taken. "Look at the wheelbase. It's much
too small for a lichen miner, isn't it, Helen Mary?"

She examined the shot for a moment, then nodded.
"About half again too small, I'd say. That wouldn't have
room for most of the equipment a miner uses. The sizes
are pretty standardized."

Joss looked at Evan. "So what, then? What kind of personal vehicle on Mars uses tracks like that, and weighs
that much?"

Evan shook his head slowly. "Nothing I ever saw."

"Helen Mary?"

She shook her head.

They all stared at the picture of the tracks for a moment. Joss began to scroll through the rest of them, the pictures becoming less and less detailed as the wind eroded the dust and gravel. Finally nothing was left.

Evan was frowning. "Anyway, that's certainly what took the prototype satellite away. The thing had been removed from its spot in cargo: the bungees were still there, and they'd been unfastened, not broken.

"And no bodies," Helen Mary said.

"No pieces of them, either," Evan said, "regardless of there having been an explosion and fire on board. No, I think the crew were alive when they came down. Where they might be now, though . . ."

He trailed off.

"Lucretia," Joss said, "is going to have six kinds of fits. If she had any doubt about SP comms being compromised locally, this should resolve it for her."

Evan nodded glumly. "And we're going to have to get a report out to her tonight," he said. "Compromised or not. It'll have to be verbal: implant information doesn't go through the same comms protocols as pad-transferred info does."

Joss was tempted to moan out loud, and refrained. A live conversation with Lucretia was not high on his list at the moment. She was one of those supervisors who, even when you had been doing everything exactly right, nevertheless had a gift for making you feel like you did it strictly by luck and the fortuitous positions of the stars.

"Well, what are we going to put in the report?" he said. "Besides the bare facts. We don't have a clue who took the prototype, or what they want it for, or how they found out. We don't know where the crew of the ship is. We don't know what made it fall out of the sky—"

"But the engine pod was shot off," Helen Mary said, looking at Joss with some surprise.

"That craft could have run on one engine with no problems," Joss said. "And as for being shot off—" He looked at Evan.

"If this storm has died down by morning," Evan said, "we're going to want to have a closer look at that ship. I take it we're carrying the full forensic pack."

"And a few extra bits I—"

"Don't tell me where you found them," Evan said, rolling his eyes. "I'm innocent as long as I'm ignorant. Meanwhile, just so we do a decent site analysis in the morning, Lucretia may let us live. She's not going to be happy that it took us so long to find the ship at all."

Helen Mary was sitting back, turning her wine glass around and around and gazing at it thoughtfully. "Who would have known about your satellite, though?" she said. "Who would have wanted to take it? And why?"

Evan and Joss looked at each other. Joss shrugged. "New technology is always worth something ... even if the people stealing it don't know exactly what it's worth. They can always take it to people who do, then just take the money and run."

"I rather think, though," Evan said, "that whoever took the satellite knew exactly what they were after. This crash site was not just fortuitously stumbled over by someone."

"And that engine pod," Joss said, half to himself. "It was awfully close to the crash."

"Yes."

They both sat quietly and thought.

"You don't suppose ..." Helen Mary said, and then stopped.

"What?" Evan said.

"No, it's a nasty thought. Never mind."

"If you've got an idea," Joss said, "don't sit on it, for pity's sake. We can use all the help we can get at the moment."

Helen Mary sat quietly for a few long breaths. Finally she said, "They were all sops, on that ship?"

"All Solar Patrol personnel, yes. Not necessarily officers on active duty, as we are. But colleagues."

"If one of them," Helen Mary said, "if one of *them* had let someone know about the satellite—"

There was a long chilly silence at the table.

"I told you it was a nasty thought," Helen Mary said.

"Our oaths—" Evan began angrily.

Joss snorted at him. "Come on, Evan. Even we have our price—pray God no one ever offers it to us. Our colleagues are no different. We're not the 'just and incorruptible force' of the SP Charter, not yet anyway; there are too many human beings working for the Patrol." His smile was grim. "Though we do our best. But it's a possibility that can't be ruled out, except by evidence to the contrary. We'll just have to see what the evidence seems to indicate." He brooded a moment. "It still leaves us the question of why they would have someone shoot them down, and take the chance of damaging the satellite, just to cover up the fact that it was an inside job. You'd think that would be too much risk."

Evan nodded, and pushed the empty wine bottle away. "You're right about needing more evidence," he said. "All this is going to be sterile until we know what we're really dealing with. Meanwhile, we ought to turn in; local dawn's not that far off. Helen Mary, you can have my stateroom."

"Take mine," Joss said. "It's neater."

Evan glared at him. Joss smiled slightly. If the truth were to be told, the only difference between his stateroom and Evan's was the color of the blankets on the beds, and the small framed picture of a red winged dragon on the wall, with the motto Y DDRAIG I CWM GOGOCH written under it.

Helen Mary looked from one to the other of them and laughed. "Best flip a coin," she said.

Joss reached over to the change jar clamped to the kitchen counter and came up with a one-cred coin. He pushed it over to Helen Mary, who looked at it with surprise. "I didn't think there were any of these left."

"The collector here," Evan said drily, "prefers money that he can hold in his hand. I wouldn't sleep on his mattress if I were you. It's probably stuffed full of Confederate dollars or some such."

Helen Mary laughed and flipped the coin. "Call it," she said to Joss.

"Heads," he said. It came up with the big 1 and the circle of stars showing. "Rats," Joss said. "Well, I tried to warn you. I mean, the man has a board under his mattress."

Helen Mary laughed, got up and made her way back to the stateroom.

Joss put the wine bottle in the recycler, folded the table

away, and followed Evan out to the front cabin. When they heard the stateroom door close, Evan turned in his seat and said to Joss, "You should see your face."

"What?"

Evan grinned at him, reached down to the clamp by the wall and took his pad out of it. "She *is* a cute one, no mistake. I wish you luck."

"What? I didn't—she—" Joss found his mouth working, but nothing useful coming out. He shut it, finally, and sat down.

"Never mind that. We've got Lucretia to deal with."

"Don't remind me," Joss said. "Let's collect our thoughts and get it over with . . ."

THE WIND HAD NOT QUITE DIED DOWN BY morning, but the sandstorm was gone. So was every last trace of the tracks that had been leading up to the crash site; the flat area was scraped as clean as if someone had run a bulldozer across it. And there had been other changes.

"Just look at this," Joss said to Evan, as they and Helen Mary stood by *Nosey*'s airlock door in the late morning light. Joss ran his hands unhappily over the ship's hull. "Our new paint-and-polish job! I just *paid* to have this surface redone!"

"Boyo," Evan said. "I would think you'd be grateful enough that we didn't go bowling along tail-over-teakettle in that wind last night. To complain about a little sand-blasting—"

"A little!" Joss shook his head. The ship had had a gloss finish yesterday. Today the finish was matte. *Nosey*'s markings, bonded into the metal, were intact; but the hull was covered with dings and bumps where stones the size of fists had been caught up by last night's wind and flung at her. "Evan, *look* at this! They wouldn't let her out of the hangar in this state, if we were on the Moon."

"I wish we were. Look, Joss, at least you have a beat-up looking ship that's in one piece, instead of shiny but strewn all over the landscape. Just think of it as having acquired that lived-in look."

"Mmf," Joss said, not particularly wanting to think about the issue of the ship being lived in. Lucretia had had a few sour words about the presence of a civilian of the opposite sex in their craft overnight while they were on duty; but she hadn't been able to really get going on that count because of the sandstorm. She had, though, taken a bit of hide off about what she considered their tardy handling of the search, and their detour into Tombstone, which she wasn't sure was entirely necessary.

"Never mind it," he said, and they headed back for the sliced-off engine pod and the crash site.

By the engine pod they paused, and Joss got out his 'Shica again and began to take pictures. "Should have gotten this last night," he said. "Look at the gravel scoring."

Evan shook his head. "Nothing much you could have done about it."

"No. Well, at least the score markings are idiosyncratic, and distinctive." He stood up and nudged the pod with one boot. "Can you pick that up for me? I want to see what the metal fracturing on the bottom looks like. There should be a fair amount."

Evan stepped up to the pod, looked it over, and bent over.

"Bend your knees when you're lifting," Joss said.

Evan glanced at him. His helm was unpolarized for the moment; the look was amused. Without bothering to bend his knees, he reached down, took the pod by the sliced end, and lifted it up the long way, so that the other end still rested on the ground. Joss began to circle it, taking pictures; and then stopped.

"Merry Christmas," he said, sounding very impressed.

Evan stared at him. So did Helen Mary.

"Evan," Joss said, "just change your grip on that and move around so that you can see this side."

He did. Joss pointed at the bottom of the pod . . . and the large, neat, clean, round hole punched into it. It was an entrance hole, and of a projectile, not a beam: the metal was bent inward all around the edges of the hole, and broken off sharply thereafter. The other side of the pod, where the projectile would have exited, was missing; the beam that had sliced the pod off the SP ship had taken the exit site with it.

"High velocity," Joss said, feeling the edges of the entry hole. "*Really* high."

Helen Mary looked at him in shock. "What could do that?"

Joss shook his head. "Evan?"

Evan ran the finger of one gauntlet over the edge of the entry hole. "Nothing that I know of." He looked over at Joss. "This is very peculiar indeed."

"Look how quickly this metal broke off," Joss said, pointing at the stretched metal around the edges of the hole. "It just *snapped.* Half-inch steel-and-composite plating. Nothing like the way the hull of the main craft behaved when it had that explosion inside; there was much more stretching before it gave." He shook his head. "Something hit this traveling, I don't know—a couple of klicks per second, maybe more. Something fairly massive, and perfectly round. What does that sound like?"

Evan shook his head.

"See if you can break me off a little sliver of that bent-in material from the entry spot," Joss said. "I want to look at the crystalline structure of the metal later. Meanwhile—"

He headed off toward the ship, with Evan and Helen Mary following. *More like a cannonball than anything else,* he thought. *Today's riddle: what flies and fires cannonballs?* Certainly nothing that he could think of. There was a big problem with projectile weapons in spacecraft. The problem was Newton's Law of Motion, which dictated that any vacuum-borne craft that tried to fire a cannonball would be kicked backward as hard as the projectile went forward. There were solutions to this problem, but they were almost all more expensive and cumbersome than they were worth. Spacecraft used beamed weapons, or at most very light projectiles that the ship's stationkeeping mechanisms could compensate for without other special intervention.

In the noon light, the SP ship's shadow pooled black around it. Joss walked carefully all around it, taking more pictures, and then stepped carefully in through the gap blown in its side, camera working all the time. Everything was burnt black, or scummed over with soot. He took careful pictures of ceiling and floor, all the walls and bulkheads, every piece of furniture, and made his way slowly back through the ship to the cargo area. There were the bungees hanging down, undone as Evan had said—not snapped, not burnt.

Not burnt. Joss looked around at the walls of the little cargo area. They were smoked black with soot like everything else, but the plastics and metals of the walls and cupboards here were not themselves burnt or warped. Joss put out a hand to one wall, having photo'd it first, and wiped with one finger. The soot came away; underneath, the wall was clean and unhurt.

Slowly he made his way back to the front of the ship, taking more pictures. He could afford to be profligate with them; after all, the camera had nearly a hundred megs of memory. When he was satisfied that he had covered every square inch of the interior, from every angle that seemed to be any use, Joss put the camera away and unsnapped the forensic sampling kit at his belt. Swabs first: of the soot on walls and floor and ceiling; and then samples of burnt plastic and fabric, and everything else that seemed to be of use, each one going carefully into its little plastic envelope.

This took him nearly half an hour. When he felt he had enough to start with, he climbed out of the hole in the ship's side and went to join Evan and Helen Mary. "That's all I need from inside," he said. "Now: the outside."

"Do you need more pictures?" Helen Mary said, with an expression that suggested she thought she had been thrown in with some kind of rabid shutterbug.

"No. I have enough of everything that shows. Now I need what *doesn't* show." He looked over at Evan. "Officer?"

"You don't want much, do you?" Evan said, but his voice was good-natured. He went over to the ship and started looking it over.

Joss chuckled a little. "Considering that I once watched

you pick up a largish section of an asteroid, this shouldn't be out of bounds."

"That was rock," Evan said, walking around the far side of the ship, and out of sight. "This is different. Rock has specific ways it breaks, predictable ones. But this thing's structure was probably badly weakened by the fire, or the crash, or both; so there's no telling what it might do. It might break in two. You wouldn't like that—"

Joss sighed. "I think we can cope with that for the moment."

There was a pause. Then the ship lurched. Lurched again. Helen Mary stood watching with her eyes wide. The nose of the SP ship began to lift, little by little, off the ground; a foot, two feet, three. Shortly Evan's greaves were visible on the other side of it, and the ship's nose boosted up higher and higher yet as he worked his way under to get better leverage.

Joss waited patiently until Evan was right under it, looking like an old picture of Atlas supporting the world on his shoulders. "Don't drop it," he said, and ducked underneath the overhanging nose, starting to take pictures again.

The servos of Evan's suit whined in complaint. "I remember when you said that to the poor girl in the pizza place at Serenity," he said. "That was a terrible thing to do."

"I didn't do it on purpose. It's just that that fourth pizza she was carrying—oh, brother."

"What?" Evan said.

Joss pointed. "Right there. The stabilization fairing should be there. It's not. Something took it off, from the side. Just scalped it off clean."

"Another one of what made the hole in the engine pod?" Evan said, craning his neck to look.

"Good question. No signs of a beam weapon being used. No need to multiply hypotheses—wouldn't surprise me if it was the same thing as did the pod. Mmf—" Joss paused to pull loose a little twisted rag of metal that was hanging away from the remains of the flattened dome that was the stabilization fairing. "We'll see."

"Oops," Evan said suddenly.

Joss didn't wait around; he simply flung himself head-first out from under the ship, and lay there sprawling on the ground, without thought for his faceplate or anything else. He waited for the sound of the crash.

None came. After a moment he scrambled to his feet. Evan was still standing there, holding the ship up, and grinning amiably at Joss. "I forgot to bend my knees, didn't I?"

"You dim-bulb leek-eater," Joss said, brushing himself off. "Helen Mary," he said to her, "whatever you do, don't turn your back on this man. He has a low sense of humor."

"Are you done with this now?" Evan said. "It might be nice to put it down, seeing it only weighs eight tons or so."

"Nine point five," Joss said. "Oh, go ahead, if it's making you tired . . ."

With some care, Evan backed up and let the ship down to lie approximately where it had before. *"Now what?"* he said.

"I want to run a few very quick tests on this material," Joss said, "and then we should go looking for some sign of Helen Mary's father. We can talk about the evidence on the way out, or back. Ten minutes for me, first."

"All right. We'll have a cup of something."

They made their way back to *Nosey*. Joss headed straight back for the little lab/utility room in front of their own cargo area-cum-brig. There was something about the way that fire had burnt in the ship that was bothering him. The pressure-proof door between the front and back compartments of the SP ship had apparently been open during the explosion, to judge from the way the soot was spread around. But there had been very little burning damage in the rear. *Could be reasons for that. The lack of oxygen might have killed the fire before it got going that far.* After all, even after years of atmosphere supplementation, there was barely a fiftieth of the oxygen in Mars's air that there was on Earth. All the forms of oxidation, from rust on up, took place at a most leisurely pace. *But still . . .*

He took his samples out and spent a few moments sorting through them. Finally he selected one particular envelope that contained nothing but the soot, pure and simple. Joss turned to one side of the lab, to the counter where his general analysis box sat. It was a clever little setup, with specific gravity, spectral analysis, even a small electron microscope for the fine work, and a visible-light counter scope good enough to do gene splicing with, if he'd felt like it.

He selected a small sample flask from a rack nearby, pulled down the bottle of nonreagent fluid medium, and put the flask into the sampling hopper; then woke the analysis box up. It dipped in a probe and sat thinking to itself for about thirty seconds. Then it displayed a string of numbers on its little LED screen, and a set of spectral lines.

Joss stared at the numbers. "Oh really," he muttered, and pulled out the reference manual to have a look at it and confirm his own memory of what that string of numbers meant.

His memory was right.

"Holy shit," Joss said, and headed straight out for the pilot's cabin.

In the galley, Evan and Helen Mary looked up in surprise as he went by. "You don't have to strap in or anything," Joss called to them, sitting down in his pilot's chair. "But I'm going to take us straight up and put us straight down again."

"Looking for something?" Evan said, coming into the pilot's cabin.

"Found something. You don't have any loose cups sitting around in there, do you?"

"I dumped them in the sink," Helen Mary said, and a moment later, came forward herself. "What did you find?"

Joss was grinning slightly, the satisfied look of a man who has been suspicious and finds out he was right. "That fire in the cabin of the ship," he said. "It wasn't accidental."

"Of course not," Helen Mary said. "Someone was shooting at them!"

"That's not what I mean. That fire didn't break out by itself." He tapped at his console for a moment; *Nosey's* engines woke up from standby and began to whine up to full.

"Someone started it on purpose?" Evan said.

"In a manner of speaking," Joss said. "That soot is full of oxidized mercury fulminate. Now hold on." He took

Nosey straight up, set her to hover, and turned to busy himself with the scan console.

"Then it was a bomb that went off in that ship," Evan said. "And not even a very sophisticated one."

"Homebrew," Joss said. "Very simple to put together. Very cheap. And fortunately, very simple to detect. Helen Mary, who mines mercury on Mars?"

She blinked and looked confused. "I havena a clue."

"Something else for us to look into. Sources of mercury, sources of sodium and iodine, processors of both of them . . . Later for that. Here we go." He told the scanner to start looking around for any sort of solid object of a particular specific gravity, or one of three densities. There were only a limited number of ways to keep merc fulminate from becoming unduly agitated before you wanted it to—gel, clathrate with a heavy liquid, or solid bricks of a density sufficiently light and full of air to keep the stuff from spontaneously igniting. Each of those gave off a specific echo to directed sound or ultrasound, and *Nosey* was equipped for such sound production—even though Lucretia, when the voucher for the installation crossed her desk, had claimed loudly that Joss was never likely to use the thing to do anything more useful than play loud classical music. *Hah,* Joss thought.

The *ping* came almost immediately, as Joss had expected it would. "There we are," he said. He grinned twice as hard as he had been. "I really love being right."

He eased *Nosey* back down and settled her on the spot from which she had risen. "There," he said when they were down again, and pointed at the screen on his comms board. "Bearing one one three, distance one hundred ninety meters. At about a ten-degree angle right of that big hole in the ship's side. There's about a kilogram of mercury fulminate out there, unexploded."

Evan looked at him with a frown. "Surely you're not thinking of something daft like bringing that in *here—*"

Joss looked at Evan sidewise, wondered if for fun he should try to convince him that that was what he had actually wanted to do . . . then decided against it. "No, but I want pictures of it; I want to see how it's made. I'll hop out and get those. And then, seeing that there's nothing else our duty requires us to do here at the moment, we'll go see if we can't find any sign of Helen Mary's father."

"Thank you," she said, sounding very relieved: sounding also as if she had been forcing herself not to mention anything about her father for a long time. Joss looked at her sympathetically.

"Won't be a minute," he said.

HE WAS TEN, BUT NO MORE. HE PAUSED ONLY TO flag the crash site near the ship with a broadcast box which said that this area contained Solar Police evidence, and tampering with it carried the usual fines and penalties. The little box had a camera in it, and was an effective enough guardian for situations such as this. It would broadcast noisy warnings at anyone who got too close, and would call *Nosey* to inform Joss that someone was in the neighborhood.

Then Joss raised *Nosey* one more time, and they started back onto the search program they had been following the day before. Helen Mary sat in Evan's seat again, and Joss in his own, and Evan in the passenger seat once more; and the hours passed.

"How we're going to explain this to Lucretia," Evan said, about two hours in, "I'm sure I don't know."

Joss stretched a bit in his seat and cast an idle eye over the screen on the comms console, on which the image of Helen Mary's father's type of skimmer was flickering. "It's a nasty reconstruction," he said, "but at least we know that the ship was actively shot down, by someone who knew where it was going to be well enough to aim at it most accurately."

"That's the problem," Helen Mary said, not taking her eyes off the landscape as they cruised over it. "They shot it out *too* accurately. Both engines. It couldn't fly with both of them gone—"

"That depends," Joss said, "on when the first shot was made, and when the second was. Let's try it this way." He folded his arms and leaned back, looking out the window again at the endless waste of red rock and sand and dust.

"Someone knows the time that the satellite is going to be delivered, and the approximate course. They have something that fires cannonballs waiting along that flight route. When they're ready—possibly, when the ship is near enough to ground forces they have waiting—they fire once, at the stabilization array. They take that out. The ship starts to have trouble holding its trim; the pilot realizes he has trouble, doesn't send a message right away, has enough control—he thinks—to put it down without too much trouble. He starts to do that.

"When he's close enough to the ground to avoid much damage being done, the people trying to get their hands on the satellite fire again. This time they fire their cannonball at the engine pod. Someone—maybe this was an afterthought—cuts the pod off, to try to hide the hole the cannonball made. Or for some other, dumber reason. The ship lands—it was doing that anyway—but now it's going to have *real* trouble getting off the ground again." Joss looked over at Evan to see what his reaction was. The big Welshman was nodding. "In the air, with these ships, is one thing; one engine can sustain you, if you can alter your trim enough. But with trim adjustment gone, *and* only one engine, and on the ground—the ship is trapped right where it lands. And unarmed, too."

"Then these people go in and take what they want from the ship," Helen Mary said, still not looking away from the window. "Maybe they tell your friends inside that they're going to blow it up if they don't come out. So they do come out—"

"I would have, in their place," Evan said. "Not sure any heap of equipment is worth dying for, no matter how much EssPat paid for it."

"Me either," Joss said. "So they come out . . . and are taken away. The satellite is removed, carefully. And then charges are planted inside the ship, to make it look as if it crashed and burned. One of them doesn't go off correctly, and is thrown out where we found it . . . but the people responsible for this theft are in a big hurry to leave, and don't notice it. Off they go, with the satellite, and our colleagues."

"Off where, though?" said Helen Mary.

Joss shook his head. "We are going to have to look into that," he said. "But that's the best I can do at this point. Evan? Can you think of anything I've missed?"

Evan stopped nodding and looked thoughtful. "One thing only. Why would they have taken the SP crew away? Why not—may I be pardoned for the wicked thought—blow them up inside it and make the explosion look that much more authentic?"

Joss thought about that one for a moment. "Bad planning?" he said. "Not having thought it through—that when the crash site was found, it would be investigated for human remains, and there would be suspicion that none were found? Though they may have been counting on the trail being long cold at that point. Or—" It was a very nasty thought, and made Joss's hair stand up a bit. "Or else someone on board the ship was involved in this plan, an accomplice—and the thieves reasoned that finding one body missing when there should have been a certain number would have been even more suspicious. So they took them all away—"

"Maybe too," Helen Mary said, "the hijackers thought that they needed the people inside to help them work out how to run the decoder or whatever it is—"

"There was one tech support person," Evan said. "It's likely enough."

Joss sat back and sighed. "It's no good," he said. "We have to find out where they went . . . and I have no idea how to do that."

Evan looked grim. "They'll hardly have filed a flight plan at Welles that says 'Unscheduled equipment theft.' Nonetheless, when we go back there, we can requisition all the plans that *were* filed, and see if anyone of interest was in this area."

Joss nodded. "I still want to know," he said, "what they shoot their cannonballs with—"

There was a noisy *honk!* from the scanner. Helen Mary jumped as if she had been shot and began looking out the window in all directions at once—then sank back in the seat, laughing weakly. "Never mind," she said. "It's just a couple of lichen-mining rigs."

Joss looked out and down. There they were, big oblong

vehicles on tracks, each one the size of a house, with a wide snowplow-like scoop on the front; huge boulders were being scraped up and swallowed whole by them.

Evan came over to the window and looked too. "There they are, all right," he said. "Why did you have the scanner set for them, though? We were looking for skimmers."

"We are." Joss looked at the comms board for a moment, touched a control and brought up the scan parameters. "Oh. That wasn't the shape-match alert—that was a map reference." He brought up a surface map on the screen. "Look," he said. "We're over one end of The Strip."

Evan looked at the screen, then down at the lichen miners, then at the screen again. "I thought there was something funny about the color of that lichen in that spot," he said. "The ground is darker than it should be. Concentrated oxides—"

Helen Mary's eyes grew wide, and she looked out again. "You know, you're right—"

Evan was leaning over Joss's shoulder, trying to figure out which key to hit. "Here," Joss said, and tapped the combination of controls that would superimpose ground scan over the map.

Evan pulled in a long breath. So did Joss. "Now that," Joss said angrily, "is protected ground—potential archaeological site! What the hell are they digging there for?"

He took the controls away from the autopilot. "Better strap yourself in," he said. "We can't just let them bulldoze through that!"

Evan went back to the passenger seat. Joss put *Nosey* into a twenty-degree dive and let her fall toward the mining vehicles. It didn't matter to him that there were eighty kilometers of The Strip stretching from here almost to Valles Marineris. The whole artifact was protected, and his scientist's heart rose up in rage to see it being scraped up. "These people may not know what they're doing," he said to Helen Mary and Evan, "but they're damn well going to find out, and stop it."

About two hundred meters up he began putting the brakes on, and with great care he brought himself to a hover over the two mining vehicles. They were bulling along their previous path with no sign of having noticed him. This by itself didn't mean anything. Evan had told him that the machines could operate completely automatically for days at a time, the owner-operators only looking into the control room every now and then to see how the yield of lichen was, and to decide whether to keep mining that particular area, or to move on elsewhere. Possibly a mistake . . .

Then the beam went right past *Nosey's* windscreen, a white-hot line of light.

Joss jerked her off to one side, more by reflex than anything else. *"That* wasn't automatic!" he said. "Damn!"

"Why are they shooting at us?" said Helen Mary in great alarm.

"I don't know, but if I have anything to say about it, it's going to stop," said Joss. With one hand he swept *Nosey* around in a wide circle, away from the first miner's guns, and with the other, hastily started reprogramming the comms console to look for weapons signatures and ready-signs. The screen changed to show the miners' silhouettes, marking the guns, reading their energy outputs and showing their types.

"All energy weapons," Joss muttered. That could be good for him, depending on how easily steerable the weapons were. He tapped at the control for the exterior sound system, keyed it up to about two hundred dB, and said, as angrily as he could, "This is the Solar Patrol! Cease fire and disarm your weapons immediately!"

There was a long pause. Then more beams came past *Nosey,* one even closer than the last one.

"Can I do anything?" Evan said, sounding worried.

"Not till we land," Joss said, working frantically at the keyboard. "Then you can bang their heads together, and I'll stand there and applaud!"

The firing was still going on. Joss moved out of its way, and noticed with satisfaction that it was following him only very slowly. The other mining vehicle was not firing at him—*Ah, damn, spoke too soon,* he thought, as it too opened fire. He jumped *Nosey* about five hundred feet straight up, ignoring the elevator feeling in his stomach, and angled off to one side. He had no desire to get caught in the crossfire between the two vehicles. Fortunately that was unlikely to happen unless he got very distracted indeed, for the miners were slow-moving and not terribly maneuverable.

Joss swung *Nosey* on around and down again, and came at the first mining vehicle from behind. Its weapons were turning, and firing as they turned. *I wouldn't do that,* he thought idly; *wastes energy, tells me where the guns are—* And indeed his computer was already quite sure of where two of them were. Joss grabbed the firing yoke, swung it around to match the computer-generated crosshairs on the comms screen, fired. First one of the guns, then the other, blew out in an impressive explosion of metal, coolant and superheated glass.

"One down," Joss said, as one more beam, not as well aimed at the others, went past *Nosey*'s nose. *Interesting: they know where to shoot to kill . . . but they don't have much practice—*Joss was not inclined to let them have any more, either. He changed his course, executing the beginning of a figure eight, and let the computer get a good fix on the guns of the second mining vehicle; then took the firing yoke again and with great care, and exactly one shot, killed the first gun; and more care, and one more shot, killed the other.

Then he put *Nosey* on hover, and waited.

For several minutes, nothing happened. Both the vehicles slowed, and eventually stopped.

"Now then," Joss said. "Evan?"

"You mentioned head-banging, I believe," he said, and went to get his suit sealed up again.

Five minutes later he was standing by the airlock. "How shall we handle this?" Joss said to him. "You want me to come in with you? Or should we stay wingborne?"

"Stay up," Evan said. And paused, and grinned a bit naughtily, for Joss was thinking of possible retorts, and could not really make any of them with Helen Mary there. "You can do more damage in the air. I'm pretty sure that those guns are the best they've got—and my suit could have taken those."

"All right," Joss said. Regardless, he was slightly nervous about letting Evan go into those tin cans alone. But

Evan didn't take needless risks. "I'll put you down, then go up and fly shotgun again."

"You do that."

Carefully, Joss put *Nosey* down about fifty meters from the first mining vehicle he had disabled, and then enabled the airlock. "Have you got your sound on?" he said.

"Yes, mam," Evan said, with a slight smile.

"All right, then. Shout if you need anything."

"I will. You'd better shift that extra case of wine out of the brig. We're going to need the space for its original purpose, I think." Evan stepped out of the airlock, and it closed behind him.

"Ah, jeez, I forgot about that," Joss said. "Helen Mary, I can't leave the hot seat right now. Would you move that case for me? Just shove it in my stateroom, or the galley, or someplace."

"Surely," she said, and went to see to it.

Joss boosted *Nosey* very carefully upward, and turned up the volume on Evan's link to him. "Any problems?" he said.

"The rocks are thick down here," Evan said, sounding slightly testy at Joss's concern. *"Bouncing will work better than walking, I think."*

Joss banked *Nosey* carefully around to keep an eye on Evan. It was astonishing how far he could leap in the suit; and in one-third gravity, Evan was going along as if he had something better than seven-league boots.

He had reached the first vehicle. "Now?" Joss said to Evan.

"Sure."

Joss brought up his own sound system. "This is the Solar Patrol!" he said, at about 220 dB this time. "Come out of your vehicles immediately!"

For a second or so nothing happened. Then, from Evan's side of things, came an appalling clatter, like hail on a tin roof. Joss jumped at the sound of it. "Are you malfunctioning?" he said, worried.

Evan laughed a little. *"No, it's just guns."*

"Guns!"

"Relax. Just a couple of slugthrowers. Rather old-fashioned. Come to think of it," Evan said, *"rather like*

what was used to ruin Tombstone's sheriff. That's an interesting development. We'll have to ask some questions about that."

"What are you going to do?" Joss peered out the window, still circling carefully. "What can I do? Do you need something shot at?"

"No need. I'm just going to walk through this. It's no worse than the wind was yesterday. A lot easier, actually."

Helen Mary came back. "Strap yourself in," Joss said. "I may need to move quickly."

There was more of the horrendous hailstorm noise. "God above us, whatever's that!" said Helen Mary, going white.

"Guns," Joss said. "They're shooting at Evan. See, there he is." They had finally come around to the right angle, and they could just see the small silvery-gray shape that was Evan coming up to face an open airlock door on one of the vehicles. There appeared to be something moving inside it, in the shadows.

"Right," Evan said, apparently to himself, and began to climb up the ladder that led to the airlock.

More clunks and whacks were heard, the widest range of catastrophic metallic noises that Joss could imagine, like a gorilla attacking the percussion section of a major symphony orchestra. Evan vanished from sight in the airlock.

There was a crashing noise, and a thump. *"What an idiot,"* they heard Evan say; and someone was pushed out the airlock to fall, relatively gently in the low gravity, on the ground at the bottom of the ladder. *"Now then,"* said Evan. *"I'm going to cycle this airlock closed. Don't have a panic, mam."*

"Never," Joss said, and restrained himself from covering his eyes.

There was a faint hiss, the sound of one airlock door closing outside Evan's suit, and then another one opening. Immediately much more rattling and banging began. *"Now stop that,"* Evan said. *"Here, give me that, you cretin."* A loud crash, followed by a thump.

More rattling, then. *"You really aren't getting the picture, are you,"* Evan said mildly, and there was another crash, a louder one; and then a bizarre whining noise, followed by a sound more like a burst from a jackhammer than anything else.

"Now put those down," they heard Evan say, *"before I do something I regret, like make pâté out of you. This fires quite a few more rounds per minute than yours does. That's right. You too, sir, if you please. Over there. Thank you. Wha—"*

Joss bit one knuckle. *"Bloody hell,"* they heard Evan say. There immediately came a heavy thump, and then Evan said, *"Oh, don't look like that. I didn't hit him that hard. But I might hit you that hard, if you don't put that down. NOW!"*

A long pause.

"Better," Evan said then. *"Get up. Get your friend there up. Him too. Get something for his head, and get him into his SHEL. You too, sir. What about the other vehicle? Oh, I see, it's slaved to this one. No one on board? Good, because I think I may blow it up once you're all on board our vessel. You're quite sure, are you—Fine. All of you, into your SHELs; quick, now. I want you out of the airlock in thirty seconds, and I promise you, if you dawdle—"*

Evan said nothing more for the moment. Joss swung *Nosey* around, brought her out of bank, and started settling her down near the first vehicle's airlock. The rocks were a little uneven; he had to lift her twice and put her down again before she would sit steady and not rock.

No sooner did he have her steady than two more people fell out of the mining vehicle's airlock, followed rapidly by two more, and another two. Then Evan was standing there, looking none the worse for wear. *"Here we are,"* he said. *"No problems."*

Joss looked over at Helen Mary. "Obviously some new definition of 'no problems' that I haven't heard before," he said, and unholstered his Remington. He tapped briefly at the control that locked the stateroom doors. "Helen Mary, do you want to be scarce for the moment, until we get these people locked away? It's up to you."

She thought about it. "Maybe I will."

"Evan's stateroom, then. I'll lock the door from here. Comm is on the wall, if you need anything."

She got up and went down the hall. Joss sealed her in, then made sure all the other doors tested positive for lock, except the one to the brig. He got up and went to stand by the airlock.

After a few minutes, the outer door hissed open. Joss keyed the safety off the Remington, and waited. The outer door shut, and Joss touched the pad that would open the inner one. One after another, six forms stumbled into *Nosey*. "That way," Joss said. "Down to the end of the hall. Straight down, gentlemen. Straight down. Thank you."

When the last one was in, Joss hit the switch by the door to seal the entry to the brig, and turn it opaque. Then the airlock cycled again, and Evan came in.

"No problems, huh?" said Joss.

Evan shrugged as he took his helm off. "A few scratches. Polishing compounds will put those right. Where's Helen Mary?"

"Your stateroom. I didn't know whether she wanted to deal with our merry band here."

"Fine . . . It's just as well if they think it's just us terrible sops."

"So now what?" Joss said, heading back for his pilot's seat.

"Now we head back to Tombstone. And we start finding out why everyone we introduce ourselves to shoots at us!"

FIVE

EVAN GLYNDOWER CLOSED THE DOOR BEHIND him, then turned the blank glare of his helmed and visored head on the half-dozen men in the holding tank built onto the rear of the sheriff's dome. He and Joss had played "good sop–bad sop" with suspects on more than one occasion, and he had been the "bad sop" every time. It was hardly surprising, given the way that most people regarded suit specialists: robots on the outside, psychos on the inside. There were supposedly no such things as suit sops with soft centers. Everybody knew that. And that was why, once the prisoners had been brought into the tank, he had removed the plastic binders from their wrists and replaced them with good old nickel-steel handcuffs.

The late Sheriff Joe must have been a man with Evan's own views on prisoner psychology, because there had been a plentiful supply of forged-metal fetters in a cupboard at the back of his office. It was an established fact that the new long-chain molecular plastics were stronger than steel; but there was something about the cold weight of metal bracelets dragging at a prisoner's wrists that let him know he *was* a prisoner, in a way that loops of plastic never could. Joe Chernavin probably knew his local perps: tough, hard-drinking buddies one day, and reluctant guests in the slammer the next morning. The cuffs probably had a better effect on lichen miners than standard binders, and hopefully made them more careful to avoid whatever offense had brought them here in the first place.

That was the theory, anyway. Whether it also rendered the present mob of suspects more amenable to answering questions remained to be seen. There had been an awful temptation to soften them up just a little on the way back to Tombstone, but the third degree would be counterproductive where such a hard-nosed lot were concerned. With only one of them, there might have been a point; but with six, each would gain moral support from the presence of the others, and would refuse to talk just from sheer stubborn pride. Besides which, beating up prisoners just wasn't done.

Officially, at least.

"All right," said Evan. "Officer O'Bannion, read them their rights."

"You have the right to remain silent," Joss read from his pad. "Anything said by you following this caution will be placed on record and considered as evidence. Under the provisions of the Solar Patrol (Limitations of Jurisdiction) Charter (revised version 1.03 dated May 18th 2080) and by the discretion of the arresting/prosecuting officers as provided for by Article Three of the aforesaid Charter, your right to legal representation has been waived as under Article Two of the aforesaid Charter." He looked up at six appalled faces. "Do you understand the meaning of this caution? Have you anything to say? No? Okay." He fed a data chip into the pad, tapped a couple of keys, then glanced up at Evan. "Book 'em, Dan-o."

Evan looked down at him from inside the mirrored helm, feeling certain that its expressionless surface was, if anything, blanker than ever. There was a twinkle in Joss's eyes that suggested he'd managed to use yet another of his obscure quotes, and this time right on cue. Evan waited patiently for the translation until Joss sighed and handed over the primed pad. "Read them the charges."

Evan scanned it once, just to make sure there had been no changes to what he and Joss had composed up on *Nosey's* flight deck while the miners sat uneasily in the small, overcrowded brig. The wording was standard enough, that unmistakable dry, pedantic officialese composed by lawyers and bureaucrats with nothing better to do than get full mileage from a dictionary, but when it issued from the unseen throat of a seven-foot human tank, Evan reckoned it had a weight all of its own.

"We, being Officers Evan Huw Glyndower and Joss David O'Bannion of the Solar Patrol of the Federated planets, do hereby exercise the rights of trial granted us under the aforesaid Solar Patrol (Limitations of Jurisdiction) Charter (revised version 1.03 dated May 18th 2080.)

"In that we, being the prosecuting authority, do at this time hold and possess *prima facie* evidence of guilt as provided by ourselves as the arresting authority under Article Three of the aforesaid Charter, and that expeditious conclusion to this case supersedes and waives all rights and privileges to counsel as under Article Two of the aforesaid Charter, you have been found guilty of smuggling in contravention of Section Seven of the Martian Penal Code; damage to property and common vandalism, Sections Four and Five; illegal distilling, Sections Four and Seven; unauthorized discharge of firearms, Section Five; breach of the peace, Section Six; common assault and resisting arrest, Section Nine; and assaulting officers of the law whilst in the execution of their duty, Sections Nine and Ten."

He locked off the pad and gave it back to Joss before taking the two steps forward that allowed the suit's armored bulk to loom properly over the handcuffed miners. "And unless evidence is presented to the contrary," he continued from behind the mirrored visor in a flat, deadly voice that worked far better than any threat, "it is my intention that you also be pronounced guilty of the premeditated murder in the first degree of Sheriff Josef Chernavin, in that on day 220 of the coordinated Martian year 2068, at or around 1130 hours, you did shoot to death or cause to be shot, the said Sheriff Josef Chernavin, against the peace and contrary to common law."

He didn't bother to threaten them with penalties, either for the murder or for the lesser offenses. Cop-killing had only one penalty, beside which fines and imprisonment wouldn't matter, and he as a sop was empowered not only to pass that sentence but also to carry it out. In his entire career, Evan had never executed anybody in cold blood—

but he was betting that since the miners didn't know it, and could see only the blackness of vented gunports let into a silver-gray graflar suit that looked capable of mayhem whether it was occupied or not, they weren't about to ask him what his present score of perps might be.

God knows it's high enough, what with one firefight and another, he thought. *But never that single slug in the back of the neck. The only occasion on which a sop has to account for ammunition expended . . .*

The miners were looking horrified. Whatever else they had been expecting once they were thrown in jail, it hadn't been this. Sometimes the dry, pedantic recitation of offenses puffed up casual lawbreakers with their own implied importance so that they laughed and made coarse jokes at the arresting officer's expense—but Evan had never seen anyone laugh at a murder charge delivered by a sop. Too many people knew about the Charter; about how it made any EssPat officer a potential judge, jury and executioner. Not so many knew about how infrequently that extreme penalty had been invoked, and of course it wasn't in SP's interest for that to come out.

Sops, and suit specialists in particular, might appear hard men, but there were in fact more soft centers to them than met the eye. Psych evaluation was tight enough and frequent enough to weed out the occasional black sheep; after transferring from the British Ministry of Defense AED with a reputation as someone perhaps too ready to use extreme force, Evan had been subjected to more than his fair share of scrutiny. It had been funny in retrospect, both that the psych people should have expected a member of the Armed Enforcement Department to be drooling triggerman with no forehead, and that they should have been so plainly disappointed when they were proved conclusively wrong, AED was descended in right line from the SAS, the Flying Squad, and—if you went back far enough—the Bow Street Runners, and reputation aside, they were too tightly disciplined by training and tradition to start a small war if an arrest would do.

Of course, if the small war were required, that could always be provided . . .

Joss was ignoring the miners, letting them stew while he

busied himself with something on his pad that seemed of vital importance. Only Evan had the proper angle to see that his partner was playing, and at present losing, some sort of computer game. "Do you want to draw up the warrants now, or wait?" he said, quietly enough that it was obviously a private comment, but not so quietly that the miners couldn't hear him if they really strained their ears.

Joss paused the game and considered, studying the six apprehensive prisoners sadly. "I'd rather wait," he replied in the same low voice. "Somebody might have second thoughts about being so bloody stubborn, and anyway, we'll need a doctor to sign the certificates afterwards. While he's here, he can act as your independent witness. I'd rather not drag any of the other locals into this; it'll be public enough as it is."

"I suppose. Why bother with more paperwork than we need?" Servos shined slightly as Evan turned towards the door. *After the strains I've been putting on them, those poor things need an overhaul. Lifting ships like Sandow. You should know better,* he thought. "Come on. We don't need to stay here. There's work to get done before . . . When?"

"Dawn's the usual time, but we're going to be busy. This is a bad business. I'd rather get it over with. Just as soon as the doctor arrives, probably." Joss glanced at his chrono, pursed his lips and nodded as if coming to a conclusion. "Say about 2000 hours."

"Fine. A round figure always looks neater on the forms." Evan opened the door and stalked though it, wondering how long it would be before they had to reveal this bluff for what it was.

About one and a half seconds, elapsed time.

One of the miners cracked as Joss stood up to leave, throwing himself forward off the bench where they had been arranged like trussed chickens on a butcher's slab. He was yelling something furious and incoherent, and it was enough to put the others over the edge of control as well. For almost a minute Evan couldn't hear himself think, and cursed whoever had designed the sheriff's cell area to be so acoustically bright. Probably the sheriff himself; it was on a par with the mindset of a man who preferred steel cuffs to plastic binders. Joss had both hands over his ears, so far as he could manage while holding his pad under one arm at the same time.

Evan looked at the scene and was reminded for an instant of one of Hieronymous Bosch's more peculiar paintings, writhing souls in torment and all. *Now there would be an obscure quote for you, Joss boyo,* he thought, and smiled. It was a contented smile, one of purest relief, because maintaining that level of soulless brutality came hard to him, even if it *was* faked. Though the sop uniform was black, there were no lightning-flashes on its collar. "I take it," he said, with the suit's voice-augmenter giving his words a little extra *oomph,* "that you lot have something to say after all?"

Silence fell. After 180 dB of raw noise, it was a wonder that part of the ceiling didn't fall as well. Joss shook his ringing head and gave Evan a dirty "why-didn't-you-warn-me?" look, then moved aside so that the suspects could get the full benefit of the suit pacing towards them. They backed away from it, but still Evan came on. The cell-dome allowed him six ponderous strides from the door until he barged into the side of the dome and flattened anything that stood in his way, and he took five of them before stopping. By that time the miners were crushed back against the wall, shoulder blades and spines pressed so tightly into its curve so that they were unable to stand upright. Staring up at the dully gleaming gray hulk was an uncomfortable business, but they did it all the same; staring at something frightening was as natural a human reaction as running away from it, and right now running away was impossible.

Evan gave himself a slow count of ten, and then depolarized his helm, taking care that the expression thus revealed on his face was no improvement on the blankness of the visor. Being somewhat craggy about the features had its advantages on these occasions: nobody questioned your sincerity, either in the suit or out of it. "I suggest," he said, "that you pick a spokesman, and then start talking. And bear this in mind—my partner and I have other things to do, so this had better be worthwhile."

The prisoners babbled among themselves for a few

minutes, and Evan could hear a lot of "You!", "No, you!",
"Tell him about the tourists!" and things of that nature, all
interspersed with vehemently-worded refusals to do anything of the sort.

He tried not to look at Joss for more than a few seconds
at a time, because there was a look on O'Bannion's
face—a tremor about the lips and a quivering of the
nostrils—that warned Evan his partner was on the edge of
an explosion of laughter. It was hardly surprising; there
was a flutter of the same sort in Evan's own belly, replac-
ing the carefully-cultivated viciousness that he had needed
for his "bad-sop" performance. At least if worse came to
worst he could always repolarize the helm and switch off
its speaker-mikes for long enough to get the guffaws out
of his system, but that wouldn't do Joss much good.

Finally one of the miners emerged from their huddle of
discussion. With his cropped ruddy-brown hair and a beard
of the same color coming in from lack of shaving, he
looked entirely appropriate for a man who'd been arrested
whilst mining rusty metal out of the surface of Mars. "I'm
Wim de Kuijpers," he said. "They want me to do the talking."

"All right," said Joss. "Wait one." He extended the little
boom mike that connected to the voder pickup built onto
the top of his pad, then set the pad itself to make both an
audio record and a hard copy transcription. "1735 hours,
day 223, coordinated Martian year 2068. This statement is
being recorded. I am Solar Patrol Officer 2624301
O'Bannion, J.D., and another officer is present. Would you
please state your name and rank."

"I am Solar Patrol Officer 4629337 Glyndower, E.H."

Joss nodded, and swung the mike's boom around to face
de Kuijpers. "Give your full name and date of birth, then
proceed with your statement."

"H'm." The man stared at the little microphone as if it
was a levelled pistol, and cleared his throat several times.
"H'rm. Uh, the name's de Kuijpers, Wim Piet de
Kuijpers—"

"Give the spelling, please, just for the record," said
Evan, knowing only too well what the transcription program was capable of doing to some names.

De Kuijpers did so, slowly and carefully, then cleared his throat again. "Born in Leiden, Nederland-Europa, 20th August 2092—that's day 232 coord-Marsyear 2036, just for the record."

"Just the facts, man," growled Evan. "Just the facts." Joss gave him a very funny look, and Evan wondered why; it was probably another of those things that would have to be explained "later"—whenever they managed time for later. "Your occupation?"

"I'm a lichen miner. We all are. About a year and a half ago, we joined up as a sort of combine—pooled our money so that together we could buy better equipment than any one individual could afford."

"I see. Equipment like beam weapons. We'll come back to that presently. Why were you mining a prohibited area?"

"We weren't. At least, we weren't supposed to. The automatics mustn't have been working properly, or we'd have turned aside well clear of The Strip."

"These automatics," said Joss. "They're the 'better equipment' you mentioned? Not much better."

"It was a glitch. Everything throws them once in a while. Today it was the autonav system; tomorrow," de Kuijpers raised his shoulders in an elaborate shrug, "who knows? The galley equipment, maybe, like it did last month. And we'll be eating cold pack-rations again until it's fixed."

"Like I say, Mr. de Kuijpers—if this is the sort of better equipment your combine provides, I'd think seriously about upping everyone's contribution. Unless you *like* cold field rations, of course."

Evan grinned briefly. Both he and Joss knew what those things tasted like, and hot or cold, they were unlikely to win any gourmet dining awards. "The guns, Mr. Wim Piet de Kuijpers. Now you're not going to try telling an old soldier like me that those were something every lichen miner needs to stop the lichen from escaping, are you?"

The miner stared at him for a few seconds, maybe remembering how Evan had cracked open the side of the crawler with the offhand ease of someone shelling a crab. "No," he said sullenly, "I'm not."

"But you're going to tell me what they're *really* for, aren't you? Well, *aren't you?*"

"They're for self-defense. No honestly, they are! There's a gang out beyond Tombstone—"

"Harry Smyth's mob. Yes, we've heard about them."

"You have?"

"Hard not to," said Joss, "considering what happened to the sheriff. He was cut in half with an auto slugthrower, just like the ones you were shooting at my partner."

"But we didn't—"

"I never said you did!" boomed Evan. He still hadn't taken off his helm or cracked its visor, and it was easy to cut in the augmentation circuits when he needed to. "Now carry on!"

De Kuijpers hesitated, trying to reconcile what he had just heard with the earlier drumhead court-martial. Then he looked up at Evan and decided to do exactly as he was told. "The guns *are* for self-defense. Smyth's boys have been leaning on everybody with a still—I think they're selling the stuff on, because there's never that much in the Tombstone bar—and since we do a little distilling ourselves—"

"I had noticed," said Evan, "That's why I charged you with it."

"Uh, right . . . Okay. Sure. Ummm . . . Oh yeah, Smyth; from what we heard, they make you an offer for the juice, and if you turn it down, or want more than they'll give you, then you have an accident. Life-support systems crash, people fall into the grinders. That sort of thing. It happens often enough for real, Mr. Sop, but it was happening to people who'd just told Smyth's 'representative' to bog off. So we decided to discourage him, if he ever came looking for us."

De Kuijpers waved his hand towards the other five men who were sitting on the bench in a hear-no-evil, speak-no-evil sort of pose. Evan spared them a brief glance and decided that butter would not only refuse to melt in their mouths, it would probably freeze quite solid. The only thing missing was a set of haloes. "My friends and I have one thing in common: our families, those of us that have them, aren't in Tombstone. Harry Smyth may be a big bug out here, but he's got no pull in—" De Kuijpers stopped short, looked pointedly at the red RECORD light on Joss's pad, and shook his head. "He's got no pull wherever our folks might be," he said finally, and stared at the two sops as if daring them to take issue with his reply.

Neither did. The miners' families weren't a part of this, even if some of them had been receiving an income supplement from the sale of hooch and stolen goods. Evan knew that he and Joss were after bigger fish than that.

"So why did you shoot at us?" he said. "You must have seen our ship's markings on whatever targeting array your weapons used, and we gave you a verbal warning on top of that. Yet you fired, and continued to fire. I'm interested in hearing your reasoning for that."

"Diego was on guns"—there was a brief noise of protest from one of the other prisoners—" but all he saw was some scruffy-looking thing dressed up to look and sound like an EssPat ship."

Evan heard a muffled explosion of outrage coming from Joss, and laid a heavy hand on his partner's shoulder to restrain him until he had recovered something of his equanimity. He cooled down somewhat as de Kuijpers continued his explanation and managed to dilute the original insult to *Nosey*.

"We all knew that EssPat doesn't have any business on Mars, otherwise why bother with a Planetary Police Department at all?" the miner said. "You tell me, Mr. Sop sir: when the local PPD badge looks like one thing and the badge on the ship heading for you looks like something else, what would *you* think?"

"I think I'd like to know why you didn't stop firing when you saw my suit."

"Because we figured that if Smyth had gotten hold of a ship and dressed it up to look like EssPat equipment, he might have gotten hold of something he could dress up like a sop suit as well." De Kuijpers gave both sops a weak little smile. "We should have realized when the slugs started bouncing off your armor. Mock-ups just aren't that good."

"Who is Harry Smyth?" asked Joss. "Where does he come from? And where does he go?"

"Don't know. Nobody does. Nobody alive, anyway. Try to follow his men when they come for the liquor pickup, and they'll grind you up with your own fertilizer. That's what people say, anyway. But there's nobody called Smyth anywhere in this mining district. A couple of Schmidts, that's all. Oh yeah, and Jan Smit. He's another ex-Hollander, like me, but no Smyths. You want my opinion, I don't think there's any such person as 'Harry Smyth.' I think it's just a name the gang use, and they pulled it out of an address book somewhere."

Evan considered that, then swore gently under his breath. "So we're looking for a John Doe's gang after all. At least the bastards didn't call themselves Jones. That would make my uncle Gareth and all his friends from up the Rhondda really *very* angry, and they'd expect me to do something painful, see." Evan grinned, but it wasn't a very pleasant expression, and he didn't intend it to be so. For just a few seconds, he too had been as angry as Uncle Gareth would have been, and he had really meant what he said, not from any reason of duty, but just that the thought of some cheap little crook using a good Welsh name to hide behind really stuck in his throat.

"It's funny about the glitch in your autonav system," he said to de Kuijpers and all the other miners. "But while you were on the way out of your ... chomper, isn't it? I took the liberty of dumping the nav data into one of my suit's onboard buffers. Fascinating stuff. It looks almost as if that navigational error taking you across The Strip had been programmed in. Now, I've never seen a glitch like that before, but I *have* heard of people trying to blame their own bad behavior on a poor dumb machine. Which is it this time, gentlemen?" Evan's grin got even wider. "As if I really need to ask ..."

DE KUIJPERS' LITTLE SIDELINE WASN'T JUST THE usual illegal distilling. Their position as a moderately well-off mining combine had enabled them to do privately what "Harry Smyth" was doing at a more public level: they smuggled out their own hooch, and then divided up the profits amongst themselves. That in itself, thought Evan, would go a long way to explain their nervousness over being caught by the gang boss. From the sound of it, "Harry" wasn't the sort of person to let them off with a smack on the wrist and a promise never to do it again. He—she, they, whatever—would make *certain* that Wim de Kuijpers and his friends would never do *anything* again.

And on top of it all, like icing on a very strange cake, was the reason why they and their chomper machines had been rumbling blithely into the protected area of The Strip. They hunted for, found, stole and then smuggled antiquities.

"Hang on just a minute," said Joss. "There's a substratum of steel nearly eighty klicks long out there—but there's not much else. So what do you mean, 'antiquities'?"

"Archaeological finds," replied de Kuijpers simply, then gave both sops a shameless smile. "A Slab of the Ancient Mars Metal, half still in the Raw State as Discovered by Intrepid Explorers of the Red Planet, and half burnished to a Mirror Sheen, all Mounted on a Sheet of Polished Stone cut from the Very Slopes of Olympus Mons Itself." He managed to give the Capital Letters their full value, and sounded altogether too like an advertisement in one of the gaudier Sunday-tabloid color supplements.

"That," said Evan, "is one of the most tasteless things I think I've ever heard."

"So why are you smiling, Mr. Sop Glyndower sir?"

Evan laughed a little. "I was just thinking that if your friends ever run short of the readies, they could sell your brass neck for its scrap value . . ."

"Why, thank you, sir!" said the miner.

"I didn't say I approved, boyo. I just . . . Oh, bugger it, you know what I mean."

"Yes, Officer Glyndower. I think I do. Thank you all the same." He straightened out of his customary slouch for just an instant and gave Evan the ghost of a bow. For that instant, Wim de Kuijpers seemed a lot more dignified, and Evan found himself wondering what reason had brought him all the way from the Low Countries to this particular part of the High Country.

"I don't approve at all," said Joss, and Evan could hear the sharp tones of a scientist with all his feathers ruffled. "The Strip could prove to be of immeasurable historical and archaeological value, and you bunch of bloody Goths are tearing it apart to make *paperweights.*"

"Not paperweights, sir," said one of the other prisoners, speaking out for the first time. He was the man de Kuijpers had identified as Diego the gunner. "They're too big for that. We build them as ornamental conversation pieces. You put a good, heavy sheet of glass on top, legs on the bottom and so! A table that's literally out of this world."

Evan found himself wanting to groan at the way this interview was turning into an exercise in hype. It was as if, once assured that the major felony charges against them carried little weight, de Kuijpers and the rest had lost any sense of guilt they might have felt. He wondered whether they were thoughtless, shortsightedly selfish, or just plain amoral; hard men on a hard world with an eye to whatever main chance presented itself. At least they were nothing like the last bunch of crooks he had dealt with over the same subject.

Until it actually happened and he and Lon Salonikis were called in on the case, Evan would never have believed that so dry a subject as archaeology could excite enough passion for one staid and sober scientist to kill another. At least, not over a length of rusty metal buried for God knows how long in the sand of the Martian high desert. Gold; now that could be a different matter. He remembered the time, long ago now, when he'd gone to see the Tutankhamen exhibits in Cardiff's big museum. Funeral goods; all that wealth, made for no other reason than to go into the ground with a dead teenage king. And not an important one, either. He didn't even warrant a pyramid. Just a hole in the rocks . . .

But there was no gold here, and certainly no artifact to match the awesome glamour of the great golden mask and mummy-case. Unless somebody made one—and he was looking at just such a somebody.

"You mean to tell me," said Joss, less enraged now than incredulous, "that people will actually *buy* these things? Surely they're not going to be taken in by something from you, when they've never heard it mentioned as part of a major find!"

"I could say that there's one born every minute, Mr. Sop O'Bannion sir, but that would be unkind to our customers." Wim de Kuijpers spread his hands in a shrug even more expressive than the last. "There are always those who buy for the wrong reasons. Some who would rather have something, uh, acquired, than something all properly authenticated . . . at a price to match. And likewise, there are those who buy for the right reasons, or a least, reasons that seem right to them. Our slab, for instance. You call it a paperweight. Not so. It's an artifact in its own right, made of Martian materials by Martian hands—at least, in a manner of speaking. When your scientists and archaeologists are done with The Strip, and it's all been dug up and ground up and analyzed and measured and dated, it's possible that they'll have to look at one of our ornamental slabs to see what The Strip once looked like."

"Humpf," went Joss, not sounding even slightly convinced of the miners' good intentions. "And is that all?"

"Yes," said de Kuijpers, then hesitated as a thought struck him. "Except for the swords, and pieces of tripod war machines, of course."

"SWORDS??!"

The miner blinked a bit; Joss wasn't using any sort of voice-augmenter, but even without it he had managed to rival Evan's volume. "Uh, yeah," de Kuijpers said, sounding rather less sure of himself than before. "The John Carter Special Saber, based on a design by Frazetta . . ."

"Oh-my-Gawwwd!" groaned Joss, and hid his face in his hands.

Evan watched him, and was unable to decide if he was crying or laughing. For his own part, he was under control; just. *Better equanimity through ignorance,* he thought. *Except that when we decided to do this Mars vacation jaunt, the entertainment expert over there would insist on showing me all those Burroughs books. Nice pictures, but . . .* Evan had recognized the artist's name, and couldn't help recalling the most prominent features of his illustration style. *I just hope this bunch of entrepreneurs don't claim to manufacture a Dejah Thoris Bum and Boobs enhancement outfit, or I'll really have to leave the room ...*

"Never mind that," Evan said. "I want to hear about your movements in the past seventy-two hours, in every detail. Begin."

" ... AND THAT'S IT, OFFICER GLYNDOWER."

Evan looked towards Joss, who tapped the voder pickup on his pad and nodded. "Got the lot," he said.

"Good." Evan turned his attention back to the miners. "You realize," he said to them, "that what you've just told Officer O'Bannion and myself adds forgery, fraud and misrepresentation to an already crowded charge-sheet? Not to mention theft of certified artifacts, plundering an archaeological site, trespassing on planetary parkland ..."

De Kuijpers nodded, giving both sops a weak little smile. "Maybe so," he said, "but none of those carry the death sentence."

"Good point, However, you still haven't given me any way in which I can prove that you lot were out mining The Strip on the dates that you claim."

"Aw, shit, Glyndower, give us a break! If you're starting to think like that, then anything we tell you could just be an alibi we set up in advance!"

"Exactly. So make it a good one."

De Kuijpers shook his head. "If you dumped our nav logs when you were in our chomper," he said, "you know perfectly well where we were. It's like I told you; we were about twelve klicks north of Planitia Arietis and thirty klicks west of Mons; and we came here pretty much straight southeast, in a straight line. No particular reason to go around anything on this planet, unless it's something like Marineris ... or Mons itself."

"Your log could have been faked," Joss said. "We've seen that before."

"If the officer here is using the log as evidence that we

meant to be at The Strip," said de Kuijpers, smiling a little, "he can't claim it was also faked."

Joss looked sidewise at Evan. "Well," Evan said, "that's right enough. Never mind that, for the moment. There are ways to check your location as of two or three days ago: and we'll be doing that. Meanwhile, you're going to have to be guests of the community, gentlemen. We'll do our best to make sure that whoever the PPD sends out will make you comfortable."

Joss nodded. "End transcript," he said to his pad. "Later, gentlemen."

They went out of the dome and stopped by the front desk, which was now occupied by an annoyed-looking young woman in PPD blue. She glared up at them as they passed and said, "I don't suppose you've got any of the paperwork on this for me, have you?"

"We'll be getting it through shortly," Joss said, smiling at her as charmingly as he could. Evan watched, amused, as the officer blinked at Joss in a manner that suggested he might as well go try to charm a rock. "We're running on interim at the moment," Joss said, not giving up yet, "but we'll have the paperwork in by the morning, I should think. Do you want a copy of the charges?"

She pushed her own pad at him, popped one of its endpanels, reeled a foot and a half of cable out of it, and handed it to Joss. He fastened it to his own pad, tapped at the control surface for a moment, and did the data transfer. Then he handed the end of the cable back.

The officer gazed at her pad while putting the cable away. "Look at all this," she said in disgusted wonder. "Didn't you forget to give them a parking ticket?"

"Couldn't," Joss said. "It's Sunday. See you tomorrow, ma'am."

Joss settled his SHEL gear, and he and Evan headed out together. "Parking tickets indeed," he muttered. "Dammit, why can't we have those new pads with the IR data transfer? I'm getting tired of this low-tech stuff. Cables. Pfah."

"You're just annoyed because the lady behind the desk thought you were an interfering, overpaid government flunky," Evan said with a chuckle, "and she wouldn't smile at you. Which reminds me: where has Helen Mary got to?"

Joss actually sighed, which Evan found hilariously funny, but still managed not to laugh. "She went off to find some dinner. Then tomorrow, after her father again." He shook his head. "I wish we could be of more help to her. She did us a good turn, in a way."

"She did, that," said Evan. They started to make their way back toward *Nosey*. He sighed too, for different reasons. "Well, we're going to have to stop tiptoeing around here, I suppose. We're going to have to go fully active, which is not going to endear us to the PPD, but it can't be helped." Evan hated situations like this. Catching the miners in the act of carving up The Strip was not a bad thing in itself; but the PPD was likely to take it as a personal affront that SP personnel had made the arrest, since it implied that the PPD was not doing its job. Professionalism aside, since the PPD was human, it meant that cooperation with Evan and Joss was going to be impaired somewhat. At a time when it really needed to work well, this was a major annoyance. *We'll just have to work around it,* Evan thought, *and do the best we can* . . .

"You're rather quiet," Joss said.

"So are you, then. What's on your mind?"

They came up to *Nosey,* and Joss put one hand against the scratched, dulled hull. "Some scruffy-looking thing," he said, and his voice was very cross.

Evan had to chuckle again. "Look, we'll get her polished up right when we get home. Right now, it's just as well she stays the way she is, because another sandstorm would just ruin the way she looks all over again."

They went in, Evan shelled out of his suit and racked it up, then went into the galley to put on a pot of tea. While it was brewing, he sat down with his pad and scrolled through its recent memory. No new messages had come in.

He keyed his implant on. "Tee," he said, "you around?"

A three-second pause. *When am I not?*

"I keep meaning to ask you about that. When do you sleep?"

I don't.

"Come on, now."

She laughed at him, a wicked sound. *I've got a REM augmenter in,* she said. *Instant REM sleep, anytime I want it. I get a three-hour mandatory rest shift so my body can do its "laundry," once every twenty-four hours. After that—*He could hear the shrug. *If I have five minutes here, ten minutes there, I take it. It rests me as well as your six hours lying there like a lump . . . maybe better. And I get much better vacation benefits than you do, you poor thing.*

Evan shook his head. It was true that he had never heard Telya sound anything less than sprightly. *Now what did you want?* she said. *I do have other things to do around here.*

"Remember those satellite reconnaissance photos I wanted from you?"

Still working on it, boss. You have no idea how tight-assed those Space Forces cuttys are.

"All right. But I need some other coordinates now."

Different ones? Or additional?

"Additional." He read her the map coordinates from his ad for a square between Planitia Arietis and the end of The Strip. "And I want these for about a week back. Tell the idiots it's in regard to a murder investigation."

I have been. I think we're going to have to come up with something bigger to get their attention, though. You don't suppose you could find evidence of some illicitly armed spacecraft or something?

Evan sighed. "I wish we could. We've found every *other* kind of crime you can think of. The place is a hotbed of illegality. But none of it is the kind we're looking for."

Well, I'll do what I can. I think you're going to have to start finding signs of what you're after, though.

"Oh?"

Uh-huh. Lucretia's on the crank.

"Uh-oh," Evan said.

Yes indeed. Some of the memos have been interesting, the past couple of days. A lot of stuff going back and forth between her office and the Commissioner's.

"She's going to love this, then," Evan said. "We need full release, effective immediately, and backdated a day. There are going to have to be backup warrants issued from

Welles, and they're not going to look on this with favor
... we've given them a couple of black eyes over the past
couple of days."

Tough on them, Telya said. *I'll take care of it. Lucretia
can't complain about this really; you're doing what she
took you off vacation to do.*

"Vacation ..." Evan said. He had almost forgotten. I really need to give the crowd at Sydenham a call, he
thought. They probably think I've fallen off the planet.
"Well, anyway, we're going to be jolly busy with search-
and-entry tomorrow morning, so I need the authorizations
ASAP."

You've got them now, Telya said. *I can sign them for
Lucretia and squirt them to Welles in about five minutes.
Dox will follow, and I'll put confirmations in your pads.*
There was a pause. *Just don't break anything that doesn't
need breaking,* Telya said. *They've been going on about
your expense account again.*

Evan was outraged. "What for? We haven't spent anything!"

*That's why. They're worried that you're saving up for
something big.*

"Wonderful," Evan said. "Well, we'll be good. As good
as we can, anyway."

*Right. I'll confirm the receipt of those authorizations for
you in a little while.*

"Thanks, Tee. What would we do without you?"

All the paperwork, she said. *Later.*

Joss came in, peered at the teapot. "How can you drink
it like that?"

"Watch me. Here, want some?"

"All right. No milk! How can you put that in there?"

Evan rolled his eyes and handed Joss his tea black. "I
hope to civilize you some day, so that I can introduce you
to my mother."

"Goodness, people will talk."

"Shut up, O'Bannion. Meanwhile, we have more important business. What are we going to do about those idiots
in the dome?"

Joss sipped his tea and shook his head. "One thing
seems fairly plain to me," he said. "They don't have any

idea about what happened to the SP ship, or its contents. Otherwise they would have gone straight for that. That's more money in one little package than a year's worth of souvenirs. And no question but they would have found someone to fence the prototype to."

" 'Smyth'?" Evan said.

Joss shrugged. "Maybe, to buy them some goodwill. Those remarks about their families being out of the guy's reach—these are nervous people. Or they might have sold it to someone else. It doesn't matter. Anyway, I don't think these boys are up to anything we need to be concerned about."

Evan lifted his eyebrows at that. "That's odd to hear from *you*. What about The Strip, then?"

"Well, they have to stop doing that, of course." Joss's eyes twinkled a little. "PPD will have to be a little more aggressive about its policing, too. But meanwhile, I suspect there are other deposits of iron-bearing rock in the area that could be used to fake material from The Strip. In fact," Joss said, his eyes getting distant suddenly, that figuring-it-out look that Evan had come to alternately admire and dread, "if you used an isotaxic oxidation compound—say something like—"

"Spare me the brand-name chemistry! What are you suggesting?"

"Well, if you put this stuff on a steel plate, and buried it, see, the natural speed of oxidation would be increased by as much as six hundred percent—compensating for the lack of oxygen in the atmosphere—and then you could take the rusted steel, and—"

"You ought to be in that dome with the rest of them!" Evan said. "You little Hiberno-Chinkish crook! It's a good thing you're on the side of law and order. I *think.*"

Joss looked rueful. "I can't help it that I think of these things. I'm creative."

"Too damn creative. Never mind that. Were you about to suggest that we let them go?"

"Well, if we can get confirmation that they weren't here for the sheriff's murder, and that they weren't anywhere near the SP ship's crash site—"

"I'm working on that. Might take a couple of days yet, to hear Tee talk."

"Hmm. Well, I don't think they're guilty. I think we should let them go."

"So do I," Evan said after a few moments. "But I'd prefer to have more evidence of their whereabouts."

"Did you actually dump their nav log?" said Joss.

"Oh yes. It's for real, I think. At least, if it wasn't, I couldn't find how it had been tampered with. I would just prefer some corroboration."

"And if none comes through?"

Evan sighed. "We do have other fish to fry," he said. "And frankly, we could use a little friendly native help at this point, since most of the other native help either seem to have their own agendas at the moment—like Helen Mary—or to be rather ambivalent."

"Like Virendra."

"Yes."

They looked at each other for a moment.

"Some more eyes and ears would be a help to us," Joss said. "We could release them. But not before I have a word with their chompers."

"Tracers?" said Evan.

"Nothing easier. Those mining vehicles are both their homes and their transport; they can't go far without them—or far from them. And they wouldn't dump them. Their entire livelihood rests in those vehicles. We can take a run out that way tonight before we turn in, and make the necessary installations."

Evan nodded. "Now," he said, "tell me how you would explain this to Lucretia."

Joss shook his head. "Just that way. Look, do *you* think they were involved in any way? Honestly."

"Not now," Evan said slowly, "no."

"Well, then. Lucretia would have to defer to us on this one. We're on the spot; she's not. This kind of situation is precisely why we're given the kind of discretion we are."

Evan sighed. "I want to think about this one for a while. But I have to admit, you may have a point. Let's see what the morning brings." He fell silent, then looked at Joss as a horrible idea suddenly occurred to him. "You wouldn't actually *suggest* that idea you had to them, would you? I mean, aiding and abetting fraud—"

"And if we let them loose without the idea, we're aiding and abetting the destruction of a priceless archaeological site." Joss sipped his tea and looked over the rim of the cup at Evan. "This way, we're making sure that people buying worthless souvenirs are getting *genuinely* worthless souvenirs ... rather than an irreplaceable part of Mars's history, which they're probably not really equipped to appreciate if they've bought something like this in the first place. Which way would *you* rather have it?"

Evan buried his head in his hands and groaned.

WHAT THE MORNING BROUGHT WAS ANOTHER sandstorm, but only a smallish one, with winds not much worse than sixty klicks per hour. There was nothing new from Telya. Evan climbed into his suit in a dubious sort of mood.

"Ready?" Joss said, coming out of his stateroom in his SHEL gear.

"Just about." He snapped his helm in place and did the usual power check. "Where first?"

"The jail, I think. And then—"

"Everyplace else." Evan shook his head. "I have to admit, searches have never been my favorite part of this job."

"No?" Joss said. They climbed down out of *Nosey* and sealed her up. "I don't know, I have kind of a—"

He stopped. On *Nosey*'s side, in big red letters, someone had spray-painted the words: SOPS GO HOME.

Evan braced himself. But, "Huh," Joss said. "Doesn't even match the markings very well."

"No, it doesn't."

Evan waited a bit longer, but no explosion seemed to be forthcoming. "Clumsy of them," Joss said, and started off toward the sheriff's office.

"Oh," Evan said, and followed.

"Yes indeed," Joss said cheerfully. "Leaving us a handwriting sample like that. Very ambivalent indeed."

Evan grinned.

In the sheriff's office they found again the young female PPD officer they had met the day before. "Good morning, madam," Joss said. "How are the inmates this morning?"

The officer looked at Evan and Joss with an expression that intimated she wouldn't mind seeing the whole lot of them locked up together. "Noisy," she said, pushing her dark hair out of her eyes and going back to work on her own pad. "Apparently they didn't care for breakfast."

"Ah. And you told them to call Customer Service, I take it."

She looked up at Joss again. "I told them, Officer, that I didn't join the police to practice making Béarnaise sauce, and if I heard any more out of them, I would stew them their boots for lunch. Is there something I can do for you gentlemen, or are you just here to throw your weight around?"

Joss smiled very slightly. "Probably there are those who'll put that construction on it," he said. "But they've never seen it happen, or they'd know better. First piece of business: we're going to be doing a search this morning. May we invite you to participate?"

"If that's an invitation," said the young officer, "thanks but no thanks. I'm supposed to be running a murder investigation here, and my supervisor will not take kindly to me running around with the visiting talent when I should be collecting evidence." The inflection she put on the word "talent" was not entirely complimentary.

"All right," Joss said, "Officer, uh, Steck is it? Well, you're welcome if you should find the time. Now, if we might have a few words with the gentlemen in the back? And then we'll be taking them off your hands."

"Good riddance," Steck said, the first thing she had said that sounded genuinely pleased. "At your convenience." She handed Joss the keycard.

They headed back into the cell area; Joss keyed the door open, and let Evan precede him in. Evan noticed that the "gentlemen" looked rather the worse for wear after a night in jail; not that they had been badly treated or housed, but they had the sobered, nervous look of people with bad consciences who had just had a good twelve hours to think about the error of their ways. He restrained his smile. This was the best possible mood for what he and Joss were planning.

Joss sat down on one of the benches; Evan remained standing inside the door, which he shut.

"We have some new information," Joss said, "which we have to decide how to act on."

The six of them looked at each other, and at de Kuijpers, and at each other again. Joss cleared his throat, and said, "We have a proposition to offer you."

De Kuijpers looked at Joss suspiciously. "That being?"

"This is something of a closed community," Joss said. "It's rather hard to tell what's going on in the neighborhood without some assistance. We're proposing that we will drop the most serious charges against you . . . in return for some help."

"Which charges?" de Kuijpers said.

"Well," Evan said, "we can let go the smuggling, distilling, vandalism, and breach of the peace charges. The assault charges," he said, as the men looked at each other, "will have to stand . . . though I will direct that your sentences be suspended. If what we want done goes well."

"Is it legal?" said de Kuijpers, scowling.

Joss looked amused. "Of course it is. In fact, there's likely to be a reward for it, if you pull it off. That SP ship we mentioned to you the other day? Well, something was stolen from it . . . and we want it back."

The lichen miners looked at each other.

"Here," Joss said, and handed them a printout sheet with a line drawing and photo of the satellite prototype. "I'm not going to tell you what it is," said Joss, "that not being particularly germane. It's obviously something electronic and complicated, and we want it back rather than having to build another one and have it shipped all the way here."

They passed the paper back and forth, peering at it.

"We would rather you didn't discuss what you're looking for," Joss said, "but if you think you need to, to find the thing, go ahead. Just don't mention who sent you looking for it. The usual reward for salvage and return of SP property is in the ten thousand credit range. I am authorized on this occasion to offer twenty-five thousand."

Eyes widened among the miners. Evan thought, *Oh God; what a thing. Telya was right. What* is *Lucretia going to say—*

"Right," Joss said. "I would advise you briefly, before you leave—don't bother trying to pass the equipment on to anyone else. We're going to be keeping an eye on you, and all these charges can and will be reapplied at our discretion. Whether we're here or not, PPD knows what's been going on, and will act accordingly. The only difference in your treatment would be that trial and sentencing would take a *lot* longer. So a word to the wise."

All the lichen miners sat mum.

"Are you agreeable?" Joss said. "All of you?"

Much nodding.

"I want it verbally," Joss said. "De Kuijpers—"

"It's fine with me, Officer."

"Valdez?"

"Yes, sir—"

Joss recorded all the assertions, and finally said, "All right. Pursuant to the special agreement made between us this day and date, you are all free to go, subject to later recall." He tapped at his pad.

"Officer—"

"Mr. de Kuijpers?"

"One more thing. If you're willing."

"What?"

De Kuijpers looked at Evan's suit. "We saw what that thing can do," he said. "And your ship. Couldn't you do something for us besides find this whatsis?"

"What sort of thing did you have in mind?" said Evan.

The miners looked at each other. "Smyth," de Kuijpers said, almost in a whisper. "And his bunch. Can't you catch them and stop what they're doing?"

Evan and Joss looked at each other. Evan was thinking, *This is PPD business, really. We have our plate pretty full already.* But at the same time, it was plain enough that the PPD had more than a full plate: they were hopelessly understaffed, and didn't have the kind of firepower to send out to deal with gangs like this, which for all Evan knew

were pulling this same sort of crap all over the planet. It
was so easy to walk away and say, "No, too busy, sorry."
But if one found this kind of thing in the course of one's
duty—

He looked at Joss and nodded fractionally.

Joss looked thoughtful. "You know, Mr. de Kuijpers,"
he said, "that an officer in our situation really needs, as it
were, sort of an excuse to do the kind of thing you're suggesting. A hint of what *specific* things are happening.
Names, dates, places."

Evan heard a slight emphasis on the word "places." He
held quite still, and waited to see what would happen.

Nothing did. The men all looked at each other, then at
Joss again, with expressions of truly angelic innocence and
ignorance.

Joss nodded. "All right," he said. "Look, I don't see
why we can't do something of the sort. But . . . remember.
We need hints."

All the heads nodded as if the same enthusiastic puppe-
teer was managing them.

"So," Joss said, looking at Evan. "Turnkey?"

Evan looked mildly at Joss. "It doesn't turn, really. It
just goes in that slot there—"

"Ahem," Joss said. The miners smiled.

Evan opened the door. "We'll drop you all back at your
vehicles later," Joss said. "Right now we have a few
hours' work ahead of us, so why not go over to the bar
and have something to eat. —Try the roast," he called after them as the men hurriedly reclaimed their SHELs.
"They have some really nice Béarnaise over there—"

The last man out left the cell-dome in such a hurry that
he stumbled over Joss and had to clutch at the doorjamb
to catch himself. Joss shook his head, watching them go
with a slight smile.

"Nice boys," he said.

"A bit of a change from your attitude yesterday," Evan
said. "I mean, that 'scruffy' remark—"

Joss chuckled. "Forgive and forget."

Evan found this a little hard to swallow, but he held his
peace for the moment.

At the front desk, as Evan and Joss made their way out,

Steck looked at them quizzically. "You're just letting them go?"

Joss looked at her mildly. "No point in them staying here any longer. Thanks for your help, Officer."

She nodded, looking bemused. "Anytime."

Joss got his SHEL settled, and they went out into the street. "Interesting world," he said to Evan as they strolled back toward *Nosey.*

"In what way?"

"That poor lad who fell on me," Joss said. "You know what he said to me?"

" 'Excuse me,' I should hope."

"Nope. He said, 'Try the north end.' "

Evan's eyebrows went up. "The north end of town?"

"That's what *my* amazing deductive abilities made of it."

Evan shook his head. "These people are *very* afraid," he said softly. "I'm beginning to think that putting Smyth's lot out of business will be a bit more than our good deed for the week."

"Yes indeed. And it could cause all kinds of local good-will. And cause certain lost things to become found, as well, perhaps."

"Well, Officer, I think we should start our search. Do you have everything we need? Or should we head back to *Nosey?"*

"Oh, no . . . I'm fairly well equipped. I think we should go and have a look at the buildings on the north side of town. What do you think?"

"Hmm." Evan considered it for a moment. "You know, I would almost sooner start at the south end."

"Oh? Why?"

"Well—if someone was seen leaving our company—and then we went straight to the place where something, mmm, sensitive was hidden, well, it might put the person who gave us the information in a bad light. Whereas if it's sort of in the middle of the search that we find the sensitive goods—or more toward the end—"

Joss looked sidewise at Evan. "I think some inscrutability is rubbing off on you," he said. "And about time, I say."

Evan chuckled. "South side?"

"After you, Officer."

EVAN HAD CALLED IT "TEN SHEDS AND A LAND-ing pad." Tombstone turned out to be a bit more than that.

For one thing, the sheds were often only indications of tunneling that had been done under the rocks. This part of Mars, as Joss had pointed out, was tectonically quieter than most, and more suited for underground storage. Since domes were expensive, and digging was cheap, several of the domes were common entrances to living quarters or storage areas.

The first dome they checked had both, separated from one another by pressure doors, and not belonging to the same people. In the living quarters were someone's pretty young wife and two children, who stared at Evan's suit with poorly disguised delight while their mother scowled. Evan left Joss to charm them and do a search, while he checked the other pressure door. It was locked, but that was not a problem for a sop: part of their standard equipment was a set of small devices for handling anything from coded-packet locks to ones that still used metal keys. If you got locked out of your house, or your vehicle, a sop was good to have around.

Evan had to start laughing almost immediately, once he was in. *Now was this why they wanted us to start at the other end of town?* Evan thought, for stacked on old rickety shelves all around the storage area were slabs of reddish rock, and of crumbling rusty stuff; there were carved stones, and small metallic models, artfully treated to look rusty, and heaven only knew what else. This was where their lichen miners were keeping some of their souvenir stock.

He strolled among the boxes, lifting out a "Martian Egg" here, a "rusted, corroded" set of warrior's harnesses there. The pressure door hissed, and he looked up to see Joss come in.

"Joss," Evan said, "look at this!" He lifted one hand. In

it was a big cup-hilted saber, so roomy in the hilt that he could hold it comfortably even with his gauntlets on.

Joss laughed. "Kaor!" he said.

"What?"

"It means hello in Martian."

"I'll take your word for it," Evan said, and started to put the thing down: then paused and looked at the blade. "Holy God," he said. " 'Wilkinson.' " He chuckled as he put it away. "Must be special order."

Joss walked around and looked at the souvenirs with the expression of an art critic at a sidewalk sale. "I wouldn't be surprised. You find anything interesting? Besides the Barsoom Bargain Basement, I mean."

"Nothing. I looked around with ultrasound when I came in . . . the floor's solid. No fake compartments, no large refined metallic masses. Nothing next door?"

Joss shook his head. "You make better tea than the lady does," he said, " and the kids want to know all about your guns."

Evan laughed. "Come on, let's hit the next one."

They climbed up the access steps and headed for the next dome, a smaller one. The door was locked again, but Evan made short work of it with his toolkit, and they shut it behind them and made their way down a set of stone steps into another storage area. The edges of the dome itself rested at ground level, but the area beneath it was excavated about eight feet further down. Another pressure door met them at the foot of the stairs. Evan opened it.

There were a couple of skimmers here, and a great number of crates and boxes, untidily piled off to one side of the area sunk under the dome. "Looks like my dad's garage," Joss said.

Evan chuckled. "Yours too?" he said. "Mine was always going on about cleaning the place . . . but it was only ever me who did the cleaning." He had had his visual recording apparatus on pause while they were between domes; now he turned it on again and looked right around the place. It was messy and neglected-looking. "Who owns this one?"

Joss consulted his pad. "George Jaruzelski, it says here."

Evan headed over to the skimmers, looked them over. "What's he do?"

"Mechanic, it says. Repairs mining vehicles, skimmers and so on. His living quarters are over on the east side of town."

Evan turned the ultrasound on and looked right around the dome again, getting many echoes of metal, not much of other materials. He looked at the skimmers—

—and paused. Something odd about the echo of the one closest to him. He bent over to shake the vehicle.

It rocked on its skids, and liquid sloshed. Not one set of sloshes, though, the ultrasound detector told him; and his augmented hearing circuits agreed. Two sets of sloshing. Two tanks—

"Joss," he said. "I think this is one of our bootleggers' babies."

"Oh?" Joss said, coming over quickly. He had been looking at the boxes. "Spare parts in those, mostly," he said, squatting down by Evan. "Perfectly innocent. What have we here?"

"Two tanks."

"Aha," Joss said. "The old false-wall trick. Let's see if we can find the other input. Under the usual fuel cap, you think?"

"That's been a favorite place," said Evan, and walked around to the back of the skimmer. It was one of those models that didn't have a fuel tank per se, but several long connected tanklets that ran the length of the craft; the trim system pumped fuel back and forth among the tanks to keep it level when it flew. Evan undid the fuel cap and peered down the intake. Usually there was a true intake and a false one, just down out of view; but Evan was using ultrasound and didn't need eyes to see the echo of the second pile running away from the main one. "There we are," he said. "Very neat. Fuel curves down toward the pod, booze curves up and away to the middle tank, probably." He turned. "Wonder what it's done to the thing's flight characteristics?"

"I don't intend to take it up and find out," Joss said, moving away to have another look at the boxes piled up all around. "The other one the same way?"

"Let me have a look." Evan went over to give it a shake.

He never made it. Joss stood up with a box lid in one hand, and something most unlidlike in the other. "Evan—" he said.

Evan's eyes widened. "That," he said, "is a Heckler & Koch G-40. Rather high-end, don't you think?" It was a slugthrower; extremely efficient, very high-speed, very low-caliber, one of the most modern of the descendants of the machine gun. *You could use a weapon like that,* Evan thought, *to cut someone in half with no problems.*

And then the shooting started, and Evan became very distracted indeed. "Get down!" he shouted, but Joss needed no encouragement in that regard; he was presumably down behind a pile of boxes.

Slugs rattled off Evan's suit. He was unconcerned: he wanted to find out who was shooting at them, and make them stop. A second burst of fire came, and a third—at a *very* high rate of fire, way higher than the guns in here, and of heavier caliber. *Military,* Evan thought. The H&K that Joss had been holding came flying out from behind one pile of boxes, and was duly and thoroughly shot at for its trouble. Immediately thereafter, Joss came diving and rolling from behind one of the piles of boxes. "No ammo, dammit," he gasped, pulling out his Remington.

"Forget that," Evan said. And something went *thump* beside him, and he looked at it, and his whole brain went up in alarm. He didn't dare kick the little round shape. He picked up Joss bodily in one arm, swinging him around in front of him, and with his other pointed his own gun at the wall of the dome.

The gun's rotaries came up to speed and it screamed, the stream of subcaliber slugs chopping the beginnings of a door-shaped line through the dome. Air began to howl past them. About halfway through the cutting, the dome gave way and blew outward in a big ragged tear only partly of Evan's making. Evan boosted Joss up two-armed, bent his knees, straightened up, and shot-putted him out through the hole.

Then the grenade went off.

JOSS HIT THE GROUND ROLLING, TRYING TO
spare his faceplate, and managed to get to his knees—

The dome did not so much blow out as up, at first,
straight up, the top of it coming off and sailing upward in
the light gravity like the sliced-off top of a soft-boiled egg.
Air plumed out silvery, and the moisture in it started to
snow down, then was instantly melted in the brief ball of
flame that erupted from the remains of the dome and blew
the rest of it away sideways. Joss covered his head, took
a few hits from flying debris, didn't care. A moment later
he was on his feet, staggering toward the dome. *"EVAN!"*

Nothing, no movement, no sign—Joss stared into the
roiling smoke and fire. It wouldn't last long, there was that
consolation: there was too little oxygen here—

Something moved near his foot.

A steel gauntlet came up and clamped on the ragged
edge of where the dome and its pressure seals had run into
the ground.

The hand simply hung on for a moment, and then the
fingers of the gauntlet began to drum.

Joss laughed out loud for sheer relief, and reached down
for Evan's other hand.

"Thanks, but I'd probably crush it," said the voice from
down in the smoke, as Evan hauled himself up into the
clear air. He looked a mess. Soot and smoke and horrible
scores were all over his armor—

He must have seen Joss's look, for Evan glanced down
at himself, did a long take of astonishment, and then
brushed at himself—so useless and impotent a gesture that
Joss had to laugh again. *"Diw,* just look at the finish,"
Evan said weakly.

Joss laughed harder than ever. "Now you know what I
felt like," he said. "Poor Evan!"

He laughed himself out, and then they both turned to
look at the remains of the dome. "I think," Evan said, "we
must be on the right track, here."

Joss nodded, wondering what the *wrong* one would look
like . . .

SIX

THE DUST SETTLED. IN THE ONE-THIRD GRAVITY of Mars, it settled more slowly than usual, but it settled nonetheless. There was no smoke to speak of, and after the first detonation, no fire: The thin Martian atmosphere could permit a rolling fireball like the one which had consumed warehouse, guns, fuel and bootleg liquor, but it would not sustain the sort of inferno that normally followed such an explosion.

That was just as well, because there was already little enough remaining to burn. Or to be examined for clues. "Damn them," said Joss as he surveyed the wreckage. *"Damn* them! If they could just have waited for another hour . . ."

"Then they might have had a chance to rig a proper booby trap," said Evan, looking around dispassionately, "and neither of us would be out here cursing the hasty way they had to blow it up."

"Yes, all right, I agree with that. But look at the mess!" Joss waved a hand towards the debris, and was forced to swing it through a considerable arc before the gesture could take in all the bits. *"Nosey*'s got a good enough forensic lab, but it's not up to a job like this. At least," he corrected himself, reluctant to belittle any part of the ship, "not as quickly as we'd need the information. If we had more time . . ."

"Which we haven't." Evan looked pointedly towards the

sky, and by implication out across the gulf of space to Earth's moon, where Lucretia was sitting, waiting for results, drumming her fingers on her desk, and running out of patience.

"Yeah." Joss grinned, a weak, crooked little quirking of his mouth. "The Borgia doesn't like repeating her 'hurry-up' instructions. And she'll have my reward offer to think about, soon enough. But at least she can't complain about our expense vouchers on this. Just for once, it's not our fault."

"I somehow don't see that as much of an excuse. Problem is, Joss-*bach*, that the longer we take about tracking down that blasted decoder, the more likely it is to go off-world by the back door. I can't see any little chummy with a titter of wit pulling off this heist without making damned sure he could make it away with the swag."

"Uh . . . right." *Sometimes it's just as well we're in the same line of work,* thought Joss. *If I wasn't able to get his meaning from the context, I'd really be in trouble.* "You think that our friend Harry is behind it after all?"

"Well, he's certainly closed down business in Tombstone. Permanently, by the looks of it. The PPD can go after him from here, once they've checked the census listings and worked out who doesn't live here anymore."

Joss grunted. After that blast, there'd probably be a few more families wanting to move out to a quieter area, like under a flight path somewhere. Evan was looking up and down the deserted street—people in Tombstone evidently knew better than to stick their heads out-of-doors when they heard firing—and Joss guessed that the suit was providing him with IR and thermographic views of the other buildings. "But I'm going to finish this house-to-house all the same. If they've got any sense at all, they won't have put all their eggs in one basket."

"I'm not so sure. Oh, sure, we should complete the search—and I'll be looking out for demolition charges, too. But we haven't heard any other explosions since this one, unless whoever was doing the firing is convinced we didn't get out. They were certainly putting an awful lot of effort into making sure this particular basket and every egg in it got well and truly trashed."

"We got out of it in one piece, though, and without our SHELs getting cracked," said Evan innocently. "Does that mean we're hard-boiled detectives?"

Joss stared at his partner in something close to disbelief; then for the next five minutes, made simulated gagging noises . . .

Apart from a certain amount of damage to Joss's sensibilities, which had a fairly low pun-tolerance at the best of times, they completed the search without finding anything else of note. In fact, they found nothing whatsoever that could be connected with criminal activity, which in a town whose cottage industries were without exception illegal, was peculiar in itself. *A really paranoid sop could find even that suspicious,* Joss thought to himself. *It wouldn't be too big a mental jump from finding nothing to starting to wonder who'd been through before you and tidied it all away.*

Evan, as it turned out, was feeling the same way. "Look you, the whole town feels like my old Aunty Gwyneth's house," he said. "Too bloody clean and neat and tidy for comfort. I don't know whether it was Smyth's mob, but *somebody* has been through here with a duster and a fine-tooth comb."

"But they missed the warehouse," said Joss, and then an unpleasant thought struck him. "Unless that stuff was left behind as bait. To keep us in one place until they could do something permanent. Evan, your suit *was* making a visual of the search, wasn't it?"

"It was, boyo. I was running on all bands. Thinking we should take a look at it, are you?"

"A close look. A very close look indeed."

JOSS'S IDEA OF A CLOSE LOOK, ONCE THEY WERE back aboard *Nosey,* was to push the datasolid's record through every enhancement circuit in the ship's systems. It took less time than it might have done, since there was only about ninety seconds of useful imagery before the firefight and the explosion. They had not only filled Evan's mind with more immediate concerns than keeping his suit-mounted camcorder steady, but they had filled the pickup lens with meaningless, blinding flares of light.

"Here we are," said Joss, and tapped the reader's GO button. He was running a computer-generated wire model over the visual imagery, and for a second or so before the circuitry took over and things settled down, the main viewscreen was a mess of colored lines. "We'll run through it once," he said, "while you make sure that the model's giving us an accurate representation of the things that the 'corder didn't pick up. Then I'll patch in overlays for IR, neutron radiograph, thermal and ultrasound scan data. That sort of thing's usually clearer on a model; certainly it's easier to watch."

Evan nodded, leaning forward to study what he had seen with his own eyes as *Nosey*'s computers made an outline sketch of it. Joss was quite correct about model analysis; data-gathering from a base image could be done, but once augmentation graphics began to fill the screen, it could become very hard on the viewer's eyes. There was another advantage: once the 3-d model had been constructed and locked in core memory, it could be manipulated in a way that a visual with just one point of view could not.

They watched until the first rounds of UHV fire struck blazing sparks from skimmer hulls and structural braces; then Evan sat back in his chair and watched while Joss began to analyze things. It was rather enlightening. The liquor and fuel tanks built into the skimmers had been drained; but not completely. Infrared and neutron radiograph imagery showed that there were about ten liters left in each tank; a significant amount, not enough that the vehicles were intended for use in the near future, but too much to have been left behind by accident.

"That was deliberate," said Joss, tapping the indicated alcohol and kerosene levels in each container. "They weren't wasting any more than they could, but they still left enough for vapor formation. After that, some bright spark—" Joss smiled wryly to himself at the aptness of that image, "—injected pure oxygen under pressure."

"What makes you so sure?" asked Evan. "I didn't have

time to take samples, much less run a spectrographic on the spot."

"The way it blew up. There's not enough oxygen in the Martian atmosphere to generate that level of explosive vapor in a volatile-fluid tank, and even if there was," he tapped the screen again, tracing the outlines of heavy pipes that ran into both the fuel tanks and those containing hooch, "they had the inert-system fitted."

"But rigged to pump oxygen instead of nitrogen, for our especial benefit. Now that's sneaky, if you like."

"How to make a fuel-air explosive when there's not enough air available," said Joss.

The inert rig on a fuel tank was meant to automatically replace used fuel with a blanket of nitrogen gas, and thus *prevent* the generation of explosive vapor. Whoever was behind this nasty little trap had turned the safety system on its head, and in so doing, had turned both skimmers into massive FAE bombs. It was quite possible that if he and Evan had taken much longer before searching the place, each of those bombs would have had a detonator fitted. It wouldn't—hadn't—done Evan any harm, but as for himself . . .

Joss felt ever so slightly queasy at the thought.

"There, look," said Evan suddenly, pointing at the screen. Joss automatically put the playback on hold, and followed the direction of his partner's levelled finger. "Here, give me that tracer, would you? Thanks."

Evan scribbled quickly with the light-pen and then handed it back to Joss. "Put the image back to a nonenhanced point of view," he said, "and then tell me if you notice anything." Joss tapped input keys and sat for several minutes looking at the stripped-down diagram before shaking his head. "Nothing? Okay. Pen again. Ta much. Right, so those Kocklers were *here*"—a few more marks appeared on the screen—"and this little widget already knows where you were standing. Rotate it to your point of view, but keep your eye on those marks."

The picture swung around to where Joss had been standing, then flipped to give his viewpoint. And the guns disappeared. He drew in a sharp breath and said, "Ah. I see."

"You were right, boyo. Those guns were bait indeed.

Not just to keep us in the warehouse, but to get us into a very particular part of the dome." Evan ran the tip of one finger along the structural supports. "Odds are, they had a directional pickup hidden up here so they'd know when we were in the right place. The guns were meant for you, the bombs for me. Little Harry likes to play rough."

"So it would appear." Joss stared at the screen for a few seconds without seeing it. Without seeing anything at all. *I've had a few close calls in my time, but that was the closest. Maybe I should transfer to the suit division after all.*

"You feeling all right, Joss?"

"Intimations of mortality. But nothing worse than intimations, so far." He shook a shiver away and reached for the controller again. "Let's have a closer look at those . . . what did you call them?"

"Kocklers. Service nickname for anything by the H&K people. It goes back a long way."

"I should have guessed. Anyway. Here we are. Heckler und Koch G-40. It's just a pity the 'corder couldn't get a better view; then maybe we could blow up the image big enough to show a serial number."

"Hang on just one bloody minute," said Evan, staring hard at the gun. "Sorry, boyo, I was mistaken. That's no Kockler-40. It's a 42. Well, shit."

"Problems?" Joss looked at the weapon on the screen. It was a darkly gleaming thing with the air of elegance that went with good design; much, much sleeker than the guns that Evan had confiscated from de Kuijpers and his merry band, and it looked just as lethal as any other firearm that Joss had encountered in his career. And it looked uncomfortably similar to the one that had been employed during the attempted hit in *Sichuan*. "I thought you said that that shooting in the restaurant was a legacy of your last case on Mars."

"Apparently not."

"Evan, talk to me and answer the nice questions. If this is a bootlegger's gun, why was somebody firing one at us in the Welles Hilton? Are they that common on Mars?"

"Far from it." Evan came out of his little reverie looking somewhat grim. "The Kockler-42 isn't common anywhere, not yet."

"Oh? You're always complaining that the villains are getting hold of military surplus gear far too easily."

"Military surplus, yes." The grimness was still there; in fact Evan Glyndower was looking almost as deadly serious as on the first time the partners had met, and to Joss's mind, that was a serious look indeed. "There's just one thing wrong about it, boyo. These guns *can't* be surplus, see, because a surplus thing's either been used already, or it's an overpurchase sold off to defray costs. There isn't any such thing where this H&K's concerned, because the damned things haven't even been issued to the Service yet."

Joss looked at the rakish, deadly slugthrower on the screen, and wondered how many of them had already been removed from the warehouse before it blew up. "Oh, bugger," he said, and as usual found swearing an inadequate expression of how he felt.

A report had come across their desks a few months back, about a rumored traffic in state-of-the-art military hardware that was more convoluted than it seemed. According to the report, research and development people in the weapons labs of three major corporations had been arrested for accepting large sums of money in exchange for examples of whatever they'd been working on. The R&Ds had claimed, during defense tribunal hearings, that they had taken care to restrict access only to what they termed "conventional" weapons and sidearms. They had, they said, monitored some use of these misappropriations "in the field," and used their knowledge to improve the product. It had been a sleazy piece of reading; the sort of rationalizations that came out during such hearings invariably stuck in Joss's throat like a badly chewed piece of bread. And now he was looking at what might well be the sharp end of such field research.

It's definitely the dark side of the Moon for me next time. I don't mind that it's dull. Dull means you don't get shot at—and especially not with guns like that *thing.*

"That report," said Evan, then looked at Joss's face and

nodded. "Uh-huh. You're there already. Great minds think alike."

"And fools seldom differ. You know, if we'd gone darkside, we wouldn't be here now."

"That's logical."

"Just remember it next time, because if I have any notions about going somewhere exciting and interesting for my vacation, I'm relying on you to talk me out of it." Joss laughed. "Use force if you have to. Now, that report; there was a lot of money changing hands to get stuff like these Kocklers out of the labs. Just how much money?"

Evan's eyes narrowed. "Indeed. And how much money have Smyth's lot been making from their bootlegging activities, that they can afford to buy military-level weapons at all?"

"If you give me half an hour with a pencil and a piece of paper," said Joss, "I think we could find out. I was always top of the class at adding things up . . ."

The pencil was a keyboard, and the piece of paper was a computer screen, and it took him more like two hours, but by the end of it Joss had a printed hard copy covered with columns of figures fit to do an accountant's heart good. "I got on line to Welles, and had them patch me into the Revenue and Excise systems," he said to Evan, dropping the printout onto the table with a thud. He was rewarded with the sort of mock-horrified look reserved for people with a thing for sheep in garter-belts.

"And what did the Undead have to say for themselves?" Evan asked.

"They gave me the basis of a computer projection based on figures from a cross-section of hotel, restaurant and liquor-store returns for the past twenty months. Input, output, purchases, sales, stock held, cash flow—"

"Yes, thanks very much, Joss-*bach*. I think I get the picture now."

"And since our bootleggers have to be selling below market price to shift their rotgut at all, they can't be making anything like enough money to justify the amount of trouble and violence they've been causing."

"Now is that so?" said Evan, sitting up straighter and taking an interest in the tax forms at last. He ran an eye down one credit/debit double-entry column, calculated for a moment in his head, and then grinned nastily. "Yes, indeed it is. Tombstone would need to be three times its size, and every person in the place working full time at their little still." He set the sheet back with the others and squared their edges neatly. "But they're not, are they? Harry Smyth and his friends must just about break even."

"So why are they such evil bastards?" said Joss irritably.

"Because it's fun. Because pushing people around is a reward in itself, and getting some money out of it is a bonus. They don't need any more reason than that."

"And the guns?"

"I've been wondering about that part of it myself. Being the military mind around here and all, see. It's not just the price that makes me wonder, but the cost of the backup."

"Backup?" Joss blinked, then eased his own Remington from its holster and studied it, trying to see the weapon with new eyes. All he saw was a gun that he'd used in the past to kill people who were trying to kill him, a gun he'd most certainly use in the same way again before his sop career was over. A heavy piece of machined metal and molded plastic that needed maintenance to keep it working; backup, if that was what Evan meant. Powerpacks and replacement chips and crystals; feeding and cleaning, like a lethal baby.

"Replacement parts," said Evan. "Same as for my Winchester. And the standard load and oil for my Webley—"

"And your Smith & Wesson, and that bespoke Holland & Holland, and the gatlings in your suit."

"Nearly right, but not the miniguns. They're too modern, Joss-*bach,* too modern by a good ninety years. And so are the Kocklers. That's what's wrong with finding guns like them in this arsehole of nowhere."

"You're going to lecture me about guns now, aren't you?"

" 'Lecture' implies that you think it might be boring. Tsk! Look on the bright side: I kept quiet when you started showing me those vids about the chap who travels about the universe in a public pay-loo. TURDIS or something, wasn't it?"

"Evan?"

"Mmm?"

"Shut up."

"Later." Evan grinned, and materialized a bottle of wine and two glasses from under the table. "It's been something of a day, Joss, and I don't think we're about to find anything or anyone in the next few hours who might add to our store of evidence. So have a drink, and let's consider background for just a moment."

Joss looked at the bottle, at the glasses, and at his partner. He'd seen Evan like this before, and it had never been an officer who was drunk on duty. More usually, it was an officer who'd pushed the edge of the envelope where suit ops were concerned, and was just glad to be alive at the end of it. Joss sat down, poured himself a glass of Chateauneuf-du-Pape Blanc that had traveled further than the Popes of Avignon could ever dream, and leaned back.

"Backup is what a firearm needs to keep it serviceable, and not just a very expensive and curiously shaped club," said Evan. "And the more modern the firearm, the more difficult backup becomes, whereas if the weapon is elderly, backup is a straightforward matter of chemistry or metalwork."

"The Earth PPD arrested a perp in Euro-España last year for shooting somebody with a miquelet flintlock pistol," said Joss. He remembered the case more because the assailant's ancestral handgun had misfired, projecting the ball with barely enough force to bruise his victim's ribs; whereupon the aggrieved party, a cousin, had taken possession of his would-be killer's antique pistol and used its butt to leave some lasting mementos of his survival.

"I remember that," said Evan. "The perp didn't corn his powder. You have to get a bishop to pee in it."

"Uh," said Joss, and left it at that. After such a statement, things could only get worse.

"I'll tell you all about it," Evan told him generously, "when you're feeling stronger. But it demonstrates backup. If that laddie hadn't had at least an inkling of how to make gunpowder from scratch, his flintlock wouldn't even have gone pop. Wim de Kuijpers and his forging friends probably do the same thing with their slugthrowers—certainly the amount of smoke they were kicking up suggested black powder, though I wouldn't have thought there'd be enough recoil to operate an automatic weapon. But whatever they put in them afterwards, they collect the spent brass."

"That's what those bags are for?"

"Right back to the Global Wars; though then they were trying to keep bits of metal—cartridge cases and links—from bringing down the skimmer that produced them. You can always refill a container with propellant if you know how to make it, and molding slugs isn't so hard. They used to call it 'rolling your own'; I don't know why. But the sort of gun de Kuijpers used will cost about a sixth the price of a Kockler, and the backup's far easier. Rolling your own."

Evan reached into one of the dozen or so pockets in his jacket and pulled out a gray-tipped yellow metal cylinder as long as his thumb. "That's what the old stuff fires," he said. "Refill the cases, crimp on the slugs, load them up—"

"And you're ready to rock'n'roll."

"If that means what I think it does, yes. Whereas the new equipment, like my suitguns and the 42, need this." He set what looked like a cube of plastic down beside the brass cartridge, then poked at it gingerly. "Caseless ammo. This block is the propellant; there's a subcaliber heavy-metal projectile embedded in it, surrounded by a full-caliber sabot. This one's depleted uranium, what they used to call staballoy. No radioactivity, just extreme weight. And very complicated; you'll not make this at home in the workshop.

"The big stuff's gone beyond it already. Liquid propellants, electromagnetic rail-guns—but from what I've heard, the men in the white coats are going crazy trying to build them small enough for sidearms. Everything so far has gone into tanks. At least if a tank goes haywire, you can always run after it . . ." Evan laughed at the thought, a contemptuous laugh, that of a suit specialist thinking, not too hard, about the linear descendant of the Galapagos tortoise.

"And what about gunrunning?" said Joss. "Suppose

they haven't been getting this quality merchandise for themselves at all?"

Evan considered the two rounds of ammunition on the table, then looked hard at Joss. "The sound of a man not blinded by the fascination of ballistic tables," he said softly. "That is a very interesting point. And extremely nasty. We should get it on file—so that it can protect us against Lucretia, when she wants to see how hard we've been working." Evan tapped the record facility on his pad, then lifted the fat heap of Revenue and Excise paperwork and riffled through it. The forms made a faint buzzing sound as their pages leafed past his thumb. "One: the Heckler und Koch G-42 is a military-issue personal weapon so new that even the military don't have them yet, despite our finding at least one here. Two: the usual sort of weapon encountered in the Martain outback—which, despite its reputation, is not usually a violent place by Solar Patrol terms—is an antiquated full-bore submachine gun, as proven by the dents on my suit and the half-dozen firearms locked up in our safe. Three: this paperwork indicates that our bad lads aren't making a great deal of money from their villainy. And four: the report whose title I can't remember—"

" 'Weapon Beta-Testing the Prohibited Way,' " said Joss helpfully, having just called it up on *Nosey*'s library file.

"That's the one. —indicates that remarkable sums of money have been involved in the illegal acquisition of advanced weaponry, even small arms. Indications are that the so-called Harry Smyth gang do not have this level of funds available from their criminal activities. The implication is therefore, that either the Smyth gang is venturing into the purchase and resale of military-surplus hardware of a very advanced nature, or that it is being funded by an outside source to act as a front for such purchases. The outside source, if any, remains unknown. End entry, transmit."

"So we will, later." Joss leaned his elbows on the table and stared at his partner. "But there was one thing I thought we shouldn't mention right now."

"That we haven't a clue where the decoder unit is? Yes, it's not what Madam Borgia wants to hear right now."

"That, Evan, and more than that. I've been thinking

about this gang. Apart from their other and more ordinary offenses, they might be simply handling stolen hardware from wherever it appears, hanging on to it for a while and then selling it to the highest interested bidder. Like the SP decoder, for instance. Bad guys don't have to be big name crooks, just *suppliers* to big name crooks. Otherwise I don't see any reason for the H&Ks. Smyth's gang would be able to do just fine with the old sluggers, and not attract anything like the attention."

"If that's the case, then I think that finding who swiped the decoder has just become more urgent than even dear Lucretia might believe. It's not even that it might be going off-world anymore. I'd be more concerned about who's got it—and what they're planning to do."

"Me, I'm more concerned about what's been shot at us since we reached Mars," said Joss with a thin, thin smile. "It's been escalating all the way, and I'd rather not wait for this business to go nuclear if it's all the same to you. God knows what else they've got stashed away . . ." His voice trailed off, and his eyes went unfocused for a second or so. Then they snapped into focus again, quite sharply, looking at Evan. "Like maybe something that can fire cannonballs capable of bringing down a sop ship." He swallowed. "What did you say the new slugthrowers used? The really big ones?"

Evan Glyndower met his partner stare for stare, then blinked as the memory of his own words came back to him. "Electromagnetic rail-guns," he said softly. "Linear motors. Supervelocity solid shot. Call them cannonballs if you like. It's close enough. Oh shit."

"And we might well be in it up to the armpits. What velocity are we talking about?"

"Bloody! The last stuff I read about, they were positing one hundred klicks a second, and sixty rounds per second."

Joss whistled between his teeth. That would give a solid projectile a trajectory nearly as flat as a beamer, but far less heat signature. And packing one hell of a kinetic-energy wallop. "Evan, I think you've got something there. I'm just glad I don't have to like it."

They sat quiet for a few moments. Then Evan said,

"Look you, though; we have to find evidence of such a thing first. We've none as yet. And they're not that easy to hide ..." It was his turn to trail off. "Though it can be done."

"They've got room enough to hide things in, *here,*" Joss said. "There's the problem." He sighed and stretched. "I think," he said, "just for my own peace of mind, I am going to do another vehicle search tonight."

"What for?"

"Mmm, to add a bit of electronic circuitry to each of them." He smiled. "This place has become rather busy since this morning, did you notice? I'm going to see how many flyers I can bug. A better sense of the movements of the vehicles in and around this area wouldn't hurt us particularly."

"You just like snooping," Evan said.

Joss blushed. "No, listen—"

"Don't bother justifying it to me, for pity's sake. Do what you need to. We've got to get *some* sort of lead on where this heavy stuff might be cached, if it's anywhere in the area at all. There's no disputing what shot the SP ship down. Now we have a good suspicion that there's a connection between the guns we almost got killed over this morning, *and* the bootlegging, *and* what shot our ship. Lucretia can't say a thing about it anymore."

Joss gave Evan a wry look. Lucretia was well known for finding things to say about *anything* they were working on. "You hope," he said, "Well, I'd better start getting my hardware together. What about you?"

Evan was looking thoughtful. "I was thinking it might be wise to check with our friends the lichen miners," he said. "Not right away; later this evening, perhaps, after you've done your vehicle work, and they've had a chance to go away ... assuming they do. I wouldn't want to ruin their usefulness as informers by being seen too much with them. Will you be needing help?"

"Ideally, no. I'd rather have you being large and obvious somewhere else than where I am—anywhere else. That suit does attract attention, bless it. It might be profitably used to attract it away from me, at this point in time."

Evan looked at him with a slightly concerned expression. "Does it concern you, being apart?" he said. "The stakes seem to have been upped somewhat as of this morning. I shouldn't like to lose another partner just as I've finally got him broken in."

Joss smiled, rather lopsidedly. "Much appreciated. I think. No, I suspect it'll be all right."

Evan nodded. "Good enough. I'll finish the work on this report, then, and get it up to Lucretia. You go get your ducks in a row, and let me know when you're ready to be distracted from."

Joss looked at Evan in mild bemusement. "What ducks?" he said.

Evan laughed and turned his attention to his pad.

IT TOOK JOSS ABOUT AN HOUR TO FINISH THE image-processing and prepare it for the pad, and another hour to put together enough bugs to make him happy; though he was a little concerned about what this operation was doing to his spare-parts store. *Maybe I ought to go over to Virendra's and see what they've got,* he thought. But no; anything he could buy there would raise questions. All the same, it was a pity.

He had a bite of lunch and then brought his pad back to Evan. They sat down and sent everything pertinent to Lucretia, along with a very respectfully worded note summing up the evidence they'd found so far, and the implications for the downed SP ship of the weaponry they'd found in Tombstone.

Evan looked over the final draft. "I notice you didn't tell her about the reward you offered for the satellite," he said.

Joss coughed. "Don't see why I should until it's found. At which point she won't mind. That thing cost thirty-five million credits in development . . . I don't think she'll grudge twenty-five thousand."

Evan raised his eyebrows in extreme skepticism. "Never mind that," he said. "Let's send it, and then go make our presence known.

"You might stop by Virendra's," Joss said. "We're a little short of tea."

"Have I been drinking that much?"

Joss chuckled. "You usually do when you're thinking hard. You might as well stock up."

"And have a chat with Virendra while I'm there."

"That had occurred to me . . ."

They suited and SHELed up and headed out. Tombstone had acquired that slightly muted, slightly excited air of a town where something interesting, and execrable, had happened. There were a fair number of people out in the street, adults and children both, many of them gathered down at the exploded dome, others standing in little knots in the street, talking in hushed voices. All their heads turned as Joss and Evan walked down to the dome; most of the conversations got quiet.

"You go ahead," Joss said, opening the flap of his forensics kit. Evan nodded, headed off toward Virendra's dome. A few people turned to look after him, but most of them looked back at Joss again as he walked past the staring group by the dome.

"Morning, morning," he said. "Messy, isn't it? Excuse me, please." He used the steps down into the remains of the dome's storage area, and paused to look around. He had understated. Everything was shattered, melted, in fragments. Cardboard ash stirred in the restless wind, blew up in little black fragments, drifted down again on lumps of metal and plastic, all fused together.

Joss got busy taking samples, more to give the people out there something to look at than anything else. The sight of a sop, unafraid—well, seemingly unafraid—strolling around in the ruins of the explosion that should have killed him—might give someone some pause. *I certainly hope so, anyway,* Joss thought. He brushed at some of the cardboard which had settled on him; it powdered away to nothing instantly. *Looks like I was right about the oxygen, too,* he thought. *Much too completely combusted. Dammit, these people are smart. Whatever happened to dumb perps?*

After about twenty minutes he had enough samples to bolster their report to Lucretia somewhat. He climbed up

out of the remains of the dome again and was mildly surprised to see Evan down the street, chatting with several
children in SHELs, while holding a paper bag of groceries.
The kids' parents were standing nearby, not quite telling
their children to come away from the nasty man—
especially since the nasty man was a policeman. *And we
all know that the Policeman is our Friend,* Joss thought,
smiling to himself. One of the kids pointed up to the arm
that housed Evan's gatling; Evan shook his head, hefted
the bag a little—apparently saying his good-byes—nodded
to the children's parents, and walked on down the street
toward Joss.

Joss looked with interest at the bag as Evan came up to
him. "You think you need that much tea?"

"I got a few other things. Sugar; we were running out
of it—"

"You're going to ruin your teeth."

"You use more of it than I do. I use milk, like a civi-
lized person—"

"Never mind that." They started walking back to the
ship. "Having a word with your fan club there?"

Evan laughed softly. "Yes. They wanted to see me shoot
something. You should have seen their folks' faces."

Joss chuckled. "And what about Virendra?"

"Nothing new," Evan said. "He's rather subdued this
morning. I think he's afraid there may be some kind of re-
prisal because we didn't get killed as we were supposed
to."

"We'll have to keep our eyes open, then."

They were passing by the police-dome when its airlock
door suddenly came open, and someone put his head out.
It was Steck, to judge by her size. She waved a hand at
them.

They strolled over. "Morning, Officer," said Joss, and
sketched a half-bow. "How are you this fine day?"

"Fine?" she said, throwing a glance down the street at
the ruined storage-dome. "Don't have any bad days around
here, then. Listen: one of your lads from this morning was
back a little while ago. Stinking of gin, I might add." She
peered at Evan's bag; he tilted it toward her, and she took
it by one edge to pull it open a little further, and looked

in. "Very nice," she said. "Those teabags are definitely end-of-the-day sweepings, though . . . anything you make from them is going to taste like rust remover."

Joss almost missed the little piece of paper she had palmed, as it fell down into the bag. "One of them left that," she said very quietly, and let the bag go. "Something important, he said, but he didn't want to give it to you directly. He had left his belt behind—on purpose, I think, so he had an excuse to come back without suspicion."

"Right, well, thank you," said Joss, as quietly, "and let us know if we can do anything for *you.*" He nodded courteously, and he and Evan headed away.

It took a fair amount of self-control to keep his hands out of the bag until they were safely within *Nosey* and out of sight. They went into the galley, where Evan put the groceries away while Joss hurriedly unfolded the note.

It said: *Smyth people here. XIJ 3396. Follow later. Trouble. dK.*

Joss showed the note to Evan. He frowned at it. "Well, well," he said. " 'Follow later.' Seems to imply that they're not going to be leaving for a while."

"I saw two or three flyers with that reg prefix over on the parking flat," Joss said. "I think I'll just run over and have a look at them." He grinned slightly, and patted the pocket that had the bugs in it. "We've done everything else *but* give parking tickets, after all . . ."

"How many ships can you bug and still keep track of them?" Evan said.

"As many as I can make bugs for. The tracking software can deal with about five hundred traces, assuming most of them are within its primary range. Fewer, if they're further away and the monitoring equipment needs more enhancement."

Evan's eyebrows went up.

"Anyway," Joss said, "if blowing up that dome attracts this kind of attention, maybe it was a good idea."

Evan's sour look at the state of his suit made Joss think he had doubts about that. "More to the point, though," Evan said, ". . . interesting that the Smyth people should turn up so sharp when that booby trap *doesn't* work."

"Yes, indeed," said Joss. "You go out a bit more and

mingle. I don't want more notice directed to the parking
flat than necessary."

THEY STAYED IN *NOSEY* JUST LONG ENOUGH FOR
Joss to make some notes and sort through his newly taken
samples, putting some of them in the analysis box's rack
for automatic attention. Then out he went to the parking
flat, while Evan went to town.

The flat was definitely more crowded than Joss had seen
it for a while. There were a couple of largish cargo skimmers there, both with Welles registrations; one of them
was being unloaded, a mixed delivery of foodstuffs and
other perishables for Virendra's place. Joss nodded amiably to the people doing the unloading, patted the skimmer
on the side as he passed it, and when just out of sight of
the unloading crew, patted it once more with the other
hand, installing the bug chip. It was a tiny thing no bigger across than the cap of a slim stylus, almost completely transparent, and matte-finished, with a one-sided
"Johannsen slip" on it, a molecular adhesive that would
take bare metal with it sooner than let go.

He went from vehicle to vehicle with his pad in his
hand, ostensibly tapping in reg numbers. No one here
would be surprised at that: there had been a murder, and
then a bomb—that was the local chat about the explosion,
and neither Joss nor Evan were going to disabuse anyone
of the idea—and of course the police would be taking note
of everyone who came in and out. But what harm in that,
if you were innocent? And even if you were guilty, what
proof was your presence the morning after a crime? So
whatever notice was taken of Joss was fleeting, and he felt
fairly certain that no one would be surprised that he
touched or brushed against the occasional vehicle as he
passed it. In fact, he touched them all, but managed about
six times out of ten to conceal it.

He came to XIJ 3396 about halfway through the tag-
ging. It was a skimmer very much like the ones that were
now scrap metal all over the inside (and outside) of the
storage-dome. Joss strongly resisted the urge to screw off

the skimmer's fuel cap; instead he went around front, tapped in its reg number as he had done with all the others, and woke up the pad's scanning functions; then gave the skimmer the same treatment that Evan's recording functions had given the contents of the dome in those ninety seconds before the place went up. He walked right around to get a good record, then added the bug as a coup de grace, and moved on.

When he was finished he strolled back to town in a leisurely sort of way, looking for Evan. He wasn't anywhere to be seen in the street, so he stopped at Virendra's, going straight in in the direct way of a man who's found that his partner has forgotten the one thing he stopped for in the first place.

Virendra was nowhere to be seen, but his daughter came out to the desk when she heard the airlock go. "Morning," Joss called to her across the dome. "Miz Virendra, would you by any chance have salt? My friend forgot it this morning, and we're right out."

"We've got it in bulk," Kathy said. "How much?"

"About two-tenths of a kilogram, if you would."

He wandered about for a moment while she weighed it out, then collected it, paid for it, thanked her. She was looking at him rather strangely, he noticed. "Something wrong, ma'am?" he said.

"You're awfully calm for a man who almost got blown up a few hours ago," she said.

Joss shrugged—then looked at her sidewise, and winked. "All an act," he said. "I'm a wreck."

She raised her eyebrows at him. "You don't look it."

"That's how they pick us," Joss said. "They just want people who can be scared to death, and not stop what they're doing because of it."

Kathy nodded, looking thoughtful. "Well," she said finally, "watch out for yourself."

"I do what I can," Joss said, and winked again. "Good morning to you."

He resettled his SHEL gear and went out. Still no sign of Evan.

Joss went down to the bar. Immediately he went in, he knew he had found his man: the place was as still as a mouse dinner where a cat was the after-dinner speaker. Evan was sitting off in one corner, his helm off, relaxing—if anyone could ever be said really to be relaxing, in a suit like that—and drinking something pink with ice cubes in it. Everyone else was drinking, and some of them were talking, but so low that there was no hearing anything but whispers; and all their eyes kept returning to Evan.

"Afternoon, all," Joss said, taking off his SHEL gear and helmet. "I assume it's afternoon here. Or somewhere. Good day to you, bartender."

The bartender they had met when they first came in looked at Joss as if he were a case of tuberculosis, but nevertheless polished the bar in front of Joss and put out a coaster for him. "Sir?"

"What my friend there is having," said Joss.

The bartender grunted and went off to get it. Joss waited for it to arrive, paid for it, sniffed it. Gin, and something else, Heaven only knew what. He thanked the bartender, picked up the drink and went off to sit down with Evan.

They chatted about inconsequentialities for several minutes, interrupted only once when Joss actually drank what was in his glass, and had to pause to keep from choking on it. "What *is* this?"

"Pink gin."

"I thought you said the dye didn't affect the flavor!"

"Not that kind of pink gin. I told you about it. It's a drink. Gin and angostura bitters."

"Bleah." He shook his head at Evan. "You people are *strange.*"

"No stranger than someone who orders a drink without knowing what it is." Evan smiled and downed the rest of his pink gin. "Are you done? We've got business to attend to."

"All ready," Joss said. Together they got up and donned their gear, and went out.

When the outer airlock door closed behind them, Joss could almost hear the conversation starting up behind them. In fact—He knocked experimentally at his helmet. He *was* hearing the conversation behind them, in the sealed dome. "You wicked thing!" he said to Evan, very quietly. "Why didn't you ask me?"

"It was an afterthought. I programmed it to record-and-store for twenty-four hours. We can command it to dump once a day, and have one or another of the pads make a transcript and scan it for tagged words." Evan grinned.

"Sometimes," Joss said, "I think you're even more of a techie than I am. Now what?"

"Got all your widgets in place?"

"Yes indeed. Nothing to do now but wait for tonight."

"And see what happens."

"BINGO," JOSS SAID, SEVEN AND A HALF HOURS later.

It was full night; the sunset turbulence had come and gone, and the stars were bright in the blackness. Joss had been sitting, gazing out the window, lost in thought, when the comms system's alarm went *ping!*

"Is that our lads?" said Evan from his seat.

"Yes indeed. Lifting now, heading—" Joss tapped at the comms console for a moment. "Northeast. Interesting."

"Why?" Evans said. "What's up that way?"

Joss brought up a map at the comms screen and looked at it, while Evan peered over his shoulder. "Nothing." He pointed at tiny labeled pinpoints. "Those are independent settlements—even smaller than Tombstone. Some of them are just one house, all by itself."

Evan shook his head. "In all those miles. What happens if those people need a doctor?"

"They call one, and hope she gets there in time." Joss shrugged a bit. "That's the price you pay for privacy, I guess."

Evan was looking out at the night sky. "Shouldn't we get going, if those boys have left?"

Joss laughed at him a little. "Are you kidding? Do you know what kind of range this thing has? We could let them get up to five hundred kilometers away before we had to raise ship. However," Joss said, getting up, "we'll head out when they've got a hundred or so on us. Even from the little look I had at their skimmer this morning, I'm fairly sure that they don't have anything as sensitive as our equipment."

He went off to see about stowing things away, preparatory to taking off. The galley was clean; Evan had cleared away his last brewing of tea. Both the staterooms were clear. Joss paused long enough to take the case of wine out of Evan's stateroom and put it back in the brig, then went to have a look in the lab.

His samples were still in the analysis box's rack, the run having finished. Joss pulled them out and put them away in the cupboard where he kept such things, then stopped long enough to have the box send its report to the main computer. It took about a second and a half over it before shutting itself down. *Hmm,* Joss thought; there shouldn't have been that much data for the thing to process. *Oh well. Burning always gives you trouble ... you wind up with these weird complex carbon compounds because of all the intercombination with the plastics. And then the combustion at oxygen levels that start off fairly high and then drop suddenly ... Never mind.*

Evan was fastening his straps when Joss came back in. "Goodness, aren't we eager," Joss said, and sat himself down too. "We won't be leaving for a little while yet."

Evan threw him a bored look. "I know," he said. "This is so you can wake me up when we get there. It's been a bit of a long day."

"Right," Joss said. About thirty seconds later, Evan was asleep, with the extreme suddenness and soundness of someone trained to get his sleep when and where he can.

Joss watched the trace of the bugged skimmer on the screen for a moment, and then turned his attention to the main computer, taking it off the ship's functions for a moment and instructing it to dump the analysis box's data to his pad. It did this, then began to beep softly, the tracking program complaining that it wanted more of the computer released to it so that it could supervise the skimmer's trace. Joss sighed, let the computer have what it wanted, and picked up his pad.

He took ten minutes or so to scroll through all the results from the sample tests. Most of them, as he had thought, showed the results of combustion at uneven oxygen levels. A lot of paper, a lot of metal with its crystalline structure ruined by intense heat and shock. And some very peculiar carbon compounds from all the plastics melting together.

Joss stopped. One page showed that a set of ring-compounds had managed to hold together despite the heat, and for the most part had refused to attach any other molecules in the area. "Good stuff, that," he said to himself. "Make a good fireproof insulator."

The computer beeped again. "All right, all right," Joss said softly, and started to warm *Nosey*'s engines up.

He took her up quietly, which was perfectly possible for a ship of *Nosey*'s vintage: Many of the newer craft had atmosphere-operation baffles in to keep the entire neighborhood from being advised of a sop's comings and goings. Oh, someone would notice eventually that they had left; but not right away. *Nosey* was making no more noise than a departing skimmer, which was entirely to Joss's liking.

He headed her off northeast, low and quiet in the dark, not hurrying. The best the skimmer ahead of them was capable of was about a hundred klicks an hour; and it wasn't doing anything like that at the moment—more like sixty. Joss matched its speed, and then spent a moment or so instructing the nav computers on the way he wanted to pursue the skimmer. "Follow that car," he said under his breath, and patted the console.

He went back to his pad for the time being and spent another ten or fifteen minutes scrolling through it, making sure there was nothing of interest in the analysis report. Finally he put it down and just sat back, watching the Martian night through the windscreen. It might as well have been night in the Asteroids, except that you could see them from here, a chain of stars that would rise slowly above the horizon with Jupiter embedded, blazing, among them, the jewel in the crown. They were down now, though. Only Phobos was in sight, just risen for the fifth or sixth time that day, hurtling as best it could. Joss smiled at it, and at the thought of those Wilkinson "John Carter

Specials." Maybe when all this was over, he would buy one from the souvenir specialists.

They went on for about an hour before the computer beeped again, letting Joss know that the traced object had stopped. "Right," he said. "Evan?"

Nothing.

"Evan!"

"What?" Evan said, completely awake on the instant.

"They've stopped. How long do you want them to have before we arrive?"

Evan thought about it for a moment. "Ten minutes or so . . . sound about right? That'll give them time to get their gear on and start doing whatever they've come out here to do." He stretched. "Whatever that is."

Joss pointed at the comms screen. It was showing a changed map, with nothing but a gridwork and two tiny pinpoints of light on it. "One of those is a house," Joss said, "called, believe it or not, 'Rose Cottage.' The other one is our pigeon."

Evan grinned and reached down for his helmet. "Fine. Here's your pad." He glanced at it. "What's this?"

"Test results from those samples this morning."

"Anything interesting?"

Joss shook his head. "Nope. It's all burnt." He paged back for the report. "Except this stuff," he said. "Pretty resistant." He was still trying to remember what it was about those ring structures that was nagging at him. *Oh well. It'll come to me eventually.*

"Oh?" Evan looked at the page Joss showed him, without any particular interest. Then paused, and looked up again. "Does this stuff have a name? I mean, besides 1-ethyl 2-gamma whatever."

"I suppose so," Joss said, taking the pad back. He tagged the chemical name Evan had pointed at, and asked for aliases. "That ring a bell?"

"Lexan," Evan said, and frowned. "Lexan . . . Nope."

Joss shrugged and put the pad away in its clamp. "Oh, well. All right, ETA in eight minutes, now. You have everything you need? Bullets? Powerpacks?"

Evan rolled his eyes at Joss. "Yes, and I went before I went to sleep, mam."

Joss snickered and undid his straps long enough to go get his bulletproof vest.

Five minutes later Joss had killed the cabin lights and was managing the controls personally again, skimming quite low over the bouldery ground. Sidelooking radar was keeping him posted on any large excrescences, but Evan was still looking outside with some concern. "Are you sure this is safe?" he said.

"Safe as houses," Joss said, paraphrasing something he had heard Evan say. He added, "How safe *are* houses?"

"Safer than this, I'm thinking!"

"Hush. Two minutes."

Joss began to slow them down; he wanted the quietest possible landing. He tapped at the comms console, checked one last time to make sure that the skimmer was still in the same spot—it was—and then shifted the display to IR.

Glowing ahead of them was the usual dome, bright with leaked heat. Next to it was a small bright spot, the engine of the skimmer. Something not as bright, but upright, was standing by a dark patch that was probably the airlock of the dome.

"Ahh," Joss said, and veered gently off to the left, to come at the dome from the sentry's blind side. "Thirty seconds," he said to Evan. "I'll keep it easy; you might want to go position yourself. I'm going to drop you right in his lap."

Evan nodded, put down the visor of his helm, and got into the airlock, shutting the inner door and opening the outer one. *Nosey* lurched a little as her flight characteristics changed; Joss corrected, trimmed, flew slow and quiet as he circled around. *Fifty meters . . . close enough.* He eased her down from altitude as quickly as he could. The sentry would be hearing something as Joss got closer, all right, but he wouldn't have time to do anything about it.

Joss felt the slight lurch as Evan dropped out of the airlock. Then there was the flash of a beam—only once.

Joss grinned and put *Nosey* down, left her on "ready," and got into the airlock himself. When it cycled ready, he leapt out. Evan was standing by the airlock doorway, his suit glinting ever so slightly in Phobos's light as it crept overhead. There was a body at his feet.

"Shot at me," Evan said. "I don't think he gave any alarm. Everything seems quiet inside."

"Good," Joss said. "Let's go in."

Evan tapped at the control on the outside of the dome. The airlock slid open for them, shut again. Each of them flattened himself against one side of the airlock; Evan peered through the window.

"Four of them. Three in SHELs. Oh, shit!"

He simply threw himself straight at the inner airlock door. It burst inward, and air began screaming out immediately. Evan went in after the broken door, firing as he went.

Joss dived and rolled in after him, getting one of those flash-picture images of the inside of the place: a lot of copper tubing, pipes, plastic tubing, big glass and metal containers; three men with heavy slugthrowers like the ones that had been in the storage-dome in Tombstone; and a fourth man, down on the ground, bleeding, clutching at his throat. The three armed men were turning toward whatever had just broken down the door. One of them raised his gun—

The silvery-gray object that had broken the door down was staggering in a stream of bullets from first one, then another of the men—but not falling down. Joss snapped off a quick shot or three at the third one, then rolled again toward one of the shelves, where there was a SHEL helmet lying. He managed to yank it down just before a stream of bullets hit where his hand had been and blasted the metal of the shelf into splinters.

There was a whining, screaming noise beginning. Joss heard it with a horrible mixture of delight and terror. *God, leave* one *of them alive,* he thought, and rolled once more, to get at the wounded, suffocating man on the floor. Bullets howled over his head again—

—then stopped quite suddenly, as the man shooting at Joss fell in two pieces. In the lessened pressure, blood spurted everywhere, making a red haze in the air like the one that one keeps hearing about in novels with too much violence in them. Joss elbowed over to the man on the floor, jammed the SHEL helmet onto him, fastened the faceplate, and did his best to get the neck seals done up—

That scream filled the air again, and the second gunman exploded apart, bisected brain to crotch. *"Put it down,"* Joss heard Evan's voice say, deadly quiet, to the third man, in a sudden silence that fell.

More slugfire burst out, this time over Joss's head again. Joss made himself as flat as he could, unable to get any shot at all, and trying to at least protect the man on the ground. *"Idiot,"* he heard Evan say. From this angle he could just barely see Evan walk right through the storm of bullets being thrown at him. One-handed, he slapped the slugthrower out of the gunman's hand. The backhand caught the man in the shoulder, which Joss thought was just as well, for even in the rapidly thinning air, the sound of the snap of the man's humerus was like a riflecrack. The gunman flew through the air, crashed into a pile of tubing and glass bottles, and slid down to the floor, tangled in pipes and covered in shards, motionless.

Silence fell.

Joss was hauling at the man on the floor. His color was coming back, but Joss still wasn't too sure of how positive the SHEL's seal was. Evan picked his way over to Joss through the wreckage. "Is he still with us?" he said.

"Yes. Come on, he needs medical attention. You take care of your friend there."

"Right." In one-third gravity, Joss could manage the man's weight; he helped him hobble toward the door. Evan picked up the gunman and threw him over his shoulder like a sack of flour, and followed Joss out.

Now then, Joss thought, watching Evan pause to pick up the other man, the one that Evan had rendered harmless before Joss got out of *Nosey. Let Lucretia complain to us about this.* He was shaking all over, with anger as much as reaction from almost having been shot.

And something came quite abruptly into his head as he helped the wounded man into *Nosey.*

Lexan.

Oh, no!!

Sometimes he hated it when he was right . . . but rarely so much as now.

SEVEN

EVAN PUT HIS MEN DOWN IN THE BRIG, ON THE floor, and waited for Joss to bring the other medical kit in. One of them, he suspected, might not respond to any treatment at all; in the dark, Evan had hit him a little harder than he had originally intended, and the side of the man's SHEL helmet was rather impressively concave. *Skull fracture, at least,* he thought, with a tinge of regret. *Just as well I hit the other laddie in the chest rather than the head.* He had been *really* angry then; but then, seeing someone try to shoot his partner—or a helpless, unarmed man down on the ground—tended to make him lose his temper.

Joss came in with the spare kit. "Here," he said, and then drew in a bit of breath as he saw the other man and the state of his head. "Triage," he said. "Don't bother with your friend's arm just yet. Do you want me to intubate your head case?"

"No, I can manage it. How's your lad?"

"Shaken, and dehydrated, and a little hypoxic, but he's alive. I've got him on the breather. The leg wound isn't too bad—" Joss grimaced a bit. "It's a kneecapping. They'll put a new one in when we get him back to Welles."

"Right," Evan said. He was working over the man with the skull fracture, trying to get the breather tube in, not having much luck. Then Joss was down beside him, and somehow the tube went in in three quick motions. The man's facial color immediately got paler, which was just as well; he had been going a nasty shade of purple.

"How are you so good at that?" Evan said.

Joss stood up and shook his head. "Had to do it once to someone at a baseball game," he said. "You never forget." He headed back out to his stateroom, where he had put the kneecapped man.

Evan made the head case as comfortable as he could, and then turned his attention to the second gunman and his broken arm. It was *very* thoroughly broken; compound, Evan suspected. He flipped down his visor and had a look with ultrasound. Yes indeed, the bone had splintered into several pieces where his gauntlet hit it; one largish chunk was sticking out through the skin, and the other was inside the muscle, herniating it.

Evan shrugged and got an inflatable splint out of the medical kit. All he needed to do about this was immobilize it. He was damned if he was going to give the man any painkillers, or at least any more than were absolutely necessary. Pain could make people very conversational, under the right circumstances. He splinted the arm, propped the man upright against the wall of the brig, and had another look at him with the ultrasound. Nothing else obvious broken that he could see; no internal leakage.

He got up and locked the brig door, leaving it transparent. Then he went in to look at Joss's patient.

The man had bled all over Joss's bedspread. Joss had gotten him out of his SHEL suit so that he could get at the injured leg, and was presently wiping the blood off his face so as to judge how badly he might be hurt there. There were ugly bruises coming up, and the skin of his face was badly torn in places; he was going to have to be sutured when they got him back to Welles. The knee was already bandaged up—just a dressing, Evan suspected; there was nothing to be done about that knee except by a surgeon—and Joss had started an IV going to one of the man's arms. The empty needle on the bedside table said that there was more in the IV than five-percent dextrose; and from the look of things, the man could use the relief.

He opened his eyes as Evan was looking at him, and started a little.

Joss patted him. "Don't fret, sir," he said. "That's my partner, the one who ruined your front door."

"Seemed better than letting those other lads ruin you," Evan said, leaning against the doorsill.

The man on the bed looked from one of them to the other. He had probably been pretty good-looking, about half an hour ago; he was in his late twenties, dark-haired, with the typically tanned and somewhat wrinkled face of people who lived on Mars and didn't use UV-screened faceplates on their SHELs. He tried to stretch himself a little, and his face twisted with the pain.

"Try to keep still," Joss said, putting a hand on him. "I know what you're thinking. You're thinking that your storage area there was full of distilling equipment, and we're going to bust you. We have no interest in that at the moment, none at all."

The man blinked at that. "What's your name, sir?" Joss said.

The man coughed. "Lew Sa-Sakarian."

Evan slipped out to get Joss's pad from its clamp in the front cabin. "Right," Joss said to him, taking it and tapping it into record mode. "By the way, remind me about the Lexan later."

Evan put his eyebrows up, nodded. Joss could come all over scientific at the oddest times . . . but then again, if it served to keep him functional when faced with the sight of a man as awfully battered as this one, he could understand it.

"Lew Sakarian," Joss said. "Right, Sir, I'm Officer Joss O'Bannion, and this is my partner, Evan Glyndower. Would you please tell us who those men are, and why they assaulted you?"

Sakarian looked doubtfully from Joss to Evan, and back to Joss again.

"I'm authorized to tell you," Joss said, "that we are empowered to make sure no charges are brought against you for illegal distilling. We're rather more interested in the people presently in our brig."

Sakarian lay still for a moment, then shook his head

slowly. "There's more of them where they came from," he said. "If I tell—"

"I can tell you what we know, or suspect," Evan said. "Does the name 'Harry Smyth' mean anything to you?"

Sakarian flinched, and then cried out with the pain.

"Please try to keep still," Joss said. "The neophine will take effect fairly quickly now; it's just got a lot of work to do on that leg of yours. Sir, you've got to understand; we're interested in keeping what's happened to you from happening to anyone else. Why were they there?"

Sakarian looked at Joss for a moment. "You drink?" he said.

Joss's eyes widened a bit. "I've been known to partake," he said.

"You've had stuff in the bars around here?"

"In Tombstone, yes."

For just a moment, even through the pain and the swelling face, Sakarian managed to look scornful. "It's crap. I thought I could do a little better."

"So you started free-lancing," Evan said.

Sakarian nodded, just a fraction. "I didn't know that you had to get—permission."

Joss nodded. "From Harry Smyth's gang."

"Yes. Some of them came around a few weeks ago . . . made a lot of hints about how good my stuff was, and how I should wholesale it to them, instead of retailing to the bar in Tombstone." Sakarian's face got briefly indignant. "I told them to stuff it! It's a free planet—it's gone through enough to be, anyway—I can sell my stuff where I want! That's what I told them."

He began to laugh—very soft, painful laughter. "I guess I didn't think it through," he said. "They came back to-night. They trashed all my stuff and told me if I wanted to make any more, I would have to buy new equipment from them . . . and sell all the hooch to them too, and pay a tithe on the profits. If they let me have any. I got angry—"

"You got shot," Evan said softly.

Another of those agonized laughs. "You hit it, sop sir. You got *that* in one. So now what happens?"

"Now," Joss said, "we take you to the hospital in Welles, to a secure ward, if that would make you feel better—I think it might. We're not going to charge you with anything. We might have some more questions for you later, if you don't mind."

"Anything that gets rid of these guys," Sakarian said. "This used to be a nice part of the world! Quiet, and nice. Till *they* started showing up everywhere people lived, and making their lives miserable ..." He trailed off. The neophine was indeed starting to work.

"Later," Joss said. "Let's get you where someone can do something about that knee. I have to fly us out of here. Is there anything else you need before we go?"

Sakarian shook his head carefully.

"Come on, then," Joss said to Evan. They went out to the front cabin and strapped themselves in.

"Keep it easy," Evan said. "Those two back there are on the floor loose ... there's nothing to secure them with."

"We ought to have something done about that," Joss said, bringing the engines up to full. "Have optional stretcher grapples put in when we get back to the Moon."

"There goes another thousand credits of Lucretia's money," Evan said. "I notice the wine was still in there, too."

Joss sighed. "I don't think either of them is in any position to drink it," he said. "I didn't see you coming in for any painkiller for your boy with the busted arm."

"No, and if I could think of some way for you to fly your cabin smooth and the back of the ship rough, I'd be tempted to ask," Evan said.

Joss took *Nosey* up and turned her for Welles; then put her on autopilot. "I suspect Sakarian there will be glad to tell us anything else he knows, after he's been fixed up. Names and addresses, I hope. If these thugs have any."

Evan nodded. "Meanwhile," he said, "what about the other two?"

Joss shrugged. "The one—I'm not sure he'll speak again. He's taken a good crunch to the frontal lobe, from the look of him. But we'll see. The other lad—" Joss stretched. "There are always the usual veridicals. But I myself would favor you standing over him in your suit and just staring at him for about an hour."

It was an unusual tone to hear from Joss: almost anticipatory. Evan raised his eyebrows and said, "I'd best not be too long about it, then. Somehow I don't think Harry Smyth's lot are the kind to sit around after someone's taken out one of their 'active service units.'"

"'He pulls a knife on you, you pull a gun on him,'" Joss quoted, sounding thoughtful. "'He puts one of your people in the hospital, you put one of his people in the morgue. That's the Chicago way.'"

"Sounds more like Cardiff after a rugby international," Evan said ruefully. "It would probably be easier if we put *all* of them in the morgue. Less paperwork. But yes . . . I think that's likely to be the prevailing sentiment. And we're going to be getting shot at more than usual." He glared at Joss's bulletproof vest. "That useless thing— you're no better off than the goats were. What are we going to do about—"

Joss blinked. "Goats? What goats?"

Evan was a little surprised; then he smiled. "I've never told you this story? I guess not. The graflar in the suit," he said, picking idly at one of the deeper scratches it had picked up from the firefight, "it had an ancestor-compound called 'kevlar.' They made it into bulletproof vests, like yours. You know how they tested them? They took them up to one of the test ranges, and they put them on goats, and they shot at the goats with .22- and .38-caliber, for oh, ever so long. The goats all did fine. Got a bit bruised, a few of them." He started to laugh. "But can you imagine how it would have looked to any civilian going by?"

He looked at the expression on Joss's face, and burst out laughing all over again, louder. Joss's face worked, and abruptly lost its grimness, and split into a grin, and he laughed like a fool for almost a minute without stopping.

About two minutes later, they were both wiping the tears of laughter away. "It still leaves the question," Evan said at last, hiccupping a little, "Of what to do with you. I think you're going to have to stay inside *Nosey* mostly, until this situation is sorted out."

"Are you out of your mind?!" Joss said, outraged. "And leave you without backup?"

"Joss, you daft bugger, these people are going to shoot you first and leave me without backup *that* way!"

The fight went on all the way back to Welles. Evan lost it; or at least, Joss fought him to a standstill. There were reasons that detective types and suit types were posted together, Joss insisted; guns and armor weren't everything. *But they are here,* Evan was thinking. It was annoying, for most of the time he would have agreed with Joss without question.

The med crew was waiting at the enclosed pad at Welles when they got there. Joss had slipped them down through the open top of the dome as lightly as a bit of swansdown, and as they settled onto the marked skirt, Evan was glad to see no less than six officers of the PPD waiting to meet them along with the medical staff. They took Sakarian away, and then the two gunmen, under heavy guard.

Evan looked thoughtfully after them. "Do you think they're going to be safe here?" he said.

Joss looked over at Evan, opened his mouth, and closed it again. "I'm not sure," he said.

Evan nodded. "That settles it," he said. "Let's stay here tonight. There are a lot of questions that still need asking. I want to be by both their bedsides in the morning."

"Planning to have yourself cloned, are you?" Joss said.

"O'Bannion," Evan said, very gently, "you are an idiot. Let's shut *Nosey* up and go take care of business. Tombstone will live without us till tomorrow."

Joss got up and fetched his SHEL gear, in case it was needed later. "It's a pity," he said, "to be here and not be able to go out and get Chinese."

"An *annoying* idiot," Evan said. "Sandwiches for us tonight, I think. Come on."

THEY SLEPT IN CHAIRS, BOTH OF THEM, EACH BY one man's bed: Evan by the gunman's, Joss by Sakarian's. Evan spent a long while that night, sitting up and working with his pad, while the gunman snored away under the combination of his sedation and the anesthesia from his surgery. The broken arm was pinned and in plaster. "What did you hit him with?" the surgeon had asked Evan, and

Evan had simply lifted his arm and said, "This." The surgeon had walked away shaking his head.

In the morning, quite early, the man began to stir. The room, being in a secure ward, had no windows; there was only the slight brightening of the lights out in the hall to indicate that day was coming on. Very quietly, Evan put his pad down on the chair, and stood up, there in the shadows, and just waited.

"Nnng—" the man said, and moved his head restlessly on the pillow. Very quietly, Evan moved around to get between him and the light.

The gunman saw the sudden darkening even through closed eyes. He opened them.

The eyes widened in terror.

"Now then," said Evan, very softly, and put one gauntleted hand on the man's chest. Not hard, but within easy reach of the throat, or of other things. "Here we are at the hour before dawn, just you and me. This is the time when people die, you know that? They just stop breathing. The old, and the sick . . . and sometimes, the not-so-sick." The hand just lay there on the man's chest, and didn't need to press.

"The nurses know you have a policeman with you," Evan said. "Someone who would call if there were any trouble. If you so much as squeaked, and I didn't want you to, you would stop breathing long before they got to you. A poor way to die, eh? No guns and glory, indeed not. Suffocation seems to take years, and you know about it all the way out. You feel your brain start dying. Nothing would be simpler to manage."

The man was beginning to gasp with terror.

"Now then," Evan said. "Possibly there is a way to avoid this. Possibly, just possibly, you'll tell me the names and addresses I'm interested in hearing about. And then you'll go to trial, and cop a plea, and serve your time. Not too short a time, after last night's work. But at least you'll still be here after sunrise." He smiled ever so slightly in the darkness, knowing the smile would get into his voice, whether the man saw it or not. "And possibly you'll decide to be strong, and brave, and a hero, and you won't tell

me what I want to hear. In which case . . . it's the hour before dawn. And these things happen."

And very slightly, very carefully, he leaned on the man's
breastbone.

Leaned.

Waited, and leaned—

"Yes—" the man gasped then, sucking desperately at
the air. "Yes, all right, yes, yes!"

"Fine," Evan said, and stood up straight, and spoke to
his pad. "0513 hours, day 225, coordinated Martian year
2068. This statement is being recorded. I am Solar Patrol
Officer 4629337 Glyndower, E. H. Admonition of suspect
follows. You have the right to remain silent—"

HE MET JOSS FOR BREAKFAST DOWN AT THE
hospital's canteen. Joss looked weary, but satisfied with
himself; he had his pad on the table beside him, and was
scrolling through it and making notations.

"Good news?" he said.

"I think so." Joss was reading what seemed to be a list
of descriptions of vehicles. "Mr. Sakarian woke up in the
middle of the night feeling better . . . and very talkative.
This one," he said, pointing at the pad, "is another of
Smyth's vehicles. And this one, and this one. Apparently
they're pretty well known in the area, but the good people
of Tombstone were, perhaps understandably, too nervous
to point them out to us. It doesn't matter now." Joss
swigged from a half-empty coffee cup. "Two out of three
of these, I bugged yesterday."

Evan nodded and sipped at his tea. "I did all right as
well," he said. "Mr. Dunston—that's his name—Mr.
Dunston woke up a little while ago."

"Much trouble?" Joss said.

Evan shrugged. "I had to lean on him a little. But he
saw the light eventually." He pushed his pad at Joss.
"Many interesting names and addresses. I'll be interested
to see how many of them are still on the census lists, and
which lists."

Joss sighed. "A good night's work, then."

"As far as the Smyth business goes," Evan said, putting down his cup and standing up. "We're still going to have to *prove* to Lucretia that the two are interconnnected. But we should be able to manage that pretty quickly now."

Joss nodded as they made their way out of the cafeteria toward the enclosed pad. "At this rate," he said, "we might even have time for some vacation before our vacation has run out."

Evan looked at Joss sidewise. *He always has time to think about fun,* he thought, *even after a night like this. I am fortunate to have this man around.*

I must make sure he stays *around.*

THEY HEADED BACK TO TOMBSTONE IN HIGH spirits. Evan was going over his list and shaking his head, while Joss piloted.

"What's the matter now?" Joss said.

"The matter," Evan said, "is that not one of these people is named 'Smyth.'"

"Did you really expect them to be?"

Evan laughed softly. "I suppose not. But Joss-*bach,* do you know how long it's going to take us to round all these people up? We're going to need some help from the PPD, whether they like it or not."

"They won't like it," Joss said. "Those lads last night would barely give me the time of day. It looks like word is spreading."

"Of what, is the question." The ugly thought had occurred to Evan several times now. The Smyth gang seemed to be fairly widely spread over this side of the planet. And to hear Dunston tell it, the police left them alone. *Why* did they leave them alone? How many of these cops did they own?

Or how many had they killed—so that the rest left them alone just for a quiet life?

"Good God," Joss said then.

"What?"

"Look at that," said Joss, pointing out the windscreen.

Evan looked. They were on their final approach to Tombstone, heading for the landing pad.

Or where the landing pad had *been*—

There was a crater there, about three feet deep from the looks of it. And everywhere, sunlight glinted bright from debris and broken metal. Evan looked out in horror and saw that most of the domes had been exploded. The Virendra's was one of them; the sheriff's office was another. There were people wandering around in the street aimlessly, or walking around near the former site of the landing pad, among the scattered and shattered skimmers and other vehicles.

"*Diw,*" Evan breathed. "What has happened here?"

Joss's face was set cold. "I have my ideas," he said.

They landed off to one side of the former pad and got out in a hurry, making their way to the center of the town. People who saw Evan and Joss coming drew away from them, and their looks were angry. Worse, when they had passed, the people gathered into a crowd behind them and followed them down the street.

Evan paused in front of what had been the sheriff's office. The dome was blown out and blackened, the airlock door lying on the ground, punctured with slug holes.

Someone came out of the remains of the dome with an armful of paperwork, all torn and charred and soot-streaked. It was Steck. On sight of Evan, she bent over and put the papers down carefully on the ground, with a blackened piece of equipment to hold them there, then walked over to him, and tilted her little head up, and shouted at him.

"Where the fuck have *you* been, Mister Goddamned Sop?!" she shouted. Evan stood there, muted and astounded, noticing through his shock that her faceplate kept fogging up when she shouted. "Where were you last night when Smyth's crowd came in here and destroyed the place? Out for the evening in Welles, were we? Having a nice meal? Taking in the sights?"

"Some of Smyth's boys were busy trying to kill Lew Sakarian up at Rose Cottage," said Joss, very quietly. "We were keeping them from killing him."

That took the wind out of Steck's sails slightly. But only

slightly. "Well, that's just lovely," she said. "But you didn't think to let *us* know about it, did you? You might have given me a call and said, 'Gee, Helvetia, we've just upset a bunch of Smyth's crowd, and now they're likely to think that you put us onto them, so you'd better move the women and children into a secure pressure somewhere'? Oh, no. You just go sailing off—"

"Helvetia?" Joss said wonderingly.

"You shut up, O'Bannion!" Steck shouted, whirling on Joss, so that he took a step or two backward. "Can I help it if my folks got married in Switzerland?? I want to know what kept you two assholes from giving us a little warning what you were going to do! You come swooshing in here in your fancy ship, with your fancy pads and your god-damned fancy invulnerable armor, and start poking into things, and the next thing we know the whole town's blown up, and about *twenty* of us are over in Welles at the hospital, and three of us are *dead* and past the hospital doing any goddamned good, and Kathy Virendra and her dad are dragged off as hostages by these sons of bitches, and then after all that, here *you* come back again—!"

She ran out of breath, or vituperation, but Evan had a clear feeling that the lack was going to be very temporary.

"Where's Helen Mary Cameron?" Joss said, into the silence.

Steck looked at him, took a breath to shout, and then let it out again. "I don't know," she said. "She took her skimmer and went out yesterday afternoon. Something about looking for her father, I think."

"Did she say when she was coming back?"

Steck looked around the crowd. One of the people standing there was the bartender. He peered past Joss and said, "She said last night some time. But she never came in before—"

Steck turned back to Joss. "I hope she's far away from here," she said, "because *this* is no place anymore. Thanks ever so much to *you.*"

She turned her back and walked away, back into what was left of the sheriff's dome.

Evan turned around to look at the crowd. They stared

back with dull animosity, but made no move, and said nothing.

"We'll do what we can to help," Joss said, very quietly.

"Spare us any more help," said the bartender.

Evan looked at Joss. Joss shook his head ever so slightly.

"Right," Evan said, as calmly as he could, and turned to go back to *Nosey*.

He did his best to pay no attention to the muttered comments that flanked them as they walked through the crowd. He refused to react to the stone that someone threw. Next to him, Joss walked steadily too, with a tight look on his face. When they had gotten out of hearing range, Joss said, "I think our popularity is going to show a slump in the next exit poll."

Evan had to laugh, though only once. "Those bastards," he said softly.

"It's not their fault," Joss said. "They're upset."

"I mean the bastards who did this," Evan said. "We are going to get them if it's the last thing we do."

"We've got a fair amount to go on," Joss said. "And the equipment to follow up on it."

"I just wish we had more armed support," Evan said. "Correct me if I'm wrong, but the local police don't sound inclined to offer us much more in the way of help."

"We've dealt with that before," said Joss. "We'll manage this time."

"Will we really," Evan said softly.

"Yes, we will. Don't go all moody on me, now, Glyndower."

Evan opened his mouth to say something rude, and then realized that the black mood *was* indeed coming for him, and would make him useless for a couple of hours if he let it get him. "You're right, of course," he said, and took his helm off. "I'm just so angry—I want to get all Smyth's bloody little tyrants together in one place and—"

"I know," Joss said.

They paused for a moment by what was left of Virendra's dome. It wasn't hurt as badly as some of the others had been; one side had blown out, taking the airlock with it.

Joss looked at it, then stepped in the gaping hole, and Evan came after him. For a moment they just stood there, looking around at the destruction. Shelves were tipped over, parts and food and every kind of goods were scattered every which way.

Evan shook his head and followed Joss toward the back of the place, where the desk was. The destruction was worse here, and there were bullet holes. There, a smudge of blood, with some dark hair caught in it. *Who hit her?* he wondered, for the hair was long: Kathy's.

Joss stepped past the desk, into the area behind it. Evan peered after him. All he could see was a litter of papers and clothes, stuff flung all over the place by the loss of pressure in the dome. Joss bent down to pick up a piece, looked at it, dropped it, picked up another and shook his head.

"Anything?"

"No," said Joss. He dropped the paper he was holding, looked over at a desk that lay overturned, its drawers spilling files and more paperwork everywhere. He picked up one piece of this and gazed at it, developing a quizzical expression. "Huh," he said. "Political broadsides." He dropped that paper too.

"Oh?" Evan said. "What kind?"

"You've got me," Joss said, handing Evan the paper over the desk. "And mimeographed. When's the last time you saw a mimeograph?"

"A what?" Evan said. He was scanning down the paper. It was a sort of political magazine that he had seen before often enough, going on about the oppressed masses and the propertied class, and so forth. Evan had had a problem with this kind of thing from his youth, when the last of the miners were still parroting it in Wales. His own experience had led him to believe that oppression took two, an oppressor and an oppressee, and that both sides had to be working at it somewhat. *Blah, blah, blah, time will come when the masses will rise up under the strong arm of the Sons of the Red Dawn, and the oppressors will be ground underfoot by their—*

Wait a moment. It had been a few years ago that he had heard that name . . . the last time he was on Mars, indeed.

At the time he hadn't thought much of them: one more ranting group. But then there had been that arms find. And the question of outside finance. It was never resolved, either—

His hunch sat up and bit him, hard. "Joss," Evan said, "help me pick this stuff up."

"What?"

"All of it. Get a box. Hurry up."

Joss looked at him in surprise, then turned and went off to search around for a box to use. A moment later he came back with two. Together they began to scoop up the papers and put them in the boxes.

"What's it about?" Joss said.

Evan handed him the broadside he had been looking at. Joss read it, his face getting more and more puzzled.

"Red Dawn?" he said after a moment. He looked up at Evan. "It was a lousy movie. The tanks were all fakes."

Evan shook his head. "I don't know what you're on about. Listen to me, though. The Red Dawn was a political group here, a few years ago. Radical. Not very nice. You remember, the government was just putting itself together, at that point. These lads claimed to be the *real* government of Mars. Or that everybody should recognize them as such. They said that the interim government was a"—he searched his memory for the term they had used—"a crypto-bourgeois de facto junta forced on the free people of Mars by the military-economic cliques of Earth and its Moon and L5 colonies."

Joss looked at Evan in admiration. "That's *good* polemic," he said. "They don't make it like that anymore."

"Yes they do," Evan said, "it's all around us. Don't miss any. What they wanted was to cause the collapse of the interim government of Mars—by any means possible, but force and violence would do just fine—and set up a democratic-socialist society run for Marsmen, by Marsmen, with no interference or entangling alliances with foreign powers— Don't miss those solids, either."

"Right," Joss said, emptying an armful of papers into his box, and picking up the datasolids Evan had pointed out, while looking around for more. "Sounds like these people wouldn't care much for the Acts of Federation, then."

Evan laughed out loud. "I should say not. Have we got everything? Good—I want to get out of here and look this stuff over."

"Got it all," Joss said.

They headed out with their boxes, and made their way back to *Nosey*. Joss rapped on the airlock, and she opened up.

While Evan was putting the boxes down, Joss divested himself of his SHEL gear and sat down in his pilot's seat, bringing *Nosey's* engines up to ready again. Then he tapped at the comms console and dumped the contents of his pad into it.

"Now, before we go any further, let's see about this," he said.

Evan sat down by him, looking at the screen. It filled with bright sparks of light, mostly centered on a more dimly lit patch at the center. "There," Joss said, "that's Tombstone. Those dots are everything I've bugged."

"A lot of them are here," Evan said, jerking a thumb at the window, and the destroyed landing pad.

"Yes. But not the one I'm after, I don't think—" Joss tapped at the comms console, looked at his pad, tapped again. All but two of the sparks vanished.

One was thrown off to one side of the former landing pad.

The other was far off to the edge of the screen . . . and moving.

"There," Joss said. "That's the other skimmer I tagged that we know is Smyth's. About—" He squinted at the screen. "Two hundred klicks out. We can catch up with it in half an hour . . . or trail it."

Evan grinned. It was not a nice grin. "Trail it," he said, "and let's see where it goes. I shouldn't like to rush things."

"Right you are." Joss took *Nosey* up, tapping at the comms console to set the course up.

Evan sat back for a moment and breathed out. There was something that had been niggling at his mind.

"Damn," Joss said.

Evan looked over at him. Joss looked back, a helpless unhappy expression on his face. "Damn," he said again. "In the middle of all this, one more thing to worry about. Where the hell has Helen Mary got to?"

"We'll find her," Evan said, as gently as he could. There was nothing else to do with Joss when he got like this.

Joss sighed and went back to his input.

"Oh," Evan said, remembering. "I was supposed to remind you about the Lexan."

Joss finished what he was doing at the console, and sat back in his seat as well, looking suddenly very shocked. "Jesus H. Christ on a unicycle, it went right out of my head. We have *big* trouble, Officer."

Evan was puzzled. "Excuse me. We've just seen a whole town blown up, and gotten evidence of an extortion and smuggling ring that seems to cover half this planet, and *now* you're telling me that we have a *big* problem?"

Joss nodded.

"What is the stuff?" said Evan. "Is it an explosive? What?"

"Not that way," Joss said. "Remember we were talking about rail-guns?"

"Yes, what about them?"

"Do you know how they work?"

"There are magnets in them, certainly," said Evan, "and a tube—"

"Good God," said Joss with a slight smile, "there's a weapon I know about that you don't. Here's what you have. There's the tube, as you say, and rails down the inside bore of it. they conduct very high-voltage currents of electricity. And inside the rails is a narrow bore. Now what you do is this. You take a slug of some high-flexibility, high-density plastic—specifically, one like Lexan, which is resistant to heat. And you attach a thin aluminum skirt to the back of this. You then use a gas gun, or some other means of propulsion, to shoot this slug into the bore of the rail-gun. The aluminum skirt on the slug hits those rails—"

"But aluminum's not a conductor."

"It sure isn't. The aluminum hits the rails, and vaporizes. In fact, it turns into a conducting plasma, which accelerates down the bore, pushing the slug in front of it. There are five or six more energy sources down the bore of the gun; each one goes off as the slug passes it, and accelerates the plasma even more, and pushes the slug even faster, till it finally comes out the other end."

"How big is this slug?" Evan said.

"Originally it was about two and a half grams," Joss said. "That was in the original versions of this, about a hundred years ago. But there's no reason it couldn't be bigger."

"Would it help?" Evan said.

"Well," Joss said gently, "considering that the thing emerged from the barrel of the rail-gun doing about eight and a half klicks a second, and an increase in mass and bore would increase the muzzle velocity . . . I suspect some people *would* think it would help. Yes."

Evan thought of the perfectly round hole in the engine pod of the SP vessel, and the bottom of the ship itself. *With something like that,* he thought, *who needs cannonballs?*

"You're thinking what I'm thinking, I suspect," said Joss.

"And you found traces of Lexan in the blown-up dome."

"I did. Before you ask, there are just about no 'normal' industrial uses for the stuff. Other, tougher materials have replaced it. It was originally designed for this use, and this only."

"Good God," said Evan.

"That's what I said."

Evan considered it. There would be no use using a weapon like that for anything but straight shooting; its trajectory would be perfectly flat. It would make nothing of atmospheric resistance; if it was heat-resistant enough, it would make it through the atmosphere in so little time that almost no mass would be lost. It would be traveling at—he did a brief sum in his head—sixty-seven *thousand* miles an hour.

Anything that it hit would be little good for anything rather shortly thereafter.

And if the example of the SP ship *was* provided by a

rail-gun, then apparently aiming and firing the thing could be handled with great accuracy. A ship in atmosphere would be no problem.

A ship in orbit would be even easier.

And if you had not one, but several of these rail-guns—in fact, a whole lot of them—and they all fired at a vessel at once—

"You know," said Evan to Joss, "if I were planning a coup, or a revolution, or something, and I thought the Space Forces might turn up—or the local police, or even the Solar Patrol—a few hundred of these things would come in handy. Wouldn't they?"

Joss was opening his mouth to say something when the comms board went off. He shut his mouth, turned around and stared at the board, and then said, "Now what on earth is *that?*"

"Malfunction?" said Evan.

"Damned if I know," Joss said. "My tracer seems to have stopped working. But it can't."

"Did it fall off?"

"It can't do that either." Joss tapped at the console again, stared at it, and then, to Evan's great surprise and amusement, banged it with his fist. "Come on, you bloody hunk of junk!" he said.

"Have you still got his last position?" Evan said, getting up to look more closely at the screen.

"Yes, he's right there. *Was* right there. The tracer's not answering the system's polls."

Evan shook his head and went off to do something he was competent to do, like start going through the paperwork they had brought back with them from Virendra's. "He can't have jammed it," Joss was muttering. "It can't be jammed. Even if that skimmer had crashed, the chip shouldn't have been hurt. And nothing is wrong with the system. Damn it all!"

"If I were you," Evan said, "I would go to where you lost touch with it, so we can have a look around."

"Mmmnh," said Joss. "You know, you're right." And he set about it.

"How long till we get there?" Evan said.

"About three-quarters of an hour."

"Good enough. Come help me go through this stuff."

IT WAS A PEACEFUL THREE-QUARTERS OF AN hour, and at the end of it, Evan was very disquieted. The violent rhetoric of the Red Dawn people had not gotten any less violent since Evan was here last. Now it was a constant litany of live-free-or-die, kill-or-be-enslaved, and drive-the-foreign-invader-from-the-soil-of-Mother-Mars-at-any-price; a pile of inflammatory nastiness the likes of which Evan hadn't seen since before the Irish problem was solved, and which he had hoped never to see again. *But it's true what they say, I suppose; root up the plant one place, you'll find it's seeded somewhere else.* He had never really imagined it taking root in this arid soil, though. Mars had seemed too practical a place, too tough to live in successfully, to encourage such aimless hatred.

And one of the Virendras was apparently a sympathizer. There had been at least a year's worth of the stuff in the file drawers there, much more polemic than anyone would willingly keep around the house unless they really liked the taste. *Now which of them, then?* he thought. Scott Virendra seemed too phlegmatic, too practical, to go in for this kind of thing. If it was anybody's style, it was his daughter's. He still remembered Kathy standing there with her fists on her hips, telling the cop off, and the relish she had exhibited while at it. "I'll take the compliment as intended rather than the insult it could be," he heard her say in memory. She had been enjoying his discomfort. "This isn't the lobby of the Hilton, and even the accidents around here tend to be messier than in town. I—"

Evan's mouth fell open.

"These," Joss said, tossing a batch of papers away from him, "are very sick people. Don't they have asylums on this planet?"

"Sometimes I wonder," said Evan. "Joss, do you remember the first day I went to see the Virendras? You know what she said to me?"

"Something rude, to hear you tell it."

"She said to me, 'This isn't the lobby of the Hilton.' How did she know where we had just come from?"

Joss stared at him. "It could have been a figure of speech."

"Oh? There are six other hotels in Welles. Why pick that one?"

"It's the biggest."

Evan shook his head slowly. "I don't think so. I think Kathy Virendra knew quite well where we had been ... somehow."

Joss looked bemused. "Gossip?"

"I don't think so, somehow. It strikes a strange note."

"Hunch?"

"If you like ... yes. A hunch."

There was another beep from the comms board. Joss got up and went to look at it, and then began clapping his hands so loudly that Evan jumped with the suddenness of it. "Hot doggies!" Joss cried. "They're here!"

"Who?" Evan said. "The cavalry?"

Joss looked over his shoulder. "You *have* been sneaking peeks at my vids, haven't you! No, not them. The satellite photos. Tee is just now putting them in my pad."

Evan threw his hands in the air in mock astonishment. "Only three days late," he said. "Hurray for Our Heroes in the Space Forces."

"Better late than never," Joss said, going for his pad.

"They'd be the ones to send for trouble," Evan said, as his mother often had to him. "They'd be a long time coming back with it."

"Hush," said Joss, sitting down with his pad. "Let's have a look. Good Lord, how much of this stuff is there?" He scrolled back to the top of the display. It said:

THOUGHT YOU MIGHT WANT SOME EXTRA COVERAGE, SO HERE IS ENTIRE AREA SYRTIS-PLANITIA-MONS-MESENTIIS TO MCD 100 THIS YEAR. T.

"That's four months' worth," Evan said wonderingly. "What did she do to get *that* much data out of those tight bastards?"

"I don't care if she did a nautch dance," Joss said. "This

is just what I wanted." He started tapping hurriedly at the pad. "Now if I can just get this pile of circuits to understand what I want it to look for, rather than having to do all the looking myself—"

"Fine. How long till we hit your lost-trace spot?"

Joss checked his chrono. "About fifteen minutes now."

Evan left Joss to it, and went back to the Red Dawn paperwork. The unchanging level of sheer screaming hatred was hard to take for long periods, but Evan wanted to make sure he didn't miss anything. He was hoping for a document that would mention the names of people involved with the organization, but there was none, at least in this batch of papers. *I should have known better,* he thought. *If one of the Virendras is actively involved with Red Dawn, they would hardly leave paperwork to that effect around their house.*

The comms board beeped again. Evan looked over at it, then at Joss. "Now what?"

"You've got me," Joss said. He put his satellite photos on hold for the moment and had a look at whatever it was that was coming in.

His face went perplexed.

"What's the matter?" Evan said.

Joss pushed his pad at Evan. "Read it."

Evan looked at the message. After the usual route codings came the header of the SP headquarters at Tethys, around Saturn. And then the message:

MESSAGE BEGINS/ADVISED BY L. ESTHERHAZY AT SP LUNA THAT YOU ARE PRESENTLY AVAILABLE FOR ADVISORY WORK. PLEASE REPORT TETHYS SOONEST. MULTIPLE MURDERS COMMITTED OVER PAST THREE DAYS. ASSISTANCE URGENTLY REQUIRED. M. LADISLAS/CMMR. SP TETHYS/MESSAGE ENDS/MESSAGE ENDS

They looked at each other.

"Now what do we do with *this?*" Evan said.

Joss made a suggestion.

Evan laughed. "No, really."

"Are you kidding? We refuse it!"

Evan studied the message. It was not an order; it was a

request—he had seen enough of both in this time in the SP to know the difference. They could refuse it. But if the case they were presently working on didn't yield results quite shortly, they would be in *deep* trouble when they got back to the Moon.

The comms board beeped again. Joss looked over at it with a "now what" expression, which abruptly dissolved. "We're near where my chip stopped working," he said. "Look: I say we refuse it. What do you think?"

Evan thought.

"All right," he said. "I'll do the reply. You go take care of business."

"Fine. Let me finish with the pad here—we have a few minutes' margin before we get into the hot spot."

Evan went for his own pad, which also had the message from Saturn in it. He composed as careful and respectful a message as he could, saying that unavoidable circumstances, hot pursuit, etc. etc., made present acceptance of the invitation impossible, and as soon as possible, etc. etc. etc. *This is one of the most mealy-mouthed things I've ever written,* he thought, when he finished, and felt slightly disgusted, slightly proud.

He sent the message off and went to see what Joss was doing. He was in his pilot's seat again, with the pad in his lap, comparing pictures on it with his screen. And he was smiling.

"Good news?" Evan said, sitting down in his seat.

"Look at this," Joss said. "Here's where that signal went missing. And look at the pad. This is the same area, over the past three months. Just hit that key there and the series will animate."

Evan hit the key in question. For a few seconds, nothing seemed to happen; he was looking at a piece of Martian landscape, all rocks, no variation.

Then the contrails began—some large, some small, crisscrossing the area. They seemed to come in batches, and then dissipate, and then return. Mostly they came at night, but the satellite had IR imaging, and seeing in the dark was no problem for it.

"Those," Joss said, "are the heat-traces of fairly large ships. What are they all doing here?"

"I was hoping you would tell me."

"I don't have a clue. But I intend to have some shortly—"

And anything else Joss was about to say was lost. Something went *THUMP!* and *Nosey* shuddered, and side-slipped, and started to fall out of the sky.

Joss leapt for his seat. Evan grabbed the tilting bulkhead next to him, hung on to it for dear life, and made his way along the suddenly slanted floor to his own seat, grabbing Joss's SHEL headpiece and bringing it with him. "Thanks," Joss said. "Get yourself strapped in." He was arguing with the steering yoke with one hand and hammering on the comms console with the other.

"What happened?" Evan said, trying very hard to stay calm. But it was hard to keep calm when one was dropping out of the sky so fast.

"No stabilizers," Joss said, his breath coming fast. "Here, hold this just like this," he said, indicating the yoke, and taking his SHEL gear from Evan. "Thanks," he said after getting it on and sealed up. "I still have downward-vectored thrust, thank Buddha or whoever. Here we go—"

There was another *THUMP!* "Too late," Joss said, almost cheerfully. Evan clung onto the seat and hoped there was good reason for the cheer.

WHAM!!

Joss cried out as they hit, and lolled back in his seat, momentarily stunned. Evan was all right; the shocks and stabilizers in his own suit had saved him. *But poor* Nosey! he thought, unstrapping himself. He stood up and looked out the windscreen—and wholeheartedly panicked.

It looked like a tank. It was about the right size for a tank. But it had hoverskirts on it, and it was scooting along smooth as a puddle of mercury about a foot above the tallest boulders; and it had a very peculiar-looking gun on top of it; something with a bore about two-tenths of a meter wide.

"Shit," Evan said, with some feeling. He pulled the straps off Joss, picked him and his pad up, tucked them both under one arm, and slapped the inner airlock door open, and overrrode the outer lock. It sprang open with the usual complaining of alarms. Evan jumped out and ducked sideways and around the back of *Nosey*—

—which was just as well, as the slug that ran through her then went in high up on her front, and out high up on her back, and hit a largish rock behind her, and blew it up—but not before setting it on fire.

Wonderful, Evan thought, and began to jump, as low and fast as he could. *Pyrophoric detonation.* And less rationally, *Well, at least they missed the wine*—

He started to bounce. Bouncing was one of the first things they taught you when you did your suit training. The problem, of course, was that everyone ever put in a suit thought they knew how to bounce already. They always found out otherwise. Years of experience have told each human being how to manage the negative-feedback systems in his own body, the sensorial data that lets one know when one's feet have hit the ground, and how to keep one's balance. But a suit doesn't have the instinctive overrides that a body does, and will do exactly what one tells it—an obedience that can produce comical results, or fatal ones.

Evan, after all his years in a suit, was expert. Trained in many environments, he knew how to bounce in heavy gravity, in low gravity, in no gravity. He could manage all kinds of terrain, and he could bounce while being shot at from one vantage point or many, and make sure he was missed. But he had never met a weapon like *this* before. Off to one side of him, barely a couple of feet away, another rock burst into flame and exploded, showering him with chips and shards that rattled off his armor.

That damn thing traverses too fast, Evan thought. *Bloody. Light barrel, light propellant and projectile; why shouldn't it be able to whip around in a second? At least the thing carrying it isn't as fast as I am. I hope.* He bounced sideways, and then high up, and then low, always heading for the horizon at his best speed. If what Joss had said was correct, if he could get over the horizon, the railgun would be useless: anything it fired at him would just keep going, right out of atmosphere. *Heaven send it doesn't hit anything else!* But he would have to *keep* the horizon between him and it. And how long could he manage it?

Over his shoulder, Joss moaned. "Sorry," Evan said. "Joss? Are you with me?"

"Oooohhhhhh," Joss said, sounding very sick and hurt indeed. Evan looked him over hurriedly, while bouncing sideways a bit, then straight ahead again. He looked all right, though. "Sorry," he said to Joss, "but the ride is going to be bumpy for a while. We've got company, and it wants us dead."

"Where—the hell—are we going?" Joss said, as Evan went up and down and sideways, as fast as he could.

Evan blinked. "Away from *that*," he said. "Past that—we've got to get some help."

"We could—call the police," Joss said.

Evan immediately started to feel better. If Joss's sense of humor was intact, so was the rest of him. "No such luck, I think. What are they going to do about *that?*" Evan twisted hurriedly aside again, as another projectile hit quite close to him on the left. He twisted as he jumped, to take the force of the boulder's explosion on his armor, and spare Joss from a hail of rock shrapnel.

"Don't know. How long—can you—keep this up?"

Evan considered the powerpack levels displayed in the status readout in his helm. "Depends whether I have to shoot too," he said. "Right now I think flight is a superior response to fight. So maybe an hour or so."

Joss gave him an unhappy look from inside his SHEL gear. "Might—throw up on you—before then."

Evan laughed ruefully. "Feel free, partner. Everything *else* has happened to this poor suit on this trip."

Joss laughed slightly at that, a peculiar sound since the bouncing kept cutting the laugh into pieces. "How far—distance-wise?" Joss said.

Evan considered his readouts again. "At this speed, we can make about five klicks a minute. Call it three hundred before I start redlining."

"What's—our friend—"

Another projectile whammed into the ground to their right, kicking up an incredible plume of fire and dirt and gravel. Evan bounced hurriedly away from it, then back again, then away in a different direction. "He's making about four and a half, five himself. Mexican standoff. Also, he can go straight as the crow flies. We don't dare—"

Evan felt the gravel kick against the backs of his legs, and responded by going straight up, at high speed. Underneath him the stones burst into flame, and the shrapnel rattled against the soles of his boots. Frantic and terrified as he was, Evan was also becoming strangely confident. He was remembering how it had been during the Second Global War, all that while ago, when the *Bismarck* had been firing at a squadron of Fairey Swordfish that had been attacking it. The Faireys were antiques—more appropriate to the First War than the Second—all the Brits had had to use for their own defense at that point. But the *Bismarck*'s fire predictors had been set for faster, more modern attack planes, and the "obsolete," slow-moving Swordfish got in under its guns and made a mess that the *Bismarck* couldn't cope with. *That thing's fire predictors haven't been programmed for shooting at people, I bet,* he said. *Ships, yes. But ships can't maneuver like I can.* That was, in fact, his only hope. He intended to squeeze it till it squeaked.

"Where—to?" Joss said.

Evan laughed. "Away from *that!*"

"Got anything—more specific?"

Evan shook his head, bounced sideways, sideways again, up, and was missed by another projectile, more widely this time. "Not a clue. Care to suggest something?"

"Phone—booth," Joss said.

Evan had to laugh out loud. "Who were you thinking of calling?"

"FAF—Sydenham."

Evan blinked. There was no calling them on the pad, or on his commlink. The people chasing them would hear. But a landline link—"You're delirious," Evan said. "There's not a phone box for five hundred klicks."

"Yes—there is."

Joss began struggling with his pad, tapping clumsily at it while thrown over Evan's shoulder. "Listen," Evan said, "would it help if I carried you frontways? I was just in a hurry when I picked you up, that's all."

"Yes—please!!"

Evan put on the brakes, bounced once in place, high, while shifting Joss around to cradle him in his arms—then took off for the horizon again as he saw another projectile go by. *Thank God that thing isn't a rapid-firer—* At least, *that* one wasn't. Who knew what else these people might have? Money, that they had for sure. Evan found himself wondering how many financiers on Mars were involved with this movement—for he was sure now that this was Red Dawn, gotten big and deadly—and how many companies who thought they might do better in an "indepedent" government than under the aegis of the Federated Planets?

Joss was banging away on his pad now, frantic. After a moment he stopped. "Right," he said. "I've got a settlement. Listing shows it has a commlink. Bearing—" He squinted at the pad. "One one five, about thirty klicks. How fast can you go over the horizon, about five klicks farther than that thing can see, and then do a ninety?"

Evan thought about it for a moment. "Six minutes."

"Go for it," Joss said, and clutched the pad tightly.

Evan went for it. It was a race such as he had never run even in training, when men on the Moon leapt rilles and bounced over whole craters and started silent landslides in the force and speed of their going. He wove less, now, and he stayed low to the ground, with no sound to keep him company but the impact of his boots on the uneven stones. The impacts of projectiles grew fewer. They could still certainly see him, but their accuracy was dropping off with distance. It as unquestionably a function of his size, and Evan was grateful for it. He ran. He ran.

And finally came a time when a projectile went over his head, and just kept on going, out of sight.

"Go! Go!" Joss shouted, like someone cheering on the winner at a race. Evan went. He was getting the hang of it now. Each terrain had its own tricks to learn. Here it was a matter of picking rocks that were too big or too deep-set in the substrate to move under his weight, precisely judging the size of an empty spot, picking the next landing site three jumps away; like a child using stepping-stones to ford a creek. Evan milked the low gravity for everything it was worth, making his suit work as efficiently as possible, saving its energy, not bouncing higher than he needed to. Speed, speed was everything—

"Good," Joss said, panting, out of breath himself just from the speed they were moving at. "Okay. Do your ninety. The place is six klicks in front of us after you do it."

Evan turned ninety degrees, kept low, and bounced fast and furious as a kangaroo with a mission from God. "What place?" he said.

Joss laughed, another weirdly disjointed sound. "Would you believe it's called 'Dunroamin'?"

"No," Evan said. "You're making that up."

Joss laughed again. "Come on, step on it!"

Evan did.

About a minute and a half later, they saw the dome. It was partially buried, a favorite building configuration here, and surprisingly large for a dome all by itself in the middle of noplace. "Who lives here?" said Evan.

"It says 'K. Downing.' "

They slowed and stopped in front of the dome, and Evan put Joss down. They were both out of breath. *I must be really out of shape,* Evan thought with some annoyance. *But then I haven't had to do a run like that for* . . .

Joss was knocking on the airlock door, hard.

No answer.

"Come on, come *on!*", he muttered, knocking again.

There was a hiss and clunk from inside. Then a hiss as the outer door slid open.

The apparition standing there was wearing half a set of SHEL gear: just the upper half—not a recommended configuration, but barely all right for very short periods. The lower half was wearing a demure gingham print dress, and fuzzy bedroom slippers.

"Come in!" said the person in the SHEL gear.

They did, hurriedly. "Ma'am," Joss said, "we're Solar Police, can we use your phone, please?"

The outer airlock shut, and the inner opened, and the lady waved them inside. "Sure, boys, you just come on in. Can I get you something while you're here?"

"An armored division would do nicely," Evan said. Joss shushed him.

"Just the phone, ma'am . . . then we've got to get out of here. There's someone coming behind us who doesn't mind blowing people's houses up if we're in them."

The lady took off her SHEL headgear. Her face was as wrinkled as that of one of the apple dolls that Evan had seen people back in Wales sell to the tourists; she had an aureole of silver hair, and a slightly mischievous look to her. "Right over there, son," she said to Joss, pointing over to a table beside a big couch.

Evan spent a moment looking around him in total astonishment. The dome was made of a translucent material, one of the old-fashioned geodesic type; and from every joint of its internal ribbing, plants hung. Green plants, flowering plants, vines; ivy climbed up the ribbing and the walls from pots on the floor. The place was carpeted in Oriental rugs, and a large dozy black cat with emerald eyes lay on the nearby settee. It looked at Evan and yawned, and then rolled over and showed him its tummy.

Joss was hunched over the lady's comm pad, dialing for access. "What's the number?" he said to Evan.

"440302886."

"Right."

Evan paused ever so briefly to scratch the cat for luck, then went to join Joss at the phone. Joss handed him the receiver. The connection was ringing.

Evan watched in momentary amusement as Joss paused long enough to look around the place, and then looked down in surprise to find the cat weaving around his legs.

"She thinks she's going to get fed now," the little old lady said. "She usually does, when company comes. It's the only way to keep her out of their plates. Lilith! Stop bring so shameless."

Lilith continued being shameless. The connection clicked. "FAF Sydenham," said a female voice.

"This is Solar Patrol Officer 4629337 Glyndower, E. H., on active assignment. *Au secours! Au secours!* Armed assistance required immediately at"—Joss was holding the pad for him, with a course indicated on it—"map coordinates HDZ 40558, LKI 4401.9, and course westbound;

seek for passive tracker at 101.776! Being pursued by unauthorized armored vehicle, armed with high-velocity
plasma weaponry, vehicle has shot down SP vessels, will
destroy private property and endanger civilians! Attention
Commander Chris Huntley! *Au secours! Au secours!* Confirm!"

"Confirmed map coordinates HDZ 40558, LKI 4401.9,
and course westbound, passive tracker at 101.776—" said
the very surprised voice at the other end. "Hold for
ETA—"

"Can't hold," Evan said. "On civilian property at the
moment, must continue to prevent damage. Out!"

"Out," said the female voice, and Evan put the phone
down.

"That's us. Let's go."

"Are you sure you don't want a sandwich?" the little
old lady said.

"Mrs. Downing," Joss said, "we want a sandwich more
than anything else, and we can't have one now. Later?"

"You young people are always in such a rush," said
Mrs. Downing. "All right, you run along. I'll see you later
on."

Lilith was rubbing against Evan now. He patted her
head and made hurriedly for the door. "You be careful
now, here?" said Mrs. Downing.

"Madam," Evan said, "count on it." He and Joss
crowded into the airlock together.

Once out, Evan picked Joss up again. Joss pointed at the
plate on the side of the dome. "See, I *told* you it was
called 'Dunroamin.' "

Evan shook his head and started bouncing. "Where's
that course leading to?"

"Away from our friend—we hope—and toward The
Strip. We have some company there, I think. And we're
less likely to be blown away in company than alone."

"You think so?" Evan said, bouncing low and building
up speed again. The sweat was standing out all over him,
and being soaked up by the neural foam in the suit. *And
I just had it replaced,* he thought. *Oh well . . .* He put that
thought aside, concentrated on putting as much distance
between him and Mrs. Downing's place as possible. "You

think our friends the 'lichen miners' are still likely to be there?"

"More than possible. It's worth a try, anyway. How long do you think your friends from Sydenham will take to find us?"

Evan shook his head and bounced hurriedly sideways as, way off to his left, he saw a projectile impact in a sudden flower of fire.

"Shit! They've found us again!" said Joss.

"At least they don't seem interested in Mrs. Downing's place."

"I hope not. Move it! What about that ETA?"

"They're three hundred klicks from here. If they scramble—twenty minutes? Half an hour."

"Oh joy," Joss said. "How's your power?"

Evan looked at the helm display. It was rather depleted, not redlined yet—but pretty soon now. "About that much."

Joss got an unnerved sound to his voice. "What about your lifesupport?"

"Oh, I'll be able to breathe. But not run."

Joss said nothing for a moment.

"You and Mrs. Downing," Evan said. "Sandwiches! I thought you said you were going to throw up."

"I will . . . later. SHIT!"

Evan simply threw himself sideways and kept himself from falling as best he could, then was up and bouncing again. Joss's face through the SHEL faceplate was white; the projectile he had seen coming right toward him had set a rock afire no more than a few meters ahead. "Are those guys getting better?" he said.

"Better hope not," Evan said, and started paying much closer attention to evasive action.

They ran. Evan was embarrassed, and upset, and frightened, all at once. Embarrassed for having had to call for help; upset because he was used to standing his ground and fighting; frightened for Joss, more than for himself. *This isn't my day,* he thought unhappily. But there was no point in wasting time thinking about it. He was better concentrating on the rocks, the projectiles, staying upright . . .

The color of the ground began to change; it got darker red. "Good," Joss said. "We're on The Strip. Just keep go-

ing the way we're going. There's always the chance—" He
paused, and then said, "By the way, what was the sudden
outburst of French back there?"

"French?"

"Au secours—"

"Oh! It's the old pickup-recall signal. 'Help, I'm stuck!'
An Armor thing."

"Ah. A secret password."

Evan jogged sideways, and it was just as well, for about
a second later a projectile went through where he had been
and blew a boulder the size of a small house to kingdom
come. "An identifier, anyway. Let's hope that message got
through a little quicker because of it. Hey—" He bounced
sideways again, and then up, and then straight ahead at
high speed.

"You see something?"

"Looks like a mining vehicle to me. The witnesses you
wanted."

"Something to hide behind, at least."

Evan grunted. He wasn't sure that hiding was going to
do any good against the rail-gun. He just poured on the
steam.

Projectiles began to come faster around them. *The range
is reducing,* Evan thought. *They were saving speed for
this. Oh, hell.* And his suit was getting low, very low indeed. *This is not a good situation* ...

He put on his augmented vision and looked at the mining vehicle ahead. Vehicles; he could now see the other
one a short distance away from it. Both were moving. He
laughed, just once.

"Something funny?" Joss said. "Do share it with me."
He was sounding very shaken.

"Yes," Evan said, and laughed again; he couldn't help
it. "Your friends up there, that you let go ... they're
digging up The Strip again."

"WHAT?" Joss cried, in sudden and total outrage. "After I went to all the trouble to tell them how to fake it—"

Evan shook his head. "Maybe the instructions were too
complicated?"

"Why, those—"

"So much for officerial compassion," Evan said. He was

looking at the vehicles again. One of them, the one that had been empty, and was slaved to the other, was slightly closer. As far as he could tell, it was still slaved. It would do to hide behind for the moment—

"Hang on," he said to Joss. "I've got to hurry a bit here. The jump juice is getting low."

"Wonderful," Joss said, and hung on.

Evan made for the slaved mining vehicle. From the air, it was surprising how small these things looked; from the ground, it was amazing how enormous they were. This vehicle alone couldn't have been driven into Tombstone; it would have covered it, from one end to the other, with only a little of the town's property sticking out on the sides. It certainly would do to hide behind, for a few minutes anyway.

Oh, Chris, Chris, come on, he thought, and pulled up to the shadow of the vehicle. It towered over them, about ten stories high, moving gently by at about five klicks an hour. Cautiously, Evan began to make his way around it—

Then the projectile hit the tank, and it caught fire.

Only briefly, of course; there wasn't enough oxygen to support the kind of conflagration that would have broken out had such a weapon been used in an atmosphere like Earth's. But the spot that caught fire promptly melted and ran down, and since part of the vehicle's tracks were involved, the vehicle started the slew around sideways—

Evan bounced off to the side. Another projectile, and then another, stitched into the vehicle behind him. He was torn. If he went out into the open, the fire of the tank might be drawn to the other vehicle—and there were people in it. If he stayed where he was—but that was no good either. He was up against a wall.

He put Joss down. "Run for it!" he shouted.

"Run? In *this* place? Are you crazy? Run *where?*

"JUST RUN!!"

Joss looked at Evan as if he were out of his mind, and pulled his Remington out.

Evan knew when he was being confronted with a crazy man. He picked Joss up again, this time under his arm, like a parcel, and bounced out into the open, away from both the vehicles. No choice but to run again. *But we won't run long—*

A projectile slammed into the ground right next to Evan, and the rock that blew up as a result threw its biggest fragment, easily five hundred kilograms' worth, straight at Evan's left leg. The leg servos screamed, overloaded and went out. Evan fell over rightwards, on top of Joss. *At least it wasn't* him *it hit—* He scrambled for purchase, tried to get up, couldn't—

That was when he saw it—the odd curved shape sticking up over the horizon. *A dome?* was all he had time to think, before he saw it move. And move swiftly, rising up above the horizon as if it were on a fast elevator: a huge rounded shape, all silvery, a great ovoid with odd excrescences and lumps all over it. From one of them Evan saw a line of light lance out, too bright to bear looking at even with though his helm polarized it. Other shape arrowed out too, smaller, darker, blue fire trailing out behind them.

The ground shuddered; a great wash of light bloomed over everything.

Evan struggled to his feet. The left leg of his armor was not working: he had to balance on his right, and leaned on Joss a bit as he got up.

Joss was staring into the sky, at the looming shape that was inching downward toward them. Evan laughed a bit under his breath. There was no question this ship was impressive. "Like it?" he said.

"Like it? I want to marry it," Joss breathed. And then he laughed. "If the queen of all the Easter eggs went to war," he said, "it would like this."

"Don't let Chris hear you say that," Evan said. "Her name is *Arnhem.*"

They stood there and waited, just feasting their eyes. After a few moments, a bay opened near the rear of the ship, and a sleek little shuttle came soaring out, to settle not too far from them.

Evan looked at Joss's face with amusement. "That *little* one," Joss said, "has more guns than *Nosey!!*"

"Annoying, isn't it?" Evan said.

The shuttle's door opened, and a figure in a suit like Evan's, but more sleek and deadly-looking, peered out. "You boys call the Triple-A?" she said.

"Did we ever," Evan said. Joss helped him hobble toward the ship, and helped the suited lady inside get him up through the hatch. Then he climbed in himself, and looked around. To the lady in the suit, Joss said, "I just want you to know that I take back *all* the bad things I ever said about the Space Forces."

"Thought somebody was talking about us again," said Chris Huntley. "My ears were burning. Sit down, boys, and let's go have a palaver."

EIGHT

JOSS HEARD THE DECOROUS CHIME AS *ARNHEM*
entered Tombstone's ILS zone, and straightened out of his
comfortable slouch. "Commander Huntley," he said, "before we set down I'd like an overflight, please. Low, and
slow."

"Nothing easier." She said a few words into her personal comm, then glanced at Joss. "Terry wants to know:
how low, how slow, how many passes?"

"One-fifty meters, two hundred knots max and four
passes ought to do it."

Evan was standing nearby in singlet and shorts; they
had taken his suit away from him and hustled it down to
the ship's armor maintenance officer, to see to its leg.
Evan nodded at Joss; evidently he was thinking the same
way he was. "Thermal can?" he said.

"Thermal, IR, motion sensor, the lot. I want to see
who's at home and who isn't." Joss swivelled his seat,
touched controls on the scanner board and watched as its
screens came to life. The assault-ship's sensor suite wasn't
as modern or elaborate as *Nosey*'s, but what it lacked in
delicacy, it more than made up for in raw power. The system was designed to locate potential hostile forces after
they had taken steps to avoid just such a detection, and a
plain old residential area was unlikely to give it many
problems. Joss finished calibrating and patched in a
dumper link to the computer core. "The problem is, that

there are twenty innocent people in the hospital, three in the morgue, and Buddha alone might know how many families have just upped sticks and gone. After we land, you and I will wander over to the sheriff's office. Steck ought to have copies of the town census, and I want to cross-refer, just to see who should be where."

"And how many non-innocent people have taken it on the fly in the past twenty-four hours?

"It'll have to be twelve." Joss stared down the hooded viewer of *Arnhem*'s infrared scanner. "If Mars was a little warmer, residual heat wouldn't bleed away so fast. As it is, the decay curve will give us a positive reading for maybe eighteen hours, but since this is going to be presented as evidence somewhere, I'd rather not push the findings that far down the line."

"Noted. I'll want a word with Lucretia, too."

"You *want* . . .?"

" 'Fraid so. We're going to need heavy-weapons fire support once we find out where our Red Dawn chummies are hiding, and though Chris and the rest are willing enough—"

"For purely selfish motives, Glyndower, as you well know!" laughed Huntley. "You sops are the only people who get to see any action nowadays. If it wasn't for the fact they'd chop the nuts off my suit before they let me use it, I'd transfer."

"Commander Christine Huntley, every inch a lady," said Evan. "Right down to her military mustache." He clanked slightly as she hit his armored shoulder with her armored fist, but didn't stop grinning. "You see why I need clearance before I let this bunch loose, don't you?"

"It's a man's life in the Triple-A," said Chris, "and don't let little boys like this one tell you otherwise."

"Uh-huh," agreed Joss. He could have been agreeing to anything, because he was staring down the scanner hood again, all but oblivious to whatever else was going on around him. His fingers were dancing with a life of their own across the sensor unit's keyboard, and he was grateful for that level of standardization. It would have made his task much more difficult if *Arnhem*'s scanner systems had been slaved to, say, antipersonnel weapons. And it would have made for another interesting afternoon down in Tombstone, where they'd already had quite enough of that sort of interest, thank you very much.

He had guessed right. Ignoring the wrecked areas which were obviously beyond human habitation until they were repaired, several of the untouched and previously-occupied domes had been vacated, and recently. Using IR and thermal, it was child's play to see the difference between a place whose owner had just stepped out and somewhere that was now deserted. If the resident had gone to the bar to drown his or her all-too-real sorrows, or to whatever now passed for a shop in Tombstone, they left their environmental controller running so that the domes, despite their insulation, glowed with an overspill of heat. The others were cold, and almost dark. There was still enough heat in the denser structural units to outline the buildings in a ghostly sketch-outline of themselves, but not enough to maintain life inside it without a SHEL—and the SHEL itself would show up on the screen as a human silhouette of heat and light. There were none.

"Jesus wept," said Chris Huntley, and she said it with respect rather than as an oath. "When you said the place had been trashed, you didn't tell me the half of it. That looks," she hesitated, as if momentarily ashamed of the profession of arms, "as if it was done by Service-trained personnel."

"It might have been, Chris." Evan stayed in his seat; he had already seen the devastation, and would see it again when he and Joss went to the sheriff's office, but he had no desire for a grandstand view. "The Sons of the Red Dawn play rough, and who's to say what their people used to do for a living."

"If it turns out that any of them are ex Triple-A," said Huntley very softly, "I want them."

Joss felt the skin at the nape of his neck twitch just a little at the cool, dispassionate way she spoke. Raw anger would have been easier to take, but Armored Airborne Assault personnel had that response trained out, as something more likely to hurt them than the enemy. "All right, Commander," he said at last. "I've got what I was looking for. We can land."

"Right," said Chris.

The comms officer looked up and said, "Ma'am, armor maintenance was just on the horn. Officer Glyndower's suit is going to have to spend about a week in the shop, Charlie says. The leg circuitry is in a bad way, and we don't have spares to match the hydraulics."

Chris put her eyebrows up. "We can lend you SHEL gear for the moment," she said to Evan. "But after that . . . well, I don't think we'd better wait a week and a half to send your suit to the Moon and wait for a new one to come back." She grinned. "I think we have a spare suit around here somewhere that will fit you in a pinch."

Joss watched Evan's expression, a curious mixture of eagerness and uncertainty. "Ahem," Evan said, "right."

"Good," Chris said, and turned to watch the landing.

Joss wondered just a little what the people of Tombstone had made of the huge dark ship that had crisscrossed their sky and now settled ponderously onto the ruins of their landing pad, ignoring the crater in the middle of it as just one of those things a military vessel was designed to take in its stride. Despite those who had fled, the Red Dawn probably had at least one spy still in town, and if he could be panicked enough, this latest development would be reported without delay.

"There are a couple of other things, by the way. Could you have a couple of squads suit up and deploy on the landing pad while we're gone?"

"There's not going to be any trouble right under *Arnhem*'s guns. Of that I can assure you."

"It's not trouble that concerns me, Commander. It's that the people of this town should see that we're willing to get heavy with the people who did this to them. And maybe it could provoke a reaction from any Marsman who's still lurking around Tombstone to see how we respond. He and his colleagues," Joss sneered the word, "might have been expecting more sops. Maybe other sops, since they shot down *Nosey*. What he'll see is the same team, alive, unharmed and this time backed by military firepower."

"I really like your partner," said Huntley over her shoulder to Evan. "He has a sneaky mind."

"That's why he was picked to partner me, since I'm so honest, direct and straightforward."

"Yes, and I can rule straight lines with a corkscrew an' all. Pull the other one if you want music, Glyndower. And as for you, Officer Joss O'Bannion, my name is Chris. Not Commander. I'll let you know the right time to call me by rank, but as of now, it's Chris. Okay?"

"Okay, Chris. Noted and logged." Joss cracked a grin. "The other thing. Can you have someone maintain a listening watch on comms, just in case there *is* somebody watching us?"

"Nothing easier. Mike's got nothing better to do today. Have you, Mike?"

The comms officer leaned out from behind an armoured bulkhead and raised a thumb. "Not right now. What you want?"

"Monitor everything, jam anything."

"Got you. An' I can put a signal trace on whichever comsat they bounce off, if you want."

Evan smiled thinly. "You have no idea how much we want. The people at the other end of that transmission have shot at us—during dinner in *Sichuan*, for pity's sake!"

Chris Huntley looked appropriately outraged at that. "After, I could forgive. *During* shows a lack of breeding and good manners."

"That's what I thought. And now they've tried to blow us up, shot down our ship . . . and managed what with one thing and another to ruin a perfectly good vacation. Quite soon I intend to explain how much that has annoyed me, and if you and the rest of First Triple-A are cleared by our boss, I'd like you to help me explain."

He put on the SHEL gear, and followed Joss to the lock.

HELVETIA STECK GLOWERED AT THEM WHEN they came into the sheriff's office. It had been tidied somewhat; at least the charred rubble had been pushed and brushed into a single unsightly heap, rather than lying all over the floor. "You two again," she said. There was a little less venom in her voice now, but that seemed more a result of weariness than any change in attitude. "What now?"

"Officer," said Joss, keeping it formal, "we need a copy of the most recent population census, and a list of," for some topics, formality was really no defense, "those killed, injured and made homeless during the recent outrage."

Steck stared at him for a long time, as if she was reading something from his face that his tone of voice had only hinted at. Her own tired, hard expression didn't soften, but Joss had the feeling that whatever she had seen had kept her from some cruel remark. He was glad of it. Evan had recovered from his own incipient fit of depression, but Joss's own was neither so deep nor so easily gotten over, and seeing the devastation wrought by the Red Dawn in Tombstone had only served to reinforce it all over again.

When Steck came back from rummaging amongst the salvaged documents that were now filed haphazardly in a stack of boxes, she had one small binder, slightly singed around the edges, and a handwritten sheet of paper whose columns of names were disfigured by crossings-out that looked horribly new. "Two more," she said. "Last night and this morning. Have a nice day."

And that was that.

Evan had said nothing since they left *Arnhem*, and it seemed likely that such a state of affairs would continue until they returned to the assault-ship. Officer Steck had shown no desire for smalltalk with any sop, least of all a suit specialist bereft of his suit, and no interest in why they needed the census. That was just as well; silence, though it grated on Joss's nerves, was safer. Both of them were growing increasingly concerned over potential breaches in security, and had agreed to operate on a need to know basis so far as the PPD was concerned. It was one matter to worry a little over the graft provided by bootleggers to keep the cops off their backs; it was quite another when the business involved an organization wealthy enough to purchase military hardware that was barely off the secrets list.

An organization with that sort of money, and worse, the idealogy of false patriotism that it tried to foster among those with no time for mercenary motives, made the Red Dawn far more dangerous than just another mob of gangsters. It was all too easy for them to attract people who would never in their lives have touched a bribe or a handout, people who were disaffected by their station in life, by a lack of appreciation for their efforts, or by simple envy of those whom they perceived were better favored than themselves.

Any PPD cop who looked sidelong at the Solar Patrol for any of those reasons was a suspect, and both Joss and Evan had encountered more than enough of them since the start of this investigation. The notion of Mars for the Marsmen, a planet set aside for those who had slaved and sweated to make their adopted world one that was worth living on, was as enticing a pipe dream as any other; but it had already attracted those to whom idealism was just another tool with which to manipulate those less ruthless than themselves.

The brutality was all too familiar. It led down a path that could end with off-worlders and those not born on Mars being segregated from the pure Marsmen, being forced to wear a badge of their home planet on their clothing for easy identification. It was a path that could end with men, women and children shivering in naked lines as they were herded off to choke, for no other reason than they were different.

Joss shivered, and turned the heater of his SHEL up another notch.

WHEN THEY GOT BACK TO *ARNHEM*, MIKE THE comms officer was waiting for them. "A message came in for you both," he said, and didn't look any too happy over it. "I don't think it's good news."

Evan rolled his eyes. "That can only mean Lucretia," he said. "She's probably heard about how much the repairs on *Nosey* will cost."

"Hardly. I haven't put the estimate in yet. Come on,

man, let's not stand around guessing or we'll be here all day. It can't be any worse that she's sent us before."

"Can't it?" said Evan a few minutes later. *Arnhem*'s communications console had been fitted with the SP decoder taken from *Nosey*, and an in-clear transcription of the message was sitting in the printer tray. Evan picked it up, looked at it, and then set it back down very carefully just as he had found it, looking as if he wished he had never touched it in the first place. "It's a recall. Lucretia's taken the case out of our hands and turned it over to the PPD."

"WHAT?" Joss grabbed for the message sheet and stared at it. "She can't do that!" Even as he said the words, he knew that they were a waste of breath. Lucretia could indeed do it, and as he scanned the tersely worded note, he realized that she *had* done it.

MESSAGE BEGINS / HAVE REVIEWED MARS SITUATION AND AM MOST DISSATISFIED WITH CONTINUING LACK OF PROGRESS IN THIS CASE. TRANSFER ALL PERTINENT EVIDENCE MATERIAL TO PPD HQ WELLES CITY MARS. YOU ARE BOTH RELIEVED OF THIS DUTY AND RECALLED TO LUNA EFFECTIVE IMMEDIATE ON RECEIPT OF THIS MESSAGE. L. ESTERHAZY / AREA CMMR / SP LUNA / MESSAGE ENDS / MESSAGE ENDS

"Well, that's it," said Joss, slightly awed by the tone of the message. "Game over, do not pass Go, do not collect 100. She must be *furious.*"

Evan looked at Joss, but didn't bother passing any comment on his partner's latest weird quote. That in itself indicated just how shocked he was at the recall. "I had a feeling we should have let her know about the Sons of the Red Dawn," he said glumly, "but did I do anything about it? No . . . Put if off until you've got something concrete, Glyndower. Impress the boss. Some impression I made, eh?"

"Get on line right now," suggested Joss. "Acknowledge this, then tell her why we can't leave straight away." Even as he said it, Joss knew he was wasting his breath again. Lucretia had issued the recall not just as a Commissioner, but as an *Area* Commissioner. That meant no excuses, no arguments, no excellent reasons why not: it meant do as you're told or wave your career good-bye. If they wanted to argue the rights and wrongs of it all, they would have to do so from the other side of her desk once they got back to SPHQ. Trying it from any longer range would only breed more troubles than it would solve.

"Joss, you know I can't do that." Evan smiled sadly and levelled a finger. "And neither can you, so you can wipe that look off right now."

"Hum. I suppose." Mind racing round and round the problem in an attempt to find a way through it, Joss let his eyes go unfocused and stared at the darkness of the cold commscreen. Then he snapped back into focus again, and snapped his fingers for emphasis. "But what we can do— what we *have* to do—is write up an eyes-only emergency squirt to let her know what happened to *Nosey*, and just incidentally include all our findings to date. And then we'll ask the repair boys to work verrrry slowly so she'll have plenty of time to change her mind."

There was a moment's silence while Evan considered the suggestion from all sides, and then he started to laugh. "Chris is right," he managed through the chuckles. "You have a very sneaky mind indeed!"

"It's the company I keep," said Joss primly, but he looked pleased all the same. It was decided, after a few minutes discussion, that Evan should draft the reply. Despite his complaints about having to compose two pieces of smarmy crap in the same day, he had the incontestable advantage of having survived having Lucretia Esterhazy as his supervisor for almost twice as long as Joss.

"That's like saying I'm better suited to train lions because I keep ferrets down my pants," grumbled Evan, but he sat down in a quiet corner of *Arnhem*'s comms area and started tapping at a keyboard. The sound was irregular, punctuated by the sharper staccato of backspace-erase, as he did his best to create something that gave all the details without reading like an excuse or a flat refusal to move, both of which would have entirely the wrong effect on Lucretia.

Then the tapping stopped altogether.

Joss locked down his own pad in mid-collate and peered around the bulkhead. Evan was holding the hard copy of Lucretia's original message between finger and thumb, staring at it very hard, and giving Joss the instant impression of a biologist confronted by a small, fascinating but thoroughly nasty specimen. "Something wrong?"

"I don't know. There might be. I can't put my finger on it, but . . . But the wording's not quite right."

Joss looked at the sheet of paper, trying to see what it was that had caught Evan's eye, and came up with a big nothing. "Are you sure?"

"No . . ." Evan put the sheet down, got to his feet and began to pace, watching it all the time. This time Joss felt he was looking at a big cat playing with a mouse, watching and waiting for it to make an attempt to escape. The sheet of paper steadfastly refused to move—but Evan pounced all the same. "Got it!" he said with great satisfaction, holding the sheet up in one hand and slapping at it with the back of the other. "Like you say, boyo, when you've had to deal with the Borgia for as long as I have, you'll start to know how she operates. And this authorization is *wrong.*"

"What?"

"All the times I've seen Lucretia's name on something, it's been 'Lucretia Esterhazy,' then the rank, then the location. It doesn't matter whether it's her signature or not—she always gets mentioned by her full name. And yet this has just the initial."

"L. Esterhazy. It's not much to go on, Evan, especially when everything else is standard—and this is a fairly tetchy message."

"When are they anything else?"

"Um. I see your point. And it's always 'Lucretia,' not 'L.'?"

"Without exception, at least in my time."

"Let me have a look at that."

Joss eyed the message sheet dubiously. Whilst he did indeed see Evan's point, it was a very small one on which to balance the success or failure of their EssPat careers. If they got it wrong, Lucretia would make certain that they paid for *Nosey*'s repairs out of their own pockets before she would authorize a single expense voucher—

"Bingo!"

"Excuse me?"

"It's a fake!" Joss waved the message excitedly under Evan's nose, and might have danced a jig had the Comms officer not glanced round the corner to see what all the fuss was about. "There's nothing here about expenses! Not so much as a murmur. When did the Borgia ever miss a chance to tweak us about expenses?"

"When there was nothing worth tweaking," said Evan.

"Oh no, no. When that happens, she goes on about 'why can't we be so careful all the other times.' I've never paid much attention to the way she signs her name, but you can't ignore having little bits pulled off yourself just because you gathered evidence by buying someone dinner!" A thought struck him, and his grin got even wider. "And look at the time stamp. When she was supposed to be writing this, she'd have known that you'd upped the information reward to twenty-five thou. Do you still think she wouldn't have mentioned it?"

"Put that way, I think in a recall worded like this one she'd have chewed my head off—and yours for not vetoing me." Evan gazed at the time stamp, then at the other six-figure routing codes, then at Joss. "You're supposed to be the smart half of this team," he said. "Prove it. Check these, and find out where this came from. And while you're at it, check that Saturn message. Now I think about it, poor Lucretia got a single-letter mention there as well."

"Saturn, then Luna." Joss abruptly stopped smiling. "If we're right about this being false, then somebody's trying to get us off Mars. I suppose we should be grateful that they're trying to persuade us to leave under our own power, rather than on top of another bomb." He sat down at the console, prepared to erase Evan's carefully worded report; then decided to take no chances, and saved it instead.

He erased it less than five minutes later, swearing softly under his breath in time with the keystrokes that replaced it with his latest findings. "These routing codes aren't right. Look at this." He pointed at one grouping.

"1:104/424. Now what the hell is this message doing coming through *there?* That's the SPNet comms node facility on Deimos. And a *primary* routing to that node, too! That's idiotic. Messages from the Moon route through 1:10/0, at Eagle Base, always; *then* outward. No one as cost-crazy as Lucretia is going to send a call straight to Deimos, when the time saving is only three minutes. You might as well send a letter down the street by way of Hong Kong! And the system won't let you. The SP would be broke in a week if everyone tried to route their messages direct. Instead they bundle them all together and send them in batches, to save money." He looked at the routing codes again, thought a minute, and said. "No. No. You know what this is?" He waved the paper happily. "We've found the decoder!"

"What??!"

Joss was almost dancing again. "Those sons of bitches have got it on-line! But they're not smart enough to have changed the software it's running. The satellite is certainly programmed to route messages out through the nearest SP comms node. So it *is!* The nearest one isn't on the Moon, it's on Deimos!"

"Fine," Evan said, waiting for the rush of technobabble to die down. "But where's the damned *decoder?*"

Joss looked at him, and deflated slightly. "Uh . . . somewhere on Mars."

"Thank you, Doctor Science," Evan said gently. "Let's go find Chris."

CHRIS HUNTLEY SWIVELLED COMFORTABLY BACK and forth in a gunnery controller's chair as she listened first to Joss and then to Evan. They were sitting in similar chairs, but embarrassment had kept them bolt upright, and comfort was the last thing in either man's mind. Huntley wasn't helping. There was a lazy, good-humored mockery in the way she swung to and fro, to and fro, with her lower lip nipped between her teeth. Then the chair swung farther than she intended and bounced from its stop so that she nipped a little too hard. "Ouch. I gotta break that habit. It hurts." She rubbed her jaw and considered options. "So none of the EssPat coded communications are safe until this thing's been recovered?"

"None." Joss tried not to sound apologetic, but in the circumstances it was rather difficult. "It's been programmed with the parameter variables for every machine-generated code we use, and a few that aren't in service yet."

"Using stuff that's not in service seems like a habit with the Red Dawn. It's another habit we'll have to break. Along with shooting people and blowing up their towns." Chris shrugged. "There's another tiny little matter that might not have occurred to you yet. Space Forces use the same code variables. Red Dawn can listen in on any damned ship in the fleet, and if they finally decide to have themselves a revolution, they can be ready and waiting for everything we try to put in orbit before the vessels even get there!"

"Oh, that's just *great!*" said Evan bitterly. "It's exactly what that mob of crazies would use it for."

"And they captured it . . . how?" Chris's voice was sweet as syrup. "Because for its field tests, it was mounted in—let me get this straight—a lightly armed, unescorted ship." Joss and Evan looked at one another, but not at her, and that was answer enough. "Cost-cutting, I guess. Hoo, boy. Way to go, Accounts and Auditing."

A "full and frank" discussion of expenditure between Lucretia and this one would be a thing to overhear, thought Joss, and only just managed to keep the resultant smile off his face. "Your Comms officer said something earlier about a signal trace," he said. "Could I find out if that was running while our supposed recall was coming in?"

"Sure." She thumbed the comm unit on the gunnery console. "Huntley to Ford. Yo, Mike. You there?"

"Here, boss."

"Did your tracer pick up on that last incoming?"

"Wait one— Uh, yeah, it did. Will I put it up?"

"On your own screen. Officer O'Bannion's coming down presently. Full assistance, Mike."

"Understood, boss. Comms, listening out."

"Out." Huntley closed the channel, then looked curiously at the sops. "Joss, Evan, indulge me. What have you in mind?"

"The satellite's still on Mars," said Evan. "The routing codes it's using prove that. And anyway, the hijackers wouldn't risk compromising their possession by putting it back into orbit while we're still searching. And if they turn out to have some connection with the Red Dawn, then their requirements are going to be sufficiently localized that it might as well stay on the surface. We already know that it works from ground level. The trick now is to find out from where. Joss?"

"If these two fake signals were transmitted from the surface of Mars, then using the comms tracer I can track it through whichever comsat bounced the original transmission, and by triangulating from the SP comms nodes on Phobos and Deimos, I ought to be able to locate the original source."

Commander Huntley grinned at him. "I love it when you talk dirty," she said, and laughed when Joss's ears went pink. "Let me know when you've got it nailed, and we'll take *Arnhem* over for a look."

"Chris, now you're forgetting things," said Evan. "Remember what I told you about the rail-gun? And what happened to *Nosey?*"

"Hm. Quite." Joss watched in fascination as the studied languor vanished as though turned off with a switch. Huntley swung both feet to the floor, sat up straight and became all cool business. "If they didn't miss your little ship, this big brute would be cold meat. But I'm not going in without recon. Suggestions?"

"It took us three days to weasel satellite photos from the Space Forces," Joss said, and did a very creditable job of keeping his voice free of annoyance at the memory. "Could you do it any faster?"

"Three days?" Chris stared at him and blinked several times. "Whose side do they think they're on? I think I could improve on that by several orders of magnitude. You go do your triangulation and give me some coordinates, and I'll give you some pictures in, say, half an hour."

Joss sat quite still for several seconds as he absorbed

that piece of information; then stood up, thanked Chris nicely, and went off to Comms before he said something about Space Forces that everyone would regret. He was back in a few minutes, swearing slightly, but at the same time looking considerably more cheerful that he had done when he left.

"Observe the detective," said Evan drily. "He has detected something, and is therefore pleased with himself; but at the same time it is a clue so obvious that he feels foolish, hence his bad language."

Joss pulled a face. Evan had defined the situation only too well, because the triangulation—which had worked perfectly—had served only to confirm that the transmission site of the false messages was in exactly the same area as the mysterious contrails on his previous set of hard-won reconnaissance photos, which in turn was the area in which his vehicle bug had gone dead. If it hadn't been for that damned tank, they might have found the decoder by now, and be away from here. Except of course that it wasn't quite that simple anymore. Not with Helen Mary Cameron still unaccounted for. And her father, of course, and the crew of the EssPat research ship. And the Sons of the Red Dawn weren't exactly something that a Solar Patrol officer could could just walk away from either. One way or another, this business had to be settled, and probably by the use of superior firepower. The only drawback was that he wasn't at all sure right now of just whose firepower was superior, and he had a nasty suspicion that it might not be the Good Guys.

COMMANDER HUNTLEY WAS AS GOOD AS HER word. The satellite images starting coming down only twenty minutes after the relevant birds had been programmed, and everyone aboard *Arnhem* who could get to the main briefing room crowded in to watch as the pictures were beamed straight to its big viewscreen.

At first there was nothing but the russet expanse of the Martian outback; but that was before Huntley's Intelligence officer started work on the screen's control console.

As Joss had done to Evan's record of the Tombstone ware-house just before its explosion, so Lieutenant Yamata fed in thermographic, radar, IR and laser scans until at last, after some twiddling, he found what they were looking for.

"Caves?" said Evan, staring. "Dammit, no wonder the bug went dead. It's not meant to transmit through solid rock."

Through at least fifty meters of solid rock, he might have said. The scanners were giving a reading of at least that thickness before the single tunnel from the surface opened out into a warren of other caves and passageways. Surface visuals showed nothing at all, not even the presumed entrance, and it was only the other sensor feeds that indicated the extent of the cavern complex. They also showed the presence of large masses of metal; some of those were tagged as possible power sources, others were unknown.

"How accurate are these deep-penetration shots?" he asked after a few minutes more of watching in silence. "Are they representations, or just estimations?"

Yamata tapped at his keyboard and studied the small readout on top of it. "Given the present atmospheric conditions, we're getting something like eighty percent accuracy over the entire scan area, with a fluctuation of five percent each way."

"Can that be improved," asked Joss, "or are the atmospherics beyond control?"

"This is a real-time link, Officer O'Bannion," said the Intelligence Officer. "I can request an optical zoom, and you'll see the effects on-screen in about twelve seconds. Name your target."

"All right, let's try a closer look at where the entrance ought to be. Set up for a two-second delay on the screen transfer, then compensate with animation. I want to see if anything's moving down there."

They watched the stop-animated images flicker past without change for a good quarter hour. Joss blinked a little, and stifled a yawn behind his hand. *This isn't working. It's always the quarter hours that get me. Long enough that you think you're wasting your time, not long enough to justify chucking the whole thing.* Apart from anything

else, it wouldn't look very good if the man who had re-
quested this close-up treatment left in the middle of it; but
it would look even worse if he should fall asleep. Then
something went *ping!* and a legend at the top of the screen
read: MOTION SENSOR ACTIVE: TRACKING.

A computer-created dot of blue light crawled along the
screen from left to right, and that was all—until quite suddenly the dot was resting on top of a vehicle that had
emerged apparently from solid rock. It was a skimmer, one
of the heavy load-bearing vehicles rather than the lighter
five-people-and-luggage versions that were more common
around Tombstone; but even in that near-vertical plan view
Joss felt a stirring of recognition. He switched on his pad,
keyed in the appropriate instruction, and whistled softly.
The sound was still enough to attract attention throughout
the briefing room, and he held the pad so that everyone
could see a tracker-trace winking on its screen. "I bugged
that one in Tombstone, two days ago," he said. "We were
trailing it this morning, when it vanished from our screens.
Now we know why. And where."

That started a flurry of animated discussion amongst the
Triple-A personnel in the briefing room. Some of them
were all for sealing the tunnel mouth with a few kilotons
delivered by missile, and then going in at leisure to find
out what was down there—a suggestion vetoed in some
haste by Joss, who hadn't thought to explain that there
were prisoners somewhere in the complex. A couple of
troopers promptly volunteered to go in and get them out.
And in all the cross-chat, nobody heard the motion sensor
go off again, until somebody happened to glance at the
screen.

"Shit on a shingle! How many of those things do they
have?"

Heads turned, and the room suddenly went very, very
quiet. There was always something primeval and unstop-
pable about a tank, and never more so than when you
knew just how much bigger, faster and more heavily
armed it was, compared to you. This one looked bigger
than most; it was certainly faster; and both Joss and Evan
had personal experience of how heavily it was armed.

"Never mind how many they've got," said Chris. "What

are we going to do about them? Bearing in mind, by the way, that there's a rail-gun mounted on that turret." She left her troopers mulling that one over, and turned to Joss and Evan. "Right. We're going in, and Commissioner Esterhazy can backdate permission for it once we're able to ask her. Until your decoder's back in EssPat hands, I'm putting this ship on strict comm silence. That all right with you two?"

"It's very all right," said Evan. Though they had both intended that the Triple-A should provide fire-support, Chris Huntley's brisk approach was giving them a definite feeling that events were running out of their control.

"Switch your pad on, then, and record this. Be it known that I, Christine E. Huntley, officer commanding 1st Battalion Airborne Armoured Assault Group, do hereby induct this unit to act in assistance of the Civil Power, being officers E. H. Glyndower and J. D. O'Bannion, Solar Patrol. Day 224, coordinated Mars year 2068, at, uh . . ." Her confidence faltered ever so slightly, and at last she turned to yell at the room in general. "What the hell's the time!?"

"I DON'T *WANT* TO WEAR A SUIT!" SAID JOSS, aware even as the words left his mouth that he sounded like some little kid refusing to be dressed up for a visit to Granny's house.

"You're wearing a suit whether you like it or not," said Evan in a tone that suggested he wouldn't listen to any further argument on the subject. "Being almost blown up once is unfortunate; letting it happen twice is inconsiderate to your employers. And to your friends. You expect me to carry you *everywhere?* Put the damned thing on."

Joss muttered something under his breath about his mother not raising him to be an armadillo, but he did as he was told. Even in the midst of his dislike, he had to be impressed by the way in which the armor fitted together, with him snugly packed at the core of it like the yolk inside an egg. The Triple-A's maintenace squad had taken as much time as they could spare to ensure that the suit's interior padding fitted with a reasonable degree of comfort, apologizing at the same time that it wouldn't be anything like a custom job. For something he'd never worn until now, it was a remarkably good and easy fit, and he found himself wondering what a proper made-to-measure unit would feel like—before he squashed the thought back into oblivion. He didn't *like* suits . . .

Much.

Then the lectures started. Weapons systems, defense systems, powerpack, life-support, feedback modulation . . . "And how do you, er, switch it on?" Joss asked innocently, halfway through the lecture on helm and vision augmentation.

Evan smiled at him. "That comes after the lectures are finished," he said. "Now pay attention!"

Joss, unable to walk, or even to reach enough of its catches to release himself from his snugly-padded prison, could only swear. *Arnhem*'s deck vibrated gently beneath the soles of his graflar-sheathed feet as the assault ship lifted clear of Tombstone's pad. They were heading back to FAF Sydenham—or at least, they would do so until the ship simulated a landing approach over the base and then, underneath whatever sensor array might have been tracking them, would head out towards where the Sons of the Red Dawn would be settling down for a good night's sleep.

"Beamers, now," said Evan briskly, and Joss didn't bother suppressing his groan.

"What about them?"

"They're not dangerous. At least, not much, and not if you keep your head—"

"Oh, very droll."

"—head *down*, Joss boyo. Let the man finish."

"All right, then. Tell me all about beamers."

"They won't and can't damage you unless you're a damn fool who likes to admire the scenery during a firefight. That's why suits have a mirror finish. Beam weapons have to nibble that reflec coating off before they start ablating the armor underneath. Even if they manage to degrade the reflec, they've got to drill through the graflar, the ceramic and the staballoy, and they can't do that unless you stand still and let them."

Joss had seen the way Evan had outmaneuvered the tank and its rail-gun—in fact the thought of it still made him slightly travel-sick—and knew just what his partner was on about. It was just that he went on, and on, and on . . .

"You'll need a respray afterwards, and about three liters of water to replace lost sweat," Evan said with a horrible cheeriness that made Joss feel like hitting him, if he had been able to move either of his arms, that is. "And you'll need to strip out the loose foam pads and the ballistic liner, to give 'em a good washing. I'm afraid all that anyone can do for the rest of the foam is a good dousing with the deodorant of your choice."

"Ah. That explains what I can smell in here. I thought it was one of those goats . . ."

Evan paid no attention. "Just remember: keep moving, or keep down. It takes a lot of beamers a lot of time to take down one suit."

"Very reassuring, I'm sure. And the rail-gun?"

There was a short silence, and then Evan cleared his throat. There might have been another joke in there, but what came out was simple and deadly serious. "Don't let it hit you."

"Uh . . . right." Joss thought for a moment of something else to say; that frightful cannon was enough to put any conversation off its stride, even a one-sided one like this. "And what does this thing carry that I can use on them?"

"More than enough. Rotary miniguns here, right and left forearms—discarding-sabot staballoy, like the one I showed you. Eight thousand rpm, with two thousand rounds per gun. That gives you fifteen seconds each. It's usually plenty. Beamer of your own up here, in this shoulder-pod. It's slaved to your helm's sight with 270x of free traverse, but remember that your head blocks it to the left and you'll need to make a sort of half-turn to clear the line of fire. Then down here, lower part of the forearm fairing, are two SACLOS minimissiles each side. Again, slaved to your helm sight: keep the target centered and the missile's guidance system does the rest."

Evan stepped back, looking up; tall as he was, he had no choice since with one man suited and the other not, Joss was almost a foot taller than usual. "Satisfied?"

"Something like that." The proper word was "horrified," although in a very small way. Joss had after all lived for some time now with a suit not too unlike this one guarding his back and, twice now during this present investigation, saving his life. He found its capability for destruction unsettling, and at the same time admired the suit itself as a masterpiece of engineering. While he was putting it on, the individual pieces had slotted together with all the precision of an antique Swiss watch, the ones with springs that had to be wound, which yet kept time as well as most quartz crystals, and which were altogether more handsome to look at.

"And now," said Evan, "you learn how to walk all over again . . ."

"SP REGULATIONS OBLIGE YOU TO DO *WHAT?*"
Evan looked thoroughly uncomfortable, as any man might when confronted by a bureaucratic foolishness. "Chris, it's the law, and for you as much as us unless this turns into a full-scale war. We have to issue the mandatory warning before any shooting starts, to give them a chance to come along quietly."

"And how likely do you think that is, hmmm?"

"Not very. But."

"Yes indeed. But." Huntley looked at the two EssPat officers and shook her head in despair. "All right," she said. "Warning it is, and you can put on record the fact the CO of your armed intervention force thinks that the whole idea sucks. So much for the element of surprise. But we'll give out the warning *my* way, understood? I don't want to hear any complaining about it afterwards. You two boys can do all the arresting that you like, but my business is to make sure that the Sons of the Red Dawn are put out of commission with minimal and preferably no damage to my own troops. Clear?"

"Clear," said Joss. "And thanks."

Huntley smiled sourly. "Thank me afterwards," she said. "Your people owe me one. And you two owe me several drinks."

Joss watched her stalk away down *Arnhem*'s troop-deck, then glanced at Evan and grinned a little bit. It wasn't because of Commander Huntley's reaction to being told her carefully planned night attack would start with a shout of "This is the police!"; there was nothing funny about that at all, and the warning rule had definitely been cooked up by one of those cretinous legal eagles with more concern for the robbers than the robbed. What amused him right now was the faintly strangulated look on his partner's face.

Like Joss, Evan was armored to the neck in the latest mark of military exosuit, and should have been the very image of a man whose dearest dreams have been fulfilled. Instead he looked just as uncomfortable as Joss, and possibly more so. Joss had his own very good reasons for not liking what he was wearing, because despite Evan's lectures, demonstrations and assistance, his first experience of handling a suit's negative feedback circuitry had become—very literally—a crash course. He had broken several things, although fortunately none of them had been bones, his or anyone else's, and now he could at least walk in the wretched thing without posing a hazard to life, limb and property.

Evan, on the other hand, was able to make powered armor do everything its specifications claimed and then a little more. He had been grousing about the inadequacies of his stripped-down suit—the "monkey model," he called it, and not with affection—since before Joss had been partnered with him. Now he was back in harness; full battle harness, with more weapons at his disposal than his old suit had places to stow them, and he looked as if he would rather be anywhere but inside it.

"Evan, what's the matter with you?"

Glyndower made a curious up-and-down bob inside the suit before he replied. "I don't like this suit," he said at last.

Joss suppressed a grin. "That's my line. Come on, it's got everything you ever saw in the movies. Guns, missiles, a beamer—you've even got the grenade launcher and the smoke dispensers."

Evan gave him a look that fell short of murderous only

because it caught its toe in the carpet. "That's the point. It's overpowered, overgunned—"

"Over here?"

"Overpowering! I never thought I'd say this about a military suit, but they've taken it just a bit far. They've made it needlessly complicated. All this stuff: you could get shot while you're making up your mind which gun to use, and if you don't remember the control functions just so, you could fry yourself to a crisp when all you want to do is light a cigarette."

"They always did say smoking wasn't healthy. It's just as well you don't."

"That's as may be. But some silly sod's still gone and changed some of the function codes." Evan glowered, bobbing up and down again. "What used to set the guns to single-shot now activates the beamer. Try disarming a perp by shooting the gun out of his hand with one slug, and you'll disarm him good and proper. Like right up to the shoulder."

Joss shook his had, saying nothing because his mouth was pressed tight shut as he struggled not to laugh out loud. Finally he gave up, threw back his head and roared until the tears ran down his cheeks.

"It doesn't even *smell* right," Evan grumbled, so that Joss only laughed the harder. "That nasty, plasticky, new sort of smell . . ."

"And what you're trying to say is that, is that," Joss fought the laughter down to an unsteady hiccuping noise, "is that your nice new suit with all its bells and whistles chafes you right in the crotch . . ."

Evan went scarlet, right up into his crewcut, and glared until the glare crumbled and became a grin. "You wait, boyo. Just you wait. But it's true." Once the admission was made, he too began to laugh. "It's a hard thing for a man going into battle to feel like he's wearing the wrong size in shorts. One jump at the wrong time, Joss *bach,* and it's me for the soprano section of the choir!"

Joss stared at his partner and friend, and a quote crept sneakily up from the back of his mind. He choked slightly; it wouldn't be fair. But then Evan wouldn't know it for a quote, now would he? "Then ... go and change your armor!" he said, and started to break up.

Evan stared at him with great dignity. "I always wondered. Just what *is* the airspeed velocity of an unladen swallow?" And having claimed game, set and match by leaving Joss without a breath to call his own, he strolled off to his drop position.

MIDNIGHT, MARS TIME. THE SKY, STAR-LADEN, had the velvety black quality that came with a thin atmospheric envelope. It softened the blackness and made the empty void less desolate. Occasionally, up in that void, a star would venture to twinkle—although more usually, it was no more than an orbiting satellite catching the distant sunlight or a ship powering up from Welles or Herschel.

Arnhem came in low and fast, with her turrets cleared for free suppressive fire should it be needed. The ship was travelling at Mach z3 less than fifty meters above the icy Martian desert, and as she passed over the entrance to the Red Dawn redoubt, her dark outline bloomed silver as she dumped micrometric chaff filaments right where they would do most good. The troopers of 1st Triple-A came down of the middle of the chaff cloud in a widely dispersed fall pattern, and for a few seconds as their braking-rockets fired, the surface of Mars seemed as full of stars as the night sky overhead.

Joss O'Bannion wriggled his way out of the rocket-pack's webbing. The thing was one-shot and disposable, fitted with an altimeter to tell it when to fire and an inclinometer to tell it which way was up and down. As Joss struggled with it in the dark, it appeared the thing was also fitted with more straps, buckles, harnesses and other inconveniences than any six seat belts, and it was growing more all the time. Finally he freed himself from the pack's elaborate embrace, and gratefully kicked it out from underfoot before dropping out of sight behind a handy rock.

Joss raised his head cautiously, wondering where Evan was, and whether the big man had managed to ease the padding in his suit before the drop. There was no sign of

life anywhere: the other troopers had all gone belly-down
a long time before him, and the Sons of the Red Dawn apparently hadn't risen yet, despite the noise of the assault
ship overhead.

His commset clicked twice, right in his ear, and he carefully went through the sequence of chin-operated toggles
that controlled its volume. *Arnhem* was coming back to
deliver the warning—and then if its pilot had any sense at
all, he would get over the horizon before something termi-
nally nasty happened to his ship.

"ATTENTION!" boomed a huge voice. Even in a suit,
even with his ears swaddled by the earpieces of a commset
that was shut right down, Joss felt as though his brain
would push its way out through his eyesockets. Chris had
warned them all before the drop that *Arnhem* would use its
onboard screamer system, linked through to a voder on the
bridge. The troopers had laughed, Evan had looked grimly
amused—and Joss had needed explanations. The scream-
ers, it transpired, were simply noise-generators; hi-fi bass
drivers bloated to obscene proportions. They were used to
suppress enemy activity around a selected landing zone in
situations where free fire was inappropriate, and they did
it at 240 dB. Joss had often been in places where he
couldn't hear himself think; but without protection from
this sort of noise, someone might not even hear themselves
exist . . .

"ATTENTION! THIS IS THE SOLAR PATROL! YOU
ARE UNDER ARREST! THROW DOWN YOUR
WEAPONS AND SURRENDER, OR WE OPEN FIRE!"
It sounded like the voice of God on a particularly bad day,
and when it fell silent, the bellow of *Arnhem*'s engines as
she accelerated down-range was a whisper in a great
clanging stillness.

As the pounding faded from his skull, Joss was consumed by curiosity. There was still no sign that Red Dawn
existed as other than a bad dream, and he dismissed the
possibility that they were far enough belowground to have
missed all the excitement. Unless they had all retired into
the heart of the bunker and killed themselves, in the tradition of fanatics whose cause is lost. That too was unlikely,
because the uproar of the past few seconds would not

merely have wakened the dead, it would have brought them out to complain about the noise.

Joss smiled briefly at the notion of a skull with its finger-bones shoved into the holes where its ears had been; macabre, but silly. Then something moved, as one of the Triple-A troopers climbed warily upright and surveyed the dark terrain. *He has to be using thermal or IR.* Resting his chin lightly on the toggles all around the bottom of the helm, Joss tried to remember how to bring up his own enhanced night-vision. *Not toggles this time. It's a movement of the scalp muscles. I think. Oh boy. Next time, if there is a next time, either Evan doesn't talk as fast, or I take notes. Now, how does it operate?*

More suited figures rose from the shadows, and Joss wondered that he hadn't heard any command to advance—then remembered, with a little flutter of private embarrassment, that he hadn't switched his commset back on yet. As he moved his head to operate the toggles, Joss let his gaze wander past the troopers and out towards where the entrance to the tunnel was presumed to be. It was well hidden, both by deliberate camouflage and by the uncertain darkness that was beginning to play tricks with Joss's eyes. *Nightsight, nightsight, where the hell's my nightsight,* he thought. Uncertain of exactly what to do, and made wary by Evan's warning about changes in the suit control functions, Joss was reluctant to try anything that might have an unfortunate result. Suits being what they were, he was thoroughly connected below the waist to some industrial-grade plumbing, and had absolutely no desire to give himself a case of hot and cold flushes.

Oh well, I'll just sit in the dark . . .

And then he sat up very straight in the dark, because night vision or not, he could see something moving that wasn't a suit. First impressions suggested a landslip; but there was no tremor in the ground, and not even in Martian gravity would loose soil slide uphill. It was sliding all in a piece . . .

"Incoming!" Joss yelled, and saw the upright suits go flat again in the instant that the first concealed beamer opened fire. Bolts of energy ripped through the darkness, and then Joss felt himself slammed backwards as somebody zeroed him with a slugthrower. The noise was more of a shock than the impact, for although he had thought no sound would ever impress him with its loudness ever again, there was a horrible intimacy about the clattering that reverberated through the structure of his suit. Pushed off balance by the stream of high-velocity slugs, Joss toppled over backwards, and only when he was safely below the line of fire did he creep forward again into the shelter of his friendly rock.

Joss raised his head gingerly and peered around him. None of the helm's enhancement gear was running yet, except for the polarization of its visor, and what he saw, he saw with the naked eye. It looked like a Breughel vision of Hell—assuming that the painter had access to a particularly bad batch of lysergic acid diethylamide. He had seen particle beamers in use before—his own Remington for one—but he had never been under fire from massed military-grade energy weapons. Despite their heavy caliber and awesome rate of fire, the military slugthrowers were almost mundane by comparison.

There seemed to be weapon emplacements everywhere; hidden beneath camouflaged lids that were apparently proof against the various grades of sensor scan as well as visual inspection, they were opening like the dwellings of a particularly aggressive breed of gopher. Lances of actinic light stabbed from them, ripping through the air with that unmistakeable sound of a point-blank thunderclap and for the very same reason. They were terrifying.

"Just remember," Evan had said, "keep moving, or keep down. It takes a lot of beamers a lot of time to take down one suit."

Great stuff, thought Joss miserably. *Very inspiring. But what the hell am I supposed to do when they've got a lot of beamers and I'm running out of things to hide behind?*

And then he saw the rail-gun, coming up out of its subterranean redoubt like a dragon from its lair. Its bore was at least a foot across, and the barrel was about as wide as a real barrel would have been; there was a great fat bulge at the far end, over its rotating pedestal—the housing for its reloading and primary firing mechanisms *Putting that part of it out would be a good thing to do,* Joss thought.

But the thing will be pretty well armored. At least it would be if I had built it— There was also a large rounded area down at the bottom of the gun's rotating pedestal. *Crew shielding?* Joss thought. *Possibly. Look at that slit there—*

It suddenly occurred to Joss that one reason he could see the bore of the rail-gun so well was that it was pointing at him.

"Shit!" he said, and jumped. He jumped too hard, and came down on the rocks with a sound like a pile of dropped Tupperware; and a slug about a foot wide and massing at least a kilogram went by over his head. It went by so fast that the thunderclap of its firing didn't come along after it for about a second and a half. *Let's see,* said the Mr. Science part of him, *a thousand one—no, never mind that. Air density makes that one useless. But at, what is it, thirty-two feet per second per second—*

He jumped again, which was just as well, because the barrel of the gun had whipped around with surprising speed to lock onto him again. *Much better traverse motors on that one,* he thought. *Has to do with it being fixed, I suppose. The ones mounted on moving vehicles have more of a problem with torque. Possibly also they haven't fully solved the recoil problem yet—*

Ouch! He came down wrong again, on his bottom this time. The bottoms of Triple-A suits, Joss discovered, were inadequately cushioned. He said bad words and got up again, wondering what to do.

The other suits were bouncing all over the place, doing their best to be moving targets, usually succeeding ... sometimes not. Joss was horrified to see that big gun come whipping around, angling down, and fire. Thunder cracked, and six hundred yards away, the suit talent at the other end of the projectile's trajectory offered no resistance to the projectile, none at all. One minute there was a man in a suit; the next minute there was a man in a suit with a burning hole a foot wide through its chest. The man fell in a fog of blood, and the suit, already fractured by the impact of the projectile, simply shattered like glass on the stones.

I'm in a war, Joss thought in increasing horror. *Not just another shootout with some crooks. A real war. The Forces of Civilization against the Forces of Ultimate Evil. Or Freedom Fighters against the Running-Dog Lackeys of the State.* He shuddered. It rarely boded well for anybody when even one side started thinking in capital letters like that. *Both* sides, and you had a real problem . . .

Joss desperately wanted to go join a group of suits, as much for advice as for shelter; but that seemed a bad idea. Staying single and footloose seemed the best way to keep from getting other people killed along with you. He kept moving the best he could, and fired at the rail-gun with his beamer. He soon realized that a peashooter would have been about as effective. The thing was mirror-finished all down its barrel and reload end, as well armored against beams as the suits were. *Something a little more solid, maybe,* Joss thought. *Have I got any missiles in this thing?*

He alternated bouncing around and trying to remember which of the controls Evan had shown him did what. It was possible Evan had a point—that there were too many of them. When he finally got the little menu to display in his helm, he had to stare at it for almost a minute before he could even begin to find the missile submenu. *Aha, there we go. Let's see. Right hand, inward, twist out, view, point—*

The rail-gun whipped around and took out another suit. The conversation on the suit channels was very terse—everyone wanted to get close to the thing, but no one was certain how to do it without suddenly being provided with a foot-wide hole in their middle. there was no doubt that this gun's firing predictors had been installed with suits in mind. And a sudden movement off to one side showed another of the "tanks" coming out, firing; firing fast, this one, slugs coming out of it about one a second. All over the area, people in suits dropped to the ground—

The barrel of the big gun swept off to one side, pointing away from Joss, and he thought, *Now here's a possibility—* He jumped out and up, hard. *Oh dear*—rather too hard; before he knew what he was doing, he was ascending to about three hundred feet in the light gravity. *Shit!* he thought, kicking gracefully though uncertainly, rather like someone playing Peter Pan on opening night. But this did him no good; he continued to accelerate until the force of his original jump petered out. Then he started to fall, gracefully again, like a leaf in the autumn; and not without seeing, first the barrel of the tank, then that of the rail-gun, both come swinging around to lock on him.

"Yikes!" he said, and did the first thing he thought of: fired something. It was his gatling, and the kick of its firing knocked him off center in the air, and slightly backwards.

A piece of the world about the size of his head went by him, and the thundercrack and shockwave of its passing knocked him right down into the ground. He fell on his bottom again.

Joss was beginning to feel physically the way he had after his father first caught him smoking in the garage when he was nine; and this annoyed him. He had thought the whole idea of suit combat was to leave *you* cool, comfortable and unbruised, while the people around you, the bad guys, got hot, bothered and black and blue. *Something isn't working here,* he thought crossly, and got up and jumped again. *Oh shit!*

He had done it too hard again, and put too much english on it; he was heading straight at the big rail-gun, on an ascending arc. *Not what I had in mind!!* He twisted and kicked again as that big barrel came around—and then remembered the gatling, and fired it again, behind him and upward, hard. The firing forced him down and forward, much faster. In fact, he was coming down next to the barrel of the rail-gun. *Oh no,* he thought, and fired the gatling again in the other direction, but it didn't seem to be helping; he was too close to the pedestal of the gun—

"Joss!" Evan shouted at him on comms. *"Jesus Christ, man—"*

"O'Bannion, what the fuck are you doing?" came Chris's voice, slightly frantic and very annoyed. *"Have you got a deathwish? GET DOWN!"*

"I'm trying, I'm trying!" Joss said: and got down, hard, on his rear end again—just to one side of the traverse pedestal of the rail-gun, and entirely too close to the shielded area in the back with the slit. All somebody had to do now was stick a missile launcher out that slit and blow his aching rear end to hell.

He scrambled to his feet and jumped again, off to one side. "Hey, I think I'm getting the hang of it," he said as he came down on his feet—

—right under the barrel of the rail-gun as it shot. He actually felt the hot wash of the plasma bloom as the gun fired, and then the shockwave of the projectile knocked him on his ass again.

He got up. "I do not like this," he said to the world at large, very slowly. Joss walked, did not bounce, around the pedestal, viewing the little menu as he went. *The gatling sure works,* he thought. *But where are those missiles? They told me there were missiles.*

He stopped not far away from the slit. Two faces with horrified expressions visible through their SHELs were staring through the slit at him.

"Right," Joss said, "sorry, guys," and he lifted his arm and raked the slit with the gatling.

The faces abruptly vanished.

He made his way around the curved wall with the slit, and found its entrance, up the back of the gun. Joss jumped up to it and went into the operators' area.

He pushed the bodies aside and bent over the controls. "Let's see," he muttered. There was a normal firing yoke, very like *Nosey*'s, with the standard thumb-trigger. Off to one side was a large targeting screen, very clear, with crosshairs and what looked like a convergent-sighting system. *Okay, I think I've got it.* Joss thumbed the trigger.

SYSTEM ERROR, said the screen, and then restored the original view. Above it was a herald that said, in blinking yellow letters, ENGAGE RELOAD CYCLE. Off to one side, a yellow light was blinking above a button.

"Made for idiots, thank heaven," Joss said, and hit the button. The whole platform shuddered as something went *clunk* in the gun ahead of him. RELOAD CYCLE COMPLETE, said the letters on the screen, now in green.

"Aw *right,*" Joss said delightedly. "Now then—"

"Joss? Joss, what's going on—"

"Not right now, Evan," he said, slewing the gun around to get the feel of it. It didn't answer its controls quite as quickly as he might have thought; the white sight-target of the gun moved to a given target before the gun itself followed. It seemed to take about three seconds.

He looked around for the tank, saw it fire and shatter another suit and its occupant. "Goddamn," he said, and wrestled the yoke around. It was fighting him: apparently the gun liked to stay sighted on one spot for a least a second or so. And suddenly he saw the tank slow to a halt, and its barrel starting to swing toward him.

"Oh jeez," he said. Out there among the stones, on the screen, he could see a suit coming toward him, low and fast: Evan. "Shit no," he muttered, and struggled with the yoke again. *Come on, come on!* "Evan, don't! GET DOWN!" He didn't want Evan to get caught in the bloom of this thing.

Evan hesitated, then dropped. Joss gave the yoke one last furious jerk as he watched the barrel of the tank coming closer and closer to being aimed at him. The white coincident-image marker edged toward the tank—edged, and then jumped—

"Fill your hands, you sonofabitch!" Joss said softly, and fired.

At twenty kilometers or better per second, anything seems to happen instantaneously. The tank caught fire, leapt into the air, and exploded, all at once; and pieces of it rained down onto the stones in a most satisfactory manner. The tank was history. Or possibly geography . . .

Joss laughed low in his throat, then wondered why the firing yoke suddenly felt so strange. He looked at it, and found that he had crushed it with his gauntlet.

"Oh well," he muttered, "easy come, easy go. Chris?" he said.

"Joss," the answer came back, *"it's plain God is saving you for hanging. You utter, complete asshole, you dimbrained, microcephalic—"*

"Chris, if it's okay with you, I think I should get down from here so you can blow this thing up."

"You do that right now. Jump as high as you like. Just jump away from Arnhem, will you please? Targeting—"

Joss scrambled out of the gun's firing area and onto the pedestal. Off at the edge of the horizon, the big dark curve of *Arnhem* was shouldering up like some deadly planet.

How can a ship that looked so friendly before, Joss wondered, *look so nasty now?* But truly he didn't mind. He crouched a bit and jumped hard and (he hoped) relatively flat, away from there.

As he passed, he saw Evan get up and jump to match him, though more skillfully, of course. Joss was becoming very pleased with himself. he was feeling a lot less like Mary Martin, and a lot more like a real suit talent—

The ground came up to meet him too fast. Joss fell down on his ass again, and began to swear most horribly.

Beside him, Evan landed neatly and crouched down too. *"God takes care of drunks, children and suit virgins,"* he said, at the same time as Chris said, *"All personnel clear. Flash warning. Five seconds."*

"What?" Joss said.

And then the world whited out, and he knew.

It was a very small mushroom cloud he saw when they stood up. *"Just a tactical,"* Evan said. *"A doorknocker. Let's go join the rest."*

Joss swallowed and bounced after Evan the best he could. *"All right, ladies and gentlemen,"* Chris said, *"let's party. Mind the equipment: there's a piece of it we want back. Not to mention the hostages. Go! Go! Go!"*

There was only one entrance to the caves, not far from the former location of the rail-gun. The suits stormed toward it, and Evan and Joss hurried after them. The entrance was a long, sloping tunnel; some of it looked original, some seemed to have been added, or enlarged. It was less crumbly-looking than much of the stone Joss had seen on Mars, and looked more igneous than sedimentary—

Then people started shooting at them, and he forgot about the rocks.

They had come out into a large cavern, with tunnels leading to other caverns further down and in. The place seemed alive with people in SHELs, shooting at them with guns and beams. But not for long. The suits were in their element here, and scattered around the place, mowing down anything that fired first. There were two or three more tanks in this big cavern, and missiles flew from some of the suits, ruining the tanks' rail-guns before they could be made useful.

Suddenly it was very quiet. Joss stood there looking around him. Nothing moved but people in suits.

More sounds of gunfire came from further down in those tunnels. *"Take your time, kids,"* came Chris's voice. *"I want the place secured in order. Find out where that gunfire's coming from. Are all the tanks out of it now?"*

"All the ones here," said one of Chris's people.

"Good. Proceed."

Joss looked around at the ruined tanks and the bodies, and started to follow Evan down into the deeper tunnels—

—and stopped, staring at the wall.

"Good Lord," he said, "what's that?"

Evan paused and looked back. "What's what?"

Joss pointed at the wall. "That."

It was an immense wall carving, rudely done. A half-circle, with seven concentric half-arcs above it, each one with a round shape strung on it like a bead. The eighth and ninth half arcs were out of skew.

"It's a diagram," Joss said. "A diagram of the solar system!"

"Yes, well—" Evan started to head off again.

Joss stopped him. "Evan, for pity's sake, look! Look at the rest of the wall!"

Evan did, and Joss heard him suck in a breath. The whole rest of the cavern wall was covered with carvings, some delicate, some bold, some simply enhancing the shape of the native stone.

"Martian!" Joss breathed.

Evan shook his head. 'If it is—" He headed off again. "We'll deal with it later. Joss, come on!"

The sound of gunfire and beams from below was getting louder. They followed the noise down the central tunnel, where the main force of suits had gone, and around a curve into another cavern.

This one was just like the first, all carved in nested spirals and geometric patterns, every inch of it—floors, walls, ceiling—but the ceiling and the walls were being pitted with slugfire, and the floors were stained with blood. More people in SHEL were firing at the suits, and even though their fire had no effect, they weren't surrendering. Some of the suits tried to disarm the people firing at them, but the gunmen shot their own people rather than let the suits have them. After a while the suits stopped trying to take prisoners.

"One and two on the second level are secure," Chris said. *"Concentrate on three. Still some people down there. Mind the hostages!"*

Joss looked around at the second-level cavern they were in. This place looked to be used for storage, though there was some machinery around, and some computer equipment. Wiring and cables ran everywhere. *"Watch your step,"* came the voice of one of the suits. *"There are some mines down in these passageways."*

As if in answer, there came a faint boom from down one of the tunnels. *"Got one,"* said a cheerful female voice. *"They go up real nice if you shoot them."*

"Try to watch out for the wall carvings!" Joss said, rather desperately. "They're not man-made!"

There was a bit of a silence after *that.* Then Chris's voice spoke in his ear, privately. *"Joss honey,"* she said, *"you're kidding, right?"*

"I don't think so," he said. "They're nothing I recognize. And these people don't strike me as the type to sit around decorating the cave walls in their spare time."

Chris swore, hard. *"Just like those goddamn Martians,"* she said, *"leaving their artifacts in a cave full of suicidal terrorists. Joss, you do me a favor. Don't talk to me about this until we've finished here."*

Joss swallowed. "Understood."

"Good boy. Sic 'em."

The sound of more gunfire erupted from further down. "Come on," Evan said. Joss ran after him, down another tunnel, this one sloping much more steeply than the last. The cavern it opened onto was much smaller, carved as the others: and there was a great welter of computer equipment in it. And something Joss recognized, sitting sideways on a table, with a Medusa-head of wires running to it.

"It's the satellite," he breathed. "Chris!"

"I have you marked," she said calmly. *"Boswell, Mick,*

go get that thing and bring it up here now." Almost before he had time to turn around, there were two suit talents pushing past Joss and Evan and heading into the cave.

Faint shudders and booms suggested that more mines were being detonated further down. *"Fergal, Joanne, Uzi,"* Chris's voice said, *"back up a bit and start clearing those docs and machinery out of the upper caverns. Everything is evidence. Get all the solids, all the paperwork you can find. All hands, the rest of the trouble seems to be down in level three, on the right of your diagrams—"*

Evan took off, and Joss went close behind him, running down another tunnel. There was gunfire; then a scream.

A woman's scream. Joss came up even with Evan. He paused at a junction of tunnels, looked left, right, heard the scream again, went left.

There was someone running ahead of him, a guy in a SHEL. The guy turned, fired at Joss. He fired back, without thinking, being more familiar with the gatling now than anything else. The person in the SHEL fell down in two pieces.

That's for poor Joe the sheriff, Joss thought, not entirely rationally, and quite aware at the same time that he wasn't making sense. It didn't seem to matter, though. He headed on past the body, toward the room it had seemed to be heading for. Evan was close behind him. He ducked through the low doorway.

The room had been separated into several partitions by what looked like the kind of portable floor-to-ceiling screens that people used to divide up open-plan offices. Lying on the floor of the partition nearest the door were three dirty, disheveled, bruised-looking people in SP uniforms. They stared at Joss and Evan in utter astonishment.

"Space Forces?" one of them croaked.

"No, SP, actually," Joss said.

"In that?" said another of the SP crew, with a captain's flashes on her sleeves.

"Never mind," Joss said. "Are you people all right?"

"If you call being shot down and kidnapped and beaten and drugged fine," said the captain, sounding oddly cheerful about it all, "yes, we're fine. We didn't tell them more

than we could help . . . and since you're here, I don't think
it helped them much. These poor people, though—"

Joss looked in shock at what he had thought was a pile
of rags. It turned out, as the SP captain leaned over to
touch it gently, to be two people under a dirty blanket.
One of them was a bearded, tired-looking red-haired man.

The other one was Helen Mary Cameron.

"Helen Mary!" Joss said.

She stirred, let go of the man, looking at Joss with confusion. "And Andrew Cameron, I presume," Joss said.

"*Joss?*" Helen Mary said.

"In the flesh," Joss said, resisting the urge to rub those
parts of the flesh that felt the most bruised.

She smiled at him. "I told you I would find him," she
said.

"You were lucky not to be killed!"

"The Virendras spoke up for us," said Mr. Cameron."

Joss breathed out. "Gosh, I'm glad you're all right.
Where *are* the Virendras, then?"

" 'Gosh?' " Evan said, looking at him sidewise.

"Right here," said Kathy Virendra's voice, and the door
in the partition opened.

And she came in carrying a Kockler: and her father
came in behind her, doing the same.

She pointed the gun at Helen Mary and smiled genially
at Joss.

He shook his head. " 'Harry Smyth's gang', indeed," he
said. "There was never any such thing, was there? They
were all your people—keeping the whole district, maybe
this whole half of the planet, under your thumb so that no
one would get wind of what you were up to here."

She grinned at him. "I'm not going to stand here and
gloat at you," she said. "They were our people, all right.
And there are always more. You may have trashed some of
our equipment . . . but not all, not by a long shot. For the
meantime, though, I think we'll excuse ourselves and take
a few months of peace and quiet somewhere else on the
planet."

Joss shook his head in disbelief. "You really think
you're going to get out of here? For God's sake, don't try
anything stupid. We're armored!"

"They're not," Scott Virendra said cheerfully, pointing at the Camerons. "The girl is coming with us. She's our ticket out of here."

"I saw that vid," Joss said sadly. "It didn't work then. It won't work now. This place is alive with suits."

"But it will," said Kathy. "We're not acting." She smiled sweetly, then glanced down, and fired.

Andrew Cameron screamed and fell back against the wall.

"Just his knee," Kathy said. "Get back, and tell your suits to stay away from us—or *she* won't be alive much longer. Or him, or them. One at a time, till you do as you're told."

Evan and Joss looked at each other. Together, they backed away. "We've got a situation here, Chris," Evan said softly. "Pull the suits back from reference three-six-left."

There was a long pause. *"Confirmed. Pull back, all."*

The corridors outside suddenly became very quiet.

Scott Virendra was holding Helen Mary's SHEL. He tossed it to her. "Put it on."

White-faced, Helen Mary did.

Kathy looked at Joss and grinned. "You two are pretty quiet, for such high and mighty sops. Aren't you supposed to say 'You'll never get away with this?' "

Joss said nothing.

On their private channel, Evan whispered: *"Go thermal. It's H1 on the menu."*

Joss swallowed, and did it. The bright-lit room went suddenly dark except for the glow of the light-fitting and the bright-burning bodies in it: three against the wall, one slumped partly over, and standing before them, two tall blurs of light, one short.

"Bye-bye, sops," said Kathy. "See you again some time."

"Joss!" Helen Mary said, almost in a sob.

He said never a word.

Scott Virendra opened the door, pushed Helen Mary through it. Kathy grinned at them one last time, followed. The door closed.

Joss found himself looking through the wall and the door at three shapes, slightly dimmed, two tall, one short.

"Fire," Evan said softly.

Evan did it with a burst almost too short to register as more than a single shot. Joss couldn't keep his that short.

Two shapes of light on the other side of the wall crumpled down, collapsed, sprayed the far side of the wall with something warm that glowed faintly. One remained standing, and covered her face with her hands.

From the other two shapes, the light began, very slowly, to fade.

"Good-bye, Kathy," Joss said quietly, matter-of-factly, and went to open the door.

"IT'S TRUE ENOUGH, OF COURSE," EVAN SAID TO him that night, back in the bar at the Hilton. "That group has been lurking around this planet for a long time. They won't be stamped out instantly. But I daresay the government will manage it, now that the level of investment in their hardware and so forth has come out so obviously. I have a feeling that several large companies are going to be asked very loudly to rebuild Tombstone, for example."

Joss was sitting contemplating a drink that for once had no loud colors or weird flavors associated with it: straight Stolichnaya vodka, the real thing, which had actually been in Great Russia once. Or so the label on the bottle had said. He looked at his chrono and said, "What I want to know is, what about the caves?"

Evan laughed softly. "Trust that to be the only thing you're really interested in."

"It's not. I also want *Nosey* back, and fixed." He grinned a bit at his glass. "And I'm not going to come back from vacation until they handle it. What am I supposed to do, take public transport back and forth to the Moon?"

Evan snickered slightly. He was happily back in civvies again, with another pink gin in his hand, looking more like a country gentleman than anything else in his tweeds and his cravat; you almost expected to see a big gun dog down at his feet with a duck in its mouth. "We both have it coming," he said.

"But what are you going to do with yours?" Joss said. "I mean, I can still sell my vids . . . the convention's not nearly over yet. And then . . . me for the caves."

"If they let you."

Joss grinned. "They'll let me. Or I'll publish such a paper, and the scavengers will be all over the place. But *you* were going to spend about a week in a big shiny new suit, as I remember—"

"I am going to spend about a week sitting and drinking *these* with Chris and the rest," he said, "and suggesting improvements, which those suits desperately need." He shook his head sadly. "I leave the Service for a moment, and everything falls apart. Well, we'll fix that."

Joss looked at his chrono again. "Where are they, anyway?" he said. "Didn't we say eight o'clock?"

"We did. Calm down."

"Mr. O'Bannion," a voice said, a little ways off in the lobby. "Mr. Joss O'Bannion—"

Joss leapt to his feet, brushing himself off, and glanced eagerly around—then looked rather crestfallen as one of the hotel's bellboys, dressed in the traditional red cutaway coat and small flat hat, came up to him and handed him an envelope. "Mr. O'Bannion?"

"Thank you," Joss said, and handed the boy a credit. He went away, looking at it in bemusement.

"You're going to deplete your stock," Evan said.

Joss shook his head and started opening the envelope. "Joss?" said another voice.

He dropped the envelope, picked it up again and shoved it in his pocket. "Helen Mary!"

She came striding across the lobby in an electric-blue dress that widened eyes and dropped jaws right across the room; and the smile on her didn't need IR to glow. She came to Joss and took his hands. "Are we ready?" she said.

He opened his mouth and closed it.

"Nice dress," Evan suggested.

"Umf, yes," said Joss. "How's your father?"

"They're putting his new knee in right now," she said.

"He told me to go out and have a good time." She cast her eyes down demurely, but the smile was too wicked to match them. "And a good girl has to obey her father."

"Umf," Joss said, sneaking another look at the dress.

"Well, isn't this a happy crowd," said another voice, and Chris came strolling into the lobby, in a red dress which covered rather more than Helen Mary's, but somehow left rather less to the imagination. "Are we all ready? I'm starving. Where are we going?"

"I know a terrific Chinese place," Joss said, "the very best in Welles—maybe on all of Mars."

"Let's go!"

They walked out, the ladies preceding and talking about weaponry and mining rights, the gentlemen following. Evan leaned over to Joss and said, "Who was it from?"

"It what?"

"Stop staring at her dress, you'll have time later. The envelope!"

"Oh." Joss fished it out of his pocket and finished opening it. Then he made half a smile. "It's from Lucretia."

"What does it say?"

"It says, 'If you think I'm paying you thirty-five thousand creds finders fee because you—' " He stopped. "This can't be from Lucretia. She doesn't know words like these."

"Check the routing codes," Evan said, as they walked out the lobby door.

Joss did . . . then sighed, folded the message up and put it in his pocket.

"So *you* pay for dinner then," he said.

ARTHUR C CLARKE'S VENUS PRIME

by Paul Preuss

VOLUME 6: THE SHINING ONES 75350-2/$3.95 US/$4.95 CAN
The ever capable Sparta proves the downfall of the mysterious and sinister organization that has been trying to manipulate human history.

VOLUME 5: THE DIAMOND MOON
75349-9/$3.95 US/$4.95 CAN
Sparta's mission is to monitor the exploration of Jupiter's moon, Amalthea, by the renowned Professor J.Q.R. Forester.

VOLUME 4: THE MEDUSA ENCOUNTER
75348-0/$3.95 US/$4.95 CAN
Sparta's recovery from her last mission is interrupted as she sets out on an interplanetary investigation of her host, the Space Board.

VOLUME 3: HIDE AND SEEK 75346-4/$3.95 US/$4.95 CAN

VOLUME 2: MAELSTROM 75345-6/$3.95 US/$4.95 CAN

VOLUME 1: BREAKING STRAIN 75344-8/$3.95 US/$4.95 CAN

Each volume features a special technical infopak, including blueprints of the structures of *Venus Prime*

BIO OF A SPACE TYRANT
Piers Anthony

"Brilliant...a thoroughly original thinker and storyteller with a unique ability to posit really *alien* alien life, humanize it, and make it come out alive on the page." *The Los Angeles Times*

A COLOSSAL NEW FIVE VOLUME SPACE THRILLER—
BIO OF A SPACE TYRANT
The Epic Adventures and Galactic Conquests of Hope Hubris

VOLUME I: REFUGEE   84194-0/$4.50 US/$5.50 Can
Hubris and his family embark upon an ill-fated voyage through space, searching for sanctuary, after pirates blast them from their home on Callisto.

VOLUME II: MERCENARY   87221-8/$4.50 US/$5.50 Can
Hubris joins the Navy of Jupiter and commands a squadron loyal to the death and sworn to war against the pirate warlords of the Jupiter Ecliptic.

VOLUME III: POLITICIAN   89685-0/$4.50 US/$5.50 Can
Fueled by his own fury, Hubris rose to triumph obliterating his enemies and blazing a path of glory across the face of Jupiter. Military legend...people's champion...promising political candidate...he now awoke to find himself the prisoner of a nightmare that knew no past.

VOLUME IV: EXECUTIVE   89834-9/$4.50 US/$5.50 Can
Destined to become the most hated and feared man of an era, Hope would assume an alternate identify to fulfill his dreams.

VOLUME V: STATESMAN   89835-7/$4.50 US/$5.50 Can
The climactic conclusion of Hubris' epic adventures.